A Deadly Éclair

Also by Daryl Wood Gerber

Cookbook Nook Mysteries

Grilling the Subject

Fudging the Books

Stirring the Plot

Inherit the Word

Final Sentence

Cheese Shop Mysteries
(writing as Avery Aames)

For Cheddar or Worse

A s Gouda as Dead

Days of Wine and Roquefort

To Brie or Not To Brie

Clobbered by Camembert

Lost and Fondue

The Long Quiche Goodbye

A Deadly Éclair

A FRENCH BISTRO MYSTERY

Daryl Wood Gerber

CROOKED LANE

NEW YORK

Published in the United States by Crooked Lane Books, an imprint of The Quick Brown Fox & Company LLC.

Crooked Lane Books and its logo are trademarks of The Quick Brown Fox & Company LLC.

Library of Congress Catalog-in-Publication data available upon request.
ISBN (paperback): 978-1-68331-604-6
ISBN (hardcover): 978-1-68331-341-0
ISBN (ePub): 978-1-68331-342-7
ISBN (ePDF): 978-1-68331-344-1

Cover illustration by Teresa Fasolino.
Book design by Jennifer Canzone.

Printed in the United States.

www.crookedlanebooks.com

Crooked Lane Books
34 West 27th St., 10th Floor
New York, NY 10001

Hardcover Edition: November 2017
Paperback Edition: June 2018

10 9 8 7 6 5 4 3 2 1

To my family.
I am so blessed.
What a wonderful support
you have been to me.
I love you all!

The pressure on young chefs today is far greater than ever before in terms of social skills, marketing skills, cooking skills, personality and, more importantly, delivering on the plate. So you need to be strong. Physically fit. So my chefs get weighed every time they come into the kitchen.

~ Gordon Ramsay

Chapter 1

"*Bonjour*, Mimi!" Heather Holmes, a lanky blonde in her forties with huge, wide eyes and long, curly tresses, breezed into Bistro Rousseau. She screeched to a halt. "Whoa!"

I stared at the chaos in the center of my restaurant—well, it was almost mine; it bore my maiden name. I would own it when I paid off my benefactor, knock on wood.

"What happened?" Heather asked.

"What do you mean?"

"I didn't know we had tornados in Napa Valley."

"Very funny." For the past hour, I had been rearranging the tables. In my haste, I had toppled a few of the cane-backed chairs.

Heather's giggles sounded so much like wind chimes, I was pretty sure an angel had just gotten its wings. "Actually, I like the way you've set things up." She shimmied down the hem of her slinky black dress; it must have twisted up on her ten-minute drive to work. "*Très* intimate." Heather didn't have a wide French vocabulary. I didn't care. She was a wonderful hostess and assistant. "Perfect for a wedding."

1

The wedding was exactly why I was rearranging. We were hosting our very first out-of-towners' dinner for our very first wedding party. Bistro Rousseau, which was located in Nouvelle Vie—an unincorporated enclave in Napa Valley, north of Yountville and south of St. Helena, which boasted upscale eateries, inns, jazz clubs, and high-end shops—had only been open three months. We were growing in popularity, but my benefactor and mentor, Mr. Baker (*Bryan*) said that in order to make a splash, we needed to open the restaurant and Maison Rousseau—yes, I *almost* owned an inn, too—to destination weddings. And he knew just the celebrity who would want to book one. Angelica Barrington, the thirtysomething talk show hostess of *Everybody Loves Angelica* fame, was his niece. Bryan and Angelica's father, a winemaker in the county, were half brothers. Same mother, different fathers.

After Bryan had spent twenty minutes boasting about how wonderful Angelica was, I agreed. Honestly, could I refuse? I had seen her on a celebrity cooking show wielding kitchen utensils like a pro and instantly felt she and I could be kindred spirits.

The wedding ceremony would be held tomorrow, Saturday, in the inn's beautiful courtyard. Oh, how I wanted everything to be perfect. Needless to say, my stomach was in knots and my *almost* restaurant was a mess.

"Do you want me to set up the wineglasses?" Heather asked as she stowed her purse in the safe that was tucked into the teensy coatroom.

"That would be great!"

The restaurant was small, but the many mirrors on the walls gave it a larger feeling and reflected the warm twinkle from the lights in the bronze-finished, candelabra-style chandeliers. The focal point, where Heather would set up the tasting, was a hand-carved pub-style mahogany bar I had imported from

France. Bryan said, *Go big or don't go at all.* I wasn't accustomed to going *big*, but this time, I had, and I was thrilled.

"Then help me fold the linens and put out the silverware," I said. "Later, I'll gather flowers for the crystal table vases and floral arrangements from the garden."

"You know," Heather said, "seeing the chaos, I thought for a second that they had come looking for me."

They being aliens. She claimed they had abducted her on numerous occasions. It seemed to happen around this time of year, during June, when the weather in Napa Valley was pitch perfect, not too hot and not too cold, and the thriving vineyards and fertile orchards were at their greenest, preharvest. *Glonkirks*, Heather called her abductors. I wasn't sure if she was pulling my leg. I mean, c'mon, I'd watched *Star Trek* reruns. None of it was true—was it? Heather related her experiences in exotic—and I mean *ultraexotic*—detail. True confession? I enjoyed the stories. They were fanciful, and I could use a dose of fanciful every once in a while.

"When do they arrive?" she asked.

They, this time, meaning the wedding party.

"Around four PM," I said. "Jo will greet them, get them set up in their rooms, and direct them here around six."

Jorianne James, a.k.a. Jo, my best friend from childhood, was the reason I knew Bryan Baker. Long story short, a year ago I left San Francisco, where I had worked as a sous chef and then chef for nearly fourteen years and returned home with my tail between my legs to live with my mother. Quickly I landed a job as a Monday–Tuesday chef at a decent restaurant, but I blew that off when Jo introduced me to Bryan Baker, a longtime friend of her father's. Bryan was a local entrepreneur in his mid-sixties who loved to help *young people with promise*. His many success stories included an art gallery owner, a vintner, a cheese-maker, and a dress designer. Somehow I qualified!

A few days after our first meeting, Bryan informed me that he had purchased a bistro and the bed-and-breakfast next to the bistro. For *me*! Both places were in desperate need of repair—the front and rear patios begged for inspiration—but he would help me get the properties on their feet. Afterward, it was up to me to make them soar. I was terrified, but Bryan set me straight: *Big risks reap big rewards.*

With his backing, I hired a staff, including a full-time chef, and we got to work. Nine months later, voilà! We had a restaurant and inn built in the style of Giverny. Monet was not only my favorite artist but Bryan's, as well. Each building boasted a pink crushed-rock facade with green windowsills and shutters. Maison Rousseau featured a number of relaxing garden areas, all of which we named after Claude Monet's family or his artistic friends: Renoir, Sisley, Bazille. In addition, behind the inn was an idyllic walkway covered by archways of climbing plants and flanked by colorful shrubs. Beyond that, a lily pond. Bryan grandly donated two of Monet's lesser works, ones he had purchased from private collections, to hang in the inn's foyer.

Three months after we opened, thanks to savvy marketing—I was learning the value of social media—we now had a steady clientele, mostly locals. In fact, we had become quite the go-to place to chat about food, the community, and, yes, each other—otherwise known as gossip. At the inn, we dished up breakfast and brunch; at the bistro, we served hearty lunches and elegant yet affordable dinners. We weren't quite ready for the Michelin review crew to come calling, but I was optimistic.

"I hope everything goes according to plan," Heather said. "What if—"

"Stop!" I shouted. A flutter flitted through my stomach. I had a horrifying fear of the words *what if.* What if the bride hated the whole affair and panned us on television? What if, *gulp*, she bad-mouthed me to Bryan and he withdrew all of his funds? What if they found out I was a fraud through and through? No culinary school degree. No college degree. No—

"Mimi, you look pale." Heather ran to me and clutched my shoulders. "Are you okay?"

I bobbed my head. *Liar.*

"Listen to me," Heather continued. "You are a talented chef, and you are an intelligent, creative being. Breathe! Remember when your dream started."

My love affair with food began when I was a preteen, twenty-three years ago. Prior to that, I was your typical picky eater. Carrots, *ew.* Pickles, *ugh.* Squiggly things like calamari, *ick.* My mother would coax me: *Mimi, try this; Mimi, taste that.* I refused. I squirmed. I made a stink. I went from thin, to thinner, to looking up the term *anorexia* and wondering whether I was a borderline case.

"Mimi, are you breathing?" Heather whispered.

I bobbed my head again. *Liar. Fraud.*

"Repeat after me—'I am an excellent chef.'" On occasion, Heather worked with a hypnotherapist, which might explain why she believed aliens had abducted her. My guess was that her doctor had implanted a false memory. I could be wrong. "C'mon," she urged. "'I am an excellent chef and a terrific, caring manager.' Say it."

"I am" was all that popped out of my mouth because the rest of the memory was hurtling at me full force. At the beginning of seventh grade, something happened, and I began to see food in a whole new light. Maybe it was because my mother insisted that I learn how to make the five mother sauces that every girl of French origin needed to know—I was second-generation French. Whatever it was, the magic that happened when you put effort into something *happened*, and all of a sudden, food and cooking became fun. Flavors and textures came alive for me. *Pow!* I adored the aromas of fresh-baked bread and sweets and grilled *anything*. I couldn't wait to handle a fresh fish or pie dough or cookie batter. And chopping vegetables rapidly? Let me tell you, it was a real turn-on. By the tender age of thirteen, I knew my destiny was to become a chef. As for property owner, restaurant manager, and wedding planner? My heart did a jittery jig.

"Mimi!"

"I'm breathing. I'm fine. Let me go."

Heather released me and twirled a finger in my direction. "Other than that wild gleam in your eyes, you look good. I like the ponytail."

I fingered my toffee-colored hair, remembering when I used to cut it myself to help make ends meet. See, at eighteen I desperately wanted to go to culinary school, but my family couldn't afford it, so I watched cooking shows, pored over every French cookbook that existed, and went to work at a local diner. At twenty, on a wing and a prayer and with stars in my eyes, I moved to San Francisco. The first job I landed was as a sous chef at a second-rate restaurant. Next, I worked as sous chef to a celebrated chef—*celebrated* was code for *crazy*—at a snazzy restaurant. By twenty-four, I had graduated to full-fledged chef at a French restaurant. Every night I went home eager to start my own restaurant. Knowing I needed seed money, I started saving twenty percent of every paycheck. It was hard; I denied myself new clothes, rode a bicycle to work (which was good for the waistline), and cut my own hair—shaggy chic was a fairly good look on me. *Fairly*. Over the past year, I had let my hair grow to my shoulders, a much better style with my oval-shaped face. I usually wore my hair in a bun so a stray hair wouldn't, you know, wind up in a salad or something, but I wasn't going near food for a while.

"I like the outfit, too," Heather added.

I didn't need to glance down. I put on the same thing every day: white shirt, tan trousers, and suede clogs. I was not a fashion horse. I dressed for practicality. I had duplicate outfits in the bistro's office in case I needed to make a quick change. My one fashion statement was the hot-pink tourmaline necklace my father gave me when I'd turned sixteen, the necklace I always wore because it reminded me of his stalwart belief in me.

"Did you put on blush?" Heather asked.

"No." I rarely donned makeup.

"Then use more sunblock," she warned.

Okay, I had to admit I liked a few minutes of unprotected sun exposure every day. I didn't want to wind up with leathery skin; I simply needed a joy boost on occasion.

"Is Chef C here?" Heather asked.

"Yes." Though I was the owner and no longer the chef, I set the carte du jour, and I would taste test to ensure quality, but Camille Chabot, a.k.a. Chef C, a talented French-born chef with twenty years' experience and no accent—she had worked determinedly as a child to lose it—would do the heavy lifting. She could be a demanding woman, but she had a lust for food that was awe-inspiring. I was lucky to have found her.

"What's on the menu for tonight?"

"For the appetizers? *Gougères*," I said, pronouncing the word correctly: *goo-zhehr*. The singular and plural were pronounced the same. They were tiny cheese puffs that could be filled with anything. "And fig-and-olive tapenade on toast triangles. For the entrées, tamarind-braised black cod set atop a vegetable ragout, filet mignon with potatoes *dauphinoise*, or my specialty, rotisserie chicken." *Poulet rôti* was a *must* for any French bistro. I used my own personal blend of twelve spices for the rub. I paired the chicken with *pommes frites*—french fries that I served extra crispy.

"*Soupe gratinée à l'oignon?*" Heather asked.

"But of course. The guests will have a choice between the onion soup or a house salad." My mother had handed down the yummiest recipe for balsamic vinaigrette. A dash of white pepper gave it its zing.

Heather stretched her long arms and yawned.

"Uh-uh, none of that," I chided. "It's not yet half past ten." We had to last until at least midnight. Luckily, I wasn't much of a sleeper, not since I had fallen in love with food. I was always up before dawn, ready to cook with a flashlight if necessary.

Heather yawned again. "Sorry. My husband insisted on reading his latest sci-fi thriller to me." She claimed she was married, but I had yet to meet the guy . . . author . . . *aspiring* author. He had never been published. Was he real or a figment of Heather's colorful imagination? Had her hypnotherapist implanted that memory, too?

"Mimi! Yoo-hoo, Miss Rousseau!" My sous chef, Stefan, a young African American in his twenties, called from the entrance to the kitchen.

I had reverted to my maiden name after the calamitous end to my marriage. Calamitous because—

Stefan flapped his arms wildly. "Red alert!"

"What's wrong?" I yelped. My heart started chugging again. "Is there an emergency?"

"Ha! Nope. I just thought it would be fun to send you into a tailspin." Stefan could be a clown at times. His laugh was a rollicking guffaw worthy of a man twice his size. He was slim, thinner than Heather, but he had spine and could stand up to our demanding chef. Stefan hadn't revealed his last name to anyone except me—he'd had to, for tax purposes—and merely went by Stefan. I understood why, and I would keep his secret. For now. For the record, he was one of the best sous chefs I had ever met. He could slice and dice like a Ginsu pro, and he had a flair for beauty when it came to plating. On his off hours, he painted watercolor landscapes. "Chef C wants someone to fetch rosemary from the garden. Stat! I would go, but I've got bacon sizzling for the salad." The chef had the commanding air of a general.

"I'll get it in a few minutes."

"Swell!" He disappeared.

The garden was located between the bistro and the inn. It was a sizeable patch, flush with summer vegetables and dozens of herbs. After fetching rosemary and flowers, I would head to the inn to check how things were going for the wedding. There was no rain in the forecast, so we hadn't needed to rent a tent, but I wanted to oversee the setting up of the chairs and the gazebo where the happy couple would say their vows.

Heather gathered a stack of linens and started folding crane-shaped napkins. I admired her skill. I could fold pastry dough with flair, but napkins truly stymied me. I couldn't do origami, either. I flapped open a tablecloth. After it billowed and came to rest on a table, I smoothed out the wrinkles.

"Is Mr. Baker attending the wedding?" Heather asked.

"He wouldn't miss it."

"He's handsome, for an old guy."

I laughed. Bryan wasn't old-old—he was in his sixties—but he reminded me of a craggy Paul Newman with brilliant blue eyes, a noble chin, and a devil-may-care smile. We met weekly for coffee at Chocolate, an adorable café a half mile down the road.

"How's your mom?" Heather often made huge jumps in conversation and rarely stayed on topic, unless she was discussing aliens.

"She's good." My father died a few years back from a heart attack. How I missed him and his wit. My mother missed him, too, but she pushed through, one day at a time, and never let me see her cry. She was sturdy that way.

"Has she met Mr. Baker?"

"Whoa, Heather! You're giving me whiplash with the U-turns in conversation. Why do you ask?" My mother owned the Nouvelle Vie Winery, a small concern, not open to the public, which produced a lovely Chardonnay. Her father had brought vines from the old country and established the vineyard on top of its own aquifer. To this day, I could remember my grandmother making bread that was light, fluffy, and rich with yeast. She would serve it whenever a new year's wine was launched. Eaten plain, it was delicious. Slathered with butter, even better. Grandmère said the quality of the water mattered, and the water in Nouvelle Vie—which meant *new life*—was the best in the valley. "Mom doesn't date anymore, if that's what you're hinting at."

"Date? Your mom and Mr. Baker? Heavens no. I was just curious about him. He seems so . . . mysterious."

"There's nothing mysterious about him. Bryan is an entrepreneur. He doesn't bite, and he's not an alien."

"He's not an—"

"Gotcha!" I laughed heartily.

Heather snorted. "Oh, you." She flapped open a fresh napkin.

The *snap* caught me off guard, and a shiver coiled up my neck. What did I know about Bryan, really? He had never married, or so I'd heard. He didn't have children, I assumed; he never talked about any. He traveled extensively. I had often seen him in the company of beautiful, mature women. And he was worth a billion dollars—that might be a slight exaggeration—all of which he made by the time he turned forty because he started a tech company in Silicon Valley long before Google was born, after which he invested well. But what else did I know about him? I hadn't pressed him for information because, well, he was my mentor; I was the student. He often bestowed what I like to call Bryanisms—his world view, captured in sayings I could repeat—so I felt like I knew him.

My lack of curiosity given my history with my secretive husband appalled me. He was the reason the words *what if* could send me into a tailspin. See, at the ripe age of twenty-five, I met the man of my dreams: Derrick Burnham, an adventurer who wrote about his escapades in many magazines. We ran into each other—literally *bam!*—at a volunteer feed-the-poor event in Golden Gate Park. Trays toppled and food flew, followed by apologies and laughter and chemistry. That night we bonded over gourmet pizza. We married a year later. Sadly, eight years after that, the love of my life died in a tragic accident in Nepal. His body broke in multiple places. He died on impact. Quickly on the heels of his funeral, creditors came knocking, and I learned that Derrick had kept a huge secret from me—he was in debt up to his eyeballs. He bought all his pitons, ice axes, and backpacks on credit, to the tune of one hundred thousand dollars. There went my seed money, my dreams, and my sweet memories. I sold everything we owned to pay off the debt, and then, unable to enjoy, let alone *cope with*, the buzz and struggle of city life any longer, I quit my job and moved home.

Was it fate? What if—

I abandoned the task of dressing tables and, obeying Heather's command to breathe, headed to the garden.

Morning was my favorite time of day. I could hear the birds' songs; I could smell the vines. The temperature was mild today even though the sun was shining. A few flecks of clouds dotted the sky.

Drawing in deep, restorative breaths, I entered the garden. Raymond Cruz, our gifted Hispanic gardener and a former classmate of mine from high school, was steady at work.

"Morning, Raymond!"

"Hiya, boss!" With his shaggy brown hair and easygoing smile, he reminded me of a Newfoundland puppy. Raymond wasn't just any gardener; he was a master gardener who gave back to the community by speaking at public events, writing articles for publications, and volunteering on Earth Day. "It's beautiful today, don't you think?" he said, his coffee-colored eyes crinkling with impish fun. "Don't you love the weather?"

"I do."

"Is Angelica on her way?"

"Soon. Are you looking forward to meeting her?"

"It would be nice."

Yesterday I learned that he was a huge fan of Angelica's. He hadn't reached out or anything, no fan mail. He simply admired her sense of humor and the way she joked around with the guests on her show.

"I put together a bouquet for the foyer." Raymond signaled with his shears. "Wait 'til you see."

"I bet it's beautiful." The miraculous displays he could achieve with begonias and azaleas when in bloom astonished me. The brilliant red and silvery-white tea roses he had planted along the walkway leading to the inn's entrance were remarkable. "I need to fetch some rosemary and flowers. Do you have a spare set of clippers?"

"Yep." Raymond pulled a pair from the tool belt looped around his hips and offered them to me. "You can use one of those baskets for your haul." He hitched a thumb over his shoulder at an array of wicker baskets and set back to work.

As I bent to retrieve one, a woman screamed, "Mimi!"

My pulse skyrocketed. I spun around.

My best friend, Jo, the woman who had bravely tasted all my childhood cooking fiascoes, the woman who had introduced me to Bryan and who had given up her high-paying CPA job to manage Maison Rousseau, ran at me full tilt, arms waving. "Help! It's horrible!"

Chapter 2

My insides somersaulted. Unlike me, Jo never lost her cool. She had an MBA from Berkley. She was dollars-and-cents rational at all times. Except now. Her short-cropped ebony hair was going in every direction. Her blue-toned floral jacket was buttoned the wrong way. Even her pencil skirt seemed in a twist.

"What's the matter?" I shouted.

"She—" Jo gasped for breath.

"She *who*? She *what*?"

"Angelica."

"Is she all right?"

"She's here."

"That's it?" I gaped at her. "That's the panic?"

"Everyone came with her. Her fiancé, his father, the wedding guests." Jo tapped a fingertip to punctuate each syllable.

"Breathe!" I said, channeling Heather.

"I'm trying." Jo inhaled and let it out. Color returned to her cheeks. Her bright-blue eyes appeared less glassy.

I laughed.

"What's so funny?" she groused.

"You never panic. Ever."

"As if," she sputtered. *As if* was one of her favorite replies.

"As if, indeed." I was the complete opposite of my pal. I didn't overreact, necessarily, but I didn't face a crisis coolly. I was a bold chef and more of a seat-of-my-pants girl, attacking life with a dash of this and a sprinkle of that and a small amount of chaos. "Tell me everything."

"Okay, here goes." In her three-inch heels, Jo towered over me. At one time she had considered becoming a model, but that desire evaporated when she realized she couldn't *eat, eat, eat* like she wanted. She wasn't heavy. In fact, she was what men called *va-va-voom*, but she would never be considered a string bean. "Angelica's private plane arrived way ahead of time. She took off in a limo to go to the jazz festival and then to see her father for a brief hello, but the rest of the guests came here, and each one expects a room ASAP."

"Not all," I countered. "Some are staying at an estate." One of the wedding guests was a renowned actress. Her second home, north of St. Helena, was more than ten thousand square feet.

"Whatever. That leaves eight—no, *nine*—rooms to prepare." Jo tapped her watch. "It's not even eleven AM. You know the drill around these parts. Nobody checks out until at least noon. And the luggage? Did I mention how many suitcases they have?"

"Store them in my cottage if you have to."

The minute the renovation of Maison Rousseau had concluded, I had moved out of my family home and into what used to be the grounds keeper's house behind the inn. It was a one-bedroom charmer that I had decorated in stylish taupe with burgundy and moss-green accents—very in keeping with the wine country motif. It had a small kitchen, an eating nook, a fireplace, and a lovely view from the rear patio of a fruit tree orchard as well as a vineyard. Neither the orchard nor the vineyard was my property, but I could dream. Practically every morning, I sat in the bentwood hickory rocker on the porch and sipped a

rich cup of black coffee as I got my bearings. The sound of birds
flitting from tree to vine and back again was heavenly. Sometimes a mouser cat that we called Scoundrel—gray and white
and sneaky as all get-out—visited me, though Heather was the
one who fed him outside the kitchen door.

I tucked the shears Raymond gave me into my pocket and
touched my friend on the shoulder. "Jo, what's really going on?"

"What do you mean?" When we were younger, Jo could
cram the night before a test and ace it, run a 10K race without
breaking a sweat, and handle crowds of people with aplomb. I
couldn't remember the last time I had seen her this thrown. It
was so . . . *cool.*

"If you're worried about feeding them, don't be," I assured
her. "I'll handle it."

"You aren't prepared for that, and heaven forbid we surprise
Chef C. Plus the kitchen staff *here*"—Jo gestured toward the
front of my charming French country–style inn—"have a full
house of brunchers." She recited the menu: French toast with
homemade blackberry jam, Belgian waffles, California omelets,
biscuits, muffins, and cheese plates. People from all over the valley regularly came to the inn for brunch. "There's not a chance
the staff can whip up something for an additional ten or twenty."

"Well, I can. I've got plenty of items in the larder: sliced
cheese, sliced meats, a bowl of fresh fruit, freshly made bread
using my grandmother's recipe. Toss in a few bottles of wine,
and I'll bet Angelica and her guests will be happier than punch."
I twirled a hand. "Set up a picnic in the Renoir Retreat. Cover
the tables with those pretty Ramatuelle Rouge tablecloths. The
red will be so pretty with the bougainvillea." In June, all of
the gardens teemed with flowers. "And set out simple white
plates, gold napkins, and everyday silverware. I'll have Heather
put together a wine selection."

Heather had as educated a palate as I did. Like me, she had been allowed to taste wine at an early age. It didn't hurt that we had a very knowledgeable and handsome wine rep, Nash Hawke, who visited every few days to introduce us to the newest treasure. I always enjoyed spending time tasting and savoring wines with him.

"I promise, when our guests enter their rooms, they will be so relaxed, they'll pass out until dinner."

Each room was designed to give the discerning traveler a country-comfort experience. The Provençal decor was inviting, the beds were plush, and the six-jet Jacuzzi and rain showers were decadently delicious. Bryan had suggested springing for those.

"Okay then." Jo shook out her shoulders and turned to go.

I yelled, "Wait!" and motioned to her improperly buttoned jacket.

She blanched. "Why didn't you—" She shook a warning finger. "Ooh. You were enjoying seeing me rattled, weren't you? *Harrumph!*"

I giggled with glee.

"FYI," she said haughtily over her shoulder as she headed off, "don't blame me if things go haywire."

Her words doused my moment of fun.

*

That evening, around half past seven and smack-dab in the middle of the appetizer course, Bryan Baker cornered me by the bar of the bistro. He looked ruggedly handsome yet casual in a dark-blue blazer, blue shirt, and tan slacks. No tie. I couldn't remember ever seeing him wear a tie.

"Mimi, Angelica is over the moon," he said.

"Even though it's a new moon and can't be seen?"

"Ha-ha." He chucked me on the shoulder. "The evening is going great!"

"We've been at it for just over an hour. Give me time to mess up," I quipped.

"Stop it. Don't second-guess yourself."

How many times had he given me a pep talk over the past year? His favorite motto was *Life is too short to wait for anything.* I must have heard him utter it a dozen times.

"What could go wrong?" Bryan asked.

He was right. The spontaneous afternoon picnic had turned out to be a huge success, and as far as I'd heard from Jo, each of the guests had loved the rooms at the inn.

"The breeze through the opened windows is fabulous," Bryan said. "Who needs air conditioning when we have perfect weather in Napa?"

I agreed.

"The flaky cheese things were fabulous," he added.

"Gougères," I said.

He repeated the word. "Yeah, those puffy things. I can't wait for the onion soup and your specialty chicken. What's for dessert? Tell me it's not cake."

"Cake is tomorrow. Tonight, it's éclairs."

"Éclairs." He frowned. "Hmm. I might have to pull the plug on you after all."

A moment of panic shot through me. "Don't you like éclairs?" I hadn't passed the menu by him. I hadn't thought that was necessary.

Stefan, dressed in a white chef's jacket, his toque straight up, strolled by carrying a tray. He was on his way to help the waitstaff collect appetizer plates. He mouthed, *Everything okay?*

I waved him on and studied Bryan's face. His mouth was twitching at the corners like he was trying to suppress a smile. I said, "You're teasing me."

"Yep. I love éclairs." He elbowed me in fun.

The evening's photographer, who had taken photos of each person entering the party and had been moving around the room stealthily ever since, sidled up to us and said, "Twosome?"

"Not right now," Bryan replied and refocused on me. "The éclair thing, Mimi? I'm simply goading you to keep you in the game, and mind you, it's all a game. Every aspect of life. Don't ever take anything or anyone too seriously."

"My mother would disagree with you. She thinks everything should be taken seriously. Grapes, love, and cards."

"Cards, really? What's her game of choice?"

"Poker."

Bryan winked. "A serious game if ever there was one."

Clink clink clink. Angelica Barrington stood at the head table and tapped the rim of her wine goblet with a spoon. She looked radiantly happy, her exquisite face framed by long dark hair and highlighted by candlelight, her blue eyes sparkling—when did she ever *not* look radiant? Her designer sheath clung to her toned body. The aquamarine earrings she was wearing matched the color of the dress perfectly. "Hello, everyone!" She surveyed the guests.

We had set four tables: one eightsome and three foursomes. Angelica and her fiancé and his sister, father, and business partner were seated at the head table. So was Angelica's best friend and Bryan. Angelica's father was to be seated next to her, but he was running late. Really late. He had called. Twice. Apologizing.

Any time, I thought.

"Angie, baby, looking gorgeous!" a scruffy-bearded man sitting at the table of four closest to the head table yelled. The others at the table echoed him.

In truth, all of the guests at that particular table had me gawking. Each was a superfamous celebrity. The bearded guy was a director who specialized in violent movies. Next to him was a renowned actress—the one who owned the estate—

who had possibly the best short haircut I had ever seen. The other two included an NFL quarterback who was overtly religious—although he'd been outed recently for using steroids—and a highly recognizable politician who had been divorced five times and was anything but religious. Angelica had interviewed each of them over the years.

Angelica laughed. "Okay, that's enough, you hooligans. It's my night. No interruptions." She tapped her glass again. "I'd like to say a word. Mimi, can you turn down the music?"

"Wouldn't you like your father to arrive before we begin?" I asked judiciously.

"He won't mind. Promise. Dad's, well, *Dad*. Mom always said . . ." Angelica hesitated. Her mother had died when Angelica was twenty-one. She licked her lips and repeated, "The music, Mimi." She twirled a finger.

I signaled to Heather to handle the music. One of Georges Bizet's best works was playing, "The Pearl Fishers' Duet," a beautiful yet haunting tune featuring a flute.

As the music quieted, so did the guests. They turned their attention to the bride-to-be.

"Lyle, sweetheart, stand up," Angelica ordered. Gossip magazines claimed she could be headstrong. I couldn't fault her; women had to be tough to climb the ladder of success.

Lyle Ives, her fiancé, who managed Ives Jewelers in Los Angeles, leaped to his feet. Hollywood hunks had nothing on him in the looks department. He was, in a word, stunning: fair hair, fabulous bone structure, and a winning smile. He and Angelica made a striking couple.

"Please raise a toast to the chef." Angelica turned to me. "Mimi Rousseau, you have outdone yourself! The decor, *superbe*," she said with a French accent and kissed her fingertips. "The menu, *magnifique*. If the appetizers are any indication, we will be dining like royalty tonight."

Embarrassment warmed my cheeks. Not for being called out—I was used to receiving kudos from my clientele when they were enjoying a meal. But being recognized by Angelica when she looked so glorious and I looked like a worker bee? Ugh! Sure, I had put on a wraparound hot-pink dress for the evening, which went well with my necklace, but I hadn't had time to do more with my hair—still in a ponytail—and I'd forgotten to put on earrings. Dumb! I got over my angst. I wasn't there to impress anyone. This was Angelica's night. Weekend. *Future.*

"Hear, hear!" said Bryan.

"Hear, hear!" Lyle echoed, raising a glass.

"Okay, then." Lyle's younger sister, Paula, who managed Ives Jewelers in San Francisco, was not nearly as polished as Lyle. Even though she had donned plenty of glitzy jewelry for the occasion, including a ring on every finger, she didn't sparkle. Perhaps it was the pale sheath she was wearing, or her limp brown hair, or her wretchedly bitten nails. Her arms were toned, however, which led me to believe she worked out, meaning she was concerned about her health and appearance to some degree. Maybe she kept them toned so she could lift the oversized flashy tote she had brought along. She elbowed her father to join in the toast.

David Ives, who was good-looking in a severe way, as if he had stared down one too many uncut diamonds—he had started the prominent jewelry business more than thirty years ago—raised his glass. "To Mimi," he said in a husky baritone, then threw me a look that was bordering on lascivious.

I didn't react. I was not in the habit of flirting with someone old enough to be my father, even if he was a well-to-do widower.

Bryan, who hadn't left my side, chuckled. "You're always turning heads, Mimi."

"I am not."

"Get used to compliments, my dear. There will be plenty along the years with those eyes of yours."

I inherited my father's chocolate-brown eyes and thick lashes.

Bryan leaned in and whispered, "I'd better get back to my seat. Keep up the good work. And I'll take two éclairs, if you don't mind."

He settled into his chair at the far end of the table, beside Paula, who smiled at him and coyly twirled a lock of limp hair around a finger. Apparently she didn't have the same qualms I did about dating someone older.

Waitstaff appeared—two men and two women dressed in white shirts and black trousers—and removed the white-and-silver charger plates, making way for soups and salads.

"Mimi!" Angelica's best friend, Francine Meister, who was seated on the other side of Bryan, beckoned me with her pinky.

Irritation reared its prickly head. The moment I'd set eyes on Francine, I realized I didn't like her. She was a gossip by trade—she wrote a society column for an uppity magazine and had a huge social media following—and I got the feeling she had been one of those mean girls all her life. Maybe my first opinion was colored by the fact that she was Botoxed up the wazoo, and not a hair on her bleached-blonde head was out of place. Someone in a coffin couldn't look as unnatural.

Cut it out, Mimi, I scolded myself. *Maybe Francine is a lovely, caring woman.* After all, she had supplied party favors for everyone—silver wine stoppers etched with the bride and groom's initials—plus she'd offered to do palm readings for free. *To gather more gossip?* I wondered wickedly. *Bad, bad, Mimi.*

Francine called my name again and pointed to her wineglass.

As I neared the table with a bottle of Nouvelle Vie Chardonnay, which rated right up there with the best Napa Chardonnays—not too oaky and flavored with notes of caramel and honey—I watched Angelica chatting with Lyle. She leaned toward him and fingered her aquamarine earrings, which were each composed of at least a dozen gems. Grinning ear to ear, she blew him a kiss and mouthed, *Thank you*. Had he given her the jewelry for her birthday? Aquamarine was a March birthstone, and I happened to know—because of an article I had read in *People*—that Angelica had been born in March. I did *not* know of what year—that was a well-kept secret—but I figured she was about my age. Perhaps this was the first chance she'd had to wear the jewelry.

I refreshed Francine's glass of wine and moseyed toward Lyle's business partner, a whip-thin man with Marine-short, yellowish hair. He covered the top of his glass with a palm. What was his name? Clark Kent? I bit back a laugh. No, that wasn't it; he was a far cry from Superman. Kent Clarke, with an *E*, that was it. Could you imagine doing that to your kid? Think about the teasing he must have endured! First of all, he didn't look like any version of Superman, and second, he was British. On the other hand, because his family was British, maybe his parents hadn't been aware of the Clark Kent/Superman connection, it being a predominantly American cultural phenomenon when he was born.

Kent's eyes narrowed and he grimaced. Was he staring at Angelica or the costly earrings? Without preamble, he plucked his napkin from his lap, wadded it at his place setting, and stood up. "I need some air."

"We're about to serve the first course," I advised him.

"I need a smoke."

My nose twitched. I wasn't a prude. Lots of people smoked, despite the surgeon general's warning. But in my humble opinion, there was nothing worse than having a cigarette in between courses; it ruined the palate.

I pointed outdoors. "The smoking area is by the fire pit beyond the patio."

Since taking ownership of the bistro, we had totally redone the two patios. The front patio offered a glimpse of the parking lot that wrapped around to St. Helena Highway plus a view of Maison Rousseau and our vegetable garden. The rear patio, which faced east, was much larger and screened in. I'd thought to include a door to the kitchen, to make service for the waitstaff easier. Along the patio's edges, we had filled planters with beautiful Nelly Moser clematis—a purple-and-white variety. Tubs of aromatic herbs like basil, chives, and dill stood in clusters in the far-right corner. A fountain with a cherub centerpiece graced the left corner. We had planted Floribunda white roses, lavender, and lamb's ears behind the fountain. Wrought-iron bistro tables and chairs gave the patio a rustic look. Beyond the patio's edge, at a distance allowable by California law, stood a smoking area and a fire pit. We had decorated the area with stepping-stones and native ground cover. Acres of grapes grew beyond it all.

"Shall I pour more wine for you, Kent, while you're outside?" I asked.

"Sure, love, but not that white stuff. Something red."

"Didn't you order the cod as your entrée?"

"Don't be barmy."

I frowned. Was *barmy* slang for crazy?

"I don't abide by rules," he continued, "especially when it comes to pairing wine and food." He attempted a smile, but his lip only lifted on one side. A shark could have done better. He strode out of the restaurant and let the door slam behind him.

"Well, isn't he a charmer," Francine said to Angelica.

"Don't look at me." She chuckled and poked her fiancé. "It's his fault."

Like a seasoned gossip, Francine regarded Lyle. "Why did you and Kent go into partnership anyway?" I expected her to pull a recording device from her Prada purse to get the scoop.

"Because he hadn't found his path in life and asked me for a favor," Lyle replied.

"And you granted it." Angelica grasped his hand. "Like always."

"C'mon, it's not like I'm a pushover, Liquey," Lyle said.

I winced. What a horrible nickname. All I could imagine was a leaky boat or faucet.

Lyle's father, David, who was scrolling through messages on his iPhone, cleared his throat. Was he making a comment about the pushover reference? Was Lyle a soft touch? Or was he also surprised by the nickname his son had bestowed upon his intended?

Angelica gripped Lyle's hand and smiled. "Of course you're not a pushover. I was teasing." To Francine, she said, "Kent and Lyle grew up together."

"They were childhood besties," Paula remarked, an insinuation in the word *besties*. "Let the US and Britain unite."

Lyle shot his sister a loathsome look.

Paula shrugged and took another sip of wine. "They played spies, if you must know. Secret agents. Kent was James Bond. Lyle was Felix Leiter. They were this close." She crossed two fingers.

"Sis, cut it out. For the last time, he's not gay and neither am I. We hung out, that's all. Now hear this!" Lyle smacked the table, totally for effect. "Kent is good at what he does. No more making fun. Yes, the man has an edge, but he knows his stuff. Without him, we wouldn't have gone international. Paula, you would never be so successful. And, Angelica, you and I"—he clasped her hand—"never would have met. Remember when you came into the shop looking for a bauble for your mother?"

"A bauble?" Francine said.

"That's right," Lyle continued. "She was dealing with Kent. He started laughing so hard, I came running from the office."

Angelica wriggled her hand free. "They were making fun of me."

"Admit it," Lyle said. "The way you say bauble . . . Go on, do it."

"*Bauble.*" Angelica's nose crinkled and her lips pursed like she was begging for a kiss.

"Yeah, that's it. Too cute." Lyle aimed his index finger at her. "Man, I was toast."

David, still scrolling through text messages, cleared his throat again. Didn't he approve of Angelica? How could he not adore her?

"My uncle recommended the jewelry store," Angelica said.

"And I will be forever grateful." Lyle kissed her cheek.

Francine said, "Okay, you two, get a room. Oh, wait, you will. *Tomorrow* night."

Though they had cohabitated for a few months, the couple had elected to sleep in separate rooms at the inn. Sort of sweet, if you thought about it.

Angelica mock-glared at Francine, who chuckled. As did Lyle. Bryan laughed, too, in a jocular, life-of-the-party way.

Realizing he was outnumbered, David pocketed his cell phone and raised his wineglass. "I'll take some of that, Mimi."

As I poured the Chardonnay, Angelica said, "Mimi, Bryan has told us a bit about what you've done to the place. What a fascinating story. I'd love to hear—"

The door to the bistro flew open, and in stumbled a weathered, dark-haired man in a sloppily buttoned shirt. His jacket was slung under his arm. "Angelica!"

Chapter 3

"Angelica!" the man bellowed again, the *G* slurring and sounding like *Sh*. He was clearly soused and nearly tripped himself as one foot crossed the other.

"Dad!" Angelica leaped to her feet.

Lyle and Bryan started to rise. "Need help?" they asked in unison.

"No, thanks. Stay here." Angelica skirted the table and hurried toward her father.

I followed, ready to assist, and signaled Heather to remain attentive to the guests. As I drew nearer to Angelica, the photographer appeared. "Want me to snap a family picture?"

Angelica threw him a sour look. "For heavens sakes, no!"

The photographer shrank back.

Angelica petted her father's shoulders. He was quite a contrast to her. They had the same color hair, but he was thick and muscular, while she was svelte. His skin was tan; hers was pale—kept that way for the cameras, I assumed. He had a dimple in his chin; she had none. Granted, my father and I hadn't looked similar either, other than our eyes. He had been a short, stout dumpling of a man. We did have the same smile, though. I

26

couldn't tell if Angelica and her father did, since at the moment he was scowling.

Angelica whispered to me, "He never drinks."

"How is that possible? He's a vintner." Barrington Vineyards was known for its scrumptious Pinot Noir. Like Nouvelle Vie, it was not open to the public, but I had been lucky enough to taste the Pinot Noir, thanks to Nash Hawke.

"He's a sip-and-spit guy. He doesn't swallow. To Dad, wine is all about the first flavors, not the effect." Angelica said softly, "Dad, what's going on?"

Her father's blue eyes flickered back and forth in their sockets. Tears pooled in the corners. "I . . . You . . ." He shook his head.

"What did you do? Bet on the ponies and lose again? Or did you sit in on a high-stakes card game?"

Aha! That was what Angelica must have thought earlier when she said, "Dad's, well, Dad." He had proclivities that might delay his arrival to an event, even one as important as his daughter's out-of-towners' dinner.

"Did one of your buddies lace your drink so you would bet foolishly?" Angelica pressed.

"No, I was—"

"You could have gone to a Gambler's Anonymous meeting. Or to the GA chat room."

"You . . ." He patted his chest, like he was in search of something. Then he realized he had tucked his jacket under his arm. He rifled through the pockets and pulled out a bejeweled wallet. A piece of paper jutted from the fold. He fumbled to secure the clasp but couldn't manage. "You accidentally left this when we . . ." He twirled a finger. "Earlier." When she had left the hotel in a limo to meet him.

"You found it! I thought I'd lost it." She took it from him, tucked in the paper, and fastened the clasp. "I bought it at the jazz festival right before I came to see you." To me she said, "Have you been there yet? It's amazing. Tons of arts-and-crafts tents. Each filled with artisanal glasswork, leatherwork, and jewelry. The music is divine. And did I mention the wine? What an assortment!"

This year, the arts-and-crafts festival had teamed up with the annual, weeklong "Jazz in the Valley" event in Alston Park. The event featured a variety of musicians plus wine tastings. Artisanal food tents would be everywhere, and balloonists would take to the sky. A bistro patron told me that I absolutely *had* to hear the jazz guitarist.

"I found this inside the wallet." Edison withdrew a pretty silver necklace from his pocket and dangled it by the chain. It was a pendant-style necklace with an aquamarine in an antique setting.

Angelica blushed. "Aw, Dad, that was Mom's and my secret. She said you gave it to her years ago as a keepsake for me. She kept it hidden and presented it to me on my twenty-first birthday, right before she—" Angelica's voice caught. Right before her mother died. "She said to wear it on the day I got married. I wanted to surprise you when I was walking down the aisle. Want to put it on me?"

"I . . . No . . . It . . ." Edison groped for words.

Angelica smiled indulgently. "That's okay, Dad. Hand it to me."

He hesitated and then obeyed. Angelica clipped on the necklace and centered the stone. Her father let out a little whimper.

Poor guy, I thought. *How he must miss his wife.* I said, "Sir, why don't I get you something to drink?"

Angelica yelped.

"Alka-Seltzer," I assured her.

"Oh, of course." She smiled. "Good idea."

Fizzy medicine wasn't a cure-all, but it might help. I touched her father's shoulder. "Follow me to the kitchen."

"Call me Edison," he said.

After we passed through the swinging door, I settled Edison at my favorite place in the kitchen—a rustic white farmhouse-style table fitted with a set of cubbies. It was where I ate my meals. He mumbled something more about Angelica and being disappointed, but I couldn't make out the gist. I figured he was trying to say he was sorry to have let her down, showing up soused like he had. I murmured something stupid like *there, there* and asked Stefan to feed him and keep watch over him until he felt Edison was steady on his feet, and then I returned to the party.

Angelica had retaken her seat at the head table. Lyle was stroking her shoulder and whispering into her ear.

Seconds later, the waitstaff emerged from the kitchen and began the process of setting out soups and salads. The zesty aroma of onion soup topped with melted Gruyère cheese wafted through the air, as did the sound of happy chatter.

An hour later, Edison still hadn't emerged from the kitchen. As the main course dishes were being removed, Angelica slipped through the swinging door. I followed but stopped at the entrance when I spied her sitting on a stool beside her father. She was caressing his hand and murmuring to him.

Deciding not to disturb their intimate moment, I made a U-turn and went in search of Heather to see how I could help with the wine and whatnot. A few minutes later, Angelica appeared with a smile on her face.

As I was pouring champagne into flutes at the celebrity table, Stefan pushed through the door from the kitchen. "We're about to serve dessert," he announced in a big, booming voice. "The chef hopes you have all saved room."

A few people applauded.

Edison shuffled in behind Stefan, his jacket on and his hair combed.

I bustled up to him and linked my hand through his elbow. "Feeling better?"

"You'd like me to say I do, but I don't. I never lie."

"Well, you fooled me. You look good. Your eyes are bright." I gave his arm a squeeze and guided him to the bride's table. I seated him beside Angelica.

She kissed her father's cheek. He muttered something about the necklace, and then he leaned behind her, clenched Bryan's sleeve, and tugged.

Bryan scowled and mouthed, *Later.*

Edison said something sotto voce and bobbed his head emphatically. He seemed to be insisting, *Now.*

The photographer swooped in. "Angelica, is it a good time for a family photo? You, your dad, and your uncle? C'mon. We need at least one."

"Okay." She grabbed her father's hand and drew him to his feet.

Bryan bounded up and flanked her on the other side. He was smiling tightly, which made me wonder what was up. What was causing the strain between him and his brother? Was he angry that Edison had shown up inebriated? Did Bryan know about his brother's penchant for gambling? What had Edison wanted to discuss? Maybe he didn't like that Bryan had taken it upon himself to set the wedding at the inn or, worse, pay for the wedding. I didn't have siblings, but Jo had an older sister, and she often told me how hard it was to keep things on an even keel. Repeatedly, her sister reminded her that Jo had wasted her college education when she abandoned her CPA job to come work for me.

"Got a good one," the photographer chimed, and the trio broke apart.

Angelica resumed her place at the table. Bryan and Edison remained standing. With a stabbing motion, Edison said something to Bryan, who batted his brother's finger away.

"We'll talk tomorrow," Bryan said gruffly and returned to his seat. Edison had no other choice but to do the same.

Eager to diffuse the tension, I chirped, "Who wants champagne?"

Kent and Bryan raised their glasses. I poured Kent's first and then Bryan's.

Lyle extended a hand toward Edison. "Sir, it's a pleasure to see you again." They shook, and Lyle introduced his future father-in-law to the others.

"Mimi," Angelica said, raising her voice to be heard above the chatter, "Bryan told me you're serving éclairs for dessert. Did you know they are my favorite dessert of all time?" Edison snorted. Angelica gave her father a cautious look, then continued. "What inspired you?"

"Éclairs are my favorite dessert, too," I admitted. "I have fond memories of my friend Jo and me, when we were old enough, riding our bicycles every Saturday morning to a mom-and-pop bakery and picking up an éclair apiece. Afterward, we would ride to a grassy park area where we could devour our goodies while watching the wine train pass by."

"How delightful!"

"I like to think so."

Kent banged the table with his palm. "Hello, everyone, your attention!" He hopped to his feet, his flute of champagne raised. "Don't serve dessert yet, please. For those who don't know me, I'm Kent Clarke, business partner and best friend to Lyle, although not best *man*. It seems Paula gets that honor." There was a sting in his tone. "So I'd like to say a word about the man of the hour now."

Lyle moaned.

Kent glanced mischievously at his pal. "Don't you think Angelica should know what she's getting herself into, old man?" He splayed his arms for crowd approval. "Am I right?"

The guests clapped. The scruffy-bearded director whistled. The football star whooped.

Kent swung to face Angelica. "Did you know, love, that Lyle is a geek?"

Angelica grinned. "Of course."

Lyle batted her.

"A certifiable geek," Kent went on. "He knows the capital of every country in the world. In alphabetical order."

"So do I," Angelica said.

Kent frowned. "All righty. But did you know he is also an ace speller? He competed in spelling bees as a child."

Paula muttered, "We were homeschooled."

"Not because I wanted you to be," her father cut in. "Your mother spoiled you with a maid and a cook and a—"

"Daddy, don't," Paula snapped, her face pinched with pain.

Bryan, who had risen to his feet, sidled closer to me and clicked his tongue.

I leaned toward him and whispered, "What was that about?"

Quietly he said, "Years ago, Lyle and Paula's mother fell down a set of stairs and died. Paula, a slip of a girl at the time, was the only one home. How could David bring up her memory at a time like this?"

"I can hear you," David hissed.

Bryan threw his hands up in mock surrender.

"He's right, Daddy," Paula said. "You're insensitive. Mama wanted us to be smart."

"That's swell. However, you can't iron or cook a lick."

"But I do windows, Daddy," she jeered. "Jewelry case windows."

"Yoo-hoo!" Angelica waved a hand and, with true journalistic skill, changed the subject. "Tonight is all about me, isn't it? Kent, I love geeks. Go on. What else should I know about my beloved?"

"He can spell antidisestablishmentarianism, as well as that word from *Mary Poppins*—"

"Supercalifragilisticexpialidocious," Angelica said, not skipping a single syllable.

"Bob's your uncle!" Kent shot a finger at her. "Plus, he knows the derivations of most words and root origins. Boring." He faked a yawn.

"Okay, that's enough," Lyle said.

Kent chuckled. "Oh, no, bucko, I'm not done. One more thing. What dear Lyle does best, Angelica, is jewels. Like everything else he has ever studied, he put his mind to jewels, and he became the most knowledgeable person in the world—next to his father, of course. Why, he even travels with a sack of gems so he can pour them out whenever he wishes to reeducate himself. There's not a gem in the world he can't identify"—he inhaled pointedly—"which is why he picked *you*."

Finally, I thought. I had wondered where he was going with his off-the-cuff, rambling speech. Good for him.

Lyle shot Kent a thumbs-up gesture. Angelica blushed. Tears pooled in Francine's eyes. Paula, on the other hand, seemed decidedly ticked off. Perhaps she had never measured up to her brother, and Kent's praise of his pal was rubbing salt in the wound. Maybe she couldn't stand the fact that Angelica was such a catch. Or was it possible that she was still upset about her father's reference to her mother? Paula stood and excused herself to the restroom. I watched her depart. As she reached the door, she swiveled her head and threw a decidedly sour look at the others. Talk about dramatic.

"Angelica," Kent continued, "I raise a toast to you, because you, you daft cow, are going to be stuck with this blowhard forever. Luckily, I hear you have the patience of Job."

Angelica cut a quick look at her father. How often had she needed to be patient with him? Did everyone know her distress? Edison, feeling her gaze, scraped back his chair and bolted from the table. He fled toward the kitchen.

Bryan said, "Want me to—"

Angelica waved a hand. "Let him go. He told me earlier that he doesn't want to give me away tomorrow. Or ever. He can be very protective."

"Or territorial."

"Don't, Uncle Bryan." She patted his hand. "I'll fix it later."

"*In post*," Bryan joshed, using industry slang that meant postproduction, the part of a show's process after principal photography, during which all the editing was completed.

"As I was saying," Kent continued his speech, "may you have the patience of Job or fleet feet if you need to cut and run!"

The guests laughed. Many toasted Lyle with a quick wisecrack. He responded in kind. Francine gave Kent a thumbs-up sign. Angelica whispered something in Lyle's ear. He grinned and responded by giving her a full-on smooch. In fact, it was so hot and heavy that Bryan, who I thought was unflappable, left my side and strode to the back patio. Did public displays of affection bother him, or had Edison's hasty exit upset him?

I hurried to Stefan. "Pour coffee. Offer brandy."

"I saw that kiss." He winked. "How about a cold shower? I've seen romantic movies with kisses that weren't that steamy."

"You go to romantic movies?"

"I'm a Renaissance guy. Why, I even read poetry."

I shoved him good-naturedly. "Go!"

Through the French doors, I spied Bryan on the patio pacing agitatedly, his mouth moving. Maybe he had hoped to give a toast and Kent had spoiled the moment. Paula, upon returning from her bathroom break, slipped out to the patio and joined Bryan. She touched his arm and smiled coquettishly. He shrugged her off and said something. Paula, clearly taken aback by his words, bowed subserviently and headed toward the French doors. She shuffled inside, slinked into her chair, and began chewing her fingernails. What a sorry sight. Had any man ever given her the respect she thought she deserved?

Her brother offered her a charitable glance. Paula jammed her hands into her lap and averted her gaze. In a flash, Lyle rose from the table and strode outside. Was he going to confront Bryan about his poor treatment of Paula?

Like a moth transfixed by a flame, I watched the action. Lyle withdrew a package of cigarettes from his pocket and approached Bryan near the fire pit. He offered a cigarette. Bryan turned him down. The golden glow of the flames in the fire pit gave both men a chiseled warrior look.

Lyle lit a cigarette for himself and took a puff. He said something to Bryan, who seemed unmoved. Lyle became more animated, gesturing toward the bistro and slapping a hand on his chest. Bryan still didn't react. Lyle stabbed his cigarette in Bryan's direction.

Whatever he said that time snared Bryan's attention. He seized Lyle's wrist. Lyle wrenched himself free and backed up a step, arms raised. Angrily, he tossed his cigarette on the ground, jammed it with his toe, and headed into the bistro.

I peeked over my shoulder. Angelica seemed oblivious to the drama that had unfolded outside. I tried to signal her, but she didn't look up. Francine had settled into the chair Edison had vacated and was gripping Angelica's right wrist. Her mouth was moving rapidly. Was she predicting Angelica's fortune? Could you tell a fortune by measuring someone's pulse?

Lyle returned and settled onto the chair beside Angelica. He seemed downtrodden. He didn't touch her, didn't whisper into her ear. After a person *huffed*, as my mother called it, a person needed time to *unhuff*.

A minute later, Bryan strolled into the bistro, his face calm and his eyes once again full of humor. He tapped Angelica on the shoulder and jerked his head. Apparently he wanted a private conversation. They moved to the front door and talked in hushed tones. Paula swiveled in her chair and stared daggers at them.

Whatever Bryan was saying to Angelica affected her. Her eyes brimmed with tears. Bryan offered a handkerchief. She dabbed the tears before they could fall, kissed him on the cheek, and made a beeline for the kitchen. Seconds later, she emerged, her forehead pinched. Her father must have exited out the rear door. Angelica resumed her place at the table, and Francine once again took hold of her hand.

Bryan clasped my elbow. "Join the party. You deserve it."

"Dessert," I protested, but he wouldn't release me.

He led me to his seat and pressed me into it. How could I refuse?

"What's the prediction, Francine?" he asked. "Will she live?"

Francine released Angelica's hand and beamed. "A happy, contented life." She faltered when she caught sight of me. "Mimi, how lovely that you could join us. It's nice when the help takes a breather."

A prickle of exasperation cut through me. *The help?* I started to rise.

Bryan held me in place. "What did I miss when I went outside to ponder the stars?"

Is that code for regrouping? I wondered.

Kent waggled his thumb between himself and David Ives. "Lyle's dad and I were discussing a bloke's real estate deal. He was a friend of the family. It occurred a decade or so ago. David said you were involved, Bryan."

"Really?" Bryan aimed a stern look at David.

Kent continued. "He said I wouldn't believe how many people go for the jugular just to seal a deal. Did you go for the throat? Did you ruin one of David's real estate deals? C'mon, old chap, spill the beans."

Bryan worked his tongue inside his cheek.

"He said you made a mint on it," Kent continued.

"I didn't, and he knows it."

David smirked.

"Bryan"—Paula fluttered her fingers—"is it true that you date hundreds of women?"

Visibly grateful for a change of topic, Bryan turned his attention to Paula. "That's a rumor."

"Angelica's father told me you like to play the field."

"My brother likes to fabricate stories."

That threw me for a loop. Moments ago, Edison said he didn't lie. Maybe *that* was a lie.

Stefan exited the kitchen, this time balancing a huge tray on his shoulder that was filled with glowing tea-light candles and plates of chocolate éclairs. "Dessert!" he announced and paraded past all the tables to a chorus of *oohs* and *aahs*. He set the tray at a serving station, and four waiters delivered the goods.

As after-dinner drinks were served, the chatter in the room became muted. The dessert course often was the time when people consumed without talking. I wasn't sure why, but over the years, I had taken heed and always had music at the ready. Debussy's "Claire de Lune" was in the queue.

I left the head table and crossed to the sound system. I twisted the volume control knob to *moderate* and found myself humming along to the music as I roamed the room, removing bread plates, extra silverware, and butter dishes. *Presentation is of utmost importance*, a restaurateur had told me when I had worked as a waitress during high school. *That includes tidy tables at all times. Don't ever forget that.* I hadn't.

As I gathered plates from the head table, David rose and exited to the rear patio. Paula scrambled to her feet and sprinted out of the bistro after her father. He acknowledged her as he stretched, arching his back. Paula said something. He flourished a hand but didn't say a word.

Fascinated, I watched the next scene as if observing a silent movie. I could have added my own captions, and no one would have known whether I was telling the proper story.

Daughter grabs father. He whirls around and starts in on her, jabbing a finger. She responds by throwing her arms wide but ultimately lowers her head and tucks her hands behind her like a chastened toddler.

Were they talking about Bryan?

Father: Don't pursue him. He's not worth it.
Daughter: Don't tell me I can't have him, Daddy. He's mine.
Father: You fool! He's twice your age.
Daughter: I love him.

Ha! I was *not* missing my calling as a screenwriter.

A hand brushed my shoulder. "Mimi?" Angelica glowed with good vibrations. *Wow! If only I could bottle the stuff.* "Lyle is talking to guests. It's almost time to close this party down. So c'mon, tell me the story of how you started all this. How did you and Bryan meet?"

"My friend Jo introduced us."

"You are so lucky. He's so fabulous. I've seen him turn people's lives around, but I've got to admit that this"—she opened both arms to include the bistro—"is amazing! So creative. Did it cost a fortune? Where did you find the bar and all the gorgeous mirrors and—" Angelica stared in the direction I was gazing. "Say, what's caught your attention?"

"Right outside, over there"—I wiggled a finger, indicating the patio—"something is going on between Paula and her father. It's very dramatic."

Angelica sighed. "They can be a little soap opera-ish. It's in their blood. Both of them dabble in community theater. I'll bet they're arguing about who will run the business while we're on our honeymoon. Kent demanded to be put in charge. Lyle nixed that. Then Paula begged, but she minces about—Lyle's words, not mine. He said *no* to her, too. She's probably telling her father to intercede."

"Who will run it, then?"

"Lyle says he can manage. So much can be done via the Internet nowadays. Oh, Mimi!" She giggled like we were the best of friends. "Two weeks with the love of my life in Australia seeing the Great Barrier Reef. Can you think of anything more romantic?"

Back when Derrick and I were together, we traveled a lot. We snorkeled in Cancun, hit all the museums in Paris, rode mules in Yellowstone Park, went pearl diving in Japan. But when I discovered his secret—*Pfft! All romantic memories vanished.* Nowadays, when I thought of romance, I couldn't help but think of Nash Hawke, but I doubt he saw me as anything more than a client.

Angelica knuckled me. "Where did you go?"

"Me? I'm on planet Earth, living in reality."

"No romance? No true love?"

"Nope."

"You'll find someone. Love is out there. And it's not always at first glance."

"You and Lyle fell in love at first glance."

"Don't let him snow you. It took him an entire year to get me to agree to a date. Granted, I kept going back to Ives Jewelers to get this or that item cleaned or reset. I didn't play completely hard to get." Angelica scanned the room. "Oh, he's signaling me. Time to call it a night. Thanks for making this evening so special. Make sure tomorrow is the same." She aimed a forefinger at me and popped her thumb. *Bang!* Then she pecked me on the cheek and trotted to her fiancé.

I searched for Bryan, but he had already left. So much for saying *Job well done* or giving me a pat on the back. Tomorrow I would make him pay. Literally. I giggled and headed for the kitchen. It would take a couple of hours to clean up the bistro. I didn't need to supervise that, but before leaving, I wanted to make sure all the prep for the big event was in place. I checked the food in the pantry and the walk-in refrigerator. I made sure there weren't any last-minute items that we needed from our supplier. Before leaving, I told each staff member how well he or she had performed during dinner.

"Chef, stunning job tonight!" I said and gave her a huge hug.

Chef C was a cube of a woman with white hair, apple cheeks, and alert eyes. She adored hugs. Her full mouth broke into a grin. "I am looking forward to the wedding. The cake will be *fantastique.*"

"How many tiers?" I asked.

"Three," Stefan blurted.

Chef C gave him a cautionary look. Stefan responded with a smirk. I screwed up my mouth in mock frustration. She hadn't let me see a sketch of the cake. She wanted it to be a surprise. Knowing that she was a marvel with baked goods and that she had obtained Angelica's approval for the design, I hadn't pressed until now.

"Don't worry." Stefan held up the *V* sign. "I've seen it. It's in the refrigerator. The roses are exquisite. And the ribbons—"

"Shh," Chef C warned.

"All I can say is ooh-la-la." Stefan kissed his fingertips.

I laughed. "Don't work too late," I said and left.

Around eleven thirty, before falling into bed, I fed my goldfish, Cagney and Lacey. As much as I would have liked to own a cat—not just the fly-by-night Scoundrel—I worried that cat hair might travel with me into the restaurant, so I adopted fish instead. Goldfish were far less demanding than a four-legged friend.

*

Around a quarter to six the next morning, I woke to the sound of a woman pounding on my door. "Mimi, it's Angelica! Open up!"

I scrambled out of bed, tugged my Victoria's Secret night-shirt over my thighs, and dashed to the door. I flung it open, and a chilly breeze wafted in. "What—"

"It's Bryan . . . He's . . . I was out running and—" Angelica was dressed in multicolored calf-length tights, a fuchsia-pink crop top, bubble-gum-pink running shoes, and a headband, and she was glistening with perspiration. She grabbed my hand. "Come with me!"

I cringed and tried to pull away. My hair was probably sticking out in every direction—bedhead hair was not my prettiest look—but she wouldn't let go. In fact, she was gripping so hard, I worried I might lose circulation. I lifted my raincoat from the wall-mounted coat rack, and we were off.

The sun had barely made an appearance as she dragged me across the cold ground to the bistro. My bare feet felt as if needles were impaling them.

"I was out for my run"—Angelica continued to tug me, her ponytail whipping to-and-fro—"so I swung by the bistro before coming to my room, hoping to catch a glimpse of the wedding cake through the kitchen window. I know. A bride should wait to be surprised, but I couldn't be put off. Then I saw—" She pointed. "There!"

Bryan was lying near the door leading to the kitchen, his body motionless, his eyes closed.

"He's dead!" Angelica released me and sucked back a sob. "Dead!"

I didn't believe her. It couldn't be true. Bryan must be dozing. He must have shown up eager to see what I had in store for the event and had drifted to sleep. Except there was no rise and fall to his chest.

"Bryan!" I called. He didn't respond. I rushed to help.

A patio chair lay beyond him, cast aside as if thrown away in haste. Had somebody struck him with it and knocked him out?

As I drew nearer, I gasped. Bryan's face was motionless and tinged blue, and something was stuffed inside his mouth—an éclair.

Chapter 4

I sat at a table inside the bistro, shivering even though I was wearing my raincoat. The chill I felt wasn't just due to deep-seated dread. My bare legs had something to do with it—the cool morning temps, too. I ran my finger around the lower rim of a coffee mug, my insides twitching with anxiety. I had drunk three cups of strong coffee, yet I craved more caffeine. I wanted to stay fully alert, and the jittery energy racing through me seemed to be keeping my tears for Bryan at bay.

Who had killed him? And why had the killer stuffed an éclair into his mouth?

Through the French doors, I watched Sergeant Tyson Daly, a Napa County sheriff contracted by the town of Yountville, supervising his investigation crew on the patio. One tall, husky deputy had cordoned off the area. Another deputy, a young Asian woman with sleek black hair, was taking photographs of an item she had marked by placing a yellow plastic cone beside it. *Footprints?* I wondered. I couldn't see any. Maybe it was dirt, or fibers, or even the cigarette Lyle had discarded the night before. She had already marked a few loose gems—a diamond, a ruby, and a sapphire—which lay on the ground near Bryan.

Why Bryan would have been carrying them baffled me. A third deputy—all Napa County deputies were trained as deputy coroners and could do the technical work required to establish that a victim had been murdered—removed the éclair from Bryan's mouth and set it on a black cloth to his right. Then he removed something else, something sparkly—another gem. An aquamarine. I gagged. The killer must have put that into Bryan's mouth. Why? Scoundrel, who had shown up about twenty minutes ago, sat perched on the fountain, staring at the deputy coroner as if inspecting his work, his tail swinging back and forth like a pendulum in a grandfather clock.

I returned my attention to Tyson, who, like me, had grown up in the area. Back in grade school, he had been gangly and bucktoothed and had kept to himself. Now he was a handsome man and more outgoing. He had a wry smile—braces had fixed his teeth—and he wore his beard and mustache in a distinctive Buffalo Bill Cody style. He had a unique gray streak down the center of his unruly flaxen hair, as if he had been greatly shocked once in his life. If he had, he never talked about it. Maybe he would tell Jo. I bet he would tell her anything; his love for her was that obvious. However, he had never asked her out, the coward.

When he had first arrived on the scene that morning, he had been all charm. He had made fun of my raincoat-over-nightgown look and teased me about my hair. I hadn't let the jesting fool me, though. He, like his father and grandfather who had served the law before him, possessed a dogged passion for discovering the truth.

Heather shuffled to my side. "Are you doing okay?" Her hair was knotted at the nape of her neck. She was wearing jeans and an *I Love Napa* T-shirt and no makeup, which was unlike her, but why dress up? We weren't open for business. The wedding was on hold. Heck, life was on hold. "Want more coffee?" she asked.

For the last hour, she had been plying me with my drug of choice. And she was the one who had scrounged up a pair of Crocs for my bare feet.

"I'm okay," I said.

"Liar."

A moan escaped my lips. "I can't believe it. Bryan's dead." I worked hard not to cry. Bryan. My mentor. My benefactor. The man who had taught me not only to trust others again but, more importantly, to trust myself. I didn't even want to contemplate how a murder on the property would destroy the bistro's reputation and end all prospects of its success.

"I'll bet he had enemies," Heather whispered. "Successful men often do."

I gawked at her. She was right. Bryan had a lot of business dealings. Had one of those gone awry? If so, why kill him at the bistro?

"Do you know why he was here so early?" Heather asked.

"No."

She stroked the back of my head. Her touch comforted me. I wondered if she was quietly calling upon her alien pals to ease my troubled soul. If it would work, I wouldn't fight it.

"Did you notice anything before the sheriff arrived?" she asked. "Did you look around for clues?"

"What? No!" The thought made my stomach roil.

"Did you touch him?"

"His wrist."

"To make sure he was dead."

I nodded. After my initial shock, I had gone to him.

"Breathe," she coaxed. "You'll probably remember things as the day unfolds. I'll get you a croissant to absorb some of that coffee."

Despite the early hour, Chef C was already in the kitchen making pastries as well as mini–bacon and onion quiches packed with extra protein for the sheriff's investigative team and the somber wedding party, all of whom had gathered outside the screened-in patio and were watching the proceedings. Lyle, in sweatpants and a hoodie, stood by Angelica's side, mindlessly stroking her shoulder. David and Paula Ives, also in casual clothes, hovered nearby. Francine and Kent lingered at a distance, each sipping from to-go coffee cups. Edison—Angelica had called her father right after we alerted 9-1-1—was pacing behind the group. His gaze was fierce, like he wanted to rip someone's head off.

Tyson crouched down. The movement caught my attention. I rose and inched toward the window. He was next to Bryan's body, inspecting something in his palm. Something hot pink.

My insides did a somersault. It was a cell phone. Mine was housed in a hot-pink case. *No blinking way*, I thought. *It can't be.* When had I last seen my phone? I didn't remember putting it in my purse last night. I was so tired when I'd left the restaurant, I might not have. Usually, I plugged it in and stowed it in one of the cubbies in the bistro's kitchen so it could charge in case of an emergency.

Tyson caught my eye and hooked a finger.

I thumbed my chest, miming, *Me?*

He beckoned me to the patio. I stepped through the doorway and paused halfway to him. There was no doubt in my mind. He was holding my cell phone. I could see the glitter I had glued to the rim of the case to make it distinctive, as if hot pink wasn't unique enough.

"Where did you find that?" I asked, moving closer.

"In the pot of basil."

"How did it get there?"

"Exactly what I was wondering."

"I didn't put it there. Moisture can ruin a phone." I splayed a hand. "For your information, I forgot to take it home last night. I often do because I don't need it, and I know it will still be in the kitchen cubby in the morning."

"Who would have access to it other than your staff?" Tyson asked. He towered over me. At six feet four inches, he stood head and shoulders above most people.

"I don't know. I don't have a—" I caught sight of Bryan, his skin pale and his limbs stiff, and I shuddered. My gaze landed on the patio chair, still lying on its side. "Did whoever killed him hit him with the—*that*? Did he die instantly?"

Tyson was working his teeth back and forth. Was he a habitual grinder? Did it help him concentrate? I wondered whether he wore a night guard to avoid getting TMJ, a.k.a. jaw pain. My mother wore a guard and had urged me to do the same because I ground my teeth when I slept.

I shook free of the off-track thought and focused. "Well?"

"Yes."

I glanced at Angelica and her loved ones, and a fleeting suspicion swept through me. Would any of them have killed Bryan? I couldn't fathom a reason Angelica or her father would want him dead. The others barely knew him, though I recalled David being disgruntled about some business deal with Bryan. Then I remembered the way Bryan had shut down Paula the previous night. Had that infuriated her? I would never forget the way she had bowed submissively and shuffled away from him.

Tyson said, "Tell me again what Miss Barrington said to you when she fetched you."

I had given him a lengthy statement already: Angelica's early morning arrival at my cottage, the way she'd tugged me to the bistro, her claim that she had been out running. I recounted my statement and added, "She said she wanted to glimpse her wedding cake, but then she saw Bryan, and—"

"Did she?"

"Did she *what*?"

"See the cake?"

"I don't think she made it as far as the kitchen window before seeing Bryan and racing headlong to my place."

Tyson set my cell phone on a patio table and pulled a small spiral pad from his pocket. He clicked a disposable pen and jotted a note. He flipped the booklet closed and eyed me.

"Was he robbed?" I asked.

"Why do you ask?"

"Bryan is very wealthy. Maybe he had a lot of cash on hand."

"His wallet seems to be intact. It's filled with fifty-dollar bills."

"What about the loose gems?"

He didn't respond.

"Many successful men have enemies," I said, repeating Heather's comment.

"We'll be checking into that." Tyson lifted my cell phone and displayed it to me. "Can you explain why you wrote this text to him?"

The text read, *Meet me on the bistro patio. Something has come up. Hurry.*

"I didn't write that. Like I said, I didn't have my cell phone with me. I haven't seen it since—"

"Since when?"

I glanced toward the bistro kitchen, trying again to think of when I had last seen it. While Stefan was dishing up salad? Or later, while I fixed Edison an Alka-Seltzer? Maybe it was when Bryan and I had discussed éclairs, I thought, but revised that notion. We had discussed dessert in the main dining room.

Tyson said, "There's a matching message on the deceased's cell phone."

The *deceased*. I groaned.

"Tyson . . . I mean, Sergeant Daly." I would show him the courtesy of using his title. Friendship was off the table for the present. "I didn't write that. I don't know who did. Whoever it was put my cell phone in the basil. I'm not that stupid."

"Where would you put it? In the chives?"

"Don't be flip," I snapped and instantly regretted my tone. "I'm sorry. What I'm trying to say is, I think the killer is framing me."

"Why?"

"I don't know. Maybe the killer thought Bryan wouldn't show up if he . . . she—" I flailed my hands. "Why would I want Bryan dead? Without him, the bistro—everything I've worked for—is going to go up in smoke. Poof!"

Tyson nodded as if I was making sense. Was I? Did he believe me?

"I wouldn't be strong enough to knock him out with a patio chair."

"Sure you would. You're a chef." Tyson jotted a note on his pad. "The killer hit him on the back of his head. He was caught unaware." He flipped the pad shut. "Where were you between four and six this morning?"

"Is that when he died?"

"That hasn't been determined yet, but approximately."

"How can you tell? By body temperature?"

"Don't you worry about the technical stuff, Mimi. Where were you? In bed?"

"As a matter of fact, I was awake. From a quarter to four to twenty to six, I was on my patio, pacing, because I was restless about today's event. I'd just gone back to bed when Angelica—" I halted. Did the killer know that I was up and about? Was that why he . . . she . . . had used my cell phone? Why me? Why frame me? I moaned. "Being alone in my yard is a pretty weak alibi, isn't it?"

"About as weak as being asleep."

"Early morning hours would seem to be an inopportune time to commit murder," I said. "It's hard to find a witness to account for one's whereabouts."

"On the other hand, it provides anonymity."

Tyson jotted another note on his notepad. I had to admit that his habit of flipping the pad open and shut was driving me nuts.

He said, "Did anyone see you, um, while you were pacing?"

"A stray cat and my goldfish."

"Very funny."

"I'm not trying to be. Look, the killer took my cell phone and contacted Bryan. Whoever it was knew Bryan would come running because he was invested in the wedding. He wanted everything to be perfect for his niece. I swear I didn't do it."

Jo bounded onto the patio and cut past a deputy who tried to stop her. "Of course Mimi didn't do it."

Tyson stood a little taller. He swept a hand over his hair and smoothed his mustache and beard. His interest in Jo was rather endearing. She didn't seem to notice, or if she did, she was deliberately ignoring the signs. She could be prickly when it came to men. Her father was a great guy who was dapper, smart, and as funny as the day was long; she had extremely high standards. I remember two boys in high school who had ended up with very bruised egos after asking Jo on a date. Not that she was nasty; she wasn't. She was terse. Maybe that was the reason Tyson still hadn't found the nerve.

"Tyson Daly, what's going on?" Jo demanded.

"I'm interrogating Mimi."

"Why?"

"Because we found evidence that is fairly incriminating."

"Give me a break. You know Mimi. She didn't do this. She has an alibi." Jo turned to me. "You do, don't you?"

I muttered that I had been on my patio, pacing. I added, "Yeah, I know it's flimsy, but what were you doing between four and six this morning?"

"Tossing and turning, thinking about all the plans for today."

"Exactly."

Jo tilted her head and whispered, "What does Tyson have on you?"

"My cell phone was found in that pot of basil."

"The basil? Not the chives?"

I sneered at her. Tyson bit back a laugh.

"There was a text message," I continued, "asking Bryan to meet me here. There's a corresponding text message on Bryan's phone."

Jo blanched but recovered quickly. Boldly she held a hand out to Tyson. "May I see Mr. Baker's phone?"

"I'm afraid I can't do that, Jo," Tyson said.

"Don't be a ninny. Of course you can."

"I can't have your prints on the evidence."

"Fine. Give me a pair of vinyl gloves. I know you have extras in your pocket."

"Listen, Jo—"

"No, you listen, mister." Without an invitation, Jo foraged in his pocket. She found a pair of vinyl gloves, blew air into them like a pro, and slid them on. She and Tyson had a relationship that went back to the playpen. I had heard stories about him smooshing oatmeal in her hair and her messing red Jell-O in his, and even more stories about wrestling matches and bicycle races down steep hills. "The phone." Jo wasn't a bully. She was dogged. "C'mon. You always say fresh eyes are important. Deputize me if you have to." Her eyes blazed with a dare.

Tyson's mouth twitched; he was fighting a smile. "Fresh eyes," he said and handed over Bryan's cell phone.

While scrolling through messages, Jo said, "Sergeant, did you review all his text messages?"

"Not yet. We just found the darned thing."

"Well, take a look at this thread." She flashed the cell phone at him. "See that? It's from Paula Ives. It looks pretty pathetic to me." She read it out loud, emoting like crazy. "'Please meet me. There's something I need to discuss.' Bryan didn't respond. So she sent another. 'I need to explain.'" Jo thrust the cell phone into Tyson's hand. "Um, explain what?"

I said, "I think she made a play for him last night, but he rebuffed her."

"Wasn't he old enough to be her father?" Jo asked.

"I know lots of women who date older men."

"Ahem." Tyson wagged the cell phone. "The message, you will note, was sent at midnight, plus Ms. Ives doesn't ask him to meet her on the patio."

"Maybe when he didn't respond," Jo countered, "Paula used Mimi's phone to lure him here."

"How would she have gotten it?" Tyson regarded me.

"I'm not sure." I felt my cheeks warm. "I suppose she could have taken it from the kitchen." I wracked my brain for a recollection of Paula entering the kitchen last night, but I couldn't conjure up an image.

"That would mean malice aforethought," Jo chimed. She loved reading mysteries. So did I, but I wouldn't presume to talk about malice or motive to Tyson.

He glowered at her. "I'll consider it."

Jo shot me a look of triumph. I sighed, but the sigh wasn't one of relief. I was far from in the clear.

Chapter 5

Luckily Tyson didn't haul me into jail. He said he didn't have enough evidence that I was the killer . . . yet. The word *yet* clanged in my head like a death knell. I shuddered. He added that I was free to go, but I shouldn't leave town. As if I would. All I could hope was that he would find something on Paula Ives, which of course made me feel awful. I shouldn't *wish* someone to be guilty. But someone was, and it wasn't me!

All day Saturday, the sheriff's team investigated the crime scene. My mother called numerous times to check up on me. She had heard the news. I promised her I was fine. I wasn't, but I didn't want her to worry.

Around eight PM, Tyson told me I was permitted to open for business the next morning. Although that was the last thing I wanted to do, I knew I had to—to honor Bryan. He had guided me to success. I couldn't let him down. Dang, but I missed him. He had been such a powerful figure in my life. Of course, Angelica didn't want to hold the wedding on Sunday; I couldn't blame her. She said she would reschedule, but when?

However, when Tyson advised her and the rest of her party to stay in town, all agreed, so it turned out that I wouldn't lose a dime on hotel fees, and they had to eat, so food wouldn't go to waste. As for the wedding cake? Chef C said it wouldn't be discarded, either. She had come up with a delectable way to serve it to our diners, topping each piece with a swirl of whipped cream, a sliver of strawberry, and a sprig of mint. I approved the idea.

After the sheriff and his deputies left, I spent hours in the kitchen checking the food supplies and throwing out anything that didn't look fresh, which were mostly vegetables. Before leaving for the night, I rang up the local vegetable grower and begged her to drop off a dozen heads of romaine lettuce in the morning, plus numerous other items. We had lots of goodies in our garden, but twice a week we needed to purchase from other local growers. Sundays seemed to draw the most diners who requested our special Caesar salad, although I didn't believe we would sell one salad this particular Sunday. People would stay away, despite the fact that tomorrow was Father's Day and people had booked reservations more than a month ago.

When I finally trudged home, I couldn't settle down. I mopped the floor, cleaned the counters, and scrubbed the sink. None of it needed to be done, but I needed to be busy. An hour or so later, I nestled into the rocker on the porch, swathed myself in a patchwork quilt my grandmother had made me, and listened to the sounds of night: frogs croaking, crickets chirping, and the wind whistling through the trees. Every sound made me miss Bryan more than I could imagine. His mentorship and his confidence in me had meant so much. I wouldn't be living in this cottage, sitting on this porch, and enjoying nature without his help.

I fell asleep in the chair and woke when a neighboring rooster crowed. Quickly I washed up; fed the fish; downed a piece of French bread topped with a slice of Brie and fig jam; threw on my uniform of white shirt, tan trousers, and clogs; and headed to the bistro to meet the vegetable grower.

After she came and went, I put on a pot of coffee, opened the windows, and set the kitchen's music system to a preset list that I had arranged for Father's Day: "Daddy" by Beyoncé, "Dance With My Father" by Luther Vandross, and "My Father's House" by Bruce Springsteen, among others.

While cracking eggs into a large bowl, I sang along with the music. My eyes brimmed with tears as I remembered my father and the fun guy he was—always ready with a joke, always ready with a hug.

When Chef C, Stefan, and the rest of the staff showed up a half hour later, I was wailing to Harry Chapin's iconic "Cat's in the Cradle."

"Should we consider submitting your name to *America's Got Talent*?" Chef C teased.

"You're a riot, Chef," Stefan said and faked one of his goofy laughs.

"And you, sweet boy, are not. Get those shallots sliced and chop the garlic," she commanded.

Stefan saluted.

I enjoyed the way the two of them sparred. It did my heart proud knowing that I had hired talented team players. Within minutes of their arrival, the kitchen smelled heavenly.

Chef C eyed me as she moved around the kitchen gathering items she intended to use for today's menu. "I think those are enough eggs, Mimi. How about dicing celery?"

"On it."

"How are you holding up?"

"I'm fine."

"Do not kid a kidder. My daughter can lie better than you." From what I'd heard, she and her daughter, Chantalle, had locked horns during Chantalle's teen years. Time and distance had softened the contentious relationship. Chantalle was now a sous chef in New York, and they talked frequently. "Relax your forehead." She brandished a wooden spoon in my direction.

"Will do, Chef." I gestured like Stefan had.

Chef C frowned, but then I caught her smiling. She was all bark and no bite.

Close to ten AM, as I was polishing the mahogany bar, the front door of the bistro opened. Nash Hawke strolled in looking like a sight for sore eyes in jeans, a crisp white shirt, and a leather jacket; it was his standard ruggedly handsome yet casual outfit. His wavy dark hair framed his face, and he offered an easy smile. "Hey, Mimi."

"Hey, yourself." I loved how comfortable he always seemed in his own skin. It was a real turn-on.

He tugged the strap of his brown leather satchel higher on his shoulder and switched the pack of wine he was carrying to his other hand. As he drew near and set the pack on the bar and his satchel on a stool, I wished I could lean into him. He seemed as sturdy as an oak yet as easygoing as an aspen willing to bend with the breeze.

"I heard about the murder," he said. "What a shame. Bryan was such a good guy. How are you holding up?"

"Not well. I'm dragging, even though I'm OD'ing on caffeine. And I'm afraid bags under my eyes don't suit me."

"You look beautiful, as always."

The compliment made me shiver, but not from delight. Bryan had said the same thing Friday night.

Nash pulled his laptop from the satchel and flipped it open to reveal an Excel-based order form. "Thought you might like to taste this wine before the place fills up."

"Fills up? Yeah, right," I grumbled. "I'm sure the story is spreading. People will stay far away. I'm betting in a matter of weeks, the bistro will go under."

"Ha! Haven't you peeked outside? You're going to be packed. Curiosity breeds intimacy, as the saying goes. You've got a lot of people who want the inside scoop."

I skirted around the bar and peeked out the front window. He wasn't kidding. The line appeared to be fifty strong. Men, women, old, young. Opening on Father's Day was going to pay off after all.

"Before you officially unlock that door, care to have a glass of this fine specimen and tell me what happened?" Nash removed two bottles of wine from his pack, both of them Grgich Hills Estate Fume Blanc. He expertly opened one using a wine tool he kept in his pocket.

"A sip," I said. I needed to keep my head about me today.

He poured the wine into a Riedel Bordeaux glass I provided, and as he swirled the wine in the glass to open the aromas, he said, "Fermented in oak casks. Fruit and lemongrass flavors. With a hint of minerality." Whenever he described his wines, he spoke as if he were writing the descriptions for the bottles himself. He handed me the glass. "It'll go great with seafood, particularly that coquilles Saint-Jacques gratin you make."

I loved that particular dish. Rich with cream and Cognac and Gruyère cheese. We made the entrées ahead of time. According to Ina Garten, a lot of dishes tasted better after they sat for a while.

I sipped the wine.

"Well?" Nash asked.

"It's got a long finish."

"That's my girl," he said. "You're getting the lingo."

I offered a wry smile. "How quickly you forget that my mother taught me about wine years ago."

"Right." He winked, knowing full well I had good taste buds. "Will your mom like me?"

"Will she—" I stopped short.

"Uh-oh," Nash teased. "You're frowning."

After Derrick died and I moved home from San Francisco, the first words out of my mother's mouth were *I told you so*. She had never liked him. She had sensed there was something off about him, but she had never been able to put her finger on it.

"We'll have to see," I said cryptically.

"She will. I'll praise her wine, and it will be well deserved." He winked again.

A flush of desire rose within me, but I tamped it down. I couldn't become mush every time he winked at me. What kind of signal would that send?

"So what happened to Bryan?" Nash rested the heel of his boot on the stool's footrail and took a sip of wine from the glass he'd poured. He let the wine roll around on his tongue.

I watched, transfixed for a moment, but quickly reclaimed my wits and told him how Angelica had found Bryan and fetched me, and together we had contacted the sheriff. I also told him about the message on Bryan's cell phone that had been sent from mine.

"I heard something about that," he said.

"You did? From whom?"

"The owner at Chocolate."

"How did she hear?"

"I'm not sure."

"Well, I didn't contact Bryan. Someone stole my phone, used it to text him, and ditched it in a pot of herbs."

"Sneaky."

I couldn't help wondering who had told the owner of Chocolate. Not any of the sheriff's people. That meant it had to have been one of Angelica's entourage. Maybe Francine or Kent. They had come to the scene of the crime carrying to-go cups of coffee. Tyson would be ticked when he found out.

"How do you like the wine?" Nash asked.

"It's great. I'll take two cases."

"Terrific. The second bottle is on the house." He typed the order into his Excel spreadsheet and saved it and then reinserted the computer into his satchel and hoisted it onto his shoulder. "I'll see you soon. Keep your chin up." He tapped my chin with his fingertip and then circled his finger underneath and let it rest there. "It's such a pretty chin."

Desire swept through me again, but I kept my cool. He wasn't interested in me; he was simply being charming. "Thanks for stopping in."

He strode out of the bistro, letting the front door close with a *clack*.

Heather glided up. "Mimi, you're drooling."

"Am not."

"Handsome is as handsome does. And Nash is about as good-looking as they come."

"You're telling me."

"We're opening in twenty. Are you ready?"

"If Chef C is."

"Is she ever! She saw the crowd. The kitchen is in high gear. Reba McIntire's 'The Greatest Man I Ever Knew' is playing full blast. She's even singing to it." That song was another Father's Day special that I had selected. "She'll tone it down, of course, the moment we open. More coffee?"

I shook my head. "How about a plate of deviled eggs? I could use some protein." One of the items on the lunch menu was a selection of French-inspired deviled eggs, rich with ham and bread crumbs, set atop a luscious pile of butter lettuce and served with toast points and a small ramekin of to-die-for chicken liver pâté.

Within minutes, Heather returned with my request, and I quickly downed my meal. Fueled and steeled, I opened the door for the crowd, which included lots of families honoring fathers.

Around two PM, as business died down, Tyson entered the bistro, his face stoic, his eyes tired. Like a process server, he was tapping a white envelope in his hand. I cringed. Was it a warrant for my arrest?

Perspiration broke out above my lip. I swiped it with a knuckle. "Hey, Sergeant." I offered a broad smile. A forced smile was still a smile, wasn't it? "What's up?"

"Can we speak in private?"

My heart sank. The smile melted away. "Yeah, sure. In my office."

The office for the bistro was small and cramped, but I loved it. I had decorated it in shabby-chic style with a French flair: cream-colored rustic file cabinets, a couple of green-tinted industrial barnwood side tables, and a gray, kidney-shaped French desk with scrolled legs. Silk flowers in tin vases stood on the desk and cabinets. Impressionistic Monet-like paintings of flowers hung on the walls.

I entered first, and Tyson followed. I cleared one of the cream-colored grain-sack chairs for him to sit on. "Please." I gestured.

He remained standing.

I did, as well. How could I sit? Adrenaline was zinging through me like pinballs. *Bad news, bad news* kept ringing in my ears. Years ago, I had felt the same way when I had opened the door of my San Francisco apartment and seen a creditor standing there.

"Mimi, I'm sorry, but my people found something in Bryan Baker's office."

"Okay."

"And it doesn't look good for you."

"May I see it?"

"I can't let you touch it." He removed a letter from the white envelope and unfolded it. He held it out for my inspection.

I scanned the contents. By the time I reached the bottom, my insides were as tightly knit as a potato basket. The letter stated that in the event of Bryan's death, his estate was to forgive my debt. My entire debt. I would owe nothing.

Emotions caught in my chest. Relief paired with thankfulness. But they were quickly replaced by unnerving fear. This letter provided me with a motive. I owed Bryan a lot of money. "Where did you find it?"

"On his desk."

"How? His desk is a mess." I had visited Bryan in his office just a week ago. It was three times the size of my office with manly furniture and expensive art—not the thrift-shop variety I had hanging on my walls. He owned art by Picasso, Miró, and Degas. He had three paintings by Pissarro set in Paris. A green, fused glass heart hung near his desk. A couple of small bronze sculptures and a collection of Fabergé eggs sat on display shelves. My favorite egg was the red one with the miniature carousel inside. Bryan confided that it was his favorite, too, because he had met the love of his life on a carousel. He had no personal pictures in the office other than one of his half brother standing beside his wife and teenaged Angelica. Countless file folders were always stacked on his desk. He wanted them at his fingertips. The day I'd visited, he could barely find the blotter when he had to write a check for the out-of-towners' dinner costs.

"The letter is dated last week," Tyson said.

"You've got to believe me; I didn't know about this."

"But it doesn't look good."

"I did not kill Bryan Baker." My eyes welled with tears and my throat grew thick. "There must be someone else who benefits more than I do," I croaked. "He sponsored others, including an art gallery owner, a vintner, a cheesemaker, and a dress designer. Did he forgive their debts?"

"I didn't find any letters to that effect."

"Can you look again? There's got to be something. There's no reason for him to do this for me."

"Was he in love with you?" Tyson asked.

"What?" I squawked. "He was old enough to be my father."

Tyson raised an eyebrow.

"No, he was not in love with me. He believed in me. That's all." My face was flaming with embarrassment. "Did he have a will?"

"We've got a call in to his estate attorney, who is on a cruise. Reception on ships can be spotty."

"What if someone killed Bryan, took his office keys, and went there to rob him?"

Tyson pursed his lips as if considering the possibility.

"Was anything missing from his office? Maybe a piece of art? Was there an empty space on the walls? Or on the shelves?" I detailed the items I could remember. "He had treasures at home, too."

"His office appeared to be intact as far as we could tell, but we don't have an itemized list of his possessions."

There wasn't much space in my office to pace, but I paced nonetheless. "Bryan shares . . . *shared*," I corrected, "an assistant with others in the building. She might have a record of his collectibles. You should get that from her."

"Good idea."

"He had to have enemies, Tyson, like people who were jealous of what he had accomplished. Plus he argued with a few of the guests Friday night. I told you about Paula Ives. I really don't trust her. There's something about her. Her brother, Lyle, had a heated discussion with Bryan, too. And David Ives—"

Tyson put up a hand. "Okay, I get it. Everyone is a suspect, but for right now, this"—he brandished the letter—"is evidence."

"Are you sure Bryan wrote that letter? What if the person who stole my cell phone forged it to frame me?"

Tyson frowned. "Does someone hate you that much?"

I was beginning to think so.

Chapter 6

"Who hates you *how* much, Mimi?" Jo asked as she entered the office, head bowed, her gaze focused on the stack of mail she was sorting through. No doubt creditors were lining up to get paid in the event the bistro went under. She set the stack at the center of the desk. She never put mail anywhere else because of Bryan's rule: good credit matters. Paying bills had to be my first priority.

I cleared my throat.

Jo peered up and locked eyes with Tyson. Like yesterday when she appeared, he drew taller and sort of puffed his chest. If I wasn't in such distress, I might have laughed. He needed to find some courage around her if he ever wanted to win her heart.

"Not you again, Sergeant." Jo cocked a hip. "What are you doing, giving my pal the runaround?"

"Jorianne James!" my mother said as she hustled into the office. "That is no way to speak to our fine man of the law." Mom and I looked similar, though her toffee-colored hair was chin length and streaked with gray. She had more wrinkles because, well, she was older, plus she smiled a lot, though she wasn't smiling at that particular moment. "Apologize, young lady." She smoothed the lapels of her gypsy-style lace vest—my mother wasn't a hippy, but she loved Bohemian clothing—and gave Jo a stern look. When Jo's mother had divorced her father and run off to *find herself*, my mother had taken up the reins to keep Jo in line. After all, what were best friend's mothers for?

But Jo would have none of it today. "Ginette, I'm sorry, but I can't apologize." She scowled at Tyson. "What are you pinning on my friend this time? What are you holding in your hand?"

"It's—"

"Something worse than the text message," I cut in.

"What text message?" my mother asked.

"I told you yesterday, Mom. Someone used my phone to text Bryan to lure him to the bistro." I turned to Jo. "Tyson is holding a letter that states that upon Bryan's death, his estate will forgive my entire debt."

"That's great!" Jo exclaimed.

"No, it's not!" my mother cried. "It establishes motive." She hurried to me and clasped my hand.

"But she didn't know about it, Tyson." Jo glanced at me. "Did you?"

I shook my head vehemently.

"Were the letter and Bryan's signature witnessed by a notary?" Jo asked.

Tyson nodded. "Last week."

My mother squeezed my hand hard. I gulped. If a notary had acknowledged Bryan's signature, it couldn't have been forged. I was toast.

Jo batted the air. "Okay, fine. Bryan Baker was benevolent. We all knew that. Big deal. What about Paula Ives? Did you question her, Tyson? I don't trust her as far as I can throw her. She's got a sour disposition and a mean streak. I've heard how she talks to the help at the inn. She's not nice."

"Who is Paula Ives?" my mother asked.

Quickly I gave her a recap of the guests at the out-of-towners' dinner. She knew Edison Barrington. As fellow vintners, they had met on various occasions.

"Poor Edison," she murmured. "How are he and his daughter holding up?"

"As well as can be expected."

"Paula Ives," Jo repeated.

Tyson suppressed a smile. "You and Mimi seem to be on the same page, Jo. She's not a fan of Ms. Ives, either."

"Well?" Jo tapped a foot.

I had to admit that my pal and I were quite the opposite when it came to confrontation. She got in front of the problem, whereas I had a tendency to sidle to the perimeter to get a better view. It wasn't that I wasn't adventurous; I was. I'd moved to San Francisco on a whim, hadn't I? But taking on a guy as big and powerful as Tyson Daly? I would do my best to impress him with my intuition.

"I'm visiting Ms. Ives next, Jo," Tyson said. "We're meeting in the library at Maison Rousseau."

"I love the library," my mother said.

I did, too. It was small but fashionable, with an eclectic assortment of comfy reading chairs and lamps. Two walls were filled with books—romances and mysteries and classics—that guests could read during their stay. If any found the need to take a book home to finish it, we provided a return stamped envelope. So far, no guest had permanently borrowed a book.

"Swell," Jo said. "I'll bring you and Ms. Ives tea."

"No, you won't," Tyson warned, "because you'll try to listen in."

Jo *tsk*ed. So did my mother and I, knowing that Jo would definitely eavesdrop, and she wouldn't have to be in the room to do so. She had the hearing of a bat. When she had learned that her parents were going to divorce, she was at the rear of their ranch-style house. I would never forget her telephone call that day. She was sobbing. Up until that moment, I had never heard her cry.

Tyson brandished the condemning letter at me. "Mimi, if I were you, I'd get some legal advice." He bid us good day and strode from the office.

My mother threw her arms around me and hugged me fiercely. "Oh, my darling girl, I'm so sorry."

"Don't worry, Mom. I didn't do it."

"Of course you didn't."

"This is merely a snag."

"Listen to you." She released me and petted my face. "Just like your father—sloughing it off as if you didn't have a care in the world."

I wasn't sloughing it off, but I didn't want her hovering over me. We were both proud, independent women. The last thing she needed was to see me become the same sniveling mess I had been after Derrick died. I had eaten bonbons and potato chips for days. Not pretty.

I kissed her cheek and said, "Thanks for coming to see me. Go home. I'm so busy, I can't see straight. I'll call you later."

She tucked a stray hair behind my ear. "I'll light a candle."

"Or two or three," I joked. She was a candle freak. Last Christmas, the fire department showed up because she had lit so many candles that the residual smoke after blowing them out had set off an alarm. I gave her a nudge, and she left.

When I headed back to the dining room, my stomach was in knots. One of our regular patrons was a defense attorney. Would she take my case?

Jo followed me. Under her breath she said, "You're going to be fine. Promise. We'll get to the bottom of this."

The place was packed with guests. Heather was seating patrons. Stefan was preparing a Caesar salad tableside and chatting good-naturedly with the customers. Two waitresses exited the kitchen with full trays of food. The aroma of onion tarts filled the air. The chatter was infectious. So far, I didn't hear anyone talking about me going to prison for a crime I didn't commit, but once the news leaked about the letter concerning my forgiven debt, all bets were off.

"Come with me," Jo said. She led the way out the French doors and across the patio to the fountain. I wasn't allowing diners on the patio yet, since Bryan had died there. It didn't feel right. Tomorrow, maybe.

Sunshine was warming the day, but the trellis across the top of the patio was keeping the sun's intensity at bay. Even so, I was roasting. Embarrassment and frustration always did that to me. I wasn't guilty of murder, and yet I felt responsible. It had happened on my property, to my mentor.

Water gushed from the pitcher that the fountain's cherub statue was holding and spilled into the basin below. I perched on the ledge and fingered the cool liquid, wishing I could splash my overheated face repeatedly with it.

Jo sat beside me and handed me a tissue. I dabbed my eyes.

"I'll bet Paula did it," Jo said, "and Tyson will be back in a matter of minutes to let you off the hook."

I wadded the tissue in my fist. "If only." Jo was more of an optimist than I was. My life with Derrick had put a damper on my rosy-eyed hopefulness. "Not all murders are that easy to solve. Rarely does the killer admit guilt."

"I heard Paula's mother died under iffy circumstances. Did she kill her?"

"Don't go spreading rumors."

"Do you know the facts?"

"I don't, but I know she was a little girl at the time."

Jo dipped her fingers in the water, too, and dabbed the back of her neck. I recalled Angelica saying that both Paula and her father were involved in the San Francisco local theater scene and told Jo.

"That's not good," she said. "Paula will probably be skilled at lying. She'll put one over on Tyson. You watch."

I knuckled her arm. "Be kinder to him. He *sooo* has a thing for you."

"He does not."

"Are you blind?" I chuckled. "He can't take his eyes off you. And if you would open your pretty blue eyes, you'd see that Tyson has turned into a good-looking man. Plus he's simply good. Good at his job. Good in his soul. You could do worse." And she had. Her high school snubs aside, during college, Jo had stretched her wings. She'd dated a few *bad boys*. Luckily none had won her heart and none had broken it, either. "Give him a chance."

She harrumphed and said, "Forget him. You're the one in trouble. We've got to figure out who killed Bryan Baker before Tyson throws you in jail. Think."

"I don't believe Kent Clarke or Francine Meister killed him. They only met Bryan for the first time at the out-of-towners' dinner."

"But you won't rule them out."

"I won't rule anyone out yet." Not even Angelica's celebrity friends, though none of them had shown up to observe the scene of the crime, and from what I'd heard, all had enjoyed quite a bender Friday night. I doubted any of them could have roused themselves to drive south to Bistro Rousseau. And what motive would any of them have had to hurt Bryan Baker? None.

I plodded to the bed of white roses beyond the fountain and aimlessly started to remove brown leaves. "By the way, there were quite a few events that occurred at the out-of-towners' dinner that piqued my interest."

"Like?" Jo popped to her feet and joined me at the roses; she cupped her hands so I could discard the dead leaves I was collecting.

I told her about the scene when Paula followed Bryan to the patio.

"You think she was throwing herself at him?" Jo asked.

"Seemed like it."

"And he rebuffed her?"

"In less than a minute. She was crestfallen and retreated to the table to chew her nails."

Jo scrunched up her nose. "What about Paula's father, David? I don't like him. He has narrow eyes."

I had thought the same thing, as if David had stared down one too many uncut diamonds.

"Cheaters squint," Jo said.

"He and Bryan have a history."

"I knew it."

"According to Kent, ten years ago, Bryan might have ruined a real estate deal for one of David's friends. Apparently Bryan went for the jugular, though he claimed he hadn't. The topic was quickly extinguished, thanks to Paula, so I don't know the half of it, but both men appeared steamed."

"So later"—Jo dumped her collection of dead leaves out of sight behind the lavender bushes—"David, fuming from the old grudge, decided to act on his rage. To avenge his friend, he met up with Bryan and bashed him with the chair."

"But why wait so long? Why stuff an éclair into his mouth? And why insert a single aquamarine?" I discarded the remaining leaves behind the bushes and brushed my hands on my trousers.

"Maybe the marriage was the last straw. David wanted Bryan to choke on his lifestyle and riches. As for the aquamarine, he intended to put in the other gems, too, but he ran out of time or he heard something and dropped them, which is why they were found on the ground."

"You know, if David didn't kill him, Lyle might have."

"The future groom?"

"He and Bryan had a heated conversation right after Paula was dismissed. It started out calmly enough." I described the encounter, adding that I hadn't heard a word of it, though I could surmise. "I'd wondered if he was making Paula's case for her, but then Lyle said something and jabbed his cigarette in Bryan's direction."

"Like a sword."

"Exactly. Bryan gripped Lyle's wrist. Lyle wrenched free and backed up, arms raised." I mimed the action. "That seemed to end it."

"It sounds to me like Lyle was jealous of Bryan."

"Jealous?"

"Maybe he was telling Bryan that he didn't like how close he was to Angelica."

I blanched. Minutes ago, Tyson had made the same insinuation about Bryan and me. "He was Angelica's uncle," I countered.

"Right, but, you know . . ." Jo let the inference hang.

"No way. Ew. Bryan and Angelica had a pristine relationship. He glowed whenever he talked about her. Lyle had to realize that." I recalled the way Angelica had fawned over her intended at the out-of-towners' dinner. "No, Lyle couldn't have been jealous. Angelica very obviously adores him. She kisses him frequently. She even snuggled him openly while cooing her appreciation for a dangling pair of earrings—" I halted.

"What?"

"The earrings he gave her. They're aquamarine. Her birthstone. The same as the gem that was found in Bryan's mouth."

"So we have a connection there. However"—Jo raised a cautionary finger—"let's not dismiss Angelica as a suspect. Are you sure she didn't kill him and fetch you to establish her alibi?"

"She was beyond grief-stricken."

"A killer can have regrets."

"Why would she kill Bryan? There's no motive."

"Yet," Jo said. "Say, what about her father? Bryan put the wedding together. Bryan arranged for the rooms at the inn. Bryan was doing everything for Angelica. Maybe her father was jealous. Basically Bryan had stepped in for him."

I shook my head. "I can't imagine. Edison was Johnny-on-the-spot when Angelica called him after finding Bryan. The moment he showed up, he seemed ready to rip the killer to shreds." I recalled him pacing behind the group as they watched the investigative team's discovery process. His eyes had smoldered with what looked like a hunger for retribution.

Jo snorted. "You said David and Paula Ives dabbled in acting. Maybe nowadays everybody is an expert at putting on an innocent face because they see how it's done on TV murder mystery shows."

"David," I grumbled. "We've got to figure out what the story was between him and Bryan."

"I know the truth," a man said.

Chapter 7

I spun around. Edison let the screen door slam and crossed the patio, making a beeline for us. He must have cut through the garden between the inn and the bistro. He was dressed in a black shirt and trousers, and his skin was beaded with perspiration. My heart skipped a beat. Had he heard us talking about him? Why should I worry? I had uttered positive things.

"What are you doing here?" I asked.

"Looking for Angelica. We have a date to meet at the inn. Have you seen her?"

"Maybe she's running."

"She never exercises midday. There's too much sunshine. She can't allow herself to get a tan."

"Maybe she went shopping and got stuck in traffic," I offered. "There's a lot of it on the main highway." There was always traffic because there were so many wineries to visit. The Silverado Trail, which ran parallel to St. Helena Highway, was a much easier route to travel.

"Sir," Jo said, "feel free to go to the inn and get some sparkling water at the bar while you wait for your daughter. It's on the house."

"Thanks." Edison turned to leave.

"Wait." I held up a hand. "Before you go, you said you know something about the history between David Ives and your brother."

Edison narrowed his gaze. "It's not mine to tell."

Then why had he spoken up in the first place? Because he wanted us to beg for the gossip?

"Give us a hint," I said, obliging him.

"Please do." Jo offered a dazzling smile. If only she would flash that smile at Tyson and mean it.

Edison peeked over his shoulder and back at us. The coast was clear. He beckoned us to draw near. "David held a longtime grudge because his wife's brother lost a real estate deal to Bryan."

I said, "Kent implied it was a friend of David's."

"A brother-in-law could qualify as a friend," Jo said.

Edison nodded in agreement. "The property, a home in San Francisco, had been in the family for generations. The brother-in-law had some financial trouble. David and his wife were trying to scrape up enough money to buy him out, but Bryan put in a preemptive bid to stave off other investors and snatched it up. He then fixed it up and sold it six months later for a million-dollar profit."

I gasped. "David said Bryan went for the jugular."

Edison nodded. "He could be ruthless."

How angry David Ives must have been with Bryan. *Mad enough to kill?* I wondered.

"Edison," I said, "do you know what happened to David's wife?"

"She fell down the stairs and broke her neck."

Jo cut a look at me and then turned back to Edison. "Was it an accident, or did someone push her?"

"Come to think of it, there were rumors, but I don't know." Edison scratched his chin. "I should go find my daughter."

"I'll go with you, sir," Jo said quickly. She winked as she moved past me, which could only mean that she hoped to glean more information.

I headed into the restaurant. Seconds later, Stefan darted up to me. He stopped me near the bar. "Boss!"

"What's wrong?" My insides did a nervous jig.

"Chef C requires fresh thyme. ASAP!"

I offered a wry grin. Did the chef think that I was *her* employee?

"Please," Stefan begged. "We need all hands on deck. The place is booming. Heather wants to open up the patio. We have twice as many customers as usual."

I scanned the bistro. Among the throng, I caught sight of Lyle sitting alone at a table for two. He was reading a newspaper. He appeared tired, his shirt rumpled and his hair mussed. Had he slept in his clothes and rolled out of bed for a meal? Where was Angelica?

"Uh, thyme?" Stefan threw his arms wide.

I glanced at my watch, which made him snicker. "Oh, you meant *thyme*." My cheeks warmed. I had to force myself to focus. "Sure. I'll get some." I could use a walk.

"Be quick about it, missy," he chimed.

"Don't let Chef C hear you mocking her," I warned. The phrase he'd uttered was one of her favorites.

"Never. What do you think I am, suicidal?" He strolled away, chuckling to himself.

I scrounged up a pair of cutting shears and headed to the garden, thinking about what Edison had revealed. He said Bryan was ruthless in business. Why did that not sync with the Bryan I knew? Sure, he'd wisecracked once that he loved making real estate deals because he had grown up playing *Monopoly*, but he was a humanitarian. He gave freely of his time and wealth. He was my mentor for no other reason than he had wanted to help a young woman find success. No, I couldn't believe it. Bryan was not the man his brother or David Ives made him out to be.

Was I too naïve for words?

When I arrived at the garden, I spotted Paula sitting on a nearby bench with her father. The scene seemed surreal, like a painting by Seurat. Birds fluttered and tweeted merrily in the nearby sycamore. Butterflies flitted happily from lavender to lantana to white spirea. Paula and her father appeared to be deep in conversation. She, dressed in a long-sleeved, ankle-length floral dress, was twisting a lock of limp hair around her finger. David, clad in a beige golf shirt, linen jacket, and pressed chinos, didn't look nearly as severe as he had at the out-of-towners' dinner.

I greeted them as I drew near.

"Hello, Mimi." Paula released her hair and smoothed her dress. "Pretty day."

"It is." The sun was so bright, I had to shade my eyes. "Did Sergeant Daly catch up with you?" I asked.

"In the library." Paula tittered. "With the candlestick."

David frowned. "Honestly, Paula. This is no joking matter."

"I know, Daddy, but when I said 'in the library,' the game *Clue* came to mind, and—"

"I got the reference," he snapped.

Paula flushed and wove her fingers together in her lap. "The sheriff is asking everyone for alibis," she said to me.

"I know," I said. "He asked for mine."

"Which was?"

"I was awake, pacing on my patio and working through the day's plans."

Paula addressed her father. "What was yours, Daddy?"

David stiffened. "I don't think that's appropriate for us to discuss in front of a stranger."

75

"Mimi isn't a stranger." Paula clicked her tongue. "C'mon, tell us where you were between four and six AM, unless you have something to hide."

I regarded Paula, who in one moment was a chastised girl and the very next moment a sassy, confrontational woman. If I wasn't careful, I would get whiplash trying to figure her out.

"Fine." David drummed his fingertips on his leg. "I was on a long-distance call. To Israel."

There was a ten-hour time difference between California and Israel, so talking to someone around four AM would have made it two PM. That sounded reasonable.

"You talked for two hours?" Paula challenged.

David's cheek started to twitch, which made me wonder if he was lying. Why take the risk? He must know the sheriff and his team could check his telephone records. "We were discussing a shipment of gems. We have been having problems, as you know, obtaining quality diamonds. Nachum"—he eyed me— "Nachum Abrams is my contact." He turned back to his daughter. "Nachum has been working tirelessly with our suppliers."

"Actually, I didn't know that, Daddy."

"If not, then you've been lax." David crossed his legs and slung an arm over the back of the bench. "Since we're being open, dear daughter, what is your alibi? You did have quite a heated discussion with Mr. Baker that evening."

Paula glanced at me.

"What's good for the goose," David said. "She's not a stranger. You said so yourself."

Paula pursed her lips and stared daggers at her father—not an appealing look for her. "If you really want to know . . ."

"Oh, I do." David smiled smugly.

Gee, was I glad I hadn't been raised in their family. Did Angelica know the kind of acidic temperaments these two had? Was Lyle similarly predisposed?

Paula said, "I wanted to talk to Bryan about becoming his latest protégé."

"His protégé?" her father echoed.

"Like Mimi and the others." She met my gaze. "Mimi, I can't believe what you've done with this place. I saw the remodeling album you keep at the inn. Wow."

I had chronicled every step of the renovation with photographs. I thought our clientele might like to see what it had taken to create a thing of beauty.

"I need a change, Daddy," Paula went on.

David gawked. "Are you saying you want out of the family business?"

"I'm tired of coddling spoiled rich people who are never happy with anything I offer, no matter how much I bend over backward to please them." Paula seemed to be working hard not to allow a whine to enter her voice. "I want a new career."

"What do you think you're equipped to do?"

"Lots of things."

"Like what?" He crossed his arms, hardly a picture of fatherly warmth. "Certainly not open a restaurant, I imagine. You burn water."

"I'm very capable, Daddy, and I'm intelligent. Lest you forget, I graduated Mills College with honors."

"Go on." He wiggled a hand without unfolding his arms.

"My dream is in the beginning stages, so I'm not going to reveal everything, but when I laid it out for Bryan, he passed, in no uncertain terms. I was mortified by how stern he was with me. I thought maybe my timing was off, so I pleaded, but he refused."

So much for me thinking she was making a play for him. Her hasty exit had simply been a matter of being cowed. Why had Bryan turned her down? Because she hadn't fleshed out her proposal? Because he thought she was too old to start something new?

"Paula," I said, "you called Bryan later that night."

"How—" Her mouth fell open. "Did the sheriff tell you that?"

"He was inspecting my phone," I said, not offering more information about it being found in the planter of herbs, "and I asked to see Bryan's cell phone to corroborate something."

Paula blanched. "Are you a suspect?"

"As it turns out, I am, for a reason that I'll keep to myself."

"Oh-ho," David said. "That reminds me of a quote: 'In nature's infinite book of secrecy, a little I can read.'"

"Daddy loves spouting Shakespeare," Paula said. "That's from *Antony and Cleopatra*."

I flashed on what Jo had told me about actors being good at putting on innocent faces, and I wondered if two expert thespians were wearing them now.

"Mimi, did you and Bryan have an affair?" David asked.

"What? No!"

"Did he renege on your arrangement?"

"No, sir. Bryan and I were on great terms in all respects."

David assessed me. "What else was on your cell phone, then?"

I ignored him and said, "Paula, in the text message to Bryan, you asked him to meet you."

She reddened.

"Why?" her father demanded.

"I wanted to apologize for accosting him—" She flailed a hand. "No, that's the wrong word. I did not *accost* him. I approached him at a bad time. 'Business,' he told me, 'should always be conducted in the office and not at social events.' I . . ." She fidgeted. "I wanted to see if he would give me another chance to pitch my idea—say, a year from now. But he never responded.

I was so frustrated that I couldn't sleep, so I went to the library at the inn and drifted off in a chair. I woke to the sound of a siren."

"Has anyone mentioned having seen you in the library?" I asked.

"Not to me, but I'm not lying."

Interesting choice of words, I mused. Why didn't she say she was telling the truth?

I glanced at David again. He was gazing at his daughter as if she were a flawed gemstone. Didn't he believe her?

"Mr. Ives," I said.

"Call me David."

"Sir, I heard a rumor about you and Bryan."

"'Rumor is like a flute,'" he intoned. "'Guesswork, suspicion, and speculation are the breath that makes it sound, and it's so easy to play that even the common masses—that dim monster with innumerable heads, forever clamoring and wavering—can play it.'" David flourished his hand. "These are the words of the Bard, as well."

"*Henry IV*, part two," Paula said, proving she was, indeed, capable of more than selling jewelry. Maybe she wanted to open an acting studio or theater. She addressed me. "What was the rumor?"

"For heaven's sake, Paula!" David rasped.

"Let's dispel it if it isn't true, Daddy."

He grumbled and glowered at me. "Go on. Tell me what lie someone is spreading."

"That you and Bryan had a falling out over a real estate deal."

"We did."

"Over a property he preemptively bought that belonged to your wife's brother."

David worked his tongue along his teeth and finished with a click. "It's true. He didn't give us time to gather the cash. He leaped in and seized it with no concern about anything or any-one, only his bottom line. It devastated my brother-in-law."

"That doesn't sound like the Bryan I knew," I said.

"It's the truth." David bolted to his feet and held out a hand to his daughter. "Paula, let's go."

She remained sitting. "Bryan didn't ruin my uncle, Mimi."

"Paula, this is not your affair," David warned.

"She might as well know the whole story, Daddy. You keep dwelling on it because you weren't clever enough to get the job done and Bryan was, but Bryan is dead." Paula said to me, "What have you heard?"

I told her what Edison had conveyed about the property.

"That's half true." Paula bobbed her head. "Yes, Bryan made a million-dollar profit, but he didn't keep the money. He put it in a trust for my uncle's children. He didn't want them to lose what should have been their inheritance. He believed my uncle would have lost the property and every ounce of value in it if he had retained the title. That embarrassed my uncle, of course, which made my mother furious. Daddy took her side."

"Why would Bryan help your uncle's kids?" I asked.

"We used to have a second home here. Our families and Bryan traveled in the same social circles. After Mama died, Daddy sold the place. We spend our time solely in San Francisco now." She smiled at her father. "There, Daddy. She knows the truth. Let it go."

Paula rose and marched away. David hurried after her.

As they disappeared, I wondered again how I could corrobo-rate David Ives's alibi. Even though Bryan had acted gallantly in the matter of David's brother-in-law, the brazen way he'd done it had ruffled feathers, and David clearly still held a grudge.

Had that made him angry enough to kill?

Chapter 8

Eager to prove one of the Ives family members guilty but knowing I had a job to finish first, I returned to the kitchen with cuttings of thyme and handed them to Stefan.

"Beautiful. Magnificent. You are a peach!" He quickly moved to the utility sink to rinse off the herbs and then hurried to his station and stripped the leaves and flowers from the stems.

Chef C, who was standing at the stove, said over her shoulder, "About time."

Stefan snorted, and I smiled. So did Chef C. She winked at me, amused at her pun. I moseyed closer and noticed the perspiration moistening her face. She was working hard, and the kitchen was hot. I peeked over her shoulder. In a sauté pan, onions sizzled in butter. There was no better aroma in the world, in my humble opinion. My salivary glands went on high alert. When had I last eaten?

"What are you making?" I asked. Thyme leaves and flowers were best suited with mild meats such as pork, veal, chicken, or turkey and worked well in dishes that did not require long cooking times.

"Your tantalizing recipe for Gruyère and mushroom quiche."

"Mmm." I adored that particular pie. I remembered the first time I'd attempted to make the crust. All the dough stuck to the rolling pin, and I nearly shredded my knuckles when I grated the cheese, but the end result had been divine. Now more adept at piecrusts and grating, it took me minutes to throw one together, and it always satisfied my appetite. "Save me a piece?"

"If you beg."

"Pretty please."

Chef C eyed the floor and then me, as if she expected me to kneel. I considered doing so but decided against it. I didn't want her to think she could *manage* me.

I added sweetly, "With a cherry on top. That's my best offer."

She muttered, "Sassy girl," and then let out a hearty whoop and waved a spatula, signaling that I was free to go. The queen of the kitchen. That was what she was. But I was queen of the establishment, and she knew it.

For the next few minutes, I roamed the main dining room, checking in on our guests. There were no complaints, as far as I could tell. Some of my regulars offered rapturous praise.

Heather caught up to me and whispered, "Mimi, bad news. We're overbooked tonight."

"That is music to my ears! Don't worry. There are always cancelations."

"I don't think so. Not this time. Lots more guests are hanging around, waiting for our second seating." She indicated the crowd outside.

"Wow," I murmured.

"They want gossip."

"You're not giving them any."

"Of course not. I would never." She pushed a curly lock of hair over her shoulder with a defiant huff. "But our guests are. Many seem to have the inside scoop." She let out a little snort.

"What have you heard?" As I was checking on the diners, I hadn't picked up any ominous chatter, but I did recall that a number of conversations had grown softer as I'd approached.

"Some say you're on the suspect list," Heather said. "Care to enlighten me as to why?"

"Consult with your aliens. I'm sure they know the answer."

"Mimi!" She threw me a disdainful look.

"Sorry. I don't mean to make fun. Promise." I crossed my heart and then sighed. "Yes, I am a suspect because last week, Bryan drew up a document that said in the event of his death, his estate was to forgive my entire debt to him."

"Golly."

"Golly is right." I swallowed hard. "He didn't absolve any of his other protégés, as far as I know." Although I wasn't completely sure about that. Tyson hadn't found letters to that effect, but that didn't mean Bryan hadn't written them. "So I wasn't kidding earlier when I said I need help."

"I know a good defense attorney."

"So do I."

"Kaya Hill!" we blurted at the same time, and then I shouted, "Synchronicity!" the word Jo and I had chimed when we were young because of how often we were in sync.

"She's won a lot of cases," Heather went on. "She handled that mess up north in Calistoga."

I knew the circumstance she was talking about. A vintner had murdered his foreman when he discovered the man had been skimming for years. The vintner used a magnum of champagne to strike him dead. Miraculously, Kaya had gotten him a reduced sentence.

"I'll call her tomorrow," I promised. "In the meantime, if you do communicate with your otherworldly pals, would you ask them if they know anything about Bryan having a will?"

"Honestly, will you cut me some slack?"

"*Honestly*, I need to find out!" I squeezed her arm. "If there is a will, I think it might be the only thing that could save me. If someone other than me benefits from Bryan's death, that would be a pretty good motive."

"Money," Heather grumbled. "Why does everyone think it's so important?"

"Because it makes the world go 'round."

"But it doesn't buy happiness."

How true.

Speaking of happiness, or rather a lack of it, through the window I saw Edison Barrington hopping into a black Jaguar in the parking lot. He seemed steaming mad. Seconds later, he peeled rubber and tore off. I wondered what was up. Had he met with Angelica? Had she said something to upset him? Had she accused him of killing his half brother? Would he, as Bryan's sole living relative, inherit everything? If he did, maybe he killed Bryan so he could pay off his own reckless debt—if he had any. That was purely supposition on my part. Angelica hadn't said as much. Not all gamblers went bankrupt; some made a decent living. But the other night, she hadn't been pleased when she'd confronted her father about his habit.

Out of the corner of my eye, I spied Angelica, clad in a smart black sheath with a clutch purse and matching heels, waving to her vanishing father from the path leading to the inn. She seemed despondent.

"I'll be right back," I said to Heather and dashed outside.

Angelica disappeared into the inn. I caught up to her as she was inserting a key into the door to her room. Steady streams of air conditioning wafted over us.

"Angelica!"

She whirled around and gasped. Hair caught on her lipstick. "Oh, it's you." She pried her hair free and then dropped her arm to her side and released the handle of the door, the antique key balled in her fist. Light from the wall sconces cast a warm glow on her face and made her aquamarine necklace sparkle. She smelled faintly of Chanel No. 5 perfume, one of my favorite scents. I rarely wore perfume, too afraid it would affect my senses in the kitchen.

"I apologize," I said. "I didn't mean to frighten you."

"You didn't. Well, sort of." She tittered. "Fans come out of nowhere sometimes. You wouldn't believe the things they do. Request autographs. Coerce me to take selfies with them. Praise me ad nauseam. Insult me beyond words."

Here in idyllic wine country, I had forgotten that she was a prominent figure on television.

"What's up?" she asked.

"I saw your father leaving."

Her eyes were red-rimmed as if she had spent the time with Edison crying her eyes out. "We met for coffee, and then we went back to my room to chat a little more, and he got upset."

"I noticed."

"He's"—she twirled a hand—"bereft."

"I can imagine. You must be, as well."

"Poor Uncle Bryan. I can't believe it." She blinked back tears. Using her pinky, she swiped at one that slipped down her cheek. "Is that all you wanted to say?"

"Um, I hoped we might chat."

"About?"

"The wedding."

She flinched. "I can't think about that now."

"Of course not." I put a reassuring hand on her arm. "I simply wanted to say that I'm sorry you had to postpone it. However, whenever you're ready, we are. Even if that's next year."

"A year." She sighed.

"Were you able to change your honeymoon plans?"

"Yes." She sounded dejected. "They allowed for special circumstances, plus we had trip insurance."

"That's good." I removed my hand from her arm. "I'm also sorry that the sheriff asked you to stick around."

"It's okay." She swept a lock of hair over her shoulder. "At least he's being cool about it. He's a nice guy."

"Tell that to my friend Jo."

"Is he interested in her?"

"Big time, but she has no interest in him. Zero."

"Love is never easy, is it?" Angelica glanced wistfully at the room next door, where Lyle was staying.

"Are you two doing all right?" I asked. "Lyle seemed quite attentive yesterday morning."

"He was, but he's been keeping his distance ever since."

"I was wondering about that. I saw him dining alone at the bistro. You know, he might still be there. You could probably catch—"

"I won't disturb him. I'll give him his space." She ran her free hand along her neck. "This is all so unsettling. When I spoke to Sergeant Daly, he asked for a detailed account of my alibi, as I expected he would."

"You told him, as you had before, that you were out running, and then you went to peek at the cake, saw Bryan, and came to find me?"

"I did. However, there's one more thing." She eyed the neighboring room again. "At five AM, I knocked on Lyle's door to tell him I was going running. I always let him know because he worries about me, it being so dark, but he didn't respond."

"Perhaps he was sleeping."

"That's just it." She lowered her voice. "He doesn't sleep past five. He goes online to see what the commodity markets are doing. I saw a glimmer of light beneath the lower rim of his door. He had to be awake."

"What are you saying?"

"What if he wasn't in his room?" A shudder rippled through her. She laid a single arm across her chest as if to keep her emotions in check, the antique key dangling from one finger. "He argued with Bryan last night. I know you know because I saw you watching them."

Oops. Guess I wasn't very subtle. "Do you think he might have killed Bryan?"

"No!" Angelica's jaw ticked with tension. "All I'm saying is, maybe he went for a walk to blow off steam."

"At five in the morning?"

"He's not a good sleeper. He never has been. He says it's because he has an overactive mind." She chewed on her lip and dropped her arm to her side. "But if he can't corroborate my alibi, then I'll be under suspicion."

"So will he, if he wasn't sleeping."

"No, that wasn't why I—" Angelica inhaled sharply. "I'm not trying to point the finger at Lyle."

"Of course not," I said and once again contemplated the plusses and minuses of an early morning crime. Witnesses were hard to come by, and alibis were impossible to establish, but a murderer, as Tyson had pointed out, could move around quite freely.

"Angelica," I said gently, "why would you be a suspect?"

"Because I'm family. The authorities always suspect family first."

Not in my case. "No other reason?"

"How could there be? I adored my uncle."

"Do you know what Bryan and Lyle argued about?"

Angelica pressed her lips together and then exhaled. "Lyle and I had a heated discussion about it later, in the garden, right before we went to bed. Everyone must have heard us arguing."

"I didn't."

"Bryan told Lyle that he was looking into Lyle's finances. Lyle was outraged. Bryan told him that he was simply trying to protect me." She shifted her weight. "It seems my fiancé's business had a slow period this past year, and he took out a number of bridge loans. Bryan found out and decided to dig deeper."

"Is that what Bryan talked to you about at the out-of-towners' dinner?"

Confusion crossed her face.

"You two chatted," I said, "right after the set-to with Lyle. Bryan escorted you to a corner. Before you broke apart, you had tears in your eyes."

"Oh, that." She flitted a hand. "It was nothing." I wanted to believe her, but the snag in her voice told me maybe I shouldn't. "Back to Lyle," she went on, ignoring my question. "As we walked to the inn, he told me about his fight with Bryan. Silly me, I defended Bryan and not—"

"You didn't know about Lyle's situation?"

"We don't talk finances. What's mine is mine; what's his is his. I'm sure everything will be fine. Lyle is a very savvy businessman."

Visions of Derrick and the way his surprising debt had bankrupted me ran roughshod through my mind. "Do you have a prenuptial agreement?" I asked.

"Bryan and my father both wanted me to have one, but I told them Lyle and I understand that our assets are separate."

"That's not necessarily true." I explained how finances got muddled if a couple paid rent together or held a joint bank account. "California's laws are quite stringent."

Angelica blanched. "Is that why my father raged out of here? He said I was blind to the truth. He said I didn't understand that a marriage was a partnership in all aspects of the word." She started to tremble. "I'm sorry. I have to go. I have to let him know that I understand now." She flew down the hallway.

I didn't budge as I pondered what else Bryan might have said to Lyle. Had he threatened him? Did Lyle lure Bryan to the patio and bash him over the head? If so, why tell Angelica about the bridge loan issue? Why not keep it a secret? I felt like I was missing something.

A door to my right opened, and Francine, wearing a body-hugging blue warm-up suit and carrying a laptop under her arm, slipped out. She closed the door quietly. When she caught sight of me, she gasped. "You!"

Apparently I was pretty fright-worthy today. If I didn't know better, I'd have thought my mascara had run or I had donned last year's Halloween mask—it was pretty ghoulish. "I didn't mean to scare you," I said.

Francine tried the doorknob but had locked herself out. She pressed her back to the wood. Did she hope she could melt through it and evade me? Why was she being so cagey?

"The front desk can give you another key," I suggested.

"Of course."

"Are you off to write one of your columns?"

She nodded.

"The Bazille Garden is my favorite," I suggested. "It's completely shaded, and the pink tea roses smell divine at this time of day." Bazille, a good friend of Claude Monet, became a painter after failing his medical exam. His work *The Pink Dress* had inspired the garden. "You can get a specialty coffee at the mini-café near the concierge and take it out there. You'll find plenty of wicker tables and chairs."

"Thanks. I'll check it out." She wiggled the knob of the door. Did she think she could pop the lock? She abandoned the prospect. "I thought I heard Angelica in the hall."

"You did. She ran off to speak to her father."

"Really? That takes guts. Me? I'd let him calm down. They were arguing something fierce." She thumbed toward Angelica's room. "I'm not saying the walls are paper thin, but"—she fanned herself with a hand—"whew! I had no idea Angelica had that kind of vocabulary. She's always so proper on TV."

I happened to know that the walls weren't thin, which meant Angelica and Edison must have really gone at it or Francine had held a glass to the wall. What could Edison have said to elicit such colorful language from his daughter?

"By the way, between you and me, I've seen things in her readings," Francine said. "Money is not fluid in her future. I spoke to her about minding her finances, but she pooh-poohed me."

I rolled my eyes. I doubted anyone could see that information in any kind of reading other than a financial statement produced by a trusted business manager. Did Angelica have a business manager? She ought to. At the very least, she needed to consult an attorney.

"Speaking of arguing," I said, "did you hear Lyle and Angelica argue after the out-of-towners' dinner?"

Francine fiddled with the zipper of her warm-up suit. It stuck. She tugged harder as she tried to edge past me. "I don't, um, recall."

Her gaze flickered up to the right, a sign that she might be lying, according to neurolinguistic programming. I might not have gone to college, but in addition to devouring mysteries, I liked to read psychology magazines. To that end, if Francine was right-handed, her glance upward could merely mean she was trying to visualize an event.

"I can't, um, remember seeing them at all," she added and then hesitated and flipped a hand at me.

I tilted my head. According to some research, verbal hesitations or excessive hand gestures might provide better indications as to whether a person was telling a lie. "Angelica claimed she and Lyle were pretty loud. She wouldn't have been surprised if the whole inn had heard their spat."

"Well, I . . ." Francine ran a finger along an eyebrow. Not to steer an errant hair into place; I was pretty sure her eyebrows were tattooed on.

The door to her room abruptly pulled open from the inside. When Kent Clarke emerged in boxer shorts and bare feet, I understood why Francine was acting so weird.

"Snookums, bring me back some—" He caught sight of me and grinned. "Hello, love. Guess you caught us shagging."

"I'm glad I didn't."

He let out a rip-roaring laugh. "Good thing you didn't catch me completely starkers."

"Well, now you know," Francine said and wagged a finger between the two of them. "We hooked up after the dinner."

Kent snickered. "To the moon and back."

Francine blushed. "That's probably why we didn't hear Lyle and Angelica arguing."

"Arguing? Poor sods. Who could argue in an idyllic spot like this?" Kent wrapped an arm around Francine's waist and pulled her close. She giggled. He whispered, "Coffee," and patted her rear end. She giggled again.

Spare me.

I left, realizing that they had just provided a solid alibi for each other. I hadn't truly considered them suspects. Neither of them had met Bryan before this weekend.

As I returned to the inn and entered the high-ceilinged foyer, Jo raced toward me, jacket unbuttoned, skirt straining at her thighs.

"Mimi! Come quick!"

"What's wrong? Is there a fire?" My heart chugged. I did not need more bad news.

"It's Raymond."

"Oh, no," I said. "Is he hurt? Do we need paramedics?"

Jo clutched my hand and tugged me through the entrance and out to the garden. Raymond, wearing jeans, a work shirt, and work boots, lay facedown on the ground near a stand of hydrangea bushes, his arms stretched above his head.

"Did he pass out?" I squawked. "Raymond!" I rushed to help him.

"He's fine." Jo yelled, "Raymond, stand up!"

Lickety-split, he scrambled to his feet. In his hands he held dead leaves. He tossed them into his portable trash can and brushed off his shirt. He grabbed his straw hat from the ground, batted it against his thigh, and then jammed it on his head. "Sorry, Mimi, I look a wreck."

"You're supposed to if you're doing your job."

He tucked his shears into his tool belt. "Yeah, if you work with the earth, you look and smell like it."

"Tell her," Jo commanded.

"Tell me what?" I faced Raymond.

"He saw you," Jo chimed.

I flinched. Saw me where? In the shower? Getting dressed? Egad. I had sheer drapes at the cottage. Did I need to install blackout curtains?

"On your patio," Jo added.

I shook my head. "I'm not following."

Jo thumped Raymond on the arm. "Tell her."

"You seem to be doing a fine job for me." He chuckled.

Jo buttoned her jacket while tapping her foot.

"Okay, then," Raymond said. "Mimi, I saw you on your patio the morning Mr. Baker died. You were walking about, muttering to yourself."

"You saw me?"

"Yep."

"Why didn't you tell the sheriff?"

He rubbed the underside of his nose with his index finger. "Well, in the first place, I didn't know I needed to. I had no idea you were in trouble. In the second place . . ." He dragged a toe across the dirt.

"You didn't want me to think you were a Peeping Tom."

"Yep."

Jo grinned. "Remember back in high school? He had a bit of a"—she cleared her throat—"reputation."

"Did not," Raymond said.

"Did too. You liked that long-distance runner, and you made a point of being there whenever she finished her run around the oval." Jo elbowed me. "She would peel off her T-shirt before heading for the showers."

Raymond's face flushed bright red.

"Jo, cut it out," I said. "I know lots of boys who peeked at Erika. She was an exhibitionist. By the way, did you know she became an ecdysiast?"

"A what?" Jo asked.

"A strip artist. She's also a pole dancer. Over in Oakland." I turned my attention back to Raymond. "Go on."

"That's not why I didn't speak up, Mimi." His voice was packed with raw emotion. "It's because we've got snails."

"Snails?"

"Not the edible kind. Real snails. They eat the plants. I didn't want you to think I wasn't doing my job, but if they take hold, they can do real damage."

"Why were you out at night?"

He rubbed the back of his neck. "Because they slither out in the dark. That's the best time to catch them, one by one. I don't want to spread snail bait because metaldehyde pellets are useless. Only ten percent of snails or slugs die when they're used. Methiocarb is better, but it's about ten times more poisonous, so it poses a greater danger to animals, and because it breaks down more slowly, it's an environmental hazard. Plus it's an insecticide, which means it will kill off insects, including the slug-eating beetle and the—"

"We got it, Raymond," Jo cut in. "You were snail hunting."

"How long?" I asked.

"About four hours. I got out there around two AM, I guess, and I finished up right at dawn. I do small patches at a time. The schedule for that night was alongside your cottage. I hope you don't mind."

"Mind? Raymond, I've never been so happy to know there were snails near my place! And I hate snails."

"You like escargot," Jo teased.

"That's different, and they had better be drenched in garlic butter." I threw my arms around Raymond and gave him a firm hug. "Thank you."

He didn't reciprocate. I wasn't sure if it was because I was his boss or because he was still embarrassed about the snails. I released him.

"We have to tell Tyson," I said. "Raymond, go wash up and meet us by my car. I'll drive." I owned a well-loved Jeep Grand Cherokee, an SUV with good handling and seats that fitted me perfectly. I liked to sit high in the saddle, as the saying goes, plus the car was great for transporting large orders of food. "Jo, I'll be right back. I've got to tell Heather where I'm headed." I whooped with glee as I ran to the bistro.

Chapter 9

When I arrived at the restaurant, Heather grabbed my hand and dragged me to the kitchen. "About time you returned," she said. "Chef C is in a tizzy."

"But—"

"No buts. You have to handle this." She pushed me through the kitchen door.

Chef C was at the menu board scribbling. She caught sight of me and thrust a marker pen in my direction. "Thank heavens. We are out of desserts. The wedding cake sold *très vite*."

Very fast!

"I am scouring my brain for a brilliant idea, and nothing will gel." She tapped her temple. "Do your magic."

"My magic? You're the magician."

"Not today. My mind is mush. I stayed up too late last night watching season one of *Downton Abbey*."

"Haven't you seen it before?"

"Of course, but my wily daughter challenged me to watch every show again before August, and if I do, she will come visit. I agreed. I miss her like crazy. Now go." She brandished the marker pen. "Be brilliant!"

With all eyes on me, I toured the kitchen. I started by looking at our baking supplies. Next I reviewed what we had in the walk-in refrigerator. A chill gripped me as I circled the space. My breath turned frosty. When I noticed a crate of raspberries, tubs of sour cream, and a dozen premade pie shells, six regular and six gluten-free—every morning one of the sous chefs prepared them—I landed on an idea.

I emerged with a smile. "Let's make that raspberry sour cream tart you're so fond of." It was one of the first desserts I had made for Bryan and one of the reasons he had decided to back my venture. "Anything raspberry," he'd said. The crumble topping gave it a tasty finish. "Add crushed walnuts to the toppings of pies that aren't gluten-free," I added, "and make sure you prepare the tarts separately. We don't want any patrons getting sick because of cross-contamination."

Chef C beamed, clearly thrilled with the suggestion, and instantly returned to being a general, commanding her troops with flair.

I headed toward the exit, telling Heather my intention, but she wouldn't let me leave without taking something along for the road. I could miss breakfast, she said, but I couldn't skip lunch, too. She collected a few bottles of Perrier and foil-wrapped three croque monsieur sandwiches that Stefan had prepared for diners—one each for Jo, Raymond, and me. The diners could wait another few minutes, she assured me.

While we sped to the sheriff's station in my Jeep, I downed my gooey, luscious sandwich, rich with Gruyère cheese, ham, and warmth. Yum. Heather had even tossed in a paper cone of crispy pommes frites. Perfection. For some reason, I was craving salt.

As it turned out, Tyson wasn't on the job. He had taken the morning off to help his mother at her ranch. Learning that he wasn't out drumming up new evidence and investigating

Bryan's murder sort of ticked me off. On the other hand, the fact that he was helping his mother highlighted how caring he was. Give the guy two brownie points.

"Isn't that sweet, Jo?" I said as we climbed back into my SUV and sped north on the Silverado Trail. "I'm telling you, he's a keeper."

"I can fix my own place, and you know it." She could. She was adept at using any power tool you threw at her, including power saws and sanders. "Plus I am independent and self-reliant."

"Whoop-de-doo."

"Besides, he's not into me. He's never asked me out."

"Keep putting up emotional roadblocks, and he won't."

She shot me a sour look. "Can it. Today isn't about me. Let's keep focused. We're getting you off the hook. Repeat after me: 'I am not guilty.'"

"I don't have to repeat it. I know it."

Tyson's mother's ranch was a one-story rustic up in the hills east of the Silverado Trail. She raised goats and made artisanal chèvre that she supplied to a few of the local restaurants. The goats kept the weeds and grass at bay. A variety of succulents, like red-tipped panda plants, spiral grass, jade, and burgundy-toned hens and chicks, thrived along the driveway and filled wine-barrel planters in front of the house.

We found Tyson replacing steps leading to the front porch. The sound of his hammering kept him from hearing us drive up, slam the car doors, and call his name.

Seeing as I was scaring pretty much everyone today, I approached from the side, waving my arms broadly, hopeful that he wouldn't be shocked by my unexpected arrival and accidentally whack his thumb. My plan worked.

"Hey, you guys." Tyson stood and stretched. Sweat drenched his face, neck, and armpits. Sunlight beamed into his eyes, and he held a free hand above them to block the glare. "What brings you here on such a lovely day?" He offered a special grin to Jo. If I wasn't so nervous about our meeting, I might have elbowed her and whispered, *See?*

"Raymond saw Mimi!" Jo blurted.

"Huh?" Tyson's face pinched with confusion.

Showing more pluck than he had earlier, Raymond said, "I'll tell him, Jorianne. Sir"—he faced Tyson—"on the morning of the murder, I saw Mimi on her patio." He explained how he was out snail hunting with a flashlight.

Throughout the account, Tyson batted the hammer against his thigh. Did he believe Raymond? Was he trying to decide whether my amiable gardener would lie to protect me?

When Raymond finished, Tyson slotted the hammer, head first, into the back pocket of his jeans. "Why didn't you mention this before, Ray? One of my deputies had a conversation with you."

Raymond explained that he had been disinclined to come forward for fear of being considered a Peeping Tom.

Tyson bobbed his head in understanding. "Snails, you say."

"Yes, sir."

"They're that big a problem?"

"It's a perception thing. We don't want customers at the inn to see them or encounter them. Snails are, simply put, the sign of an untended garden." Raymond's attention to detail and his willingness, after hours, to help the team was starting to amaze me. Talk about a keeper. "That's what Mr. Baker always told me," he added. "'Maintain appearances at all cost,' he said."

My breath caught in my chest as, once again, I realized how much I was going to miss Bryan. He had always considered me the owner of the property, but he had never failed to offer his two cents. He saw the big picture. He was vital to the success of both the inn and the bistro. And me.

"Mimi was there the whole time?" Tyson asked.

"Pacing and mumbling to herself," Raymond replied. "I wondered if I should check on her because she was talking non-stop. Sometimes that's a sign of mental illness, folks say. But, well, the staff gossips, and a few have reminded me that she mutters when she's working through issues, so I kept my distance."

"A sign of mental illness?" I exclaimed.

"I didn't believe them," he said as if that pardoned the staff for rumormongering. "But then when I saw it happening . . ." He splayed his hands.

Tyson grinned. "I assure you, Mimi is not mentally ill."

"Yes, sir."

I did, in fact, talk to myself—to clear out extra thoughts that were cluttering my mind—but I was a far cry from schizophrenic. How could I get that across to my staff without letting on that Raymond had blabbed? *Forget about it*, a little voice chimed in my head.

"Hooray," Jo knuckled my arm. "This means she's off the hook, right, Tyson?"

I looked at him expectantly. "Do I still need an attorney?"

"I think you're good."

Jo did a fist pump. "Tyson, we'll leave you in peace to finish your duties. Happy hammering. Nice work, by the way."

In response to the compliment, he grew a little taller.

Jo grabbed my elbow and steered me toward my Jeep. "Tonight after we close the bistro, we're celebrating."

Raymond didn't budge. "Sir, I don't know if it matters . . ."

Jo and I turned back. Sheer panic flooded her face. Mine warmed with alarm. What more did he have to say?

"Ray, stop calling me *sir*," Tyson ordered. "We've known each other too long. Heck, we played on the same soccer team."

I recalled sitting in the stands and watching them. Raymond played center back; Tyson played forward. Raymond had thwarted numerous goals, and Tyson, with his long legs and incredible speed, had scored plenty.

Raymond shrugged a shoulder. "Sure. If you say so."

"What's up?" Tyson asked. "Out with it."

"I don't know if it matters, but I think I saw someone running from the restaurant around a quarter to six."

Tyson cleared his throat. "Didn't you say you were snail hunting by Mimi's cottage at that time?"

"Yes, sir . . . I mean, yes. But, actually, I quit around half past five."

Uh-oh. My insides tensed. Did that mean I needed a lawyer after all? Quickly I said, "That's about when I went back to bed, Tyson. Remember? I told you that."

Raymond studied his fingernails. "I heard Mr. Baker died before five thirty, so I didn't think anything of it when your deputy interviewed me."

Tyson scrubbed the side of his head with his fingertips and then held a hand out to Raymond, palm up. "Can you describe this person?"

"I'm not sure if it was a man or a woman. The sun hadn't crested the mountains. I heard the gate on the patio bang. That was what caught my attention. Whoever it was ran fast."

I moved back toward the porch. "Maybe Raymond saw Angelica," I offered. "After she found Bryan, she fetched me."

"I can't believe she killed him," Raymond said. "She's so nice."

"I remember seeing her on her TV show," Jo said, "with a celebrity chef."

"I saw that," I said. "Could she ever wield a frying pan!"

Jo concurred. "Her arms are supertoned."

I eyed Tyson. "Anyone could have swung that patio chair at Bryan. Isn't that what you told me? The significant items are the éclair and the aquamarine. Why stuff them in Bryan's mouth?"

Raymond gagged. Apparently he hadn't known the details of the crime scene.

"What if it was Lyle running away?" I said.

Tyson frowned. "Why make that assumption?"

"Lyle and Bryan argued the night before, and according to Angelica, Lyle might not have a verifiable alibi. Mind you"—I aimed a finger at him—"she was quick to say that she didn't think her fiancé killed Bryan. She was simply concerned that he wouldn't be able to back up her alibi."

"And he can't," Tyson admitted. "I spoke with him. He was sleeping."

Jo said, "Being asleep isn't a very compelling alibi."

I tilted my head. "If he was even in the room."

Tyson moaned. "Let's get out of the sun. It's hot." He climbed onto the porch and beckoned us to follow. He sat on the cedar swing. The chains holding it creaked beneath his weight. He gestured to the cedar Adirondack chairs.

I remained standing and leaned against the railing. Tentatively, Jo joined me and settled in close, making us metaphorically connected at the hip. Whatever hurt me, hurt her. Raymond held back and inspected the succulents, automatically plucking dead leaves off a few and turning the soil with his fingertips. Once a gardener, always a gardener.

Tyson leaned forward, elbows on his knees, and tented his fingers. "Go on, Mimi, regarding Lyle. What do you know that I don't?"

"I ran into Angelica at the inn earlier, and she said she was concerned because before she went running Saturday morning, she knocked on his door to let him know she was on her way out. She said she always tells him because he worries about her running in the dark. Except he didn't respond."

Tyson unfolded his hands. "Like I said, he was asleep."

"That's just it. Angelica said he always conducts business at that time. He looks at what the commodity markets are doing. She saw a glimmer of light beneath his door."

Tyson leaned back and scratched his chin. "I'm not happy that you're questioning witnesses."

"I wasn't questioning anyone, Tyson." I let my arms hang neutrally at my sides; I didn't want to appear defensive. "I was conversing. There's a difference. And Angelica was offering. By the way, she and Lyle quarreled the night before, too. It seems Bryan was investigating Lyle, and Lyle wasn't happy about it."

"Investigating him about . . . ?"

"His financial situation. Lyle—his jewelry business—has taken out some bridge loans."

"He didn't mention that."

Recalling how many times Derrick and I had talked about things and he simply hadn't told me the truth, I said, "Some people don't offer the whole story if the question doesn't prompt them to."

Tyson frowned.

"Angelica took Bryan's side," I went on. "Lyle stormed off. But, like I said before, Angelica was quick to add that she didn't think the bridge loan thing was an issue or that Lyle was angry enough to lash out at Bryan, although she did admit that she and Lyle don't have a prenuptial agreement."

"What's your point? Lots of people get married without one."

I stepped closer to Tyson. "Bryan wanted her to have one. What if Lyle got sick of Bryan sticking his nose into their affairs? At the out-of-towners' dinner, Angelica said how much she liked éclairs, and Bryan said they were his favorites, too. Maybe all that buddy-buddy relationship between uncle and niece irked Lyle and pushed him over the edge. 'It's him or me,' he thought. When he plotted to kill Bryan, éclairs came to mind. He stuffed one in Bryan's mouth to make a point."

"Don't forget the gems lying about," Jo said. "Lyle would have access to loose stones."

"Exactly." I lowered my voice, imitating Lyle. "'I'll show you, Bryan. Don't mess with me. I'm plenty rich.'"

"'Choke on this!'" Jo intoned.

Tyson suppressed a grin. "You two should write a soap opera."

Jo gave him a dirty look.

"How about the ones found on the ground?" Tyson asked. "Why would Lyle leave those behind?"

"Because he heard something and thought he might be caught, so he raced away." Jo sat in the Adirondack chair to the right of the swing. "I repeat: being asleep isn't a very good alibi."

I said, "David and Paula Ives's alibis aren't much better."

Tyson cut me a stern look. "What did you do, interrogate them, too?"

"No, I did not," I said. "We were chatting. It came up in conversation." I told him how I had run into them in the garden, and each had pressed the other for an alibi. "It wasn't my fault. I merely happened to be present."

Tyson scoffed. "Give me a break. You were a reporter on the Vintage High School newspaper."

I chuckled. "I wasn't a reporter. I wrote a food column. Big difference! I shared tips on how to make the perfect piecrust or how to bake soft, gooey cookies."

"Go on." He folded his arms, resigned to listen.

I relayed what I believed Paula's and David's motives were and recounted their alibis—Paula being so overly distraught at Bryan's snub that she couldn't sleep and went to the library and David claiming he was on the phone to a gem dealer in Israel.

"Apparently that's where much of the gem trade takes place," I said. "There's a ten-hour time difference, so calling him at four in the morning makes sense, except . . ." My voice trailed off.

"Except . . ." Tyson echoed.

"I'm not sure I believe him."

"Why not?"

"It seemed like he was trying to convince his daughter of his actions so she would corroborate them later on, yet she was asleep in the library."

"With the candlestick," Jo teased.

I giggled. "That's what Paula said, riffing on *Clue*."

"I love that game," Jo cried.

I added, "Both of them could have had access to loose gems, too."

"Okay, I'll follow up." Tyson stood, putting an end to our interview.

As I moved toward the steps, I said, "One more thing." I glanced over my shoulder. Tyson had put his hand at the small of Jo's back to guide her. I suppressed a smile and continued. "You haven't seen Bryan's will yet, have you?"

"No. His attorney is still on the high seas."

I descended the steps and headed toward my car. "I assume Edison Barrington will inherit. Bryan had no children, no spouse. If he died intestate, Edison should get everything, correct?"

"Probably," Tyson said, "although I'll bet Mr. Baker included Angelica in his will. She's his niece. He obviously adored her. He was putting on her wedding. Besides, Edison Barrington has plenty of money. He wouldn't need it."

Jo gazed at him with admiration. "I hadn't thought of that."

"That's why I get paid the big bucks." Tyson flicked her arm with a finger. He didn't make a huge salary, but he didn't need much. He was a man of the earth. His pleasures included fishing and hiking, same as Jo.

"Edison might need the inheritance," I said. "He could be in debt."

Like a gentleman, Tyson opened the driver's door for me. "In debt?"

"He's a gambler, and Angelica is worried about his habits. She did her best to hide her concern at the out-of-towners' dinner, but I heard them exchanging words. He had arrived a little worse for wear, and she grilled him about whether he had been at a card game."

"Mimi, I'll say it again: let me do the conjecturing, okay?"

Jo sashayed around the front of the car and said over the hood, "Tyson, it won't make you any less macho if you accept help. Promise." She winked.

Tyson's face flamed red, but Jo, who was climbing into the passenger seat, missed his reaction entirely.

Chapter 10

Back at Bistro Rousseau following the conversation with Tyson, I felt hollow as I delivered the evening's specialty menu to a few diners. Many guests asked for the raspberry tart, which made me miss Bryan something fierce. How I craved his sage advice. As smart as he was, he would have solved his murder in a matter of minutes. What was I missing?

Deciding I needed fortification to think, I went to the kitchen and fixed myself a cup of strong Earl Grey tea. When I returned to the dining room, I spotted Lyle sitting with Kent and Francine. Lyle and Kent were dressed casually in button-down shirts and khaki trousers. Francine had gone to town, styling her hair into an updo, applying a trowel's worth of makeup, and donning an expensive-looking silk dress. A fourth place setting was made up but untouched. Maybe Angelica was still consoling her father. Was Edison making plans for his brother's funeral? Would Tyson release his body soon?

I sipped my tea and scanned the rest of the room. Paula and David Ives were seated at a separate table. Both seemed as blue as the outfits they wore. They were talking, and Paula's gaze perused the room whenever her father spoke. I wouldn't presume to ask why they weren't dining with Lyle and friends. Relationships were strained, I imagined.

Heather waltzed toward me, the skirt of her chiffon dress swinging in a bell-like motion. "How are you holding up?"

"I'm fine." *Liar, liar.*

"Need honey?"

"No thanks." I preferred my tea unsweetened.

"I'm happy the sheriff let you off."

"Me, too." As we drove away from the ranch, I determined Tyson must have had a firmer time of death, which was why he had cut me some slack, given Raymond's iffy timeline. Had Bryan died before Angelica went for her run? Would that change the list of suspects?

"By the way"—Heather leaned in close—"my husband said he's getting vibes and Tyson should check into all of Bryan's business contacts."

I threw her a look. "Your husband is getting vibes, or *they* are?" The aliens.

She mock-scowled. "I have a husband."

"I'd like to meet him."

"He's private."

I winked. "I can keep a secret."

"Someday you'll meet him."

I frowned. What was up with the guy? Was he for real? Why hadn't he stopped by his wife's place of business for even a nanosecond? I bit back a smile as I paired up the words *nanosecond* and *aliens*. An image of Robin Williams giving his *Mork & Mindy* greeting—"Nanu, nanu"—flitted through my mind. I had to hold myself back from offering a Spock-like salute to Heather.

"What's so funny?" she asked.

"Nothing." I didn't want to tease her. There was only so much ribbing a person could handle, and I was not mean-spirited.

Besides, the fanciful thoughts of aliens had perked me up. I handed her a pair of menus. "Take these to David and Paula Ives, will you? See if you can hear what they're talking about."

"You want me to snoop?"

"Be attentive. Offer them something to drink. Try to make at least one of them smile. Consider it a challenge."

In a quasi-British accent, Heather said, "Detective Holmes, at your service. Get it? My last name is Holmes. Too bad my first name isn't Sherlock."

"Go." I shooed her.

She flicked her curls over her shoulders and sashayed away.

As I watched her leave, I wondered about her husband's vibes. What was he picking up, if indeed he existed at all? Had one of Bryan's business associates or protégés bumped Bryan off? Was Tyson working that angle? What about people other than David Ives who might have felt that Bryan had pulled a fast one on them? Maybe the killer had known about Bryan's art treasures and murdered him to get hold of a key to Bryan's home or office. I had suggested to Tyson that he get a tally of the art he owned from Bryan's assistant. Had he done so yet? If only I had remembered to ask him while we were at the ranch.

Tiring of tea and thirsty for sparkling water, I headed toward the bar. I paused halfway there and revised my thinking. Bryan's death couldn't have been a theft. The killer had used my cell phone to contact him. Granted, everyone on my staff had access to it, but I trusted each of them implicitly. So who else might have had the chance to swipe it? None of Bryan's associates would have known about it; therefore, someone at the out-of-towners' dinner would be my best guess. Why lure Bryan to the patio? Because it was a neutral, accessible location from which it would be easy to flee. It dawned on me that Bryan would have suspected something was up if he had seen a car in the parking lot that wasn't mine, so whoever murdered him had to have either parked out of sight or arrived on foot, the latter suggesting that the killer was staying at the inn or was a local.

Location, location, location, I heard Bryan chanting from beyond the grave. It was a real estate motto, one he had uttered when he had bargained for the restaurant and inn. He said being on the main highway between two of the hottest towns in Napa Valley would give us more free advertising than we could possibly imagine. He had been right. Had being in a good location backfired on Bryan? Had it helped the killer manage a quick escape?

An icy sensation zipped through me as I gazed around the bistro. Was the killer present? Did he or she know I was trying to figure out his or her identity? Whoever it was must believe I was doing all I could to exonerate myself.

The abrasive noise of a chair scraping the floor startled me. Lyle was on his feet. He hurled his napkin on the table and stormed out of the restaurant. *What was up with that?* Kent was glowering at him. Francine was giving Kent the evil eye. Maybe Kent had learned about the bridge loans and demanded a reason for them. I could imagine the conversation:

Lyle: I'm the boss; how dare you question me?
Kent: I'm your partner; I have a bloody right to know.
Lyle: No, you bloody don't.

Like I said, Hollywood would never come calling for my screenwriting skills.

The door to the bistro opened, and I caught sight of Nash Hawke entering. Dressed in a black shirt and jeans, he looked enticing and mysterious, all at the same time. My breath snagged in my chest, and I instantly forgot about the turmoil between Lyle and Kent.

I reached up to make sure no stray hairs were sticking to my cheeks and then blew into my hand to make sure my breath was still fresh from my most recent raid on the Altoids mints I kept in the office. Assured it was, I offered a discreet wave.

Nash grinned and held a hand out to someone entering behind him. A redhead took hold and glided in. She was stunning with a capital *S*, wrapped in a Diane von Furstenberg purple-toned animal-print dress that hugged every curve. It ended six inches above her knees, revealing legs a pin-up girl would covet. Nash walked with her toward me.

"Hi, Mimi," Nash said.

The woman extended a long-fingered hand with a perfect manicure. "Mimi, *bonsoir*. It's so good to meet you."

Well, rats. Her voice sounded like honey and butter all melted together. Circe, the goddess of magic, couldn't have sounded sexier.

"Mimi, this is my ex-wife, Willow."

"Willow Hawke." She petted Nash's arm while emphasizing the last name. "And, ahem, darling, we aren't quite exes yet."

"We're meeting our attorney for dinner," Nash explained. He seemed pretty casual about a fairly serious meeting. Even his jaw appeared relaxed.

"I simply had to dine at the hottest place in Nouvelle Vie," Willow cooed. "What a find." She released Nash's hand and turned in a circle, taking in the restaurant. "So quaint. So lovely. You have an exquisite eye, Mimi."

"I had help," I said.

"Don't be modest. As the owner, you could have put the kibosh on anything. It's lovely."

Nash said, "Willow is an artist."

"*Was* an artist, darling." Willow wrinkled her pretty nose. "I'm a hack, but I have an eye for the real thing. There I was, a freshman at UC Davis—where Nash and I met—and I believed

I was going to light up the art world, but then I got a dose of reality when I saw my fellow students' works. They were brilliant; I was so-so. But I do have an eye."

For some reason, I would bet she was a pretty good artist and was simply being modest, although her dress certainly wasn't modest. Neither were her bold glances at Nash. I wasn't missing the signs. She was totally in love with him.

"Willow owns an art store in Yountville," Nash said. "You've probably seen it."

"Fruit of the Vine Artworks," Willow offered. "We have some blown-glass vases that would be ideal for your restaurant." She gently touched Nash's arm. "You know the ones I mean. They would be so colorful and fun, don't you think?"

We had perfectly fine cut-crystal vases with white roses in them. Bryan had thought they were classy.

"They'd be nice," Nash said, "but the ones she has are great, too. Like prisms, they reflect the light from the chandeliers."

I grinned. How very diplomatic. And how astute.

"Of course." Willow flitted a hand. "Well, we have many other things. Wind chimes, pottery, one-of-a-kind mirrors. I love all the mirrors you have hanging about. You must visit." She spun again to take in the restaurant. "This is simply delicious."

Snarkily, I wondered whether she was truly interested in the view or whether she wanted to show off her exquisite derriere. *Bad Mimi.*

I said to Nash, "May I show you to a table?"

"That would be great. I made a reservation for three. Our attorney is almost here. He hit traffic."

As I led the way to a table set for four, I leaned into Nash and whispered, "I didn't know you were married." I needn't have worried about speaking softly. Willow had hung back to appraise the etched-glass front door.

"We've been separated for nearly a year," Nash replied. "I was waiting for the divorce to become final before I asked you out."

"Asked me—"

"On a date. You know, where two people get to know one another better."

"Oh," I croaked and hated that I was revealing myself to him. I liked him. I didn't want him to know how much. If I could help it, I didn't want to be that vulnerable again in my lifetime. "Well, let me know when it's final." I gestured to the table. "Here we are."

Willow caught up. "How charming. Mimi, the exterior lighting along the paths is *très* dramatic." She brushed Nash's arm with her fingertips. "Darling, did you arrange this? A table right by the window? How romantic."

She sure was the touchy-feely type, I noted. Nash didn't seem to mind, or perhaps he was merely tolerating it. Maybe he didn't want to make a scene.

"Mimi, please bring us a taste of everything you love to eat," Willow said as she sat and placed a napkin on her lap.

"That might be a feast for twenty," I joked.

"Okay, then, whatever you think we'll like." Of course her laughter sounded as melodious as the burble of a gentle brook. Was there anything wrong with her? Why were they divorcing? "Nash, I forgot my shawl in the Mercedes, and it's a little chilly in here. Would you mind?" She flicked a finger at him. Like a dutiful puppy, he headed for the exit. When he was out of earshot, Willow said, "Between us girls, tonight I'm hoping to convince him that we should get back together."

I knew it.

"I miss him," she went on. "What better place to snare him than your lovely bistro? My attorney is in on the ruse."

I sighed. Nash would fold. I had no doubt. His almost ex-wife was quite an enchantress. Guess that date he'd promised was already in the mist.

Tucking my feelings safely away, I crossed to Oakley, a bubbly, carrot-topped waitress, and asked her to bring a bottle of Nouvelle Vie Chardonnay to Nash's table with three glasses—compliments of the house—and I retreated to the kitchen.

The savory aroma of roasted chicken wafted to me, and I breathed easier. There were few things that could soothe the soul better than the smell of good food. I moseyed to where Chef C was supervising the preparation of soup. We served two selections nightly: always French onion soup, regular or gluten-free—many diners were requesting that option nowadays—plus a specialty soup. Tonight's was split pea loaded with chunks of artisanal ham that the chef made using pork sirloin tips, which she had placed in a brine of fresh herbs, garlic, and onions for two weeks. Then she slow-cooked them by smoking them over applewood chips for twelve hours. Talk about heaven! That was what I was having for dinner when we closed.

"Promise to save me a bowlful," I said.

"Have some now," she replied.

"I can't. No time."

"You're not taking care of yourself."

"Don't mother me."

"If I don't, who will?"

"My mother."

Chef C grinned. "Two mothers might be better than one, missy."

"Not in my world." I grinned. I put in an order for an array of her best selections for Nash and Willow, which in the future I would add to the menu and call a tasting platter, and headed toward the dining room.

At the same time, Heather pushed through the swinging kitchen door and scuttled toward me. "I heard something between, you know . . ." Her eyes sparkled with intrigue. She clutched my elbow and dragged me to the rear of the kitchen by the dishwashers. "I brought David and Paula drinks, like you suggested . . ." She mimed the action. "Prosecco, on the house."

"Go on."

"David was talking about Angelica. He said he didn't trust her."

"Did he say why? Did Paula defend her?"

"Are you kidding? She hates her."

"I didn't know that."

"Neither did I, but the way they were talking—as if I was as deaf as a lamppost—they couldn't say enough bad things about her. They don't want her to marry Lyle, claiming things like she's too cocky and flamboyant and why does Lyle want to be chained to a celebrity, anyway? Paparazzi stalk celebrities, according to Paula. David suggested this whole affair should be called off. Paula said it's got bad mojo."

To be fair, a murder on the morning of your wedding did scream *bad mojo*.

"Did you hear more?" I asked.

"Paula said Angelica is using Lyle to get his money."

"But she isn't," I said. "She's got her own money. Not to mention Bryan was investigating Lyle because he's in the hole. He has business bridge loans up the wazoo."

"Mimi!" Stefan hurried toward me. "You have a gentleman caller at the door." He hitched his chin toward the swinging door leading to the dining room.

Nash was standing there. A halo of light backlit him and added to his gorgeous allure. My knees wobbled.

"Don't blow this," Stefan whispered. "He's a hunk."

I nudged him fondly. "Get out of here."

"You're getting up there in years." He aimed his index finger at the ceiling. "Just saying."

"And you are pushing your luck at being employed by the end of today."

Stefan chortled. So did Heather. I squeezed her elbow. "To be continued," I whispered and hustled to Nash. "Is something wrong? I've ordered your meal. It might take a few minutes. We're slammed."

"Everything's fine. Okay if I come in?"

"Um, sure."

He edged through the opening and sidled to his left. He reached for my hand. "I want to ask you on that date now."

"The divorce is final? So quickly?"

"Not yet. But I'm not waiting any longer to ask you out."

Apparently Willow's charms weren't as captivating as I had imagined, or the lawyer, who was *in on the ruse*, had arrived and doused her plans.

"Will you go to the jazz festival with me?" Nash asked.

I couldn't imagine a better first date. "Yes."

"When's your day off?"

I grinned. "I'm the boss. I can take any day. But we're closed Tuesday."

Though restaurants were typically dark on Mondays, because Napa was a tourist destination and tourists often stayed in the area through Monday, we decided that Tuesday would be a good day to close. You could get lots of errands done on a mid-week day when there was less traffic. Most Fridays, I took over the lunch shift in the kitchen, and the assistant sous chef who reported to Stefan served as my sous chef so that Chef C and Stefan could rest up for the busy weekend crowd. Last Friday had been an exception because of the out-of-towners' dinner.

"Great. See you Tuesday." Nash kissed me on the cheek and quickly returned to the dining room.

A warm glow ran from my head to my toes. *Is Willow going to be a problem?* I wondered. I sure hoped not because, throwing caution to the wind, I had to admit that I really liked Nash. A lot. I didn't know him very well, but what I did know, I enjoyed.

The swinging door flew open again, and Jo scurried in. Her short-cropped hair stuck out like a porcupine's quills, and her blue blazer was unbuttoned and flapping. She was smiling triumphantly while waggling her cell phone. "Guess what? Tyson called me."

"For a date?"

"No. Are you nuts? He's not . . . we're not . . . how many times do I have to tell you—" She wiggled her cell phone again. "He didn't want to disturb you because he knew you were in full swing on a Sunday night, so he called me with the news. Bryan's attorney returned from his cruise, and get this: Angelica Barrington is Bryan's *sole* heir."

"Are you kidding?"

"As in, her father is cut out. My dear friend, you are definitely off the suspect list!"

I shook my head. "Being his heir doesn't mean she's guilty. She has plenty of money."

"True. But she can always use more, especially if Lyle's business is under water. And let's face it, her alibi is iffy. Out running in the dark?" Jo rolled her eyes.

"I'll bet she didn't have a clue she was his heir."

"I'll bet she did."

Chapter 11

In my cottage later that night, unable to sleep, I flicked on the wireless speaker that I kept at the ready in my kitchen, opened iTunes on my iPhone, selected the album *The Phantom of the Opera*, hit *Shuffle* so all the songs would play in a random sequence, and let the music fill my soul.

Back when I was a teen, my father turned me on to musicals. He wasn't a pianist by trade—he did the bookkeeping for the winery—but he did play occasionally at a variety of restaurants in the valley as well as at the music festivals. He believed, like Shakespeare, that music was the *food of love*. I felt the same. When I lived in San Francisco, every few months I would attend a show in the theater district, which was situated between the Union Square shopping area and the Tenderloin neighborhood. After Derrick died, when my purse strings were temporarily tied in a knot, I squelched the luxury of going to a musical, but that didn't mean I couldn't rock out on my own time.

As I sang, my stomach growled, and I realized I had missed the bowl of pea soup Chef C had promised me. To keep suspects' faces from flickering through my mind like a film, I decided to create one of my favorite meals. I moved around my kitchen, singing at the top of my lungs while setting items on the granite counter.

My goldfish, Cagney and Lacey, which I'd named accordingly because I not only liked reading mysteries but also liked watching classics on television, eyed me with fascination, their snouts pressed to the glass, tails fanning to and fro. What was their crazy human doing? Sure, they had seen me cook in the cottage before. Often. But not with such frenzy. And not while belting out "The Point of No Return."

I fetched an English muffin from the refrigerator and split it in two using a fork, making sure the little holes remained intact. Then I pulled out eggs, butter, chives, and Tabasco. Hollandaise sauce should be made with care. Tonight I was going to make my mother's speedy yet consistently good version.

First, the sauce. I added the ingredients to the blender and let it whirl. I melted butter and drizzled it into the blender. Perfect. I put the blender into a pot filled with hot water and set it aside.

Next came the difficult part—the poached eggs. I had no trouble making them, but poaching eggs was not easy. Way back when, it took me many tries to master the task. A tablespoon of vinegar in the simmering water was key.

After broiling the English muffins and browning the Canadian bacon, I assembled my masterpiece on a Limoges France–pattern dinner plate. I sprinkled chopped chives and cracked red peppercorns for color on top—I happened to own four peppermills, each holding a different color of peppercorns: white, green, rose, and red. A sprig of parsley completed the presentation.

As the track for "The Music of the Night" started up, I set the dish on the antique oak kitchen table, flapped open my linen napkin—I always treated myself to a pretty table—and dug in. Heaven.

I took the next bite a little too hastily. Hollandaise sauce dribbled down my chin. "Slob," I muttered as I swiped it with a fingertip and licked it off.

Cagney, who was a common, or feeder, goldfish—orange in tone and fairly bug-eyed—seemed to be saying something. Her mouth was moving.

"What?" I asked as if she could speak.

More mouth movement.

I knew she wasn't talking to me—I wasn't crazy—but I sensed that she wanted me to focus on the investigation into Bryan's death. I kid you not. If cats and dogs could persuade their humans to do things, why not fish?

I set my fork down. "You think I should write down everything I know."

Cagney's mouth opened and closed, as if agreeing with me.

"Okay," I murmured. "When I'm done eating." I savored every bite of my dinner. The trouble with eggs Benedict was that it was gone too soon, and I instantly wanted more. But I wasn't going to splurge, and I knew it was time to face the demons in my mind.

If I didn't kill Bryan, who did?

I set my dish in the sink, soaked it with water, and moved to the dry-erase board that stood on an easel in the corner of the kitchen. I regularly used it to brainstorm new menus. I picked up the marker.

"Okay, let's start with Paula Ives."

Cagney wiggled her tail as if telling me to go for it, so I wrote down Paula's name and scribbled her father's name below. I added what I suspected would be their motives. For Paula, *Rejected*; for David, *Vengeance*.

Seeing their names paired together made me think of Paula's mother. She had fallen to her death. Was it really an accident? Paula was the only one home at the time. Had she deliberately pushed her mother, or had David sneaked in while Paula was sleeping, murdered his wife, and claimed he was nowhere in the vicinity? I scribbled *Paula's mother/David's wife* on the board and drew arrows between the phrase and Paula and David's names.

I recalled my theory at the restaurant earlier. Whoever killed Bryan had used my cell phone to lure him out. Who could have swiped it? David Ives sprang to mind. Right after dessert was served, he went in to pay his compliments to the chef. Camille loathed intruders and had booted him out, of course, but before she had, he could have taken the phone. The cubby where I stored it was right near the entrance. I jotted the note by his name.

What about Paula? I couldn't recall seeing her enter the kitchen, but I hadn't kept a strict eye on her. I wrote *Access to cell?* by her name and moved on.

"Who else could be a suspect?" I asked the fish.

Lacey, who was a slim matte goldfish, meaning she lacked any reflective pigments and the pink of her muscle showed through her white scales, became more animated. She flicked her tail and swam in a quick circle. For some reason, her eagerness reminded me of Angelica on the morning of the murder, dressed in her pink running outfit and hyped up on fear.

"Yes," I sighed. "Angelica should go on the list." I recalled her entering the kitchen to check on her father. She could have nabbed my cell phone then. She stood to inherit. Plus, if my notion about Tyson cutting me slack because the murder had happened a lot earlier was correct, Angelica's running alibi might not hold up. Reluctantly I wrote down her name and the words *motive = money* beside it. I really liked Angelica. I didn't want her to be the killer. I wondered whether there were speed cameras in Napa that would register if a person—say,

Angelica—was running around the area before dawn. I made a mental note to ask Tyson.

Right below Angelica's name, I scribbled Edison's name. I couldn't rule him out. I had seated him in the bistro kitchen at the table with the cubbyholes. If he had learned that his half-brother was planning to leave his money to Angelica and not to him, he could have grown incensed. Also he might have feared that Angelica would begin to favor Bryan over him because Bryan was more stable and hadn't gambled away his fortune—if indeed Edison had blown through his savings. That was still an assumption on my part.

I revisited Angelica's name and added *Inheritance, when might she have learned of it?* I recalled her speaking with Bryan at the out-of-towners' dinner, out of earshot of the others. Had he revealed that he was leaving everything to her?

"Don't be silly," I murmured. A celebratory dinner was not the place to talk about death and wills and life-altering matters. But if Angelica was to be a true suspect, she had to have known about the inheritance. Otherwise, she had no motive that I knew of.

My cell phone rang. I glanced at the readout. My mother was calling. She always went to bed at ten. Worry spiraled up my neck as I answered the call.

"Are you okay?"

"Darling, I'm . . ." She hesitated. "I hate to bother you, but . . ." She stopped herself again.

"Mom, what is it?"

"You'll think I'm overreacting, but I think there's a ghost in the house."

I didn't believe in ghosts, although one time after Derrick's death, the bedroom had grown incredibly chilly, as if he had entered. I'd noted the event in my diary to be sure I hadn't fallen

121

asleep and dreamed the scenario. But nothing happened. Derrick hadn't materialized. We didn't have a chat.

"Can you come over?" she asked, her voice barely a whisper.

Lightly I said, "Is it a scary ghost or a *Casper the Friendly Ghost*–type ghost?"

"Don't make fun."

I squelched a giggle and took her seriously. She never let spooky things get to her. She was one of the few people I knew who adored scary films.

"Do you want me to spend the night?" I asked.

"No. Just come check things out. The house is so big without . . ."

Without my father. "I'll be there in a few."

I promised the goldfish I would return soon and sped to Nouvelle Vie Vineyards.

The tires of my Jeep skidded on the gravel driveway. I didn't bother locking the doors. I raced up the path leading to the house, a beautiful farmhouse-style home in moss green with cream trim. My love of a wine-colored motif came from my mother. Low lights cast a warm glow along the path and the abundant red roses bordering it. Exterior lights highlighted the columns and the blooming crape myrtles.

A dog barked as I trotted up the stairs to the porch, and the aroma of freshly baked bread wafted through the screen door. Riesling, my mother's fluffy white midsized Goldendoodle, stood sentry. As I entered, he nearly tackled me with love.

"Four on the floor," I ordered.

Riesling planted his feet, but his rear end wagged as hard as his tail as he waited for my caresses.

"Mom?"

My mother rushed toward me. Flour from late-night baking dusted her black cotton flannel pajamas, which were decorated with multicolored wineglasses and wine bottles.

I drew her into a hug. "Mom, you're trembling."

"I am not."

"Okay, you're not," I said, feeling like the parent trying to calm the quaking child. "Show me the ghosts. 'I ain't afraid of no ghosts,'" I chanted. Bill Murray couldn't have delivered the line better.

"I feel so foolish," she said as she climbed the stairs to the second floor.

I followed. Riesling trailed me.

"Maintaining the vineyard has become so daunting. Maybe . . ." My mother stopped outside a room that used to be my father's study. When he wasn't working or playing piano around town, he loved to read. "In there."

I gulped. I hadn't been inside the room since we had sorted through things the week after Dad died. Emotions raced through me. Would I cry? I hoped I wouldn't. I needed to be strong.

I tried the doorknob. It was locked. "Do you have a key?"

My mother plucked a key from above the doorjamb and handed it to me.

"Tell me what you saw," I said as I inserted the key and twisted.

"Nothing."

"I'm sorry?"

"I haven't gone in. I *heard* things."

"Woo-woo things?"

"Clattering. But not typical clattering."

"Typical?"

"You know, not like a thief rooting through your father's treasures. It was specific clattering."

I raised an eyebrow. *Specific* clattering. For a woman whose business required being precise—just the right amount of *this* grape paired with just the right amount of *that* grape—she was being pretty darned vague.

"I'm going in. Want to hide in your room?"

"No."

"All right. I'm going—"

"Wait! What if—"

"Don't say it!" I held up a warning finger as a frisson of fear crawled up my spine. "There is a perfectly good explanation for whatever you heard." My father was not floating around this house causing a ruckus, and no ghosts from previous owners were, either. "No what-ifs," I said. "Only what *is*. Let's solve this."

I unlocked the door. My mother sucked in her breath and pressed herself against the hallway wall as if she wanted to become one with the plaster. Riesling snuggled against her legs. I pushed the door open and flicked on the light switch. The overhead light flickered and popped.

My mother screamed. Riesling yelped.

"Calm down, both of you," I cried. "Lightbulbs often blow because of loose connections or a slack light switch. The electricity causes an arc, which produces heat. It happened all the time while we were sprucing up Bistro Rousseau." I assessed my mother, who was shivering. "It doesn't help that adrenaline is rushing through us as well as the dog at warp speed. Stay here. That means you, too, Riesling." I flattened my hand, signaling for him to stay. Obediently he sat on his haunches, but he didn't stop whimpering.

I tiptoed into the room. It was cold. I tried not to think about that. A chill did not signify the eerie presence of a ghost. I switched on a light by the desk. A warm low-level glow filled the room. My father's desk appeared untouched. He had been methodical. All his files stood in neat piles. The file cabinet was intact. No drawers hung open. His reading chair, where he had read me many a book growing up, was in the proper place. I turned on the floor lamp beside it and pivoted to take in the entire room. A book lay on the floor by the bookshelf. I bent to inspect it and suddenly felt a whoosh of air and heard a clatter.

A bust of Edgar Allen Poe fell off the bookshelf, nearly hitting me on the head.

I leaped to my feet.

Something skittered. Then the drapes began to flutter.

I tore to the window and pulled back the curtains. The window was slightly ajar. In the glimmer of what little moonlight there was, I spotted a squirrel making its escape down the tree outside the room.

"I see you, you varmint!" I yelled. "Mom, come in. It's not a ghost. You left the window open, and a squirrel was taking a tour of Dad's things."

She entered, her face white with fear. It turned pink with embarrassment pretty quickly. "I had the windows washed last week," she murmured. "One of the crew must have left the window open. Silly me for not checking."

"For your information, the squirrel had good taste. It was attempting to read *The Fall of the House of Usher*." One of my father's favorite stories.

My mother laughed, which elicited a happy yip from Riesling.

I returned the book to the shelf and picked up the bust of Poe. The tumble had nicked the base but not the face. Dad would be relieved. Then I secured the window and followed my mother downstairs. She put on some music—Chopin to relax us both—and set a teakettle on the stove. When the water was boiling, she made us each a cup of soothing chamomile tea and offered me warm bread slathered in butter. How could I refuse? We ate in companionable silence. She didn't ask me about the investigation. I didn't press her about her emotional state. She had been my rock before; she would be my rock again.

An hour later, she told me to leave. I assured her I would do so when she was soundly asleep.

Around midnight, I returned home. Too wound up to rest my weary brain, I slipped out to the patio to drink in the night air and stare at the stars. Thinking about what lay beyond the stars always calmed me. A few minutes after I was nestled in my chair, I heard a rustle.

"Scoundrel?" I whispered. The cat didn't emerge.

I scrambled to my feet and peered into the dark. Off to the left, a couple walked along a path. I could barely make them out in the light of the waxing crescent moon, what my mother liked to call God's thumbnail, but on closer inspection, I realized it was Angelica and Lyle. They were holding hands. Angelica was talking, but I couldn't make out anything she was saying. Suddenly she turned to Lyle and jabbed her finger into his chest. He grabbed her wrist and pulled her close. He planted a kiss on her mouth. For a moment, she struggled to get free, but then she melted into him.

"Lyle," I whispered, realizing I had forgotten to add his name to my list. I raced inside to the dry-erase board and jotted down his name plus his possible motive: *Money trouble.* Bryan had investigated Lyle and had found his finances in shambles. Lyle had challenged Bryan. What if he knew ahead of time that Angelica would come into money? She had plenty of her own, of course; she was a well-paid celebrity. But what if Lyle was banking on paying off his debt with his bride's inheritance?

If Angelica had learned about the inheritance from Bryan or otherwise, had she told Lyle? I circled his name, believing he had the strongest motive. Then I stepped away and paced the floor. My goldfish studied me as if I was a specimen in their human experiment.

I muttered, "Bug off," and returned to the board. I tapped the marker on Lyle's name. Was he really the most likely suspect? If Bryan had intended to break up Lyle and Angelica, why had he thrown an out-of-towners' dinner and planned an elaborate wedding? Had he hoped to embarrass Lyle at the wedding by speaking up when the pastor asked if anyone wanted to protest the happy union? Had he told Lyle as much? Had Lyle blown a gasket?

How would he have gotten his hands on my cell phone? I pondered his movements and had an "aha moment." Lyle had spilled a glass of water and hurried to the kitchen for extra napkins. Had he spilled the water on purpose? Had he known that my cell phone was in the kitchen, or had taking it been an impulsive decision? He saw it, decided he could use it to further his plot, and grabbed it.

Then he returned to his hotel room, remembered his stash of loose gems, and thought exactly what Jo and I had said to Tyson: *I'll show you, Bryan. Choke on this.*

Chapter 12

At my usual predawn time, I woke, showered, and dressed. I drank my coffee, fed the fish, scanned the dry-erase board to give myself a mental picture that I could work on throughout the day, and zipped to the restaurant. I skipped breakfast because, as we did every Monday, Chef C and I spent the early morning hours preparing specialties for the coming week that we would taste-test with the staff. I loved working in tandem with her. We moved about the kitchen with the same tempo. She whistled; I hummed.

Around nine AM, we assembled our crew at a rectangular table in the bistro. The table was preset with place settings, multiple wineglasses, and menus. Stefan and Oakley worked in tandem to serve the dishes.

Meanwhile, Heather, who had taken charge of pairing each course with an appropriate wine—another job at which she excelled—was moving around the table and pouring a swallow of white wine into Bordeaux-style glasses. "This week," she said, "Mimi is serving chicken roulade stuffed with brussels sprouts, pine nuts, and pecorino."

A roulade was rolled meat or pastry filled with a stuffing. The dish's name originated from the French word *rouler*, which meant "to roll."

The staff murmured its appreciation.

"I'm pairing that with a crisp Cakebread Sauvignon Blanc," Heather continued. "As you all know, they're some of the best around because Dolores Cakebread loved her Sauvignon Blancs. Take a sip." Everyone obeyed. "I know you taste the citrus and the melon. What other flavors do you detect?" She eyed me. "Mimi?"

I frowned. All I was getting was citrus. Stress, I decided, was doing a number on my palate. I could usually rattle off three or four flavors. "Tell me."

"Guava?" Heather asked. "Peach?"

I swirled the wine over and under my tongue. "Um, okay. No matter what, I like it."

Chef C agreed. "It will go nicely with the savory cheese and pine nuts."

Next up was one of her specialties, Boursin-stuffed chicken. I happened to love Boursin cheese. A man named Philippe Boursin had created it in France in the 1950s. A long-standing traditional dish called *fromage frais*, which translated to "fresh cheese," had inspired him. Ages ago, guests could season their fresh cheese using herbs provided by the host. Boursin made it a household product.

Heather said, "I like a Chardonnay with this dish. I've chosen the Flora Springs Family Select, which has been sourced entirely from the family's estate-owned vineyards."

Chef C grinned. "Love it."

Heather went on, "It opens with mango. After that, you get the flavor of Asian pear."

Stefan snorted. "Really? Asian pear?"

Heather scowled at him. "And notes of caramel."

"If you say so." Stefan didn't drink alcohol and loved to tease Heather.

We carried on for an hour, with Chef C occasionally challenging Heather's selection and Heather holding her own. As I sipped moderately—I needed to keep my wits about me—I thought of Bryan. He had joined in many of these taste-testing sessions. His frank opinion and his passion for food would be greatly missed.

When the time drew near to get things into gear for the lunch crowd, I stood and said, "Thank you, everyone. Let's all have a positive day. No gossip about Mr. Baker—or anybody, for that matter. Make our menu shine. Encourage every customer to have the best dining experience ever."

My staff saluted like career soldiers and marched off to do what they did best while chatting among themselves about which dishes they liked and which words they would use to describe them, like *succulent*, *creamy*, or *heavenly*. I coveted their lightheartedness.

At noon, I stood near the hostess podium, where Heather was welcoming guests, and I drank in the good vibes. People were entering with smiles. Laughter abounded in the bistro. With the sun directly overhead outside, a golden glow emanated through the windows. Many of the hotel's guests had come in for lunch. I heard a few say that they intended to load up on rich food because they were going wine tasting afterward. Fats helped keep alcohol from being absorbed into the system. One diner said she had heard that the duck confit, which was essentially duck preserved and baked to a crisp in lard, would be the perfect pretasting dish. I wholeheartedly agreed.

"Hello, Mimi," a woman said.

I turned and saw Angelica entering the bistro with her father. Dressed in a sheer black blouse, gray cigarette pants, and low-slung black heels, with her hair swept off her face and secured in a hairband, she appeared sedate and solemn. Edison's attire, however, surprised me. He was wearing a yellow plaid shirt tucked into jeans. Don't get me wrong. I knew the world had changed. A mourner no longer had to wear black for a year, but his yellow shirt seemed a bit too cheery a mere two days after his brother died. Was I being prickly?

I scooted around Heather and met them at the door. "Let me take you to your table."

Heather handed me two menus.

"How are you holding up, sir?" I said to Edison.

"I'm okay. Thanks for asking."

Angelica said, "Dad and I are trying to fill the hours until the chief deputy coroner signs off on the cause of death and releases the body. Then we can have a proper funeral."

"Has anyone given you a clue as to when that will be?" I asked.

"No. A few days, they said. They did toxicology reports but promised the results of those wouldn't delay the release of his body." She sighed. "Neither of us is really hungry."

"I understand." I guided them to a table near the door leading to the patio.

Angelica grew pale. "Can we sit elsewhere? I don't want to look out—"

"Of course," I said hastily. What an insensitive dolt I was. "This way." I showed them to a table nearer the kitchen. "How's this?"

"Perfect."

Once seated, they immediately opened their menus. I told them about one of the specials, a leek-and-Fontina quiche with a side garden salad—all herbs and vegetables picked from our garden. "If you wish to go light, why don't you have French onion soup?" I offered them a glass of Prosecco on the house. Both declined.

Before leaving the table, I said, "Angelica, I spotted you and Lyle walking last night. I imagine you mended fences if your kiss was any indication."

Her cheeks reddened.

Edison gaped at his daughter. "Mimi knows that you and Lyle argued?"

"Uh-huh." Angelica unfolded her napkin and placed it on her lap. "She's the one who set me straight about California law."

That seemed to placate Edison.

I said, "May I ask you a question about Lyle?"

Angelica tilted her chin up, her mouth slightly open and her eyes receptive.

Knowing what I knew about their previous argument and sensing that I could be treading on dangerous ground with what I intended to ask, I softened my pose and tried to look more like a friend than the Grand Inquisitor. "Kent mentioned that Lyle carries gems with him everywhere."

Edison clucked his tongue. "I heard him say that. How reckless. Your young man is tempting fate." He aimed a finger at his daughter. "Thieves are lurking everywhere."

Angelica threw him a dismissive look. "Lyle locks them up in a portable safe, Dad." She said to me, "It's actually a gun safe with a steel security cable and everything. No one could remove it from the room."

"Well, then," Edison said, "that certainly points a finger at him as the murderer, doesn't it?"

"Why?" I asked.

Edison splayed his hands. "A gemstone was stuffed into Bryan's mouth, correct?"

All who had watched the crime scene crew collect evidence had picked up on that tidbit.

"B-but," Angelica sputtered, "Lyle isn't the only one with the code to the safe. Kent has it and so do I."

I would bet David Ives had it, too. He owned the business.

"You couldn't possibly be the murderer," Edison said.

"How can you be sure?" Angelica said. "I've got the best motive. I'm Uncle Bryan's sole heir."

"What?" Edison's mouth fell open.

Aha! So he knew about the argument but not about the will. Had Angelica planned to tell him during lunch?

"Bryan claimed he didn't write a will," Edison said.

"Well, he did." Angelica's eyes sparkled with defiance.

"Who told you so?"

"Sergeant Daly."

"Really?" I said. "I thought Bryan might have told you when the two of you had your private chat at the out-of-towners' dinner."

Angelica clapped a hand to her chest. "How horrible that would have been! Can you imagine? As if he'd foreseen his murder?" She took a sip of water and blotted her lips.

"What did you discuss, then, if it wasn't about his estate or what he and Lyle argued about on the patio? You told me the other day that it was *nothing*."

Angelica blushed. "Bryan simply wanted to tell me how beautiful I looked. Like my mother, he said. He admired the necklace I was wearing and said it suited me." She eyed her father, who was working his tongue inside his mouth. "Dad, about the inheritance, I guess he left it to me because he thought you had plenty of money." She reached for his hand.

Edison pulled away and smashed his lips together. Was he upset because his gambling addiction had emptied his coffers, as I suspected, and he was going to be financially ruined? If Bryan had died intestate, Edison, as his brother, would have inherited.

Had he counted on that? Or maybe he was ticked off because Bryan had chosen Angelica over him?

Abruptly he rose to his feet, tossed his napkin down, and headed toward the restroom.

Angelica blanched. "Poor Dad. I should—"

"Don't go after him. He'll return." I placed a hand on her shoulder. "Let's focus on you for a bit. You need to pin down your alibi. You said you were out running. Are you sure no one saw you?"

"There weren't any other runners. Most people like to run when there's sunlight. They feel safer. Me? I like the anonymity of darkness. In Los Angeles, I hate running when everyone else is out and about. Plus the paparazzi can be incredibly cruel. I do not want a picture of my *derriere* in jogging pants plastered in the *National Enquirer*."

I smiled. I wouldn't want that, either, even though Derrick had once told me that I had an attractive derriere. "Did you see any cars on the road?"

"A few passed by, but I doubt anyone would have recognized me."

"What if you took out an ad in the local papers or posted flyers on the road and in some of the food stores?" I suggested.

"Good idea."

"Have you asked Sergeant Daly if there are speed cameras on the main roads that might have captured an image of you?" I had yet to touch base with Tyson on that.

"No, I haven't—"

"She doesn't need to." Edison returned and took his seat. His face looked moist, as if he'd splashed it with water. "She's innocent."

"Mimi's right, Dad. I might need proof. I'm going to put up flyers to see if a witness might come forward."

"Take a picture of yourself in your running clothes," I suggested. "Your pink top was pretty distinctive. And remember your hair was in a ponytail."

"Right." Angelica gazed pleadingly at her father. "Do you mind if I go, Dad? You stay, have lunch. Mimi, put the check on my hotel bill, please." She rose and kissed her father on the cheek and petted his shoulder fondly. "I'm sorry if the news about the inheritance upset you. You know I'll split whatever Uncle Bryan gave me with you."

"I don't need his money," Edison snarled. "I don't *want* his money."

"We'll talk." Angelica tore out of the restaurant.

As the door whooshed closed, Edison's shoulders sagged. "Well, write me up as father of the year. I sure handled that wrong. But I meant what I said. I don't need the money. She worries too much about me."

I offered a supportive smile. "Disregard how quickly she left. She's on a mission."

He reset his silverware—the knife next to the oversized dessert spoon and the smaller spoon next to that.

I perched on Angelica's chair and leaned forward, elbows on the table. "Sir, forgive me, but I sensed tension between you and Bryan."

"Yep, you did. Brothers fight. We went at it as kids. We argued as adults. But we also liked one another. He was one of the few people I could talk to about anything. Granted, he didn't appreciate my lifestyle."

"The gambling," I murmured.

He regarded me with caution.

"When we met Friday night, I heard Angelica chastise you."

"Not my finest hour." Edison screwed up his mouth. "That's probably why Bryan cut me out. He didn't want me to run through his estate like water. He worked hard for it. He gave up a lot to be wealthy and carefree."

A gloom seemed to consume him. His shoulders curved forward. He set his napkin back on his lap and smoothed it repeatedly.

"Were you jealous of Bryan because he was paying for Angelica's wedding?"

"Jealous? No. I was annoyed. There's a whole world of difference. It's emasculating, what he did. He knew I didn't have the cash. Sure, I'm in hock, but I'll get out of it. I always bounce back. I've refinanced the winery many times. It's profitable as long as I don't run it into the ground. The grapes are good. The product sells. I'm resilient."

"My husband used to say he was resilient. I believed him, until I didn't."

Edison leveled me with his gaze. "Again with the innuendoes."

"No, I—"

"Do you really think I could kill my own brother? You're wrong. I loved him. Besides, where would I have gotten those gems? I suppose Bryan could have been carrying them, but why? That makes no sense." He leaned forward and folded his arms on the table. "As for my daughter, she couldn't have killed him. She's the sweetest, gentlest person I know. Like her mother." His eyes brimmed with tears. "My money is on Lyle. I don't trust him or his family."

"Sir, you stormed out of the dinner that night. Where did you go afterward?"

"Are you asking for my alibi?"

"No, I—"

"It's all right. I don't mind. I'm just yanking your chain." He sat back in his chair. "I went home. I was dog-tired. I fell into bed. I woke early. It's one of the hazards of being a vintner. There was no frost, of course, not at this time of year, so I didn't need to check on the vines. Even so, I stayed up and read a book." He held up a warning hand. "And don't—"

A waiter added fresh water to both glasses on the table and departed.

"Don't go asking me which book," Edison finished. "I don't remember. A wine primer, probably. I have a pile of them next to my bed." He rasped out a laugh. "I know it's a weak alibi, but it's all I've got." He picked up his menu and perused it.

I tilted my head. Was he avoiding my gaze because he was lying? Did he go out gambling after the out-of-towners' dinner? Was he afraid I might tell Angelica and she would lower the boom on him? Or was he telling me this so *I* would corroborate his alibi? Maybe he believed I would put in a good word for him with Tyson. What if Edison knew before that night that Angelica would inherit from her uncle? He claimed that he and Bryan talked about everything. Had Bryan given him a heads-up about what he intended to do in the event of his death? Maybe they had discussed it when Bryan told him he was footing the bill for the wedding.

No—that didn't make sense. Edison wouldn't have killed Bryan in that case; he would have tried to persuade him to change the will back.

On the other hand, what if he knew his daughter would freely offer half the inheritance to him? He said she was the kindest, gentlest soul he knew. Except she planned to marry Lyle, the love of her life, and if Lyle's business was in trouble, Angelica would be hard-pressed to choose between helping her father and helping her beloved.

"I'll take the French onion soup." Edison handed his menu to me, dismissing me.

As I moved away from the table, a gruesome thought hit me. Would Bryan's estate revert to Edison if Angelica were out of the picture?

Chapter 13

A while later, I was in the restaurant office reviewing the orders for the upcoming week's supplies when Jo entered, a flush to her cheeks, her black leather notebook opened wide.

"Everything okay?" I asked.

"Busy." She unbuttoned the single button on her stylish peacock-blue jacket and consulted her notebook. "Lots of guests checking out today." She gestured with her thumb. "Say, I saw Angelica Barrington pinning flyers on telephone poles. What's up with that?"

"She's intent on finding a witness to corroborate that she was running on the morning Bryan was killed."

"Who put her up to that, her father?"

"Me. I don't think she killed Bryan, in spite of how it looks with the inheritance."

"Right, the inheritance." Jo flipped her notebook closed, her curiosity piqued.

"Angelica said she'll split the money with her father no matter what."

"Unless that fiancé of hers has something to say about it. I don't like him very much. He's sort of arrogant, you know what I mean? Nose in the air. Giving orders to the staff."

"I'm not sure if he's arrogant or simply thrown off course by what happened." I signed the order form and handed it to Jo. "Will you see that this gets handled?"

"Sure. Speaking of business, I've booked the inn for a number of events. I didn't consult with you. I hope you don't mind."

"As if I would." I steered her out of the office and into the bistro. "What did you agree to?"

She stopped beside the hostess podium and opened her notebook to a specific page. "Vanessa Marshall's fiftieth birthday bash."

"Vanessa Marshall of Vanessa's Vineyard? She's the most flamboyant woman in Napa. How big will the bash be?"

"She has fifty friends coming in from all fifty states"—Jo rubbed her fingers together, signifying big money—"and they're going to do fifty outings, all of which we're to book for her."

"Whew. We had enough rooms available?"

"It's a year away."

"Maybe we should hire a concierge after all." I had been putting off creating that official position, believing that Jo could handle everything, but if our little enterprise continued to blossom, we might need a full-fledged employee. "What else?"

"We have an anniversary for a pair of ninety-year-olds. They're calling it their one hundred and eightieth birthday. They want to go hot-air ballooning."

"How romantic. May they both survive the thrill."

Jo winked. "I'm sure any balloon company will require them to sign waivers."

I pointed toward the window with the view of the inn. "What's going on?" People in colorful smocks with easels slung over their shoulders and canvases hooked under their arms were streaming up the front path.

"Because of the wedding—it being our first—I didn't book any additional events over the weekend. I didn't want the staff overextended. However, since the wedding was postponed, I jumped all over a spur-of-the-moment art affair this gal pitched to me. I figured we could recoup some of the lost revenue. You and I both know that groups rarely schedule events on a Monday. We're setting up in the Sisley Garden. Each artist has paid a handsome fee to participate. It's for charity to buy art supplies for local schools." Jo tucked her notebook under her arm. "Can you take a break? Come see."

"Sure. Just a sec." I hurried to Heather. She was involved in a lively conversation with two of our regular patrons, telling them what she had planned for her day off. I said, "I'm heading to the inn with Jo."

"Hang on." Heather excused herself from our diners, dashed to the kitchen, and quickly returned with a to-go bag. "I told Chef C you hadn't eaten, so she made you lunch."

I grinned. "My mother was never this conscientious."

Heather patted my arm. "You need someone to look out for you."

Maybe Chef C was right; two mothers were better than one. Losing Bryan had left me off-kilter.

As Jo and I strolled to Maison Rousseau, the sun blazed overhead, but a gentle breeze cooled the air. Chatter abounded as we rounded the bend toward the Sisley Garden, which was rife with white roses.

"This way," a woman said in a booming, authoritative voice. I couldn't see her. She was hidden among the throng of artists. "Right over here. That's it. Set up and we'll bring out the model."

"Model?" I glanced at Jo.

"Don't worry," she said. "A clothed model. She'll be dressed like Venus—with arms." She waved as she proceeded toward the woman in charge. "Willow! Over here."

I clutched Jo's arm. "Willow Hawke organized this?"

"Is there a problem?"

Willow forged through the crowd, looking as exquisite as she had at our first meeting—hair flowing, floral dress fitting her like a glove. How she could walk on the gravel path in four-inch spike heels was beyond me. She extended both arms. "Jo, darling. Isn't this fab? The wine tasting is set up over there. The harpist is almost ready to begin." She turned a keen eye on me. "Mimi, you never change."

Okay, that stung. Like I said, I wore the same work outfit daily. I centered the gem of my necklace in the hollow of my neck and lifted my chin. *Sticks and stones . . .*

Idly I wondered if Nash and Willow had severed the knot or if she had changed his mind about the divorce. He hadn't called to cancel our date. No matter what, I would not—*not*—date a married man. And I refused to be jealous of Willow if they stayed married. My father always said that jealousy undermined confidence. All my life, I had worked hard not to be green with envy if a girlfriend liked someone I did, and I had tried not to be resentful of those who wished to follow my same career path. The world had plenty of room for terrific chefs and entrepreneurs. I would not be envious of Willow. I was attractive, I could probably cook rings around her, and besides, she seemed nice. Truly nice. Maybe the clothing comment wasn't meant to be a barb.

"Don't you love it?" Willow swept her hand in a grand gesture. "Look, there's Venus." A long-limbed woman draped in a silver one-shouldered gown glided into the center of the garden. "Climb on, darling!" Willow gestured with a flick of the wrist. "I brought a pedestal for her," she said to us and motioned to the center of the garden, where a preset foot-high white column with ionic lines stood.

The model climbed onto the base and swept her long black hair over her shoulders. She struck a pose, one hand on her hip.

"I hope she's wearing sunblock," Jo teased.

Willow said, "Mimi, when the artists are finished, you'll get to pick one of their pieces for the inn."

I gulped, not sure what to say. What if the artists were terrible? What if the art turned out to look like a mash-up of a Picasso and a Jackson Pollock?

Jo said, "It'll look nice in the library."

"That's great," I murmured tepidly. "Um, Willow, sorry, but Jo and I have work to do, so we'll leave you to it. Nice to see you."

"You, too. And don't forget to stop by Fruit of the Vine Artworks. I'll show you those vases I mentioned."

As I hustled Jo out of the garden, I whispered, "Willow is Nash Hawke's wife."

"Nash as in hunky, gorgeous Nash?"

I bobbed my head. "They're getting a divorce. Or I think they are. I'm not sure. They met at the bistro for dinner yesterday to sign papers. Before he left, he asked me out. On a date."

"Ooh," she said, realization dawning in her eyes.

"But Willow doesn't want to divorce."

"O-o-oh," Jo said, in a much more ominous tone. "So you think she went to all this trouble to get under your skin?"

"I don't think she knows about us. Heck, I don't know about us." I waved a hand. "It doesn't matter. I can't think about it. Not with everything else that's going on. I need to eat. Come with me to my place."

I jogged toward the cottage, the to-go bag rustling loudly.

Jo hustled to keep pace. "Speaking of everything else, have you heard anything from Tyson?"

"Nothing."

As I reached the front door, Scoundrel darted across my feet and disappeared into the bushes. I shrieked. So did Jo.

"That cat," she muttered.

I giggled. "He keeps us on our toes."

"Found any, um, *gifts* lately?"

"Nope."

Scoundrel was a successful mouser. He loved bringing heads or tails of mice and other rodents to the bistro's kitchen door—his *gifts* to us for feeding him. Luckily I wasn't the one who had to dispose of the body parts. I let Heather take care of that lovely duty.

I unlocked the cottage door, slung the to-go bag on the kitchen counter, and unpacked its contents. Chef C had packed enough food to feed an army. The aroma from the quiche made me salivate. "Hungry?" I asked my pal.

"Starved."

I set the kitchen table with two decorative green-and-gold-paisley placemats, matching napkins, and two Forsyth by Royal Doulton plates, their green-and-gold pattern going well with the paisley. I asked Jo to fill a pair of crystal goblets with ice water.

"What's with the notes on the dry-erase board?" she asked.

"I couldn't sleep. Even though I'm no longer a suspect, I care about who killed Bryan, so I—" My voice cracked. I started to shake. I gripped the kitchen counter to keep from sinking to my knees.

Jo raced to me and slung an arm around my back. "Are you okay?"

"Yes. No. I—"

"You haven't cried yet, have you?" She clucked her tongue. "Just like with Derrick. You held it in for weeks, remember? You silly goose. Let it out."

"I . . ."

"C'mon. I'm here. You're safe."

I sank into her arms. Tears gushed out of me.

"Talk it out," she coaxed.

"Oh, Jo. Losing my dad"—I hiccupped—"ripped me to pieces. And then to lose Derrick?"

"I know. I know."

"And now to lose Bryan? He . . ." I could barely breathe. "He believed in me. He instilled me with such confidence. He . . ." I sniffed and pushed away. "I feel so robbed. So cheated. It's like all the men in my life are vanishing. One by one. I don't want to . . . to . . ." I drew in a deep breath and let it out.

"You don't want to risk giving your heart to anyone ever again."

"Yes. No. I don't know." I shuffled to the counter and grabbed a couple of tissues from a box. "All I know is I want to find the killer. I want this to end. I want—"

"Closure."

I nodded and then blew my nose and wiped the tears off my cheeks. After a long quiet moment, I said, "Whoa. That took me by surprise. I must look a mess."

"You look fine."

"Liar."

"I hear the red, splotchy look is in." She twirled a finger near my face.

I stuck out my tongue; she blew me a kiss.

"If it makes you feel any better, I miss him, too."

I sighed. Of course she did. She had known him all her life. "Jo, what are we going to do?"

"What do you mean?"

"I've heard that if a murder doesn't get solved in the first forty-eight hours, it often never gets solved."

"Where did you hear that? On TV? Maybe that's true in a big city where they have to abandon cases and move on to new ones, but not here." She petted my shoulder. "Don't worry. Tyson will crack this."

"What if he can't?"

"He will."

I tossed the tissues in the garbage beneath the sink, sanitized my hands, plated the quiche and salad, and took a seat at the table. Eating a meal suddenly didn't sound as good as it had minutes before, but I knew I needed to refuel.

Jo joined me and waved at the dry-erase board. "Okay, I'm game. Explain what your thinking is."

I shrugged. "I know it looks like a bunch of mindless scribbles."

"Actually, it looks pretty organized for you. Remember, I've seen some of your menus before they're finalized." She shot her hands in every direction.

I laughed. She was right. I was pretty good at using arrows and indicators when I was in "create mode."

"It all started when . . ." I recapped seeing Paula and David Ives in the garden. "I told you about that at Tyson's mother's ranch."

Jo nodded. "David said he was on a long-distance telephone call to his diamond broker in Israel. You suggested to Tyson that he follow up. Did he?"

"I don't know."

"If he didn't, we could help. If David used the hotel telephone to make the call, we could review the records and get the guy's number."

"Given the scope of his business, David probably has an international cell phone."

"You're right." Jo ate a few bites of quiche, hummed her approval, and reexamined the notes on the board. "You know, I've got a jeweler friend I can touch base with. Maybe she knows this Abrams guy. What does the *spilled water* note next to Lyle's name mean?"

"Whoever killed Bryan used my cell phone to lure him to the patio. I've been wracking my brain trying to figure out who had access to it and when. I forgot to take it home that night. I often leave it because I know it will be there in the morning. Lyle knocked over a glass of water and rushed to the kitchen to get something to mop up the mess. I didn't think anything of it at the time, but looking back, he could have tipped the glass on purpose."

Jo read what I'd written on the board aloud: "'David Ives entered the kitchen to pay his compliments to the chef.'"

"He did. Chef C booted him out."

Jo guffawed. "I can just picture that scene, with Chef waving a wooden spoon and verbally reducing him to mush."

"Close. She pounded a metal spoon on a twelve-quart pot."

"Ouch! The noise. She hates when a stranger enters her domain."

"Even so, he might have had time to spot my phone and swipe it."

"I suppose."

"Angelica went into the kitchen, too, because her father was there, seated at the table with the cubbies. He arrived slightly inebriated, so I fixed him an Alka-Seltzer, trying to sober him up."

Jo folded her hands on the table. "How about Paula Ives?"

"I never saw her enter, but that doesn't mean she didn't."

Another thought came to me. I rose and wrote a note at the top of the board: *Who had the code to the safe?*

"What safe?" Jo exclaimed. "And when did you get so good at this sleuthing stuff?"

I grinned, accepting the compliment. "A chef is always trying to figure out what's in a recipe. Investigating comes naturally to me. As for the safe . . ." I explained how Lyle traveled with gems and kept them in a portable safe. "He and Angelica knew the code." I wrote their names under the question. "So did Kent, but I've ruled him out as a suspect because he hooked up with

Francine for the night, and why would either of them have a reason to kill Bryan?"

"How did you find out that they hooked up?"

"I caught them sort of cohabitating in one of the rooms."

"Aha." She skimmed the board again. "Wouldn't David Ives have the code? He's the boss."

I grinned. "You and I think alike." I added that note.

Jo tapped her lips with her forefinger. "My money is on him."

"Minutes ago, your money was on Lyle."

"Okay, so I like to cover my bets." She grinned.

"The one snag is that stealing the gems required sneaking into Lyle's room."

"That wouldn't be hard." Jo polished off her quiche and dabbed her mouth with a napkin. "I know you went for quaint when you designed the inn, but the old-style key locks are definitely not high-end security. A novice could pick them."

I sighed. "I said as much to Bryan and argued for magnetic strip–style keys, but he believed in the beneficence of man. Plus he believed using antique keys would make guests feel like they were living in a gentler time."

"Murder definitely isn't a gentler time," Jo quipped. She let that sink in and then said, "I imagine knowing the safe's code rules out Angelica's father."

"Possibly, although he knew that Lyle traveled with gems. He said it was reckless."

Jo checked her watch. "Yipes. I've got to run. The art class should be winding down, and I've got to get the staff prepared for our next event."

"You booked another one for today?"

"Yep. We have the Agatha Christie Society coming tonight for a reading under the stars. Tonight's book is *And Then There Were None*."

"We're certainly busy."

"Never a dull moment. I want us to be a success so I can stick it to my big sister. How dare she say I'm not achieving my potential!" Jo gave me a fierce hug. "Are you going to be okay?"

"Only one pity party allowed per day."

When she left, I felt empty down to my toes. I ate my quiche faster than I should have. Cagney and Lacey stared at me as if trying to figure out why I was in such a rush. I couldn't give them an answer.

All I knew was that I was feeling anxious because something was missing on the dry-erase board. But what?

Chapter 14

Heading back to the bistro, I glimpsed Tyson and Joshua James, Jo's father, sitting at a table on the dining patio. I entered through the patio gate and went straight to their table. Joshua was a striking man in his early sixties with a square jaw, bright-blue eyes like Jo, and salt-and-pepper hair. After Jo's mother ran out, he dedicated himself to his girls and his career, though I'd heard that he'd recently started to date again.

Menus were set in front of them as well as glasses of ice water. Joshua was slathering butter on a slice of bread. Tyson was jotting notes on a pocket-sized spiral notepad.

I strolled to their table. "What are you two doing here?" I asked. "If Jo sees you, she's going to think you're conspiring."

"Conspiring about what?" her father asked.

"Yeah, about what?" Tyson echoed.

"Oh, I don't know. Her hand in marriage?"

"Ha ha, very funny," Tyson said. "As if."

"Gee, Sergeant, that's one of Jo's favorite sayings," I teased.

He blushed and cut a quick look at Joshua, who was smirking.

Quickly, Tyson waggled his finger between himself and Joshua. "We're talking business."

"It's true. Tyson wants to purchase a property." Joshua had a good reputation as a real estate broker. His firm managed a number of business parks, a half dozen outlet malls, and most of the retail properties in Nouvelle Vie. In addition, his company listed houses, ranches, and wineries.

"A house built for two?" I teased.

Tyson glowered at me. "A small ranch."

"Are you going to retire and raise goats like your mother?"

"Maybe. Not yet. For now, I want someplace where I can kick up my feet when I'm not hunting murderers." He lifted his glass of water and took a sip.

"We're also discussing Bryan's murder," Joshua offered, his face growing somber. "Tyson's trying to get a feel for other people who did business with him."

"I'm so sorry for your loss," I murmured. "I know you were close." Joshua's grief showed in the lines that pinched his face.

He nodded his thanks. "I was telling Tyson that Bryan couldn't have had any enemies. He was as decent a guy as I've ever known."

"He had enemies, all right," I said. "David Ives, for one."

"The man who owns Ives Jewelers?" Joshua asked. "How would they have known each other?" He took a bite of his bread and set the rest aside.

"David used to own a second home here, and he and Bryan ran in the same social circles. I would have assumed you ran in that same circle."

"Me?" Joshua scoffed. "I've never been social. I'm a home-body. After a long day in the field, I like watching ESPN and catching up on the news. Maybe an occasional meal out at a nice restaurant."

"Well, as it turns out, David and Bryan had a business deal that had nothing to do with jewelry."

Tyson set his water glass down. "I know of the matter. It involved his brother-in-law." He recapped what I knew. "I've spoken to him about it. He swears that it was water under the bridge, and he didn't hold a grudge."

"Could have fooled me," I countered. "When I overheard them talking about it at the out-of-towners' dinner—"

"Mimi"—Tyson tapped the notepad with his fingertip—"don't worry. I've got this handled. Joshua has given me a list of other people to follow up with."

"Speaking of following up," I said, "I've been meaning to ask if you—"

I stopped midsentence, distracted by the sight of Lyle and Paula Ives on the patio, at a table close to the door leading inside. Lyle was rising. His face looked as ominous as his dark shirt. He threw his napkin down and shot a finger at his sister. Golly, he had a temper. What was going on? Lyle said something and beat a fast retreat through the bistro to the exit. Paula lowered her head and pulled a credit card from her purse.

"I'll be right back," I said and rushed across the patio. I would return in a minute to ask Tyson about David's call to the jeweler in Israel. If their untouched menus were any indication, he and Joshua hadn't ordered yet.

I reached Paula's table as she was opening the check presenter that held her bill. She glanced up. Her cheeks were flushed pink, as if she had taken too much sun. "Hello, Paula."

"Mimi."

"Is Lyle okay?"

"Yes, why?"

"He left in a hurry."

"He needed to walk. He's"—she worked the credit card between her fingers—"Lyle. If things don't go his way, he gets perturbed. Once, back in grade school, he upended a chessboard

151

because he wasn't winning. He likes to win and gets embarrassed when he doesn't."

"What isn't going his way?"

"A high-end client decided to take his business to Tiffany's. It happens all the time."

Even though it seemed like a reasonable answer, I wasn't sure I believed her. "Did you spend the day outdoors?" I asked.

"Not the whole day. Why?"

"You look"—I flicked my fingers near my face—"sunburned."

She clapped the check presenter closed and held it up for her waitress to retrieve. "I like getting a little color."

"Me, too." I slipped into Lyle's vacant seat and leaned forward, trying to act like one of her closest confidantes. "So what's really going on with Lyle?"

"I told you—"

"He's Lyle. Got it. He's upset. But it's not about losing an account, is it? Is he worried about Angelica? After all, she's the heir to Bryan's estate."

Paula remained tight-lipped.

"That makes her the main suspect in Bryan's murder," I said.

Paula frowned. "I heard *you* were the main suspect."

"I've been cleared."

"By whom?"

"The gardener who works for me."

"Raymond?"

"You know his name?"

"I make it a point to know the names of the help."

The *help*. How I hated that term. All my staff were *family*.

Paula waved the check presenter in the air and said, "Psst," to Oakley, but she missed the signal. "If you want my two cents, my brother never should have gotten engaged to Angelica."

"Why not?"

"She's a gambler and short on cash."

My ears pricked at that information. "Who told you that?"

"I overheard a conversation." Paula waved the check presenter again.

"Does she gamble on cards or bet on the ponies?"

"Let's simply say she's high-risk." Paula tilted her head and stubbornly pursed her mouth. Either she was spreading a nasty rumor or she didn't want whomever she had overheard to know that she had eavesdropped. *Daddy,* perhaps? "I heard Angelica and Bryan talking privately at the out-of-towners' dinner. They pulled off to one side after my father and Bryan had an argument on the patio."

"You were nowhere near that conversation. You were seated at the head table, as was I."

Her nose flared and her eyelids fluttered. "So?"

"Admit it. You didn't actually *hear* them."

She shimmied her shoulders. "I can read lips."

"Can you really?" I had the impulse to mouth something silly to test her ability but curbed it.

"Bryan told her he was leaving everything to her. She *knew*."

"He said those words exactly?"

She bobbed her head.

"Funny," I said. "Angelica told me their conversation was about Bryan telling her how pretty she looked."

"He did, but he also said he would always take care of her."

Okay, I'll grant that if Paula *could* read lips and she had picked up those words, she could interpret them to mean Bryan was leaving everything to Angelica. Still, I continued to have a gut feeling about Angelica being innocent, even if she had prior knowledge of the will. I said, "Your father held a grudge against Bryan."

"That was years ago."

"Grudges have a tendency to hang around."

"Daddy told you his alibi. He was on a call to a broker in Israel at the time."

"Speaking of which, do you happen to have Mr. Abrams's telephone number?" I jutted my chin in the direction of Tyson. "I think the sheriff might like to follow up with him."

"Of all the nerve. Keep your nose out of our business." Paula huffed, slapped the check presenter on the table, and marched out of the restaurant without finalizing her bill. No matter. I would make sure the charge plus gratuity showed up on her hotel account, and I would return her credit card in a pretty envelope.

"Mimi!" Heather raced up to me and clasped my elbow. Quickly she told me about a gentleman in the main dining room who was complaining that his steak au poivre was overdone. Steak au poivre, pronounced "oh-pwahv," was a classic French recipe featuring a steak crusted with cracked peppercorns and served in a creamy Cognac sauce. Needless to say, Chef C was peeking out from the kitchen and watching my exchange with Heather. She seemed ready to go to war.

I sidled up to her. "It's okay. I've got this. Go back to your post."

"I never overcook my steaks. *Never.*"

"I'll handle it."

"The nerve." She disappeared into the kitchen muttering a string of French curse words.

I approached the diner and drew up short when I recognized him. He had come into the bistro the first week it was open and had ordered the same meal. He had complained then, too.

"Sir," I said with as much graciousness as I could muster. "How are you?" I acknowledged his fluffy-haired female companion with a nod. She smiled at me but didn't say a word. She was too busy eating the french fries that accompanied her rotisserie chicken. "Why don't I get you another dish, sir? You don't seem to like the way our chef cooks steak au poivre, although I have to say, I think she cooks it to perfection."

I reached for the plate.

He put a hand on the rim. "Don't take it."

"What do you want me to do?" I asked solicitously.

"Bring another properly done."

"Fine, but I'll remove this one." I reached for the plate again. He flicked my wrist with his fork. I flinched. "Sir, I'm not letting you have two meals for the price of one. Either this one returns to the kitchen or I'll ask you and your guest to leave."

He gaped at me. "You wouldn't dare."

"I would."

He spanked the table with his palm. "I'll ruin your reputation."

I lasered him with a glare. "I highly doubt that."

Haughtily, he raised his pudgy chin. "I write for the *Napa Culinary Circle*."

"What is that? I've never heard of it."

"An online group of gourmets."

"How big is your following?" I asked, trying to calculate the possible negative impact. "More than one thousand?"

He balked.

"I didn't think so." I offered a tight smile. "Sir, do what you like, but I won't bring you another steak unless you surrender this one."

"Fine." He tossed his napkin on the table and stood, fully expecting his companion to join him. She didn't. "Get on your feet!" he commanded. "We're leaving."

"For heaven's sake, you old codger," she hissed between bites, "don't be a pill. Stop making a fool of yourself. Sit down and eat." She gazed at me. "Pay him no mind. Everything is divine. He's a cheapskate."

The man huffed. His companion threw him a baleful look. He resumed his seat. Deciding to let the two of them hash it out, I moved away. A minute or two later, I peeked over. He had finished his steak. She was ordering dessert. Crisis averted.

I returned to the patio to chat with Tyson and Jo's father, but to my surprise, they had split. Rats.

The rest of the day disappeared in a flash. The afternoon crowd kept us hopping. The dinner crowd was even busier. We ran out of every special. We had to make an extra assortment of desserts. Even our most expensive wines were selling off the rack. Was the spate of activity simply because a murder had occurred on the premises, or was word getting around that Bistro Rousseau was delivering quality meals? I couldn't be sure. I hoped the latter.

Around ten PM, I settled on a stool in the kitchen at my favorite table. Stefan brought me a plateful of mini–onion quiches.

"I've got to feed you, boss. Chef's orders. And you know I never disobey orders."

"Unless they come from your father."

"Shh." He held a finger to his mouth and grinned.

I downed a miniquiche and hummed. It was melt-in-your-mouth delectable. Stefan fetched a plate of peasant-style chicken kebabs made with olives and fennel, set it beside the quiches, and went back to work. I dove in. The combination of the orange juice marinade and the whole-grain mustard gave the kebabs an assertive French personality.

Chef C settled onto a stool beside me. "Are you doing okay?"

"As well as can be expected. How about you?"

Her skin glistened with perspiration. Her eyes gleamed with pride. "Now that the rude man has departed, much better. In fact, I am wonderful. It was a very successful day." I adored her passion. "Heather has become quite the pit bull. She does not take guff from anyone. She is a great hire."

"Yes, she is."

"By the way, she made a few suggestions for tomorrow's menu."

"Did she really?" Until now, Heather had been reluctant to offer her two cents regarding the food we served because she wasn't trained as a chef, but she was an admitted foodie. "Like what?"

"She suggested chicken cordon bleu roll-ups. She said they are not fussy, and they would make a nice compliment to a simple green salad, for the lighter eaters. I agreed." Chef C gestured to the dry-erase board.

As I took in the menu, my mind flew to the suspect list and the unanswered questions I had written on the board in my living room. "Camille, on the night of the out-of-towners' dinner, do you remember if Paula Ives entered the kitchen at any point?"

"I do not remember seeing her, but I was fully focused on the meal. Mr. Baker"—she sighed and shook her head—"had made it very clear that nothing could go amiss. Stefan might recall."

"Stefan!" I yelled.

He was standing at the dessert station, handing two plates of chocolate soufflé—decorated with white chocolate shavings and sprigs of mint, all set within a chain of white and dark chocolate hearts—to Oakley. He glanced up.

I beckoned to him.

He loped toward me while tugging on the collar of the white shirt he wore beneath his chef's coat.

"I'm sorry to interrupt your artwork."

"No problem, boss. A gifted artist can always pick up his brush and start anew." He offered a self-assured smile. "What's up?"

"On the night of the out-of-towners' dinner, do you remember if Paula Ives entered the kitchen?"

He scrubbed his chin. "Matter of fact, she did. She was keen on getting the recipe for the fig-and-olive tapenade."

"She asked for a recipe?"

"Yep. She wanted to make it for her father."

"Huh. According to him, she doesn't cook."

He barked out a laugh. "Well, she fooled me, because in the course of our conversation, I learned she had attended an all-female college, had considered a career in the medical field, and had even dabbled with the idea of going to culinary school. I would bet her father nixed the culinary idea and steered her toward the family business. Fathers can be mighty persuasive."

I smiled. His father and Paula's, maybe. Mine had been a pussycat; he had granted me his blessing for whatever I had wanted to do. "Did you give her the recipe?"

"Sure. I figured you wouldn't mind. There's no mystery to that one. No secret ingredient."

"Where did she wait while you fetched it?"

He pointed exactly where I expected, to the stool upon which I now sat. Right next to the cubbies.

Chapter 15

When I arrived home, my cell phone held a text message from Nash: *Are we still on for tomorrow? Don't bail on me. Pick you up at ten.*

Bail on him? Was he nuts? I was thrilled we were going on our date, but I would make it clear that if he was not getting divorced, we would be friends, and that would be that.

I rose Tuesday morning with a spring in my step. Because the day was going to be sunny, I applied sunblock and dressed in white capris, a floral tank top, and comfy sandals. I left my hair loose and donned my adorable pink-and-white-striped sunhat.

Nash arrived at ten on the dot, which pleased me to no end. I liked a man who was reliable. He appeared relaxed in a white polo shirt and khaki shorts, his wavy dark hair tucked beneath a Giants baseball cap. And he smelled good, like warm honey and vanilla. I didn't launch into the question of his availability right off the bat. I decided to let the day unfold. Later on, I would pin him down. I blew good-bye kisses to my goldfish, and we were off.

Jazz in the Valley was in full swing when we arrived at Alston Park. Hordes of people walked in streams toward the balloon-festooned archway. The strains of a sizeable jazz band rang out from inside the gated-off area.

The parking lot was jam-packed, so we drove to the alternate parking and took an open-air shuttle bus back. Everyone on the bus seemed as eager as we were to enjoy the day.

We paused at the entrance to the festival beneath the green and white balloons and planned our route. To the right stood white tents filled with artists peddling their wares. To the left was the food court. The aroma of barbecue, freshly baked bread, and numerous other delectables made me hungry. A protein shake for breakfast hadn't quite nipped my appetite.

The musical stages were directly ahead of us, including a large venue and two smaller ones. In between and surrounding them, vintners were offering wine tastings.

Nash said, "According to the official online program, every two hours, a large band will occupy the main stage. In between, individual artists can play to their hearts' content on the smaller stages. Let's browse the shops and get a bite before your guitarist goes on."

On the way over, I had mentioned that I wanted to hear the guy that my customer had recommended. As it turned out, he had an early slot.

Nash steered me to the right. Barkers dressed in green festival T-shirts and jeans roamed the crowd announcing the next musical events and locations.

"Hey, Nash," a freckle-faced woman selling jewelry called.

He waved.

"Who's that?" I asked.

"She's the daughter of a vintner whose wines I sell. She makes nice stuff. All silver and natural stones. We should check it out later."

Beyond her tent stood another in which a pretty redhead was selling leather items. On the table by the entrance, I spotted a bejeweled wallet like Angelica's and tugged Nash closer so I could take a peek.

"Hey, Nash," the redhead said.

I shot him a look. "Don't tell me. Another daughter of a vintner?"

"Nope. She's the sister of the woman who sold me my house. Part-time, she answers phones at the real estate office." He addressed her. "How's business?"

"Jazzy." She giggled at her own play on words. "If you see anything you want to purchase, let me know."

A couple carrying stemless wineglasses decorated with glazed confetti passed us. "Where did you get those?" I asked. They were adorable and would be a perfect birthday gift for Jo. In a little more than a month, she would turn thirty-five, like me.

The woman jerked a thumb. "Three tents down."

We continued on, passing an art booth filled with paintings and a woodworker's booth featuring chessboards, and found the tent with hand-blown glasswork.

"Mimi, how about we come back to this one?" Nash said. "It's nearly eleven. You don't want to miss your guy."

"You're right." I took the glasswork artist's business card and promised to get in touch.

Near the guitarist's stage stood dozens of bar-style tables, each fitted with an umbrella and wooden stools. Nash sat. I excused myself and headed to the restroom.

The upscale mobile restrooms, which were trailer-sized and seated three, were situated near the front of the venue. When I arrived, there wasn't a line. As I entered a stall and closed the door, I heard another patron enter. The person shuffled toward my stall and stopped. I saw blue tennis shoes appear beneath the rim of the door.

The person tapped on my door.

"Occupied," I said.

"I know," the person replied in a Wicked Witch–style voice. Was it a man or woman? I couldn't tell. "If I were you, lady," the intruder continued, "I'd be careful. You should stick to what you do best—running a restaurant. You'll be safer that way. Understand?"

Safer? What the heck! My breathing constricted. I felt so vulnerable sitting in such a compromising position. "Who are you?" I stammered.

No answer. Whoever it was exited, and the door to the trailer banged shut.

Hurriedly, I pulled myself together and raced back to Nash. "Are you okay?" he asked, his face concerned.

"Yes, I . . ." I swiveled my head, looking for someone I could identify. Someone in blue tennis shoes.

"Mimi?" Nash clasped my hand.

At the same time, a perky blonde server appeared. She set down a Plexiglas menu. "Hey, Nash."

I recognized her. She was a tour guide at Cakebread Cellars, though this particular venue featured a smaller vineyard more on the scale of my mother's.

"Two flights?" she asked. "One red, one white?"

Though I was tighter than a top after the exchange in the restroom, I said, "Let's start slow. How about we share one flight of white? We don't want to get plowed."

"Sounds good," Nash said. He also ordered a charcuterie platter and a cheese platter. When our server left, he said, "Want to tell me what happened? Did you see a mouse by the restrooms?" His gaze held a hint of humor.

"More like a rat," I said, refusing to let the incident ruin my day. I had been hassled twice when I'd lived in San Francisco. Knowing that those kinds of freaks thrived on attention, I'd learned to ignore them and hadn't gone running to Derrick or even my father to solve the problem. I wouldn't start now.

The blonde returned with four small wineglasses, each holding two ounces of a different wine. She suggested we start with the Pinot Grigio, which was the lightest and fruitiest; the Chardonnay was supposed to be buttery and rich with oak-toasted scents. The platter of charcuterie—*charcuterie* was a French term referring to prepared meat products (*chair* meaning "flesh" and *cuit* meaning "cooked")—turned out to be a variety of gourmet salami. My mouth started to water. Nash paid in cash, and our server glided to the next table.

The guitarist, a hunk from Sweden, was as good as promised. His fingers flew up and down the neck of his guitar. His long hair flopped as he swayed his head in rhythm to the music. I listened wide-eyed as he took us on a journey through what he called jazz with a Nordic flare. Incredible. While my father had introduced me to Broadway musicals, my mother was the one who had introduced me to jazz. She regularly played CDs of a wide variety of jazz guitarists with names like Lenny Breau, Joe Pass, and Wes Montgomery. Keeping to her French roots, she also liked the chanteuse Edith Piaf, a far cry from jazz. I knew plenty of her songs by heart.

When the Swede ended his set, I took a sip from our final tasting glass and leaned forward on my elbows. "Okay, Nash, I've got a question, and don't be evasive. Promise?"

He crossed his heart.

"Willow and you. If you two are going to stay married, then I can't—"

He put a finger to my lips to quiet me. It tasted salty. It took all my willpower not to lick my lips . . . and his finger.

"I knew you'd ask," he said. "I was waiting to see how long it would take you."

"You rascal." I swatted him and then sat back and folded my arms across my chest. "Well?"

"Don't worry. Everything is done. I'm officially divorced."

Something zinged inside me. Relief? Excitement? "Really? Willow let slip that she was hoping to make it work between you two."

"Hoping and *doing* are two entirely different things." He reached forward and looped his fingers over my arm. "Don't be mad at me for not telling you at the outset."

How could I stay mad at him with that mischievous twinkle in his eye? Wow, but I was going to be toast if I didn't watch out. Derrick had charm; Nash had mind-blowing charisma.

I polished off the wine. "Why didn't you and Willow, um, make it—if you don't mind me asking? She seems so nice."

"She is, but we weren't a good match."

"You met in college."

"We did. We married right after we graduated and moved here for my career, but a few years into the marriage, we realized it wasn't working out."

"How come?"

Nash hesitated.

"I'm sorry." I ran my finger along the rim of the wineglass. "I have a bad habit of being curious."

"Let's just say there was no physical attraction on my part. There never was, but since we got along so well, I figured we should get married."

"You married even though you weren't in love?"

He winced. "I was young and inexperienced." He took a sip of wine and savored it for a few seconds. "If you must know, Willow spends too freely on clothes and such, and she was always maxing out our credit cards. When I discovered she had a few secret credit cards that I didn't know about, that was the beginning of the end." He swirled the wine and took another sip. "I like to pay for things in cash. I hate paying the banks a dime of interest. It became a bone of contention. You've probably noticed by the tally sheets I keep that I appreciate orderliness."

I had. He never made a sale without opening his computer and logging the details of the order into his Excel program.

"I'm not a perfectionist, but the way I do things, I guess you can chalk that up to my upbringing. My father was always borrowing money with no consideration for my needs or the needs of my mother." He tilted his head. "Why so much interest in my ex?"

"She held an art class at the inn yesterday."

"Did she?" He seemed surprised to hear that. "Spur of the moment?"

"Yep."

He offered another sly grin. "She's keeping an eye on you. She must be jealous."

"Should I be worried? Does she have any *Fatal Attraction* tendencies?" I teased, wondering for a fleeting moment whether Willow had been the intruder in the blue tennis shoes. No way. She would never be caught in something so pedestrian.

Nash laughed. It was a glorious laugh, filled with a love of life. "Nah. She's complicated, but she's not lethal." He stood and offered a hand to me. "Let's walk."

What the heck does complicated *mean?* I wondered. There was something he wasn't telling me. *Dare I ask?*

He continued to hold my hand as we weaved around tables and back to the aisle filled with artists' tents. As we walked, he regaled me with the story of the start of his career. At first he had attended UC Davis to become a veterinarian, but in his sophomore year, he fell in love with wine and the dream of owning a winery. He then moved to Napa and landed his first job—a tour guide at a winery. He claimed he stunk at that. I couldn't imagine him stinking at anything. Luckily, he had a good palate and could pitch quality. A couple months later, he landed a job as salesman for a large vineyard. A year after that, he chose to go independent so he could represent a variety of vineyards.

At one point, he had hoped to become a vintner, but that hadn't materialized. He hadn't been able to find backers.

"What about you?" he said. "What's your story? Bryan told me a bit about your husband."

Bryan. Hearing his name cut me to the quick. My shoulders tightened. My stomach did a nosedive.

Nash squeezed my hand. "I'm sorry. I didn't mean to upset you. You must miss him."

"More than you know. My father passed away a few years ago. He was my rock. Bryan sort of filled that void." I hastened to add, "They were nothing alike. My father was a small man with a quiet demeanor and a gentle soul. Bryan, as you know, was a larger-than-life, take-charge kind of guy. But they both encouraged me to be the best I could be. Bryan instilled confidence in me after it had been stripped away."

"By your husband."

I frowned. "Bryan believed in me when no one else did, including me. He never let me doubt myself." I sighed. "How I wish I could find his killer."

"You?"

"I've been wracking my brain to see if I might have noticed something, like a clue I could give the sheriff."

Nash's eyes narrowed.

I elbowed him. "As I already told you, I'm plagued by curiosity and a sense of justice because—" I stopped myself, not willing to add *because of Derrick's deceit.*

"Tyson will solve this."

"I know," I murmured, but I wasn't so sure.

We walked for a long time, peering into the artists' tents without speaking. Our strides matched. It was beyond nice. A sense of calm filled me again. Wouldn't a life where I felt this good all the time be wonderful!

But then I sensed something . . . *off.*

I turned and saw a person in blue jeans, a blue hoodie, and blue tennis shoes trailing us. Was it the person who had warned me in the restroom? His hands were in his pockets. I was pretty sure it was a *he*. He walked like a guy, but I couldn't tell for sure with the hoodie drawn tightly around his face. Abruptly he turned his head to the side as if to avoid my appraisal.

"What's wrong?" Nash asked.

"Nothing." I slipped my hand around the crook of his elbow and told myself the person in blue wasn't a threat. If he were, he would have hurt me when he'd had the chance. I did not need to chase after him.

"Are you sure?"

I peeked over my shoulder. My stalker was gone. "Yes. I'm certain."

The music on the main stage kicked into high gear again, the fusion-style sound reminiscent of my mother's favorite jazz violinist, Didier Lockwood, who was known for his experimentation on electric violins. Someone turned up the amplifiers. Cheers from the crowd ensued.

When the music died down, Nash picked up an earlier thread. "Your husband's name was Derrick, right?"

I looked sideways at him. He gazed into my eyes, and I realized he wasn't making small talk. He really wanted the scoop.

"Mm-hmm." For the next few minutes, I shared my story: how Derrick and I met, where we traveled, what we liked about each other. "We were totally in love, but when he died suddenly . . ." I shared the one-minute version of his exorbitant debt and how he had let me down. "At his burial, his mother sobbed. I didn't shed a tear. My love for him fizzled the instant I found out the truth. My mother never liked him. She couldn't put her finger on why, but she—"

"Mimi!"

I whipped around. Speak of the devil.

"Darling, wait up." Mom hustled toward us, her ecru vintage Bohemian lace dress flouncing around her calves as she moved. When she reached us, she was out of breath. "Whew! What a beautiful day, isn't it?" She peered at Nash, and her eyes lit up with interest. "Who is this?"

"Mom, meet Nash Hawke. Nash, this is my mother, Ginette Rousseau."

"*Enchanté.*" Nash extended a hand.

My mother giggled and allowed him to take her hand. He lifted it to his lips and gallantly kissed the back. She giggled again. I gawked at her. Never in all my years had I seen her act so girlishly. Maybe the live jazz was making her feel like a free spirit, or maybe she'd had a few more sips of wine than she usually permitted herself.

"What do you do, Nash?" she asked as she looped her hand around the crook of his arm and guided him forward. I kept in step.

"I sell wine."

"Do you really?"

"I've tasted yours. It's incredible."

My mother gave me a knowing look.

"Mom, are you here alone?" I asked.

"I came with a group of women." She chuckled. "Heaven knows where they are."

"How long have you been here?" I asked, wondering again about how much she might have imbibed. Her cheeks were flushed, and her eyes sparkled with impishness.

"Since the opening. Don't you love it? These festivals bring back such lovely memories of your father and me when we were young and unfettered by—" She hesitated.

"Me?"

"No, darling, not you. Never you. Obligations. You were never an obligation. You were the fulfillment of my dreams and will always be the light of my life. But enough of this sappy talk. Nash"—she thwacked his arm—"tell me all about you."

He gave her a longer version of what he had shared with me. He had grown up in Berkeley. He worked small jobs throughout high school. His family wasn't well-to-do. They lived paycheck to paycheck. His father drove a semi and delivered tires all over the West Coast. Because his father hated his job, he spent his off hours racing motorcycles. Nash had no taste for fast bikes or fast cars. However, he did like animals, which was how he had ended up at UC Davis. Its veterinarian program was renowned. I listened, fascinated by how my mother could coax people to talk. At various private tastings at the winery, I had seen her wheedle information out of guests. A therapist couldn't have done a better job. She had never tried with Derrick, or if she had, she had kept whatever she had learned close to her chest.

When we completed the circuit of the festival grounds, winding up by the food court, Nash suggested we get another bite to eat. He asked my mother to join us. She bowed out and said that although she'd had an absolutely wonderful time getting to know Nash, she had to hook up with her friends again. She didn't want them thinking she had been swept off by some exotic stranger.

Before she left, I asked quietly if she had experienced any more ghost sightings. She swatted me playfully and, in singsong fashion, said, "Have a fun time!"

Not ten feet from us, she ran headlong into Edison Barrington, who was wearing a white linen shirt, cargo shorts, and sandals. He steadied her by the shoulders and smiled. He said something. My mother bobbed her head. He released her and they continued talking. He appeared flushed. His shirt was stained with perspiration. Could he have been the man in blue? Had he changed clothes and ditched the others to appear innocent?

Honestly, Mimi, I chided. *You have a fertile imagination.*

In response to something my mother said, Edison motioned broadly to his right. The action made me gaze in that direction, and I gasped.

"What?" Nash asked me.

Tyson Daly was sitting at one of the food court tables with a woman. Not Jo.

"Are you okay?" Nash asked.

"Yes, I thought a bee was after me," I lied and swatted an imaginary pest while continuing to stare at Tyson, irritation nicking my insides. Not because he wasn't with Jo—maybe I had picked up the wrong signals and he wasn't interested in her—and not because he and the woman seemed to be having a great time. She was laughing hysterically while he told what was obviously a hilarious story. No, my peeve came from the fact that he was idling away the day and not hunting down a killer. How dare he have fun while Bryan lay in the morgue, his case unsolved.

On the other hand, maybe Tyson was here on business. Maybe he had just questioned Edison, which was why Edison had gesticulated in that direction to my mother. If so, what had Tyson grilled him about?

Chapter 16

For another hour, Nash and I roamed the festival. Along the way, I purchased two of the multicolored wineglasses for Jo and a bedazzled wallet similar to Angelica's for myself. The one I carried was plain and ordinary, and a girl could always use a little glitz.

On the drive back to my cottage, we listened to jazz on the radio. When Nash walked me to the door, he drew near, cupped my face with one hand, and gave me a pristine but lovely kiss on the lips.

"I had a terrific time," he murmured.

"Me, too."

"We'll do it again soon."

"Wait!" I grabbed his hand. "Um, would you like to come in and—" *And what, Mimi? See your etchings?* I grinned. "Meet my fish."

He laughed wholeheartedly. "Sure."

I gave him the grand two-minute tour. At the aquarium, nose to the glass, he made eyes at Cagney and Lacey, who became instantly fascinated by him. After their introduction, I guided him to the patio to show off the view.

"Nice," he said and then slipped his arms around me. "May I kiss you properly now?"

I didn't object.

The kiss lasted a good minute before he ended it and held me at arms' length. "I had a great time, but I'm going to take off."

"But—"

He put a finger to my lips and then clutched my hand and walked me to my door. Before leaving, he whispered, "For your information, I am completely smitten."

After he exited, I closed the door and leaned against it. He had been the perfect gentleman. Why? Had I scared him off?

Get real, I berated myself. He didn't run away because he feared I would take advantage of him in front of the goldfish. He left because the timing wasn't right merely days after Bryan died—not to mention it was a split second after his divorce was finalized as well as our first date. Plus he did say he was *smitten*. It was such an old-fashioned word, but it had sounded authentic and made me grin from ear to ear.

I sped to the inn to tell Jo about the date. To my disappointment, she wasn't there. She was in town doing errands. I made a U-turn to head back to my place but paused when I spotted Paula Ives in the Sisley Garden. She was sitting on a wrought-iron bench, texting on her cell phone using both thumbs.

A notion occurred to me, something I wanted to clear up with her. I drew near. The aroma of white roses wafted on the air. I drank it in. "Hi, Paula."

Like someone caught in the act, she flipped her cell phone facedown on her thigh.

"I heard you like to cook," I said.

"No, I don't."

"My sous chef told me you wanted to go to culinary school."

"Wanted to. In the past."

"What changed your mind?"

"Circumstances."

Gee, she was being curt.

"Why did you ask Stefan for a recipe, then?"

"I want to make it for my father. He enjoyed it. I thought I might show him that I can do something other than sell jewelry." Paula tilted her head. "Why are you snooping around?"

"Snooping?"

"Talking to your staff about me."

I grinned. "Talking to my staff isn't snooping."

She narrowed her gaze. "Out with it. What do you want?"

"I'd like to know if you swiped my cell phone from the cubbyhole in the bistro kitchen on the night of the out-of-towners' dinner."

She sprang to her feet. "How dare you. I've never stolen anything in my life!" She palmed her cell phone and rushed into the inn without looking back.

Slick, Mimi, I thought. *You need to work on your subtlety.*

At the same time, Francine and Kent exited. He was looking over his shoulder at Paula. When he swiveled and saw me, he waved. Francine bussed him on the cheek and hurried past me, hotel key in her hand.

Kent slowed as he neared me. "Oho," he crooned. "What put our sweet Paula in a tizzy this time?"

"I asked an extremely blunt question."

"About?"

"It doesn't matter."

"I would wager it does. Paula likes to get her way. She despises it when someone mucks up the plan."

I pondered his choice of words. What was Paula's plan? Had Bryan Baker mucked it up? "How long have you known her?"

"Since she was in the third grade."

"That's right. I forgot. At the out-of-towners' dinner, Paula said you and Lyle were best friends. She hinted at a relationship."

"She did, did she? That's her way. Sticking in a sword"—he mimed the action—"and twisting to the hilt." He pulled the imaginary sword from his chest and slung it into an imaginary sheath. "I'm not gay and neither is her brother. Truth? Paula had a thing for me. I wasn't interested. Ever since, she has tried to drive a wedge between Lyle and me. She is perpetually jealous of him. He got the brains and the looks, but in the end, she won Daddy's heart, and let's face it, that's what counts, is it not?"

Had she? I wondered. David seemed particularly hard on her. On the other hand, he did hang out with her. Some parents weren't good at being affectionate, I supposed.

"By the by, anything new from the sheriff in the matter of the murder?" Kent asked.

"I don't know."

"That's pure rot. I've heard you're asking a lot of, um, *blunt* questions."

"I don't mean to—"

"I would be careful if I were you, love. Paula can be quite unpredictable, and David Ives will protect his family at all costs. Take heed." He saluted with two fingers and moved on.

I watched him leave, wondering what his angle was. To plant seeds of doubt in order to divert suspicion from Lyle to Paula? Or from himself? I revisited my assumption that he wasn't guilty. If he knew, prior to Friday, that Lyle had taken out bridge loans, which affected his future as well, and if he learned that Angelica would inherit, then he had every reason to want Bryan dead. Simply because he had hooked up with Francine didn't prove that he hadn't found the opportunity to slip out in the wee hours of the morning, kill Bryan, and return. But when would he have swiped my cell phone?

My brain ached from theorizing. I exited the garden and headed toward the bistro. It might have been my day off, but I could always take the time to pay a few bills and review sales.

On the way, I spied Lyle sitting on a scrolled stone bench in front of Maison Rousseau. A trio of books and a brief-case sat stacked on the bench beside him. He appeared to be preoccupied—one leg bent at the knee, ankle resting atop the other leg. He was plucking at something on the bottom of his shoe. I flashed on two notes I had written on the dry-erase board about him. First, had he spilled the water at the out-of-towners' dinner on purpose so he could steal into the kitchen and take my cell phone? Second, who else, besides him, had access to the gems he carried in his portable safe?

With plenty of sunlight left before dusk fell and being out in the open where any passerby could see us, I felt emboldened and approached him. "Hi, Lyle. How are you?"

He peered up at me. "All right, I guess."

"What did you do today?"

"Nothing much. Checked in on business. Read. Took a nap. I'm drinking in a moment of sun before I return these books to the library." All his selections were mysteries.

"Where's Angelica?"

"Posting more flyers. So far, no one has contacted her about seeing her running. She's obsessed with finding one person who can corroborate her alibi." He stopped attacking the sole of his shoe and raked his hair with his fingers. "I feel awful that I didn't hear her knocking that morning."

"Because you were sleeping."

He nodded.

I said, "Do you know if she asked the sheriff if there are speed cameras that might have captured her run?"

"I don't. I'll remind her." He rubbed his neck and sighed. "I can't believe they think she's guilty. She didn't have a clue about the inheritance she was going to receive."

"Your sister seems to think she did."

"Paula?" Lyle grunted. "Man, she doesn't know what end is up most of the time."

I tilted my head. "Do I sense hostility?"

He fanned the air.

"The two of you sure had a tiff yesterday," I said.

"When?"

"At the restaurant. You left in a hurry."

"Mimi!" a man called.

I swung around.

Raymond was pedaling past in his eco-friendly gardening cart. His tools clattered in the rear container. "I saw Tyson in the parking lot. He's looking for you."

"Thanks."

As Raymond rode off, a flurry of red-breasted birds twittered overhead. They made a beeline for Lyle. He flapped his arms to shoo them away. Many flew into nearby trees; two settled on the back of the bench. Lyle swatted the air around them. They didn't budge.

"Dumb birds," Lyle muttered.

"Cheeky, Kent would say." I helped bat them away. "Oh, my, one got you." I pulled a tissue from my pocket. "May I?"

Lyle grumbled.

As I wiped the bird poop off his shoulder, I said, "Don't you like nature?"

"In Los Angeles, we don't have nature. We have concrete."

A friend of mine who lived in Los Angeles boasted about the vast assortment of nature the area had to offer. She loved to surf or go on bird-watching hikes. The palm trees were, to use her word, mind-blowing, and the variety of flowers cohabitating with cacti were downright out of this world.

Lyle dropped his right leg to the ground with a smack.

The sound made me look down. Around his feet lay remnants of decaying basil. "That's a nice little mess," I said.

His gaze flitted to the debris and up to me. "I went walking in the vegetable garden."

"That's odd. There isn't any basil in the garden. It's solely in the pots on the bistro patio."

He jutted his chin. "Oh, yeah, that's right. I was sitting on the patio yesterday. I must have tracked the leaves from there."

"Uh, Lyle, sorry, but you were nowhere near the pots of basil. They're only in the right corner of the patio where Bryan was found."

"I don't have to stand for this." He leaped to his feet.

"And yet you did." I chuckled, trying to be as friendly as possible. "Stand, that is."

He glowered at me and worked his tongue along the inside of his cheek. "What do you want?"

"Are you going to let your fiancée get dragged to prison for murder?"

"I didn't do it! I was in my hotel room. Sleeping."

"If you were sleeping, then why did Angelica see a light beneath the door?"

"I fell asleep with the light on."

I frowned. "She mentioned to me that you usually go online at that hour to see what the commodity markets are doing."

He heaved a sigh. "Okay, yeah, I was up, but I didn't respond when she knocked because I was on the phone and knew I would see her when she returned. She always goes running for an hour."

"Why didn't you tell Sergeant Daly that you heard her knock?"

"Because . . ." He shifted feet.

"Because you weren't in your room, and you weren't on the phone. You were on the bistro patio."

He splayed his hands. "It's not what you think."

"Try me."

"Angelica and I argued the night of the out-of-towners' dinner. I hate fighting with her. We're in love. We shouldn't quarrel. Not the night before our wedding." He rubbed the back of his neck. "I didn't sleep at all. I tossed and turned. Around four AM, I took a walk. At first I strolled through the inn, hoping to find another night owl who I could bum a cigarette from. Except the place was as quiet as a tomb. So I went to the library, thinking that reading a book might help me fall asleep."

"Did you see your sister there?"

"Yeah. She was knocked out in a chair."

Was he making that up to corroborate her alibi or to give himself one of his own?

"Then I remembered that I'd tossed a half-smoked cigarette on the bistro patio, so I moseyed over there. I should quit. I know. It's a disgusting habit."

I had seen him stub the cigarette out during his disagreement with Bryan, but something didn't ring true. "Lyle, it was dark," I argued. "Plus it was a new moon." In Napa, when there was no visible moon, the valley could be pitch black. "How did you intend to find that cigarette?"

"A single light was on by the kitchen door, which gave enough illumination."

He was correct. We had security lights lining the perimeter of the parking lot and installed in front of the restaurant, as well.

"Plus I had my cell phone. If I needed to, I could use the built-in flashlight. When I got there, the gate to the patio was ajar. I was halfway across the patio when I saw Bryan. He . . ." Lyle began to twist an ornate ring on his hand.

Emotions clogged my throat. I whispered, "Go on."

Lyle met my gaze. "He was lying there. Out cold. I ran to him."

"Did you feel his pulse?"

"Are you kidding? I didn't touch him. Up close, I could tell he was dead. I'm not stupid enough to mess with a crime scene. I abandoned the cigarette and charged to my room. I locked myself inside and ignored Angelica's knock because I could barely control my breathing. I felt so vulnerable. That must be where I picked up the—what is that junk called?" He pointed to the debris on the ground.

"Basil."

"Right." He continued to fiddle with the ring.

"Angelica said Bryan was looking into your business practices. She said you were furious."

"I was. That's why she and I argued, but I wasn't angry enough to kill him. I'm being straight with you. I'm almost out of the hole. I told Bryan as much. He said he didn't trust me. I told him, in no uncertain terms, that he could trust me, and I would prove it to him." Lyle sighed. "Liquey . . . I mean Angelica . . . was furious that I would quarrel with him, but she trusted that I would do the right thing in the end."

"Lyle," I said softly, "do you think Angelica could have killed Bryan?"

"Are you nuts? She adored her uncle. He was good to her. He helped pay for college. He paid for her move to Los Angeles. He gave her money for rent when she was getting started."

"Didn't her father support her?"

"Sure, when he could, but Edison has a gambling problem." Lyle dropped his hands to his sides. "He runs short every once in a while."

"Does Angelica gamble, too?"

"No way! She never spends a dime she doesn't have."

"Paula thinks Angelica is a high-risk gambler."

Lyle moaned. "Like I said before, my sister doesn't know what end is up. She really shouldn't be in the jewelry business. She doesn't understand finance. Don't get me wrong. She's a great saleswoman, and she has a good eye for what looks pretty on someone, but she doesn't get the numbers part of business, and she can't stand the uppity-ups."

That was pretty much what Paula had told her father. She wanted out.

"Does she have a good eye for which gems are the better ones?" I asked.

"Sure."

"Does she have the code to your portable safe?"

Lyle squared his shoulders and raised his chin. "What are you hinting at?"

"A couple of gems were found next to Bryan. Didn't you see the crime techs pick them up?"

"I must have missed that."

"You carry jewels with you at all times. Are any missing?"

He sputtered. "I . . . I don't know."

How could he not know? Didn't he check them daily? I would.

I said, "Did you mention to Sergeant Daly that you travel with them?"

"He didn't ask."

That seemed like a gross oversight on Tyson's part, but I wouldn't point fingers. "You might want to take account."

"I will."

"And contact the sheriff."

"Will do. What else?"

I gazed hard at him. Suddenly he was being so compliant. "Could someone have slipped into your room and accessed your travel safe without your knowledge?"

He scratched his head. "Man, I guess it's possible. That night, I fetched my cufflinks from the safe, but they wouldn't insert into the cufflink holes. I was so ticked and running late, so I smacked the safe closed. But I'm sure I spun the lock. I must have. I always do."

"You have the code to that safe. I assume Kent and your father do, as well. Does Paula have it?"

He blinked, which I took as a yes.

I said, "Angelica told me she has it, too."

"Ha!" Lyle chuckled. "She does, but she can never remember it."

"So basically, any one of them could have picked the lock to your room and taken the gems, either before the out-of-towners' dinner or afterward, while you and Angelica were arguing."

He moaned.

"When you found Bryan, you say he was dead. If you're telling the truth, that sets the time of murder before five AM, which means Paula could have killed him and fled to the library and feigned sleep as you passed by."

Lyle's mouth fell open. "Paula? A killer? I can't picture that. She—"

"Doesn't know which end is up?" I said, finishing his dismissal.

He winced.

Of course there was also their father. Had Paula told David about the conversation she supposedly lip-read, when Bryan promised to always take care of his niece? Like Kent, David could have figured that Angelica's inheritance would bail Lyle out of his financial problem. Plus there was the matter of avenging his brother-in-law's honor.

As I left, I glanced back at Lyle. He looked pale, though whether from guilt or worry, I couldn't decide.

Chapter 17

I jogged to the parking lot near the bistro in search of Tyson, but I couldn't find him anywhere. I raced to the entrance of the bistro, but he wasn't there, either. Maybe he realized we were closed on Tuesdays and had driven away. Why hadn't he called me on my cell phone? Didn't he have my number? I had his. I dialed him. He didn't answer. I left a voice mail for him and then, too wound up to do the bills I knew I should be doing, I returned to my cottage, showered, and ate a light dinner—an omelet filled with bay shrimp, avocado, and French herbs.

Following the dishes, I moved to the dry-erase board to make additional notes about Lyle's alibi. Cagney and Lacey studied me as I paced in front of the board.

After an hour of frustration, not knowing what I was missing, I went to bed. I tried to wait up for Tyson's call, reading a mystery, but my eyes wouldn't stay open. Not because the mystery wasn't good; it was, but the method of murder—death by blunt instrument—made me think of Bryan, and I didn't want to fall asleep crying again.

At ten o'clock, Nash sent me a text message that brought a smile to my face: *I enjoyed the day. Hope you did, too. Sleep tight.*

I texted back that I had and fell asleep thinking of our long, delicious kiss.

Wednesday morning arrived quickly. I sped through my routine and was ready to leave to meet our local fishmonger when there was a knock on my door. I peeked through the peephole. Angelica was standing outside in an aqua-blue running outfit, arms hanging limply at her sides. My heart skipped a beat. I hoped no one else had died.

Cautiously, I opened the door. "Is something wrong?"

She swept past me. "I saw the light on. I hoped we could talk. I was—" She halted and scanned the dry-erase board.

I hustled over and gave the leg of the easel a nudge, enough to turn the board from view. How much had she seen?

"What is that?" She aimed a finger at the board.

"Tomorrow's menu," I said quickly.

"I saw my name."

The aquarium tank burped. I glanced at my fish.

Angelica took the opportunity to skirt around me. She gawked at the board. "Motive? Are you trying to . . ." She shook her finger. "Kent said you were investigating. Why? Don't you trust the sheriff and his deputies to do their jobs?"

"I do," I sighed. "But I really cared about Bryan, and I can't sit by—"

"I didn't do it." Angelica's eyes brimmed with tears.

"I don't think you did."

"Then why is my name there?" She whacked the board with the back of her hand.

"Because I was trying to theorize the way the sheriff might. I wrote down things I knew, as well as things I'd like to know."

Like what clue was missing! Something niggled at the back of my brain, but I couldn't bring it forward.

"My father shouldn't be on there. Neither should Lyle."

"Angelica, I'm—"

"Whatever!" She turned on her heel. When she reached the door, she reeled around and said, "I'd be careful if I were you."

My insides snagged as the door slammed. Kent had given me the same warning. So had the blue-shoed creep at the festival.

By the time I entered the bistro, everything and everyone was in motion. The windows were open. A cool, refreshing breeze wafted inside. The kitchen door was ajar. I loved the sounds coming from within: chopping, whirring, and happy chatter.

"Where's Heather?" I asked Oakley, who was inserting the day's specials into the menus.

"Hounding Stefan. As always. Those two." She snickered.

I crossed the kitchen threshold and spotted my lanky hostess tailing my sous chef as he moved from the walk-in refrigerator to his station.

"Rossi?" Heather asked.

"Nope," Stefan replied.

"Ferrari?"

"Uh-uh."

"Bianchi?"

For the past three months, Heather had been trying to coerce Stefan into spilling his last name.

He cocked his head. "Heather, you yo-yo, have you checked out the color of my skin? I'm not Italian."

"Maybe your mother was."

"Last names usually come from the father," he retorted as he set celery hearts on the counter and began to dice.

"Beaulieu? Belrose? Bertrand?"

Stefan barked out his rollicking laugh. "Not French, either. Give it up."

"Acosta? Aguado? Alvarado?"

Where had she collected all the ethnic names? I wondered. Did she intend to go through the entire alphabet? She could be relentless.

"Let the boy be and get out of my kitchen!" Chef C cried.

"I'll figure it out, you scamp." Heather wagged a finger at Stefan. "I always do. I have a knack."

I happened to know that she had started her quest by testing dozens of African names, thinking maybe Stefan came from African royalty and thus needed to keep his name a secret. A month later, she turned to Middle Eastern surnames. When I mentioned that Stefan had no accent whatsoever, she reminded me that our country was beautiful and strong because of our colorful immigrant population.

"Morning, everyone," I sang.

Chef C offered me a cockeyed look. Clearly Heather and Stefan were driving her nuts. I stifled a laugh.

"Mimi!" Heather approached me. "Did you hear? A food critic is coming to dinner tonight." She pinched my arm fondly.

"How do you know? Food critics don't usually reveal that they're visiting a restaurant. They show up in secret, unannounced."

"I know that, but I'm such a good sleuth, I figured it out." She buffed her nails on her dress. "See, I happen to be friends with a hostess at a restaurant in Yountville, and she told me how food critics often make reservations under an assumed name, and then she shared some of the real names and who went with which name. Well, I memorized them—you know how I like to memorize facts and figures—and, voilà, I now know which critic goes by the name John Dough. Get it, *D-o-u-g-h*?"

"Clever. So what's his real name?"

"Pierre Dubois."

I gawped. "You're kidding. From *Gourmet's Delight*?"

"You've heard of him?"

"Have I ever! Oh, I know many critics like to remain anonymous, to the point of never allowing a picture of themselves to surface, but Pierre is a big guy with a big appetite and a wee bit of an ego." I pinched two fingers together.

Heather laughed.

"He brags about how he has built up or taken down a few restaurants with his spicy reviews. We have to talk to Chef C," I said. "We have to get cracking."

"Don't worry. She's already on board. Just to be sneaky, she's preparing a set menu for everyone tonight so Mr. *Dough* will have to choose what she offers."

"Brilliant. What's on the agenda?"

"She's cooking bouillabaisse as the appetizer."

"Perfect. One of her specialties."

"The entrée will be *la clapassade d'agneau*." Heather stumbled over the word *clapassade*, which, loosely translated, meant "cup of stones." I wasn't sure why the word went with the dish. It wasn't like it had rocks in it. The recipe that Chef C would use was my recipe—actually, my grandmother's recipe—and one of my favorite dishes, made with lambs' necks, carrots, honey, and licorice root. The latter gave the dish real character.

"For dessert, a *gateau mille-feuilles*." Heather snapped her fingers, looking for the typically known term.

"Napoleon?"

"That's it."

Mille-feuille translated to a "million leaves" and was created by layering puff pastry and pastry cream. It melted in the mouth. Chef C iced her creation with fondant and brown chocolate stripes. Divine.

"That sounds terrific." I yelled across the room, "I like the menu, Chef!"

"Of course you do. It is *magnifique*." She twirled a long-handled spoon at me and continued making her soup. Steam rose in big billowy clouds nearby.

"Heather"—I beckoned to her and then guided her toward the main dining room—"if Sergeant Daly calls for me, please track me down. I'll be in the office. I want to talk to him."

She frowned. "Is everything all right?"

"I hope so. He was trying to find me yesterday. We didn't hook up."

"Do I need to contact that lawyer for you after all?"

"Gosh, I hope not. Raymond can corroborate my whereabouts, even at four AM."

"Four?"

"It turns out Bryan died earlier than we thought."

Heather shook her head. "The reality of him being gone still makes me cry."

"Me, too."

"Remember how he bustled around here during that last month of construction?"

"Wearing that ridiculous tool belt."

"Packed with seven different hammers." Heather giggled.

Bryan had wanted to make sure every nail was tapped into place. The week after, he had followed the painters around. At one point, the supervisory painter pleaded with me to teach Bryan to cook so he would get out of their hair. Bryan had proven to be pretty adept at making piecrust and was an expert with a mandolin slicer.

I smiled and squeezed Heather's arm. "Let's hold onto those fond memories." I left her to manage the dining staff and headed for the office.

Before I reached it, the front door flew open and Jo rushed in, the flaps of her royal-blue jacket catching the breeze, the ruffle lapel fluttering like it might take flight. When had she started moving so quickly? She used to be the epitome of calm.

"Mimi! You'll never guess what happened." She steered me into the office and closed the door. "Lyle and Angelica got married!"

"What?"

"They had the license, of course, so they went to the county clerk."

"When?"

"This morning."

"Wow." I crossed to my desk and set my purse in a drawer, my cell phone tucked safely inside. I was never going to leave it in the kitchen cubby again. "That seems rash."

"And suspicious." Jo braced her arms on the desk, palms flat. "Think about it. Maybe they got married so they can claim spousal privilege when questioned by the sheriff."

I wondered if Angelica had married him because, after seeing the board in my living room, this was her way of showing me how much she believed he was innocent. "Does that law apply if they weren't married at the time of the crime?"

"I don't know. I didn't go to law school, remember?" After giving up on her modeling idea, she had considered law for about a New York minute but decided she understood money better than rules. "We should let Tyson know." She picked up the receiver to my landline telephone and offered it to me.

I set it back in the cradle. "I would, except he hasn't returned my call. He must be busy."

"Why did you call him?"

"Because he came looking for me yesterday when the bistro was closed. We didn't touch base."

"Are you in trouble?"

"I can't be. Maybe he wants to ask me something about Bryan's business or . . . I don't know." I threw up my hands and slumped into the desk chair. Since yesterday, I had come up with dozens of reasons Tyson would need to see me, none of them good. My stomach felt raw with the acid that kept churning inside it. "Whatever it is, I've got so much more to tell him."

"Like what?" She pulled one of the grain-sack chairs closer and perched on it.

"Yesterday, after the jazz festival, I ran into Lyle and—"

"The festival. O-M-G, I forgot to ask you about it." She reached across the desk for my hands. "How was your date with Nash?"

"Nice."

"That's it? Nice?" She released me with a sigh.

"We're—" I paused, realizing I hadn't told her about the intruder in the blue tennis shoes. *Why worry her now?* I decided. It was water under the bridge.

"Go on." She motioned for me to hurry up with my story.

"We're getting to know each other."

"Has he . . ." She rubbed her ring finger.

"Ended it with his wife? Yes. We listened to fabulous jazz. The guitarist was amazing. And we drank wine and chatted about a range of topics until . . ." I intentionally didn't finish to lead her on.

Jo moaned. "Until what?"

"We ran into my mother."

"Of course she would be there. Do you know how many times she asked me over for dinner when you were living in San Francisco so she could play some new jazz artist for me?" Jo laughed. "Did she, you know"—she flapped a hand—"throw cold water on things?"

"No. Get this: they hit it off."

"Yay! A first."

"I know. It didn't hurt that Nash knew his wine."

Jo clapped her hands. "Okay. At least you won't get any friction from her this time. Cool. Back to Lyle."

I told her how I'd met up with him in front of the inn and how he was digging basil out of the bottom of his shoes.

"The only place where it grows is in the pots on the rear patio," she said.

"Exactly. I mentioned as much. Ultimately he caved and told me his entire alibi."

"He wasn't sleeping?"

"Nope. He said he was edgy after the argument with Angelica and needed a smoke." I replayed the conversation. I finished by saying he locked himself inside his room and lied about being asleep because he didn't want Angelica to see him trembling.

Jo raised a skeptical eyebrow. "I'm sorry, but wouldn't you want to see your fiancée at a time like that?"

"He claimed he felt too vulnerable."

Jo coughed and mumbled, "Bull," into her fist.

I folded my arms. "I think so, too. But if it's the truth, that puts Angelica in the clear."

"Does it? Maybe she went to the patio before five AM, killed Bryan, and afterward, knocked on Lyle's door to give herself an alibi, hoping the sheriff would think he was killed between five and six."

"Wow, I hadn't thought about that."

"Because you want her to be innocent."

"I do."

"Call me a skeptic, but she's inheriting Bryan's entire estate."

"And she knew it," I whispered.

"She did?"

I bounded to my feet and paced while telling Jo about the conversation Paula claimed to have lip-read—if Paula could be trusted. When I was through, I smacked my hands together. "What if David Ives counted on that?" I applied my earlier rationale regarding Kent to David. "Let's say Paula told him about the inheritance, and he thought the money would help his son avoid financial ruin."

"Did he know Lyle was struggling?"

"I don't know. It doesn't matter. There's something about David Ives I don't trust. I still feel he's lying about his alibi. A two-hour phone call to Israel? C'mon. How convenient."

190

Someone knocked on the office door and opened it. I spun around. Tyson strolled in, hair groomed, shoulders square. He greeted Jo and me.

She popped to her feet and took his hand. "Boy, do we have a lot to tell you." She guided him to the chair she had vacated and made him sit. Watching her manipulate him made me laugh. "Lyle Ives wasn't sleeping when he said he was." She repeated all I had told her, not missing a detail. When she concluded, she said, "That means Bryan died before five AM."

"Unless Lyle killed him and wants us to believe that," Tyson argued.

"According to Paula Ives"—Jo gave me a confirming look—"Angelica knew about the inheritance she would receive. Paula lip-read a conversation."

Tyson rose to his feet. "Okay, that's enough, ladies. I want you to stay out of my investigation."

"I'm not doing anything," Jo countered. "Mimi is. She's the one writing theories on a dry-erase board."

Tyson wheeled on me. I flinched and glowered at Jo with a very distinct message: *Thanks for throwing me under the bus, pal.*

She splayed her hands and mouthed, *Sorry.*

"Is that why you called me, Mimi?" Tyson asked.

I squared my shoulders. "Raymond said *you* were looking for *me.*"

"Right. I was. I wanted your opinion on the ranch property next to your mother's winery. It's for sale."

"The Lincoln estate?"

Jo gawped. "You're buying an estate?"

Tyson frowned. "Hardly. Not every piece of land around here is estate-sized, but people like to call their properties estates. The place is modest at best. It's all I can afford."

I said, "It's about a sixth of the size of my mom's property, and it's never been properly tilled. In fact, it's overgrown."

"Which is just fine with me," Tyson said. "I don't want to raise grapes."

"You want to raise goats." I gave him the thumbs-up sign. "Perfect."

"Back to you two." He drummed his fingers on his thigh. "All this theorizing. It's got to stop."

"A chef is a natural-born sleuth," I said.

"Yeah," Jo chimed. "She breaks down recipes on a regular basis."

"I notice little things, Tyson. It's the details that matter, you know?"

He huffed.

So did I, mimicking him. "C'mon, cut me some slack. I really cared about Bryan. He was my mentor, my friend. And now I'm worried about Angelica, because she married Lyle—"

"She what? When?"

"This morning. They blew off a real wedding and went to the county clerk, and seeing as how Lyle is in bad financial straits, I'm wondering whether he might have married her to get his hands on her inheritance."

"They were planning to get married anyway," Tyson reasoned.

"That's true, but couldn't they have waited a bit longer? By the way, did I mention that Lyle's mother fell down the stairs and died?"

"When?"

"When he and Paula were kids."

"Go on." Tyson twirled his hand, urging me to continue. "What's your point?"

"What if her death wasn't an accident? What if Paula, Lyle, or their father caused it?"

Jo nodded. "It's easier to kill a second time."

Tyson cracked a smile. "Doesn't that sound a little melodramatic?"

"I don't know. Does it?" She cocked a hip.

"I'll check into it." He headed for the exit.

"Wait," I called. "I almost forgot. The gems."

He pivoted. "What about them?"

"I'm not sure Bryan was the one who was carrying them." I explained how Lyle traveled with gems and how he claimed he hadn't mentioned it to Tyson because Tyson never asked. I told him that Lyle was going to check to see if any were missing and added that it was a safe bet some were. "The inn's locks would be easy to pick." I explained why. "Therefore, anyone with the code to the safe could have stolen the gems and put one in Bryan's mouth."

Jo said, "Speaking of gems, did you follow up on David Ives's alibi about talking to that jeweler in Israel?"

Tyson swung his gaze between us, his teeth clamped tightly.

"No?" Jo said. "Well, I know a jeweler who might help. I'll contact her." Without asking his blessing, she dashed from the office.

Tyson raised a hand to protest, but Jo was already gone. He sighed and turned to me, his eyes steely. Clearly he wasn't pleased. I flinched.

"E-mail me whatever you've written on that board of yours," he ordered. "I'll take a look."

"Will do," I said and solicitously moved ahead of him to show him out. "Hey, before you go, who was that woman you were with at the jazz festival?"

"Which woman?"

"In the food court. She has a big laugh."

"That's my cousin on my mother's side. She's thinking of moving to town." His mouth twitched at the corners. "Why do you ask?"

"Because—"

"Because you thought she was a date?"

"Yeah, and because I'm looking out for my pal. I think you're interested in Jo, and I really do believe that was why you were meeting with her father. I think the real estate thing was a ruse."

He let out a low chuckle. "Nope. I am truly interested in purchasing the Lincoln estate."

"My bad. Sorry."

Softly he said, "But you're not wrong about Jo."

I perked up. "I'm not?"

"I am interested, but I find it hard to talk to her, and when I do, she's always in my face, like she doesn't trust me to do my job."

"She trusts you, Tyson, but like me, we both want the killer caught—sooner rather than later."

"Dang it, Mimi." He stiffened.

"What?"

"Stay out of my investigation. You do not want me to slap you with an injunction."

His warning miffed me. I drew up taller and raised my chin. "I am not *in* your investigation, sir. I am theorizing. A citizen is allowed to theorize. And if that's worthy of an injunction, then slap away."

"Whoa!" Tyson backed up a step and let out a low whistle. "When did you become so feisty? You were never like this back in school."

"Bryan gave me the courage to stand up for what I believe in." I pointed to a poster on the wall with the phrase *A strong woman is one who is able to smile this morning like she didn't cry last night*. I added, "That's me through and through. And don't forget that I'm a Gemini, like you, which means I have a curious disposition."

"I'll say you're curious. Curious as in peculiar. Be careful."

I glowered at him and then decided to hit him with another zinger: "At the jazz festival, did you question Edison Barrington?"

Tyson grinned but didn't respond. As he stepped through the doorway, glass shattered in the main dining room.

Chapter 18

I whizzed past Tyson and darted to Heather, who was already sweeping up the remnants of a sunburst-shaped mirror. Diners were on their feet, gazing at the commotion. Waitstaff seemed to be reassuring them that everything was fine.

Heather peered up at me, mortified. "It . . . fell. I'm not sure how." She blew a hair off her face. "You know what this means? Seven years—"

"Don't say it!" I snapped. I was not superstitious, but a mirror falling for no reason sent a shiver down my spine. I didn't want to hear the words *bad luck*.

"Do you think Bryan's spirit is hanging around?" she whispered.

I shook my head, but if I didn't believe that, why had I shuddered? Because a murder had occurred on my property—not to mention my mother and her nonexistent ghost had put me on edge. To lighten the mood I said, "Maybe it was one of your Glonkirks, Heather."

She clucked her tongue. "They're not ghosts, Mimi."

"Are you sure?" I grinned.

"Maybe the broken mirror is a warning to keep out of my investigation," Tyson wisecracked.

I threw him a caustic look.

"Just saying." He grinned. "There are stories about mirrors that go way back to when the first humans saw their reflections in a pool of water. They believed the image was their soul, and to endanger the image—you know, like roiling the water—would mean risking injury to the inner self. You don't want your soul to suffer, do you? I repeat: be careful." He winked and exited.

As he left, another shiver coursed through me. What were the odds that multiple people would warn me to be careful in the same twenty-four-hour period? First the jerk at the festival, then Kent and Angelica, and now Tyson.

No, the mirror falling to the floor was an accident, pure and simple. Picture hanger hooks gave out. A shift in the earth could make something topple, too. And I would argue that Glonkirks, if they were real, could make themselves invisible to toy with us mere mortals. Just to be sure, I inspected the hook on the wall. Oddly enough, it was a weak sawtooth style with teensy nails, not the hefty kind I typically used with a nail rated to hold one hundred pounds.

Heather was on her way to the kitchen to discard the mess.

I said, "Psst. Heather, c'mere."

She made a U-turn and scurried to me. "What's up?"

"Did you change out this hook?"

"No. Why would I—" She glanced at the front door and back at me. A panicked look crossed her face.

"What's wrong?"

"This morning, when I came in, the door was unlocked. I asked Chef C about it. She was the last to leave Monday night, but she said she exited through the rear door. I always lock doors. You know I do." She was fastidious when it came to safety. "Do you think someone stole in on our day off and rigged the mirror to fall just to mess with you?"

"To mess with me?"

"To warn you because you're sort of, you know, asking pointed questions about the murder."

"No," I said hastily. "Of course not." I fanned a hand. "Uh-uh."

She narrowed her gaze. To be honest, I didn't believe me, either. I trembled as my thoughts flew back to the encounter at the festival and the person in blue who had put me on notice.

Boldly I said, "I'm going to town to buy another mirror." The incident was juvenile and most likely carried out by a prankster, I assured myself. Shopping would calm my nerves, and I knew the exact place to go: Fruit of the Vine Artworks. Willow said she carried one-of-a-kind mirrors. While I was there, I'd get to know her better and see if I could find out why Nash said she was *complicated*. A spendthrift wasn't complicated, just reckless. "Make sure everyone remains upbeat," I said as I fetched my purse. "We want tonight's mood to be blissful when the food critic arrives."

On the way to my car, I spotted Raymond crouching in the vegetable garden. Someone else was with him: a woman in a sunhat, ecru linen shorts, and a white linen shirt with the sleeves rolled up. They were inspecting the tops of carrots. I yelled to him, "Raymond, I'm going to town. Need anything?"

He popped up, looking like a wide-eyed meerkat on the alert. The woman did the same. It was Paula Ives. She looked better than I had ever seen her. Her cheeks were tinged pink from the sun, and her eyes glistened with excitement. One could almost say she was pretty.

I drew near. "What are you doing?"

Raymond grinned. "Showing Miss Ives which vegetables are ready for picking."

"Miss Ives? Honestly." Paula swatted him with a trowel. Raymond blushed. "Paula."

"Raymond has made me fall in love with Napa Valley and gardening and, well, everything." She threw her arms wide. "In fact, I'm thinking I'll do something like you have, Mimi. Not open a restaurant, of course, since I'm only a fair cook, but maybe I'll open a B and B. I can manage a business rather well." She laughed in a thin, almost choked way, as if she hadn't laughed in years. "That'll slay my father, don't you think? Me, owning my own business."

The word *slay* caught me off guard and made me glance at Paula's forearms, which were surprisingly muscular. I wondered again whether she, even though she was a slip of a girl at the time, had pushed her mother down the stairs so she could be Daddy's girl. Those arms were also strong enough to have hoisted a patio chair and smashed Bryan in the head. Did she kill him to win her father's favor by avenging the family on his behalf? Her alibi of sleeping in the library seemed tenuous at best. Somehow, though, I couldn't reconcile the giddy woman before me with a killer.

"Mimi!" a woman cried.

I turned around and saw Jo running toward me, waving a sheet of paper.

"You won't believe what I—" She skidded to a stop and fixed her gaze on Paula. "Oh, it's you."

"Oh, it's you," Paula parroted, not in a mean way—more like she was trying out Jo's voice.

Jo crumpled the paper in her fist. "What are you doing?"

"Learning to garden," Paula said. She winked at Raymond, who blushed again. Had he developed a crush on her? Was she pretending to be interested in him and gardening so we would all have a more positive opinion of her?

"I'll be back soon," I said to Raymond. "Bye, Paula. Sunblock!" I warned, and then I grabbed Jo's elbow and steered her toward the employee parking lot.

"Where are you off to?" she asked.

"Town. We broke a mirror."

She gasped. "That's—"

"Don't say it. Why did you crumple that paper?"

She smoothed the wad and waved the paper beneath my nose. "My jeweler friend had Nachum Abrams's telephone number. She deals with him, too. Nachum is a big deal. Anyway, I called Nachum, and after I explained my query, he told me point blank that he did not speak with David Ives that morning." She knuckled my arm. "Is that the best? We've got him. He killed Bryan Baker. Go to town. I'll call Tyson."

"You'll risk incurring his wrath?"

"You're rubbing off on me. I'm becoming daring."

"Warning!" I opened and closed my hands like an alert signal. "Be prepared for sparks to fly!"

"Don't worry. He'll be doing cartwheels when he gets this info."

The image of Tyson Daly doing cartwheels brought a smile to my face.

*

Yountville, named after George Calvert Yount, who established the first vineyard in Napa Valley, was upscale and colorful and home to the famous French Laundry restaurant as well as a number of other well-known establishments. The town always drew a crowd, and today was no exception; it was buzzing with activity. Swarms of people strolled along the main boulevard. Traffic was thick, as cars proceeded slowly so the passengers could drink in the avant-garde artwork that decorated the area, which included a huge basket of tomatoes, a life-size version of a previous mayor, and a field of stone mushrooms.

All the metered parking spots were taken, so I hunted for a few minutes until I found a space a couple of blocks away. Sunshine blazed down on my head as I made my way back to Fruit of the Vine Artworks on foot. I silently heard Heather admonishing me for not applying sunblock but reasoned that I wouldn't be in the sun for long and pressed on.

As I was passing the high-end jewelry store next to Willow's shop, a woman called, "Mimi!"

Past Fruit of the Vine Artworks was an artisanal cheese shop. In front I spied Kaya Hill—the lawyer I had intended to call if I'd needed representation—a beautiful American Indian of the Hopi tribe who had moved with her husband to Napa ten years ago. She was sitting at a hardwood bistro-style table with a blond man. She waved at me. The man swung around, anchored his arm over the back of the chair, and smiled. *Lyle*. Why was he meeting with Kaya? Especially since he and Angelica had just gotten married. *Short honeymoon*, I thought snarkily. Maybe after telling me his alibi, he felt the need for a defense attorney because he knew gems were missing from his safe. Perhaps prior to our meeting, he'd never imagined Tyson would put two and two together, but once I pointed out the obvious, he realized how guilty those missing gems would make him look.

A jug of iced tea stood on the table, as did a sizeable cheese platter. Lyle picked up a tumbler decorated with a sprig of mint and peered menacingly over the rim of his glass at me. A frisson of fear shot through me. If looks could kill . . .

"Join us?" Kaya asked.

"Can't. On an errand."

"Let's catch up soon."

I shouted, "Will do," and turned back toward Fruit of the Vine.

Its display window was gorgeous. The glass had been painted with a stencil of white flowers, clouds, and teapots. In the display nook stood a beautiful oak table set with scrolled candlesticks that formed a heart, yellow paisley place settings, and golden goblets. On the walls flanking the nook hung a selection of red, blue, or green mirrors and miniature oil paintings in gold frames.

Inside the doorway, I stopped and tried to collect myself. My heart was racing. Slowly, in a Zen-like manner, I drank in the rest of the shop, which was a compilation of stall-type areas, each defined by a vine-covered wire barrier. In the center of the shop stood a massive floor-to-ceiling sculpture of a grapevine. The walls, like those of the display nook, held a variety of watercolor paintings and oil paintings. In addition, there were tables filled with smaller pieces of art and display cases holding jewelry.

Willow was standing behind the antique sales counter finishing a transaction with a customer. She wiggled her fingers at me and then splayed her hand, signaling five minutes.

I roamed the shop looking for a replacement mirror. I hesitated by a starburst-shaped mirror, but it didn't measure up to the one that had broken. I wouldn't replace it with an inferior facsimile. I moved on and audibly gasped with pleasure when I spied a three-foot-wide, tealeaf-shaped mirror outlined with hundreds of tiny glass tiles, faceted beads, and patterned metal. Nearby was a similarly sized rectangular mirror bordered with a mosaic of iridescent glass. Both were beautiful. Neither was cheap.

Willow, who was wearing a form-fitting burgundy dress and another pair of outrageously high heels—*ouch* was all I could think—joined me. Her dangling silver earrings clinked merrily. "Mimi, darling, I'm so glad you came in."

"Your place is fabulous."

"I told you I have an eye for quality."

"Is any of this art your own?"

"Are you joking? I hide all mine in my workshop. The world will never see it." She slipped a hand around my elbow and drew me close, like we were best buddies. "By the way, did you see the artwork Jo selected from the charity art class? It's incredible. Quite impressionistic."

"No, I haven't yet." Again I hoped it wasn't some mash-up of Picasso and Pollock. "Things have been incredibly hectic."

"Well, it's in the library and looks fabulous. I love the green and blue tones. They go well with the furniture. The artist loves Monet, as you do, so we thought that would be the best one to choose. Come this way." Willow beckoned me to another section of the store. "Before you start shopping, I wanted you to see my favorite spot. Occasionally I give art lessons here. Would you care to join a class?"

"I'm not sure I could find the time. Besides, art has never been my strong suit unless it involves food. I'm great with a squeeze bottle and tongs."

"You're being modest."

"I assure you, I'm not."

We laughed.

Near the rear of the store, Willow had set up a small area with easels and a couple of tables. All sorts of art supplies were arranged on shelving: stacked canvases, paint brushes, oil paint, watercolor paint, clay, pencils, X-ACTO knives, and dozens of empty wine bottles. She even had a blowtorch and a Jenkins kiln.

"Come on. Say you'll give it some thought. I see you eyeing the kiln."

"I tried to do pottery in high school," I admitted, the memory still fresh in my mind. *What a fiasco!* "Most everything came out at a tilt. Even the urn I attempted was out of whack. Heck, as a girl, I flunked Mr. Potato Head 101."

"Forget pottery." Her laugh was as melodious as her voice. "Let's do something fun like melting wine bottles. There's no right or wrong. You can come to one of the parties I host. They all involve wine, and"—she elbowed me—"we all know art gets better, or at least easier, after a glass or two of wine. We become less judgmental, you know what I mean? Hey, I'll even order food from your bistro for snacks. Think about it."

"I will."

"Superb. Now, let me show you those vases I mentioned." Willow ushered me to a stall that featured vases. Releasing my arm, she gestured like a display model to a grouping of tiny three-inch-high vases, each a different color. "Wouldn't they be perfect in the bistro? Notice the delicate patterns. Each one is hand-blown and unique."

"Mmm." How could I be diplomatic? They were pretty, but I didn't need them. "I like the crystal vases we have."

"Of course, crystal is elegant, but color is so important to one's appetite. Neutral tones do nothing to get the juices flowing. I've done a lot of study on this." She picked up a green-toned vase. "Green, I've learned, arouses the appetite. It is a color that is associated with health and well-being." She set it down and lifted a yellow vase. "Yellow is a cheery color, don't you think? It simply makes people happy."

Not me. Food presented on yellow plates spoiled my appetite. A hint of yellow was okay, like a floral yellow border on bone china. But bold yellow anything? Granted, maybe I could serve brunch or a sandwich on yellow, but not an elegant entrée.

Willow motioned to the next two. "According to research, orange stimulates the brain, which increases mental activity and often makes the stomach churn." She winked. "That would make people order up a mound of food, right? And red, of course, increases the heart rate, which"—she giggled—"stimulates the hormones. Think about all the luscious desserts you'd sell simply because diners are getting . . ." Her mouth quirked up sassily on one side. "Need I say more?"

"I really didn't stop in to buy vases. I want to find a mirror."

Willow pressed a hand to her chest. "Heavens. Did you break one?"

"No," I lied. I was becoming quite adept at lying lately, but I didn't want her talking to me about bad luck. "I like mirrors around the restaurant. You must have noticed. They reflect the light in the chandeliers and give a feeling of spaciousness."

"You know, I heard a myth about mirrors. They have magical powers, including the power to see the future. Some say breaking a mirror would end its powers, and therefore, the soul would flee the body and hard luck would be brought upon the one whose reflection it last held."

A quiver of worry flitted through me. Was everyone a scholar about mirrors except me? Why hadn't I heard all these ancient tales? Was I wrong to hang so many in the bistro? The notion of someone entering the bistro and deliberately rigging the mirror to fall flashed in my mind. I nudged it aside.

"It sort of sounds like something out of Grimm's fairy tales, don't you think?" Willow spun in a circle, tapping a fingertip on her chin while perusing the shop. "Okay, ix-nay on the vases. The customer is always right. Mirrors. Hmm." She opened her arms, gesturing to the entire shop. "As you can see, we have quite a selection of mirrors. Aha! I know what I'd like to show you. This way. There is one in particular that I think you'll love."

Once again, she took hold of me and led me to a stall where each item had been made out of melted, reshaped wine bottles.

"Are these products of your students?" I asked.

"Are you kidding? No, these are quite professional." She lifted a piece that had been fashioned with a mirror in the center. A sentiment was etched onto the lower rim: *Love fully before love leaves.* "The artist is an art teacher by day at Napa Valley College." Willow plucked a colorful business card from a bronze cardholder and handed it to me. "She said a student of hers inspired the words she etched. I love that, don't you? Student inspiring teacher."

"Nice."

"It's like the perfect balance. If I were the teacher and you the student, who knows what we might be able to offer each other." She gave my arm a little squeeze and edged to the other side of me. "But back to the story at hand. It seems the student fell in love with a man who was quite a rover. He could never make a commitment and broke the woman's heart. Isn't that sad?" Willow gazed at me, her eyes misty with emotion. "My artist—the teacher—decided to etch the saying into her mirror, and every day, from that day on, she has looked in the mirror and reminded herself to protect her heart. I'm with her, aren't you? The world is full of rovers."

Why was Willow telling me this? Did she know the history of every piece of artwork in her shop and relate it to customers, or was she targeting me because—my heart did a hiccup—she was suggesting that Nash had strayed and that was why their marriage had fallen apart?

I flashed on the multitude of pretty women who had said hello to him at the jazz festival and had a sinking feeling.

The door to the shop opened. A chime over the door tinkled.

"I'll be right with you," Willow called.

"That's okay. I'm browsing," a man said.

Recognizing the voice, I turned and saw Lyle running a finger along the side of a picture frame. He smiled at me. There was no warmth in it.

"Mimi, are you all right?" Willow asked. "Do you need to sit down? You look pale."

"I'm fine," I whispered.

"How about a little tea? I'll brew you a cup of Tazo Refresh tea. That always perks me up. I'll be right back."

"Don't go," I said quickly. "I'm ready to make my selections. Then I have to split. Big night tonight."

I heard the door chime again. Lyle was exiting. He yelled, "Thanks a lot," on his way out. The moment he was gone, I breathed easier. Had he entered simply to unnerve me? If so, it had worked.

Chapter 19

I succumbed to buying two mirrors: the tea-leaf-shaped mirror with glass tiles for the bistro and the wine-bottle mirror for my cottage. The sentiment on the latter, I realized, reminded me of my time with Derrick. Though duped by him in the end, until the day I discovered his deceit, I had loved him fully. I hoped to love like that again.

As I was exiting the shop, a parking spot opened up in front. Rather than haul the mirrors a couple of blocks, I hurried back inside, set them down, and begged Willow to protect the spot outside. She fluttered her fingers and said she would be more than happy to comply.

On the walk to where I had parked, I kept my eyes peeled for signs of Lyle. I didn't see him anywhere. Maybe I was making too much of his appearance at the shop, and perhaps I had it all wrong as far as his meeting with the attorney, but that didn't mean I wouldn't remain vigilant.

Minutes later, I pulled my Jeep in front of Fruit of the Vine Artworks and, with Willow's help, stowed the mirrors in the trunk. When I slammed the hatch, I spotted David Ives exiting the neighboring jewelry store with a bag in hand. He spied me, called my name, and sauntered in my direction. Willow pecked me on both cheeks and returned inside her shop.

"Did you hear the news?" I said.

"About?"

"Your son and Angelica eloped."

David's gaze turned dark. "That boy. He never did learn patience."

"I'm sure he's pleased that Angelica is coming into money."

"Why?"

"Lyle's business—your business, I imagine—is struggling. Didn't he tell you he has a number of bridge loans that need to be paid off?"

"We operate independently. What he does with the Los Angeles store doesn't affect the San Francisco store." He rummaged in his pocket for car keys and pulled out a set.

"What did you buy?" I indicated the gift bag.

He smiled. "A long time ago, I purchased a necklace for my wife. I had it shortened for Paula. She prefers a higher neckline than her mother did. Yours is pretty." He defined the shape of the stone in my pendant with his index finger.

Automatically I touched it. "My father gave it to me."

"Very nice. Simple. It hangs well," he said like a veteran jeweler. "Paula . . ." He fell silent for a minute, as if working through conflicting emotions. "Paula has been through so much. Ever since her mother died, she's had a tough time of it. I hope having this necklace will make her feel good about herself. She and I can be at odds, as you've no doubt witnessed, but I adore her. A token to remind her of her mother might do her good."

After a moment of awkward silence, I said, "I don't mean to intrude, but the way your wife died sounds so tragic. Can you tell me what happened?"

David grimaced. "She got an inner ear infection, which threw her off balance. She suffered from them often. We visited many specialists. No one could figure out the source. That day, she must have teetered on the top step and tumbled to the bottom. Paula has always blamed herself."

"Why?"

"Because she was the only one home." David sighed. "There was nothing she could have done. She was in bed with a broken leg. I'd carried her there earlier before heading to work. We believe her mother must have been heading downstairs for Paula's crutches. She doted on Paula and Paula on her." He switched the package to his other hand.

"Lyle is pretty hard on her."

"He was at one time, I'll admit that. I think he knew early on that she was smarter than him. Better at math. Better at reading."

Funny. I recalled Kent saying that Lyle had gotten the brains.

"But my son was headstrong and, realizing his sister was a sensitive little girl, bullied her into submission. I take the blame for not curbing that early on, but he has reformed and loves her fully now."

I nodded indulgently. "I heard at one point that Paula wanted to go to culinary school, but you nixed that idea."

He *tsk*ed. "I didn't nix anything. I merely suggested she had a good brain and it would be best applied to more respectable prospects. She followed my lead."

"What will you do if Paula insists on leaving the family business?"

"She can't be serious about that."

"She's quite confident in the garden," I said and told him about seeing her being tutored by Raymond.

"Really? Her mother loved to garden, too." David sighed. "You should have seen her hybrid tea roses. She had dozens of varieties—all of them red. Gypsy, Gentle Giant, Mister Lincoln. She could talk about them for hours." He gazed at me.

"If gardening makes my daughter happy, I will encourage that hobby."

Hobby, I noted. *Not profession.* I didn't correct him. It wasn't my place to tell him that Paula was considering opening a bed-and-breakfast.

"We all want our children to be happy, don't we?" he added.

I didn't have children. I probably wouldn't at this point. I had hoped Derrick and I would have some. I had gone off the pill, but I didn't get pregnant, and a few months later, he died. I wasn't a woman who could raise children by herself. I would need support. Plus I craved the kind of loving relationship my father and mother had shared. It had been magical.

David hitched a thumb at the black Mercedes parked directly behind the Jeep. "I should get going."

"Sir, one more thing. Did Sergeant Daly contact you?"

He tilted his head as if wondering where this line of questioning might lead. "As a matter of fact, yes."

"Did you tell him about your call to Israel?"

"I did."

"Did you also mention that it, um . . ." I screwed up my mouth. "Gosh, how do I say this?"

"Spit it out."

"Well, sir, I'm not sure it was entirely true. You see, a friend of a friend talked to Nachum Abrams, and he didn't corroborate your account."

"Ah." David lowered his head and ran his tongue along his teeth. After a moment, he reconnected with me. "Fine. You caught me."

"I wasn't trying to—"

"For your information, I do have an alibi, and it is solid. It's humorous, really." He forced a smile. "You know how Bryan was investigating Lyle?"

"Your son told you?"

"We have no secrets."

I could dispute that. If Lyle hadn't told his father that he'd eloped or had bridge loans, I would imagine he had kept other things from him.

David continued, "As it turns out, I was doing the same thing—trying to get dirt on Angelica."

"Why?" I asked, again wondering whether he had killed Bryan to make sure that Angelica would inherit and thus be able to salvage Lyle's business. But how would David have known about the inheritance? Angelica swore she didn't know, which would mean Lyle didn't know, and even if he did tell his father *everything*, he wouldn't have been able to share that tidbit. Had Paula related her lip-reading story to her father, prompting him to take action?

"To be honest, I've never trusted Angelica," David said. "I believed she was after Lyle for his money."

"She makes a good living—not to mention he's the one in financial trouble."

"A bridge loan doesn't connote financial trouble. I've taken out many over the course of the last few decades." He brandished a hand as if swatting a wasp. "Angelica is the one who is up to her neck in debt."

"According to whom?"

"The investigator I hired to find out more about her financial situation. He was the person I was speaking to that morning."

Doesn't anyone trust anyone else? I wondered and then bit back a laugh. Given my history, I probably should have been less trusting.

"Does this investigator have a name?" I asked.

"Seamus O'Brien."

"Seamus? You're kidding." I mentally amended the typical spelling of Seamus to *shamus*, slang for investigator, and snorted.

"Yeah, go ahead, have a good chuckle," David said. "He laughs about his name, too. He's a good old Irish boy from New York."

"Why hire someone from New York when Angelica lives in Los Angeles?"

"Seamus lives in LA, but he happened to be in New York visiting family last weekend. Here, have a listen." He pulled his cell phone from his pocket and pushed buttons until he could broadcast a conversation. He displayed the screen to me and talked over the beginning of the digitally recorded conversation. "We talked nonstop for two hours, starting at four."

I listened for a good ten minutes as David and his investigator conversed rapid-fire about Angelica. Neither spoke for longer than a minute at a time. The investigator said Angelica had a propensity for making high-risk investments.

"Is that enough?" David paused the recording.

I hadn't heard how much Angelica was in debt. Perhaps the investigator went into detail later on in the conversation. According to the image on the display screen, the length of the conversation ran one hour and fifty-five minutes.

"For now," I murmured.

It dawned on me that if Paula had eavesdropped on her father talking to Seamus and gleaned that Angelica was involved in high-risk investments, she might have lied to me about lip-reading Angelica's exchange with Bryan. Why? Because otherwise, if her father learned that Paula was aware of his conversation with the investigator, she would have to confess to him that she had listened in. I doubted he would appreciate that kind of sneaky behavior. If that were the case, it also meant that Paula hadn't been asleep in the library when she said she was. *One lie breeds another*, my father used to say. Taking my theory a step further, if Paula hadn't stuck around to hear the entire exchange between her father and Seamus, she could have sneaked out, lured Bryan to the patio and killed him, and then raced back to the library to establish her alibi of being asleep in the chair. Of course, there were a lot of *ifs* in my speculation.

David wiggled the phone. "This proves my alibi."

"Why didn't you say so in the first place?"

"I didn't want my son to know what I was up to."

"But you said you and he have no secrets."

"I was protecting his interests."

"Yet you didn't. He married Angelica anyway."

"Impulsive," he muttered.

"Um, perhaps you should share that recording with the sheriff."

He nodded.

"By the way, I saw Lyle a bit ago. Right over there." I gestured to the tables outside the cheese shop. "He was dining with a very attractive woman."

"Who?"

"Kaya Hill. A defense attorney."

David's gaze turned dark. "Back off my son!" A viper couldn't have sounded a more threatening warning. I flashed on the person in blue shoes at the mobile trailer. Had it been David? He dabbled in acting. Had he also stolen into the bistro and jimmied the mirror hook?

I held up my hands. "Whoa, sir, I'm sorry. I only mentioned it because I suggested to Lyle that the gems found at the crime scene could have come from his portable safe, and an hour later, there he was with Kaya."

"Out in the open," David managed to rasp. "Maybe he was talking to her on behalf of his new wife. Did you consider that?" He jammed a finger at my nose and, without further ado, marched to his Mercedes. The force with which he slammed the door after entering was deafening.

Chapter 20

I strode into the bistro carrying the tea-leaf-shaped mirror. Later, on the way to my cottage, I would collect the other from the car. The restaurant was packed with diners, Francine and Kent among them. Kent noticed me instantly and said something to Francine. Was he whispering that he had warned me? Was there a threat behind his warning like there had been from Lyle? Or the person at the festival? Or whoever had caused the mirror to crash? Were they all acting in concert?

Am I supremely paranoid?

My stomach growled. I inhaled the aroma of onion soup and promised myself a bowlful after I got settled.

In the office, I set the mirror against the wall and crossed to the telephone. I dialed the sheriff's station. The receptionist put me through to Tyson.

"You didn't e-mail me," he groused.

"I'm getting ready to do that right now." And I was. I'd thought about it on the drive back to the restaurant. My computer was switched on, my e-mail open. I started a draft as we chatted. I told him about running into David and listening to his recording with the investigator. "That changes his alibi."

"Mimi, I warned you. Do not get involved."

"And I told you, I'm not getting involved on purpose. There I was on the street, and David and I bumped into each other."

"Mimi."

"Tyson." I tried to sound as firm as he did. "Look, I cared about Bryan, and if I have a gut feeling and I happen to run into someone, I feel it's my civic duty to follow up on that gut feeling." I took a deep breath. "Might I ask who you have your sights set on? Someone must top your list."

He sighed.

"C'mon, Tyson, tit for tat."

"There will be no tit for no tat. I'm in charge. You're not."

I quickly mentioned having seen Lyle with Kaya Hill and added that I believed Lyle and Paula had the lamest alibis.

He didn't disagree, but he did hang up.

I stared at the phone and wriggled my nose. Okay, maybe I hadn't handled that conversation well, but at least I had relayed pertinent information. I should get brownie points for that.

After finishing my e-mail outlining the thoughts that I had jotted on the dry-erase board, I hit *Send*.

"There," I said to no one. "Duty done." Then I remembered that I hadn't asked Tyson about the itemized list of Bryan's valuables. Had he checked whether anything was missing? Was Bryan's death a simple case of theft? I sent a quick follow-up e-mail.

Heather entered the office and noticed the mirror. "Ooh, you found one," she gushed. Her face glistened with perspiration. A stray hair clung to her cheek and chin. She brushed it away. "Let me see."

I removed the bubble wrap that Willow had carefully used to cover the mirror. Sunlight streaming through the office window bounced off the mirror. The tiles glistened like jewels.

"It's beautiful!"

"I think so, too." I set it on the floor near the wall. "We'll hang it when the lunch crowd disappears," I said, exiting the office. I paused by the hostess podium and surveyed the bistro. There were lots of people I recognized and plenty of new faces. "The place is busy."

Heather joined me. "Sure is. We haven't had a lull since, well, forever. By the way"—she lowered her voice—"I've got vibes about Angelica Barrington . . . I mean Angelica Ives."

"Vibes?"

Heather tapped a finger on her chin. "At least I think she would be called Ives, since they're married now, although I don't know if she took Lyle's surname. Do you?"

"I don't."

Heather hummed her concern.

I poked her gently. "Go on. Why do you have vibes?"

"Right!" She clapped her hands. "Because Angelica was here today having lunch alone, and she constantly checked her phone and looked over her shoulder as if she thought someone might be following her."

"Maybe she's hoping one of our diners has seen her flyers and will vouch for her. Or maybe she expected Lyle to show up for a postwedding celebratory lunch."

"Uh-uh." Heather shook a finger. "Trust me. She was definitely acting suspicious. You should have seen the lines etched into her forehead." She fluttered her fingers near the top of her face.

"Is she still here?" I searched the crowd.

"Nope. She left a half hour ago. She seemed in a hurry. Just saying."

The front door opened. Heather grasped menus and expertly greeted a couple entering the bistro. As she led them to a table on the patio, I pondered Angelica's situation. Was someone after her? Who? A moneylender? Had she borrowed money to pay off a gambling debt and welched on the loan? My stomach clenched as another thought struck me. *Did whoever had loaned her money take out his or her anger on Bryan?*

The front door opened again, and Nash strolled in carrying a single bottle of wine. He motioned to the bar. "Hey, beautiful. Care to join me for a sip of something extraordinary? I'm not selling, simply sharing."

Pleasure zinged through me. I smiled. "How can I turn down an offer like that? I haven't eaten, have you?"

"Nope."

"I'll have Oakley bring us bowls of onion soup. I've been craving it since I walked in a few minutes ago."

"Excellent."

He strode to the far end of the bar, set the wine on top, and perched on a stool. He pulled the neighboring stool close and rested his foot on the footrest.

After putting in our order, I joined him. He smelled yummy again, but different, like warm grass and almonds, and he looked rugged, dressed in jeans and boots with the sleeves of his green Pendleton shirt rolled up.

He said, "Do you think Red will mind if I do the honors?" He removed a wine opener from his jeans pocket.

Our bartender, who had gorgeous paprika-red hair—hence the nickname Red—was gregarious and always upbeat. She lingered at the far end of the bar, tending to a group of very discerning wine tasters. Flight glasses were set in front of each of them.

"Go ahead. She's superbusy." I slipped behind the bar, selected two Riedel Bordeaux wineglasses, and returned.

His forearm muscles flexed as he popped the cork. He poured two short portions of wine into our glasses. "This is a Joseph Phelps 2008 Insignia."

"I can see that."

He held the stems of both glasses and swirled deftly. "It's eighty-nine percent Cab, seven percent Petit Verdot, and four percent Merlot, aged for twenty-four months in new French oak casks. It boasts fragrant layers of dark-roasted coffee and graphite."

I giggled. "Graphite? I'm supposed to taste pencil lead?"

He chuckled. "Okay, call it minerality. Take a sip." I obeyed. "Do you taste the flavor of black fruit?"

I let the wine float on my tongue and swallowed. "Definitely. It's incredible." On my days off, one of my favorite excursions was to visit Joseph Phelps Vineyards for an outdoor wine tasting. The view of Napa Valley from the vineyard's patio was incredible. "What's the occasion?" I rarely opened a wine of this caliber unless there was something to celebrate.

"I landed a terrific account."

"Good for you."

"Nouvelle Vie Vineyards has taken me on to rep all its wines."

I gaped. "No way. My mother hired you?"

He clinked glasses with me. "I told you I'd win her heart. And now to win yours." He poured more wine into each of our glasses and whispered, "I've missed you." He cut me a sideways look. "Have you missed me?"

"A bit," I said coyly. I wasn't ready to tell him that I had dreamed about him last night. Given all the drama going on in my life, I had been surprised to note it was a deliciously sensual dream. He definitely didn't need to know *that*.

Oakley brought our soup, said, "Bon appétit," and hurried off. We ate in silent companionship.

Later, when she took the bowls away, Nash said, "Any word on, you know, the investigation?"

I shook my head.

"Mimi!" a woman called. "There you are."

Swiveling on my chair, I spotted Willow striding toward us. She was still dressed in her form-fitting burgundy dress and ridiculously high heels. She was carrying a Fruit of the Vine Artworks tote bag. Glittery ribbon decorated the handle.

I glanced at Nash. "Are you meeting her?"

"No."

"Is she following you?"

A curious look swept across his face.

Again I wondered, as I had kidded the other day, whether I should be worried about a *Fatal Attraction* kind of situation. Driving back to the bistro, I had reviewed my interaction with Willow at her shop, certain that she had been trying to warn me off Nash. Was it to protect me, or was it to keep him for herself?

Willow said, "Hi, Nash. Funny seeing you here."

"Laugh out loud," he muttered.

She removed an item from the bag she was carrying. It was well protected in ecru-colored paper. She unfurled the wrapping to reveal three of the vases she had shown me. She set them in a row and put the bag on the floor. "Mimi, I know you said you didn't want these, but I figured you might change your mind. They would look so darling on the patio tables. Think about it. They're on me. See how your guests like them. If they don't or if you don't, take them to your cottage as my gift." She bumped shoulders with Nash. "What better way to display my wares than at a hot new restaurant, right?"

Willow perched on the stool to Nash's right and reached for his wineglass. "What are you drinking?" She didn't wait for an answer. She sniffed and took a sip. "Mmm."

Heather appeared at my side. "Mimi, Chef C needs to see you. She's getting nervous about tonight."

"What's going on this evening?" Nash asked.

"Thanks to Heather's powers of deduction, she figured out that a food critic is dining with us. I'll just be a minute."

At the door leading to the kitchen, I glanced over my shoulder at Nash and Willow. She was leaning into him and laughing, her hand on his shoulder. Her eyes glistened with excitement. A pang of jealousy shot through me. Was it a mistake to like this guy? He said he was officially divorced, but would Willow ever let him go?

As I entered the kitchen, my jealous thoughts made me think of Paula Ives. On the night of the out-of-towners' dinner, she had flirted with Bryan. I was sure of it. Granted, she could have been doing so purely to get him to sponsor her new project, or she might have been doing so to rankle her father because he had brought up the memory of her mother in such an awkward way. On the other hand, what if Paula really had been into Bryan? When he rejected her, had it made her feel as jealous as I was feeling now? I wasn't ready to kill Willow or claw her pretty eyes out, but I was definitely edgy. Later that night, when Paula had texted Bryan and asked to meet and he had shunned her a second time, had that sent her over the edge?

I shook my head. No, if she were the one who had swiped my cell phone, she would have had to plot her murderous plan earlier, before their confrontation.

Think, Mimi. Why would Paula stuff Bryan's mouth with the éclair? Because she was fed up with coddling the rich. Did the éclairs represent the rich? Did the jewels signify her career?

Raucous laughter cut through the kitchen. I searched for the noise. Of all people, David Ives was standing with Chef C near the pastry table. She was wielding a silicone spatula like a sword and relating some story that was sending David into hysterics. What had gotten into her? I couldn't remember her ever acting so frivolously. Had someone spiked her tea? I knew she was nervous about the food critic's visit, but fencing in the kitchen?

I strode toward them.

Chef C thrust the spatula in David's direction. "It is true," she said with a French accent. "He fathered his own grandchild."

Okay, she wasn't fencing; she was making a point.

"No way," David exclaimed.

"What's going on, Camille?" I asked.

She reined in her spatula. Her face flushed. With no accent, she said, "I was merely telling Mr. Ives—"

"David," he said, still chuckling. "She was telling me the story of Napoleon. It seems he went behind Josephine's back to father a grandchild with their daughter."

"He what?" I blurted.

Chef C beamed, the story giving her great pleasure. "He wanted a male heir."

"I didn't want to believe her," David said, "but she made the story so colorful." He burst into more laughter.

"It is the French accent," Chef C said, employing an even broader French accent. "The French are always good at storytelling. You should hear my sister tell a story. She is the best." Her sister owned a local chicken and egg farm with her husband. "She gets bawdy." Chef C winked at David.

Honestly, I had never seen her so flirty. Had David's visit the other night when he had come into the kitchen to compliment her cooking won her over? Maybe he hadn't sneaked in to filch my cell phone. Maybe he wasn't the man in the blue shoes who had threatened me in the mobile restroom. He did seem to have a reasonable alibi. Maybe I should write him off my suspect list. If not for the tension I'd felt at the end of our tête-à-tête in front of the jewelry store, I would.

"Back to business," Chef C said. "Shoo!"

"Aw!" David pouted. "But you promised to show me how you create a Napoleon."

The makings for a Napoleon lay on the pastry counter: flaky dough, pastry cream, and three squeeze bottles filled with

Chef C's decorative sauces. Beyond them lay a dozen caramel-iced éclairs on a tray.

"You have to swear you will not distract me," she said. "I must get this right for tonight's guest."

David twisted an imaginary key on his lips.

"Chef," I said. "Heather told me you needed to see me."

"I did?" She turned to face me, her lips pursed in concentration, and then realization hit. "Aha! I did! I want your approval of tonight's menu." She flicked a finger at the menu posted on the wall.

"I already gave it to you."

"I have revised it slightly. Check out the appetizers."

I moved closer to the menu board and scanned the list. The only thing she had added was a vegetarian pâté served with toast points. "Looks good, Chef," I called.

"*Merci beaucoup*," she responded.

At the same time, Jo rushed in so fast, the door banged the wall before swinging into place. "Mimi, I was hoping you were here. I wanted to give you an update on how Tyson took the news regarding David—"

I shot a warning finger.

Jo cut a look across the room and beckoned me with her index finger. I followed her to the dishwashing area. Lowering her voice, she said, "Tyson is following up with the jeweler in Israel to confirm what I already learned—not that he doesn't believe me, but he wants to have all the facts—"

"He doesn't need to." I told her about my conversation with David outside the jewelry shop and how I'd called Tyson and brought him up to date.

"David played the recording for you?"

"Readily. He also told me how his wife died." I explained in brief detail.

"Well, doesn't that beat all? An inner ear infection made her lose her balance and plunge to her death? Poor thing. And how sad that Paula felt responsible." She clucked her tongue. "Now I feel awful for having assumed the worst." She glanced at David, who was still toying with Chef C. "So he's actually a nice guy?"

"Camille seems to think so. She's as giddy as a schoolgirl. I, on the other hand, am still reserving judgment."

"Why?"

I recapped the chat in front of the jewelry store.

"Mimi"—Jo gripped my arm—"you've got to watch out. David Ives—"

"Is a wily one," Stefan said as he swept past us. "A real charmer. He brought Chef a single rose from the garden." He pointed to a wine bottle–style vase, which was standing by the posted menu.

"The devil," Jo said. "Raymond won't be happy to know guests are stealing roses."

"I won't tell." Stefan grinned. "I've never seen Chef C so animated. It's like she's never had a man pay her attention."

What is David up to? I wondered. "Let him watch you make one Napoleon and boot him out."

"You got it, boss."

"And tell Chef C that I love the idea of a vegetarian pâté. She is brilliant."

He saluted and made a beeline for her.

"Also," Jo said to me, "Tyson is following up on Paula's and Lyle's alibis. I'm not sure why, but he leaked that to me."

Maybe because I had given him guff earlier.

"By the way"—Jo rocked back and forth on her heels, looking quite girlish—"Tyson asked me out."

"He did?"

"Be honest. Did you goad him into it?"

"Me? No!" Well, maybe I had when I'd questioned him about the woman he was with at the jazz festival—his cousin—but I wouldn't admit it to my pal. I could see Tyson and her living happily ever after. They matched in energy. They both liked the outdoors. He was smart; she liked bright men. "I told you he was into you. I'm glad he finally found the courage. Did you say yes?"

Jo bobbed her head. "Because I know you would give me grief if I didn't at least go out with him once."

"When are you going? What will you do?"

"After the sheriff's investigation is concluded, we're going hiking."

"When will that be? Next year?"

"Be nice. I think he's homing in on someone."

"Who?"

"As if he would reveal that to me. You know him. He doesn't like to tip his hand. By the way, when we do go on that date, he's fixing us a picnic. He claims he makes a mean deli sandwich."

"You love deli!"

"Almost as much as French food." She giggled and then gasped. "Is that the time?" She stared at the kitchen wall clock. "I've got to run. A busload of people are checking in this afternoon, and they've all been wine tasting. Wish me luck." She held up crossed fingers.

I did the same and then we tapped fingertips, the way we had done for years. She dashed out.

Stefan swung past me carrying a tray of Napoleons ready for the walk-in refrigerator. "Lately that woman is always in a hurry."

"She is a multitasker, which is why I love her." I spied the desserts and a thought occurred to me. "Stefan, were there any leftover éclairs after the out-of-towners' dinner?"

"A few. Not many. Can't run a successful business with waste, my father always says."

I grinned. His father would say something like that. Bryan had said something similar. I sighed just thinking about him and wondered how he would have felt about his brother's gambling habit. Had he known about it? How would he have reacted if he had learned that Angelica had the same weakness? What exactly was high-risk investing?

Following Stefan to the refrigerator, I said, "You told me Paula Ives came into the kitchen that night asking for a recipe."

"Yep."

"Which you gave her."

"I did. You told us to be nice to everyone in the wedding party."

"I appreciate all you did."

"Should I expect a bonus?" he quipped.

"At Christmas and not before."

"Hey, did you know Christmas comes early this year? Fa-la-la-la-la," he crooned.

"You wish."

He barked his rowdy laugh and disappeared into the refrigerator.

I was a good boss, and I gave decent bonuses. When I'd worked as a chef in San Francisco, my boss was a bit of a miser. Bryan said—

I curbed the thought. When would I stop remembering everything he'd said?

Focus, I told myself and surveyed the kitchen, thinking back to that night. While Stefan retrieved the recipe, Paula could have easily stolen my cell phone and filched one of the remaining éclairs. She could have hidden both in a napkin and stuffed them into that flashy tote of hers when she returned to the table.

But then I saw the flaw in my theory. Anyone who had ventured into the kitchen could have done the same. Both David and Lyle had pockets in their jackets, and either Angelica's or Francine's totes would have been able to hold the loot, just like Paula's.

Which meant anyone could be guilty. Anyone.

Chapter 21

I hurried back to the bar to chat a bit more with Nash, but he was on his feet, ready to take off. Willow stood across the room, talking animatedly to one of our customers. The vases that she had brought rested at the end of the bar. Sunlight hit them and made them sparkle.

"I'm sorry," I said when I reached Nash. "Business—"

Willow laughed loudly, drawing my attention. Her arms were spread wide, and she was flapping them, as if pretending to be a bird.

"Forget her." Nash clasped my elbow and drew me close. "She likes to make a display."

I scanned the bistro. The customers around her seemed to be amused. I decided not to rein her in unless she went on too much longer.

Nash placed a warm, gentle kiss on my lips. Desire shot through me. "I've got to get going," he whispered. "I'll call you and we'll set another date. How about going ballooning? I've never done it. Have you?"

"Never. Sounds great."

"Not afraid of heights?"

"Only steep mountaintops without rappelling equipment."

"Is that how your husband—"

"Yeah. He decided to freestyle in Ama Dablam, one of the most challenging regions in the Himalayas. He fell and died instantly."

"Wow. You'll never catch me doing that."

"Dying?" I teased. "Good to know."

He allowed a moment of silence to end that topic and then gestured to the bottle of Cabernet. "Cork that up. Have a sip after work and think of me." He offered a cocky grin and headed off.

As the door swung shut, I let out a sigh, realizing how much I liked him, but it was all *first glance*. I needed to learn more about him. *One date at a time*, I told myself. I would not rush headlong into a relationship like I had with Derrick.

Willow let out a whoop. I was about to shush her when I spotted Paula sitting at a table beyond her. She was on her cell phone, mouth moving rapidly. Who was she talking to? Lyle? Was he filling her in on his meeting with the attorney? Was he recommending that she do the same? Maybe she was talking to her father. Perhaps he had alerted her that I'd run into him outside the jewelry store. In a conspiratorial way, she jotted notes on a yellow legal pad. She glanced over her shoulder as if she felt someone spying on her from behind. When she caught me staring, she covered her pad like a student not willing to share answers on a test.

Dang, but I wished I knew what she was up to. Talk about secretive.

Heather nudged me. "Hey, can you give me a little help?" She was holding tablecloths and numerous place settings. "I've got to clear off three tables pronto. We're one waitress short and booked until two thirty."

"What happened?"

"That new girl had to pick up her sick daughter from school. This way."

I followed her to the first table. She put the linens and settings on a chair and, like a magician, whisked away soiled dessert plates and coffee cups in an instant. I moved the vase to a chair and collected the wineglasses and water glasses. By the time I returned from the bussing station, the tablecloth was on, and the napkins were folded and set in place. I arranged the silverware and fetched fresh glasses.

"How many do we have coming for dinner tonight?" I asked.

"Three early-bird foursomes at six thirty. Four duos at seven. The house is full by eight, and then we have a large group at nine to take the tables of the early birds."

I loved how she could keep the list straight in her head. Prior to working for me, she had taught high school math, which was one of the reasons she was so good at memorization. However, she had given up teaching after her third alien abduction because the Glonkirks convinced her that she really didn't like teenagers. I figured the real reason she walked away was because her hypnotherapist had suggested she find a job more geared to adults. Math had played a part in my hiring decision, since she did most of the preorders.

"Chef C seems pretty calm about tonight's visitor," I said.

"She should be. She's put a lot of work into the meal." Heather moved to the second table that we needed to reset. I trailed along. "By the way," she said as she removed the linens, "you made me curious about Pierre Dubois, so I did some digging on the Internet. He's a food critic by night, but did you know he's a data warehousing specialist by day?"

"What is that?"

"Data warehouses are storehouses of integrated data from one or more sources. You know, they stockpile info to create analytical reports."

"Boring."

"But necessary. He's all buttoned up during the day. At night, he lets his hair down and visits restaurants. He's been married once and has two grown children. He's originally from France, but he now lives in San Francisco. FYI, I read a few of his reviews. He's a fair critic."

"Good to know."

"And get this. On his bucket list, he wants to visit every three-star Michelin restaurant in the world."

"Yet he decided to visit us?"

"Our reputation is growing because of—" She balked.

"Bryan's murder." Thank heavens I was no longer a suspect, or else earning notoriety for my business might prove to be a convincing motive.

As we tackled the last table makeover, Heather said, "Say, did I tell you my husband got an agent? He's very excited. I'm trying to keep him realistic and not get his hopes up. He's had an agent before, but the guy was a loser. He charged all sorts of fees and didn't submit the novel to anyone. I've heard authors shouldn't pay an agent a fee."

"I believe most work on spec."

The door to the bistro opened, and Angelica breezed in. In white trousers and a shimmering white silk blouse, she looked like an angel. She headed straight for me. "Mimi, we did it. Lyle and I got married."

"I heard."

"I'm sorry we won't be having the official wedding at the inn. I hope you don't mind. Maybe we'll do an impromptu celebration. Would that work?" Words were speeding out of her. The joy on her face was beyond ecstasy.

I smiled. "Whatever you need, we can accommodate." I set the last two water glasses to the right of the place settings.

"Want to see my ring?"

"Of course."

"Me, too," Heather chimed.

"Lyle didn't give me an engagement ring because he was superstitious."

"Why?" I asked.

"He got engaged a few years ago, and she jilted him. She was an actress with a fragile ego."

"My husband was superstitious about the engagement ring," Heather said. "Supposedly, a secondhand engagement ring from a family member will pass down the joy or suffering of the previous marriage. Well, he had his heart set on giving me his grandmother's ring, but when he found out his grandfather, whom he had never known, was a ridiculously mean man, he decided to skip it."

"I'm so sorry," Angelica said.

"I'm not. I got this cute little diamond-studded band." She wiggled her fourth finger.

I laughed. "It's lovely." To Angelica I said, "C'mon, show us yours."

She flashed her ring, which featured a beautiful aquamarine stone in a diamond halo setting. "An aquamarine is believed to encourage a long and happy marriage."

"So is a sapphire," Heather said.

"Well, it's gorgeous," I said, trying to mask the bittersweet tug on my heart.

"What's wrong?" Angelica asked. "You look like you're in pain."

"I . . ." I shook my head. "The killer put an aquamarine in Bryan's mouth. I can't seem to shake the memory, and I can't make sense of it."

Heather said, "That sure didn't encourage a long and happy anything."

Angelica's eyes grew teary.

"The ring goes nicely with your mother's necklace," I said, trying to lighten the mood.

Instinctively, she touched the pendant.

"May I ask why you eloped?"

"Lyle said he didn't want to wait any longer, and I agreed. It's horrible that Uncle Bryan died, but he would have wanted us to be together. He would have wanted us to share a happy moment, despite the tragedy. He always said, 'Life is too short to wait for anything.'"

"He said that to me, too." I smiled, the memory fresh.

"He also said, 'No matter what, follow your heart. I didn't, and I'm sorry.' I'm not sure what he meant, but those words hit me right here." She knuckled the left side of her chest.

Heather cleared her throat. "May I ask a question? Just you and Lyle went to the courthouse. Why didn't you include his father and sister in the ceremony?"

"Lyle figured Paula would object, and his father, well, he doesn't hold me in high regard. We wanted good vibes around us."

"What about your father?" I asked. "Did he attend?"

Angelica shrugged. "I called him so he could give me away, but I couldn't reach him. He was probably . . ." She mimed dealing cards.

"Does he gamble every day?"

She shrugged.

I patted her arm in encouragement and then centered the vase with the white rose and headed back to the bar. Heather left to attend to business at the hostess podium. Angelica followed me and settled onto a stool.

I sat on one beside her. "Angelica, this might be indelicate, but are you sure Lyle isn't marrying you for your money?"

She laughed. "Don't be ridiculous. He loves me. And for your information, we wrote up a prenuptial agreement."

"I'm glad to hear that. You did that before you got married?"

She nodded. "We had it notarized at the courthouse."

"Lyle wasn't resistant?"

"Not in the least. In fact, he was so furious that his father had investigated me like Bryan investigated him, he wanted to get married just to show David that he was his own man."

I gawped. "You know what David did?"

"Do I ever! Doesn't anyone trust anybody nowadays?" She hissed in righteous indignation. "I suppose he and Bryan were being protective because they cared about us, but Lyle and I are adults with thriving careers. Plus we can handle anything that comes at us. We're in love."

"Sometimes love is blind." I raised my hand. "Been there, done that."

Angelica set her purse on the bar beside the miniature vases. "I'm expecting Lyle to join me. He had some business errands to run."

Like meeting with a defense attorney, I mused.

"Is it okay if I wait here?" she asked.

"Of course." I drummed the bar with my fingertips. "So, um, I heard what David Ives discovered."

"You did?"

"He and I were chatting, and he let on that you're a gambler like your father."

"What? No, I'm not!" Angelica exclaimed.

"He said you were high-risk."

She clucked her tongue. "Sure, I have a few high-risk investments, but that's not considered gambling."

"What is it then?"

"It's speculative." She explained how she used the barbell approach to investing, meaning the big portion of her estate was placed in index funds and value plays. She had a few smaller investments in rip-roaring trades that she hoped would pay out as soon as possible. She was a collector, as well—she had acquired a few art pieces that she was particularly proud of. Lastly, she invested a small portion of her income in high-risk investments like gold because although those investments might pay off big if gold prices rose, if the value of gold plummeted for some reason, she would lose big. Not to mention that the initial buy-in cost was steep, and gold didn't pay dividends or earn profits. "It's not considered gambling. My mother always advised me to invest in gold. She said that's what my father would say to do."

Over the past year, Bryan had said the same to me, although I didn't have any wealth to invest. Yet.

"I'm not rich," Angelica said, "but as a talk-show host, I make a good enough income that I don't want for anything."

"So you're not in debt like your father?"

"Heavens, no. Sure, I have a pretty hefty mortgage and I use my credit cards, but I pay those off every month. Dad, on the other hand, plays cards and loses regularly. He's had to refinance the vineyard seven ways from Sunday."

"Didn't you say he invested in gold?"

"If he did, it's long gone. He stays afloat because, luckily, his product is excellent. Someday he might not be so lucky, but until then . . ." She trailed off.

During her silence, I reflected on what I'd just learned. Angelica had her own fortune. She didn't need her uncle's. Would that alone exonerate her?

"Angelica, someone heard Bryan on the night of the out-of-towners' dinner saying he would take care of you."

She smiled. "Of course he would. He always took care of me. He helped me get into college. Got me my first job. Helped me meet Lyle."

"Meeting Lyle wasn't an accident?"

"Well, it was." She blushed. "He wasn't supposed to be working that day, but I happened to go to that particular jeweler because Uncle Bryan had said it was a well-known and well-respected establishment."

Interesting. Despite the feud between Bryan and David, Bryan had still recommended Ives Jewelers. Out of guilt or out of honor?

"Was his promise to take care of you what made you cry?" I asked.

"No. I . . ." Fresh tears sprang to her eyes. She seized a cocktail napkin and dabbed at the moisture. "I cried because he mentioned the necklace I was wearing. I told him its history. He said how proud my mother would have felt about the way I had turned out."

A cool breeze wafted in. I turned toward the front of the bistro. Lyle, wearing a jaunty fedora, linen shirt, linen slacks, and sandals, entered with Francine and Kent. Francine appeared rested and less made up than usual. Kent's grin was a mile wide. They were holding hands, his thumb caressing hers. Love was definitely in the air.

Lyle strode to Angelica, kissed her cheek, and plopped an envelope on the counter. "Take a peek."

"What's inside?" she asked.

Kent said, "Out-of-towners' dinner and wedding photos, love."

"Not the real photos," Lyle said. "Only the proofs."

"The dinner ones were delivered to the inn," Francine crooned. "Jorianne gave them to us. We've peeked at them. They're great."

"Lyle sent me to the courthouse for the others," Kent said. "They're a little grainy, if I do say. They must have been printed on a subpar computer."

"They'll do for now," Lyle said. He turned to me. "Mimi, something smells remarkable. Do you have a table for four?"

"Absolutely." I beckoned Heather and held up four fingers.

"On it," she said. "I'll be right back."

"Before you go to your table, Angelica, may I look at the proofs?" I asked. Seeing as we had hired the out-of-towners' dinner photographer, for future reference, I wanted to make sure the quality was up to par.

Lyle slipped the photograph proofs from the envelope and handed them to Angelica, who handed them to me.

The quality of the wedding photos taken at the courthouse was definitely inferior, as if the assistant had used an ancient iPhone in the dark, but Angelica and Lyle seemed blissful, and ten years from now, they would laugh about their elopement and hopefully not recall with bitterness why they hadn't waited to have a formal ceremony.

"Aw, look at this one," Angelica said, displaying a picture of her, her father, and Bryan. I remembered when our photographer had finally corralled them.

"Blimey, the three of you look alike," Kent said.

"It's the eyes," Angelica said. "Grandma had the same eyes, too."

"My father and I had the same eyes," I said.

"Huh." Francine tilted her head as she regarded the photograph. "Angelica, I always thought you looked more like your mother, with your dark hair and the shape of your face, but now—"

"Dad, through and through," Angelica said.

Heather reappeared with menus. "Follow me."

Angelica hung back, and Lyle returned to the bar to fetch her.

She eyed the vases Willow had brought. "Those are pretty, Mimi. Where are you going to put them?"

They were pretty, and I was warming to them. "I'm not sure."

"My mother made stuff like this. Each piece is unique."

"She was an artist?"

"Yep. She worked out of a studio at the house."

"Liquey's father hasn't touched the place since her mom died," Lyle said.

"Mother made so many beautiful things with glass and clay. She even did a few oil paintings. She never sold any of it. She said it wasn't good enough. I would beg to differ." She knuckled my arm. "You might even like some of it for the bistro. She made a mirror or two. Do you want to see her work?"

"I'd love to."

"How about tomorrow morning?"

"I have a standing breakfast with my mother every week."

"Let's meet after that. Please? It would make me happy to see someone else appreciate her art." Her voice grew faint and almost needy. Had Francine and Kent's hookup deprived her of a confidante?

Heather returned to fetch Lyle and Angelica and, overhearing the conversation, gave me a thumbs-up sign. "Go. See her mother's stuff. I'll cover for you in the morning."

"Ten AM?" I said to Angelica.

"Perfect."

Before moving toward their table, Lyle said, "Hey, Mimi, have you talked to Sergeant Daly? He's a friend, right? Has he learned anything new about, you know . . ."

"Bryan's murder?"

He cleared his throat. "Yeah."

I hesitated. Had Lyle come into the bistro to show photographs or to get a bead on the situation? Had he come into Fruit of the Vine Artworks earlier to look at the items in the shop or to intimidate me?

"I don't know anything new," I said coolly. "I have a call into him." I turned to Angelica. "By the way, did you ever find out if there are speed cameras in the area that might have captured you on film?"

"I forgot to ask."

Lyle nudged her. "I reminded you."

"And then you hustled me to court to get married."

"Babe, you really need to firm up your alibi."

"I'll do it after lunch. Promise." She petted his cheek.

I gazed at Lyle curiously. "Say, Lyle, forgive me, but did you ever tell Angelica your, um, *real* alibi?"

His bride's eyes went wide. "Lyle, what is she talking about?"

He threw me a dark look and, without another word, guided her by the elbow to their table. His mouth was moving the whole time.

Oh, how I would have loved to listen in on the conversation.

Chapter 22

Later that night, as Pierre Dubois, the food critic from *Gourmet's Delight*, ate, I felt like I was watching a scene from *Who Is Killing the Great Chefs of Europe?*, one of my family's all-time favorite movies. My mother adored George Segal. My father was particularly fond of Jacqueline Bisset. I loved Robert Morley, the overweight foodie who needed to kill the chefs because they made such fabulous creations that he couldn't resist and therefore was morbidly fat.

Pierre, a portly man of sixty with a shock of dark hair that kept falling down the middle of his forehead, was definitely into food. He relished every mouthful. As he *ooh*ed and *aah*ed over the bouillabaisse, I heard Heather snicker. I shooed her away. We did not want our guest to feel intimidated about his verbal expressions of obvious delight. Besides, she had already made a big gaffe by revealing to Pierre, when he first arrived at the bistro, that we knew who he was. She had stumbled over the name *Dough* by saying *Dubois* and correcting herself. *Oops.* Luckily Pierre had laughed heartily, adding that he wasn't very good at subterfuge.

The assistant Pierre had brought along was as thin as a rail—the tank top she was wearing didn't do her bony shoulders any favors—and she ate like a bird. One teensy bite of the soup was all she tasted. She murmured her appreciation, but I doubted she had savored it. Hers was a job, not a calling. When she set aside her spoon, she added Pierre's whispered notes onto an iPad.

Neither of them was drinking wine. Flat water was all they had requested. They didn't want to dull the flavors with liquor.

After he finished his soup, Pierre said, "Might I see the chef?"

"But of course."

I strode into the kitchen and begged Camille to follow me to the table. She spruced her hair, smoothed her splattered white chef's coat, and checked her face in the mirror beside the time clock before exiting.

"Chef"—Pierre rose halfway as a greeting and resumed sitting—"after a single dish, I am pleasantly delighted. The flavors are big and bold, and from such a petite woman."

The compliment nearly made Chef C swoon. I doubt anyone had ever called her petite. "Wait until you taste our next appetizer," she said. "It will delight and challenge you."

"Challenge me? Ho-ho. I enjoy a good challenge."

"As do I." When given the opportunity, Chef C loved to tantalize customers. Chuckling, she exited and then returned a minute later to hand-deliver the plates of green-toned pâté with toast points to Pierre and his assistant.

Pierre scooped the pâté onto a toast point and bit into it. His eyes fluttered. "Turmeric?" he whispered.

Chef C nodded. Her mouth widened in a smile.

"And garlic. And sundried tomatoes. And"—he gazed into her eyes—"pumpkin seeds? It's vegan?"

"Indeed." She clapped her hands. "My word, you have an excellent palate."

"You have an exquisite touch, madame. Next dish, please."

As he finished his pâté, I caught Chef C peeking from the kitchen. She spotted me watching her and ducked back to her station.

When Oakley, who had been assigned to his table, brought out the *la clapassade d'agneau* and Pierre dug in, he exclaimed, after one bite, that it was exactly as he remembered from the Old Country. He beckoned me.

I hurried to his side.

"Mimi, my sweet girl, have you been spying on my mother? I swear this is her recipe."

"No, sir. That is an old family recipe."

"I adore the licorice root. It's not overbearing."

"My grandmother always told me to go lightly with it."

"The crunch of the carrots is just right. I hate soggy carrots."

"Me, too."

"Scrumptious." He tucked the napkin tighter beneath his chin and didn't stop for a breath until he had finished the entire portion.

The pièce de résistance was, of course, dessert. Stefan delivered the *gateau mille-feuilles*—a.k.a. the Napoleon—and stood by to await Pierre's approval.

Pierre gazed at Stefan and back at his dessert plate. His lower lip pushed out. Was he pouting?

I hurried over. "Sir, what's wrong? Is it not to your liking?"

He swiveled his head and peered up at me. "It is beautiful, but it is not what you, my dear Mimi, are known for. I have heard exquisite remarks about your crème brûlée. I had hoped to enjoy that."

"Don't you worry." I shot a finger at him. "I'm on it."

Crème brûlée was, indeed, one of my specialties. I prided myself on finding the best vanilla beans available. We always had ramekins of the dessert on hand, and we invariably set one or two on the counter so they could warm to room temperature before applying the heat to the top.

I hurried to the kitchen, placed a ramekin on a pretty white plate, and added a thin layer of vanilla sugar to the top. Then I powered up the blowtorch. Yes, I kept a blowtorch in the bistro kitchen. There were plenty of fancy cooking torches you could purchase at a variety of culinary stores, but I was quite fond of the regular blowtorches found at your typical home improvement store. I switched it on and heated the sugar to a fine crisp.

When I presented the dish to Pierre, he was more than impressed. His assistant, to my surprise, finished her entire dessert.

By the time the two of them departed, the waitstaff, Chef C, Stefan, Heather, and I were as tense as the characters in a Hitchcock movie. The moment the door closed behind them—by then, the dining room had cleared completely—all of us let out deep sighs of relief. Then we shared high fives all around.

"Success!" I said to my chef and threw my arms around her. Her taut frame melted into me.

She broke free and said, "It is always a task, but I love it."

Stefan said, "My mother would've adored that guy. She loves to cook, but she can't get my father to eat more than the assistant did."

"Who is your mother?" Heather said, sidling into Stefan and bumping her hip against his.

"My father's ex-wife," he countered.

"You two," Chef C chided. "Stefan, you cannot keep us on tenterhooks forever."

"Yes, I can. I am a master!" He shot a hand into the air.

Heather persisted. "I'm going to find out who your parents are. I'm determined. Is your mother a famous singer or a movie star? Is your father a drug lord or a mob guy or a—"

"Enough!" I shouted. "We're here to celebrate."

Something went *clack* in the kitchen.

"Who heard that?" I asked.

Chef C and Heather raised tentative hands.

Stefan guffawed. "Relax. It's the wind. The back door is loose. I'll fix the hinge in the morning. And yes, I'll lock the door."

Our glee settled into something more sober.

Heather said, "Not to dampen our spirits, but will Mr. Dubois's review matter in the long run? I mean, it's not like he reviews for, you know, the big guns."

I smiled. "Of course it will. The magazine is well respected. Granted, a good review from Pierre isn't like earning a star from Michelin, but it's a beginning. One good review breeds another." Thankfully, I hadn't seen nor expected to see a review—good, bad, or indifferent—from the dissatisfied diner who wrote for the *Napa Culinary Circle*.

An hour later, once the bistro was spotless and ready for tomorrow's lunch crowd, I slogged to my cottage. On the way to the bedroom, I scanned the dry-erase board and spotted Angelica's motive: *Money*. I picked up the marker and added *High-risk investor—gold*.

Something niggled me as I wrote the words. I tapped the capped end of the marker against my chin. Was Angelica's story about investing in gold true? If she was lying about that and she was actually in debt, how might that alter her motive?

I scribbled *When did she learn about inheritance?* and circled the words. If she was in debt, knowledge of her inheritance did matter. I then drew a line from that cluster of words to Lyle's name. If Angelica had learned about the inheritance before Bryan died, she might have revealed as much to Lyle. If only I knew what Lyle had discussed with Kaya Hill. Had he met with her to exonerate himself or Angelica? Was he worried because Angelica had told him she'd caught me theorizing? Or had Kent told him to protect himself after challenging me in the garden?

As I set the pen down and took a step back, I heard a creak. By the front door. I whipped around. "Who's there?" I yelled.

No one said a word.

My breath snagged in my chest. I grabbed the hand-forged iron poker from the stand of tools by the fireplace and tiptoed to the door. I heard a faint *meow*. I jerked the door open and in vaulted Scoundrel. He yowled at the top of his lungs. I slammed the door and locked it and scooped him into my arms. "What's up, buddy?"

His heart pounded like a sledgehammer. Something had given him a fright.

I peeked through the curtains. I couldn't make out any figures. No one was peeping from behind a tree. No squirrels were dashing about like they had at my mother's house pretending to be ghosts. I set Scoundrel on the floor. Like an eager scout, he scampered through the cottage, checking corners and closets. A minute later, he returned to me, circled me once, and then headed to the door leading to the patio. When I didn't open the door, he glanced back at me, his tail hooked in a question mark.

"Time to leave?" I asked.

He mewled.

"Not hungry?" I had a can of tuna in the cupboard.

He didn't respond.

"Okay, fine." I opened the door.

He tore off, bounded over the rear wall, and disappeared into the night.

Nervous laughter bubbled out of me as I replayed his sudden arrival. The mouse he had preyed upon must have turned out to be more vicious than anticipated.

Water gurgled inside the aquarium. I swooped around, still on alert. Cagney and Lacey goggled me from within. Did they care whether I was okay, or were they worried that I was losing

244

my mind? Maybe they knew I was slaphappy and were trying to convince me to go to sleep.

I waved to them. "Yeah, yeah. Bedtime."

Just as I was about to enter the bedroom, I heard another sound at the front door. Not a creak. A *clatter*. "Scoundrel, stop it!"

I stomped to the door and whipped it open. Scoundrel wasn't there, but on the doorstep was a white plate with a caramel-iced éclair set atop a paper doily. I glanced right and left but didn't see any movement. I didn't hear retreating footsteps, either. I flashed on the sound I'd heard at the bistro. Had someone stolen into the kitchen while we were celebrating and taken an éclair from the walk-in refrigerator? Who? And why leave it for me? I peered at the éclair again and saw a corner of a folded piece of paper peaking from beneath the pastry.

Heart pounding, I snatched the plate, backed into the cottage, and slammed and bolted the door. I withdrew the paper and unfolded it. Written in what looked like red lipstick were the words *Back off!* The same words David Ives had said to me. My insides knotted as I recalled the recent turn of events: the encounter at the festival, the warnings from Kent and the others, the mirror breaking, the run-in with David outside the jewelry store . . . and now this.

Someone pounded on the door. I jolted. Would a killer knock?

"Who is it?" I asked tentatively.

"Raymond."

Relief coursed through me. I set the plate with the éclair and note on the kitchen counter, raced to the door, and peeked through the peephole. My wonderful master gardener was standing there holding a lit flashlight.

I threw the bolt and opened the door. "I'm so happy to see you. Come in. Have you been snail hunting?"

"It's slug night." The knees of his coveralls were filthy. "Are you okay? You slammed your door."

"I'm fine." I tugged his sleeve, drew him inside, and then closed the door and locked it. "Okay, that's a lie. I'm not fine. Did you see anybody running from my cottage?"

"No."

"Someone left that for me." I pointed to the éclair and the note.

Raymond strode to the counter and inspected the note. "We should call Tyson."

"And tell him what, that I'm freaked out? He already wants me to butt out of his investigation."

"You should."

"I have."

Raymond eyed the dry-erase board. "Uh, no, you haven't, if that's any indication." He ran his hand through his thick dark hair. "Mimi, get real. This note is serious."

"It's nothing more than a bully trying to strong-arm me, and I refuse to be manipulated."

Raymond barked out a laugh. "Ha! Yeah, that sounds like you. I remember a time in high school when you took the same stance. You were running for class treasurer. You had the best slogan: 'Chocolate bar—$3, class T-shirts—$12. Mimi for treasurer: Priceless.'"

"My father came up with that."

"You were running against Erika, remember? She was always in your face, telling you how you weren't pretty enough, and you were . . . *pretty enough*"—self-consciously, he licked his lips—"which all your friends kept reminding you, so you retaliated and said she wasn't smart enough to be treasurer. Then you posted a sign that said 'Erika makes no cents.'" He thrust a finger like a sword. "Score! Everyone laughed. She cried. Bully conquered."

246

"So what do you think I should do?" I glanced at the éclair. The murderer had stuffed one in Bryan's mouth. Was this him or her saying he or she would shut me up, too?

Raymond shoved a hand in his pocket. "You look tired. Go to sleep. I'll be glad to keep watch outside. In the morning, you can come up with a plan."

Sleep. Right. As if that was going to happen.

Chapter 23

I slept fitfully. When I woke, I showered and dressed, and after my morning cup of coffee, I felt bold and clearheaded. Whoever had left that éclair had run off. It was a warning, that was all, like all the other warnings. I didn't need to tell Tyson. Yet. I didn't relish an early morning lecture from him. I would face the day the same way I had since starting my new venture with Bryan as my benefactor—with confidence. Later, when and if Tyson touched base with me about Bryan's collectibles, I would give him a full recap.

My mother and I always met for a weekly breakfast at Chocolate, the café where Bryan and I used to talk business. Mom had gone there regularly with my father, so it held a special place in both our hearts. A terrific jazz club called Dizzy G's and Forever, a bridal shop that carried some of the most gorgeous and whimsical gowns I had ever seen, flanked the café on either side.

At eight thirty, Mom and I greeted each other in front of the café. She had taught me from an early age to be prompt to all occasions.

Chocolate was an adorable, light-filled place, decorated with white coffee-cup-shaped chairs seated around rich walnut-topped

248

tables. The white-toned granite counter was fitted with six white stools that were invariably filled. Crystal pendant lights hung over a second counter, upon which sat glass-topped cake plates filled with delectable goodies.

The owner, Irene, was as adorable as her café. She had eyes the color of Hershey's kisses and invariably wore her pink-highlighted hair in a loose braid. She had never married, and she didn't have children, but she loved dogs with a passion and kept a contribution jar on the counter to help strays. Her own rescue dog, a chocolate Labrador named Chip—get it, chocolate chip—played all day long in a tarp-covered yard behind the café. Diners who brought their dogs were invited to let their pets play with Chip as long as the canines were friendly and had the appropriate vaccinations.

Always positive, Irene hung signs with wonderful sayings on the wall by the register. Today's was *When the plan fails, change the plan*.

My mother, who looked quite chic in leggings, lacy sandals, and a loose-fitting gauze top, strode to a table by the window. Irene kept it reserved for us. Ragtime music was playing through the speakers. My foot tapped beneath my chair as I peered at the chalkboard that held the day's specials, wondering whether I would eat something other than my usual.

Seconds later, Irene, in a white smock dress and brown apron, brought us two glasses of ice water, two hot chocolates, and two croissants. *So much for choosing something different*, I mused. How well she knew us. Her croissants were so flaky and buttery that neither my mother nor I could resist.

"Morning, ladies. Hot enough for you?" The temperature outside was barely seventy degrees, but Irene liked it cool. She had grown up by the ocean but had moved inland when her aging parents retired in Napa. "Let me know if you need anything else." She sashayed back to the counter.

"How are the ghosts, Mom?" I teased.

"You're a laugh a minute."

"Maybe it's time to start dating and rediscover that plucky spirit of yours. Think of how many squirrels you could tackle."

"Not yet." She grew quiet and sipped her chocolate. When she peered up at me, her eyes brimmed with tears. "Every time I come here, I miss your father."

"Then let's stop coming here."

"Are you kidding?"

"I miss him, too." I caressed the tourmaline stone on my necklace. "I bet he would help me solve Bryan's murder."

"You?" My mother dabbed her mouth with a chocolate-brown cloth napkin. "Darling, I'm sure Tyson will solve the case. He's so handsome."

"Mom, c'mon. Really? Handsome doesn't make him smart."

"It doesn't hurt." She winked at me. "Speaking of handsome, I really like your new man, Nash."

"He's not my *new man*."

"You went on a date, didn't you? When was the last time you did that? Not since—"

"I know." Since Derrick died. I had been busy starting a business and healing a broken heart.

"By the way, you looked charming in that outfit you wore with your hair loose and that cute hat. Why don't you—"

I gave her the evil eye. She bit back the rest of her critique. She didn't need to say it out loud. She was never happy with my self-dictated uniform, but after our visit, I was going to Angelica's to see her mother's art and then straight to work.

Using a knife, she cut her croissant into eight equal bites. "Nash is charming and a bit of a rogue, if you ask me. That smile and those dimples. Mmm." She blew a kiss.

"I heard you hired him."

"I know a good salesman when I meet one. I've been waiting for someone like him to come along." My mother swallowed a bite of croissant and tilted her head. "What's with the face?" She mimicked me, and I laughed. In that regard, we were quite alike. She could match the way I screwed up my nose better than anyone. "Are you worried about something?"

"You said he's a bit of a rogue. Someone else mentioned he might be a rover."

"A rover? What an out-of-date word. Darling, don't even go there." She plopped another croissant bite into her mouth.

Irene, who was taking an order at a nearby table, whirled around. In three quick strides she was on us. "Are you talking about Nash Hawke?"

"You know him?" my mother said.

"Everyone in town knows Nash. Sweetest guy around."

"But does he play around?" my mother asked.

Irene chuckled. "Doesn't every man?"

"No," Mom said. "Mimi's father didn't."

"Has someone told you he's a player, Mimi?" Irene asked.

"His ex-wife, Willow, hinted that he wasn't to be trusted."

Irene laughed. "She's cagey, that one. Imagine her calling the kettle black. Ha!" She leaned forward and put both palms on our table. "Willow can't help herself."

"With men?" my mother asked.

"No, Mom, with money," I said. "Nash confided they got divorced because Willow overspent."

Irene chortled again. "That's a nice way of saying she's reckless, but not merely with money." She lowered her voice. "Look, I know it's not nice to spread rumors, but this isn't a rumor. You should take what Willow says with a grain of salt because, well, she has mood swings that trigger the buying sprees."

"How do you know?"

"Because Willow and I are friends."

My mother muttered, "You won't be after she learns you told Mimi her secret."

Irene laughed again. "Sure she will, because she can say the same thing about me. I really have to watch my spending. Why, I often freeze my credit cards in a cup of ice so I can't get to them until the ice melts. That seems to nip the urge."

My mother said, "Why would Willow lie and hint that Nash was a playboy?"

"I have no idea. Mind you, she has a heart of gold, but she's capricious."

As Irene ambled away, a series of thoughts ran together in my mind. Not of Willow or Nash but of Angelica. Not because of her investments in gold—although Irene saying the word *gold* was what had made me think of her—but because Angelica had mentioned that she was an art collector, which steered my thoughts to Bryan and Tyson. I opened my e-mail on my cell phone. Tyson hadn't responded yet to my query about accounting for the valuable items in Bryan's home or office. Drat. I set my phone faceup by my mug in case he did.

For the next half hour, my mother and I tabled the conversation about Nash and discussed life in general. She remarked how pretty Napa was at this time of year and how she was planning to take a trip to New York to see a few musicals in the winter. Would I like to join her? I told her I would love to, but I would have to see how my schedule turned out. I mentioned that she looked tired, but she pooh-poohed the thought.

When we finished our meal and she and I parted, I called Tyson. He wasn't at the station. He was out viewing real estate properties. "Really?" I muttered, irked that he wasn't devoting 100 percent of his time to solving Bryan's case. I dialed his cell phone number, but he didn't answer. I groaned and ended the call without leaving a message. It wasn't like he was obligated to tell me anything. If I wanted information, I would have to get it another way.

And get it I would. My curiosity was at an all-time high. On my way to my Jeep, I rang Bryan's assistant. She answered on the first ring.

"Yasmine, hi, it's Mimi Rousseau."

"Hello, Mimi." Yasmine was an Indian woman from New Delhi with the most beautiful accent and the most glorious black curly hair. We had met on numerous occasions. Once she'd asked if I wanted to learn to belly dance. Before moving to the States and marrying her American-born husband, she had performed in a Bollywood-style movie. I passed on the private lessons. If I didn't feel comfortable in a bikini, I certainly wouldn't feel comfortable in a belly-dancing outfit.

"I am sorry about Mr. Baker," she said. "I know you were close."

"Thank you."

"It is terrible, the injustice. What is this world coming to?"

"I don't know." I truly didn't. "Did you speak with Sergeant Daly?"

"I did. He asked me about Mr. Baker's business associates. I couldn't think of anyone who would want to hurt him. All his recent deals were going amazingly well."

"Did the sergeant ask you for a list of Bryan's art collection?"

"Yes." Yasmine was all business all the time. She dotted her i's and crossed her t's. Accounting sheets were never incorrect. And she had been instrumental in getting all the permits in place when we were undergoing construction—not an easy task.

"Was anything missing?" I asked.

"One of the Fabergé eggs."

"Which one?"

"The one with the carousel inside. I mentioned it to him. He said he would follow up." Yasmine clucked her tongue. "Isn't it odd, Mimi? Why did the thief take that one? I know it was your favorite."

I sputtered. "I didn't take it."

Yasmine's laughter came out in little spurts. "Of course you didn't. Did you know it was Mr. Baker's favorite, as well?" She repeated the egg's history, which I already knew. "It is sad, is it not?" She sighed. "The office lock was picked, so anyone could have taken the egg, I suppose. A deputy dusted for prints, but I don't think they found anything. I warned Mr. Baker he needed better security, but he didn't listen to me. He said in Napa Valley, people were to be trusted."

I sighed. Bryan and his old-fashioned beliefs. "Yasmine, I don't know much about Mr. Baker. You worked for him for, what, ten years?"

"Eleven." Her tone was filled with regret.

"Was he a good boss?"

"The best. Generous. Good hours. He didn't mind if I worked three hours or eight hours, as long as I got the work done."

"Was he ever married?"

"Not that I know of."

"Was he being sued by anyone?"

"Not to my knowledge. He has been, of course. Our society has become quite litigious. But he always settled matters quickly and fairly."

"Has anyone ever threatened him?"

"Once. A while ago, a man came into the office. Distinguished looking, though he had a peculiar way of staring at me, as if I were a specimen. His name was David—"

"Ives," I cut in.

"That's the one. He and Bryan yelled for quite a while, but when he left, he seemed, what is the word"—she hummed—"mollified. I told Sergeant Daly about him."

I thanked her and, unable to come up with any more questions, ended the call.

As I opened the door to my Jeep, a man behind me said, "Hello, Mimi."

I turned. Edison was walking my way, looking quite put together in a wine-toned plaid shirt tucked into jeans.

Beyond him, I spotted Paula Ives idling in a dark-blue BMW. She was staring at me while drumming the steering wheel. She seemed conflicted. Was she upset that I had stared at her in the restaurant when she was acting cagey with the legal pad, or was she still fuming that I had questioned her about stealing my cell phone? Maybe Kent had told her that I was theorizing about the murder. He had warned me to be careful. A shudder ran up my spine. Was she the one who had taunted me at the festival and put the éclair and note outside my door?

"Is Angelica inside?" Edison asked. "I heard she was having breakfast with you. I need to talk to her."

"We didn't meet for breakfast. My mother and I did. Angelica asked me to stop by her mother's art studio afterward. I'm headed there now. Want to come along?" I asked. Having him by my side might thwart whatever dastardly plan Paula was hatching.

He shook his head. "I've got to swing by the bank. Tell her I'll catch up with her later."

"But if you need to talk to her—"

"No, no, no." He wagged his head and grinned. "I won't intrude on girl time. If my wife taught me one thing, it's that women like their privacy." He turned to leave.

"Edison . . ." I hesitated.

He spun around. "What's on your mind?"

"One of Bryan's Fabergé eggs has gone missing, the one that held a carousel. I was going to ask Angelica—"

"Ask her what?" he snapped. His face turned cold. "If she stole it?"

"No, I—"

"What on earth would she want with a stupid egg?"

"That's not—"

"Do you think she killed her uncle to cover up the theft? Are you out of your mind?" He jutted a finger at me. "Angelica is innocent, do you hear me? She is just like her mother, beyond reproach."

"Sir, please." I held up two hands to placate him. "All I wanted to ask her was whether she had any idea who might have taken it, but since you're here, I thought I'd ask you."

"I'm s-sorry," Edison spluttered and then blanched. "I can be overprotective."

"Can't we all?" I smiled, trying to smooth over my misstep. "I was thinking that whoever took the egg must have known about it, seeing as Bryan had more valuable collectibles. Why single out—"

Paula revved the engine of her car as if to let me know she was nearby. Through the windshield, I saw her grinning. Was she trying to scare me? It was working.

Edison said, "Hey, isn't that Lyle's sister?"

"It is."

Paula's face drew tight. Seconds later, she ground the car into gear and tore off.

"What's her problem?" Edison asked.

"Where do I begin?"

He laughed. "Back to the matter at hand. Where did my brother keep this Fabergé egg? I don't remember seeing it at the house."

"In his office. He had a collection."

Edison shook his head. "I'm sorry. I can't be of any help. I don't know any of Bryan's clients. He had an assistant, didn't he? Did the sheriff question her?"

"They did. You know what puzzled both of us? Bryan told us that he'd acquired the egg because it had reminded him of the time when he'd met the love of his life. Do you know who that might have been?"

"Bryan? In love?" Edison chuffed. "My brother never gave his heart to anyone. He wasn't cold, mind you—simply too busy building his empire. His father . . ." He worked his lower lip between his teeth. "The man roamed the world without ever making a dime or putting down roots. That's why our mother left him and married my father. Bryan was out to prove to the world that he was a better man. As a consolation for never giving in to love, he sponsored entrepreneurs like you."

"You must miss him."

"More than I can say." Edison stroked his chin. "Did his assistant tell you how the thief got into the office?"

"The lock was picked. Bryan wasn't keen on high-tech security. He liked to believe in humankind's good nature."

"The idiot," Edison muttered. "If I didn't know better, I'd think it was my daughter's new husband. Lyle had his eye on the brass ring from the very beginning."

"The brass ring?"

"I was using the carousel metaphor. Don't you go for the brass ring on a carousel ride?" He stretched his arm, miming the gesture. "Angelica is the brass ring. She earns a good living."

"You presumed that Lyle was after Angelica's fortune?"

"Let's just say, I don't trust him. I might gamble, but he lies."

Chapter 24

On my way to meet Angelica, I used the hands-free system in my Jeep and called Tyson again. Still no answer. What was up with him? Was he doing anything to solve Bryan's murder? House hunting, honestly? I waited through his message and this time left one of my own: "Call me or come find me. I heard about the missing Fabergé egg. I have an idea. I'm meeting Angelica at her mother's studio, then I'll be back at the bistro. Plus, I have to tell you about a few warnings—"

The call ended abruptly; no cell reception.

"Shoot," I muttered, instantly regretting my message. I should have been nicer. I should have said *please*. How I wished I could erase it and start over. Tyson didn't deserve my wrath.

As I made the turn onto St. Helena Highway, sunshine glinted through the windshield, making me blink. Luckily traffic was better than normal. No workmen fixing potholes. No tourists stopping in the middle of the road for a less-than-ideal photo op. No llamas. Yes, one time there had been a forty-five-minute delay because a llama had escaped from its farm and was taking in the sights while walking down the median.

Halfway to Barrington Vineyards, my cell phone rang. I pressed the telephone icon on the steering wheel. "Tyson?"

"It's Nash. Should I be jealous that you were hoping to hear from another man?"

I smiled. "Not a whit. What's up?"

"I was wondering whether you thought about me while you drank the rest of the wine last night."

I gulped. I was so tired that I had forgotten to take the wine to the cottage. Then I saw the dry-erase board, got spooked by Scoundrel, found the éclair and the note, shared my fears with Raymond and, well, all thoughts of Nash went out the window. What to do? Lie?

"Mimi?"

In the rearview mirror, I caught sight of a dark-colored car speeding around another car. From this distance, I couldn't tell the make. Was it Paula in her BMW?

"Mimi? Are you all right? Did I lose you?"

"I got distracted. Traffic is sketchy." I continued to watch the car behind me. It didn't make another pass. There was too much traffic heading south. "I did think of you in my dreams," I said. That wasn't a total lie. I had been dreaming about him with regularity.

He chuckled. "You forgot the wine."

"I was so exhausted."

"How did the evening go with the food critic?"

"Terrific."

"And my ex-wife. Did she behave herself after I left?"

"She did."

"Listen, about Willow—"

I cut him off. "Nash, can we talk about her another time? I'm on my way to a meeting."

"Sure, of course."

We ended the call right as I arrived at the entrance to Barrington Vineyards.

Like Nouvelle Vie Vineyards, the property was modest in size, but the sweeping driveway leading to the estate at the top of the hill offered incredible views to the north and south. Pinkish roses grew at the end of each row of vines. They had been planted to attract bugs that might destroy the grapes.

The Barringtons' main house, which abutted the building where salesmen would be received, was a traditional two-story farmhouse, all white with a wraparound porch and plenty of dormer windows. Angelica, dressed in a summery white halter dress, met me at the front door and gave me a hug. She smelled like lilacs.

"I'm so glad you came. I'm making some tea that we can take to the studio. Follow me."

She led me through the foyer into the kitchen. On the way, I peeked into the adjoining rooms. Each was decorated with an artist's touch. There weren't any works by famous artists on the walls—no Picassos or Mirós like at Bryan's—but the art that hung there was colorful.

"Your mother's work?" I asked.

Angelica smiled. "She painted it during her red period."

Even the kitchen, though mainly white—white counters, white floors, white cabinets—was accented with red: red pots, red utensils, red trivets. Through the windowed cupboards, I spied red plates and mugs.

"Dad hasn't seen fit to change anything. He hates the color red. He prefers blue. But he lives with it. I don't think he has the heart to remove anything."

On the counter was a tray set with two stunning red floral china cups on saucers, a matching teapot, two silver spoons, and a tiny bowl filled with sugar cubes.

"My mother treasured this set. It's antique French Limoges hand-painted china. She bought it when she was twenty-one. She was lucky enough to travel to Paris, and she found it at an antique fair. She fell in love with it."

My mother collected tea sets. This one reminded me of a Limoges set she had.

A teakettle on the stove whistled. Angelica turned off the burner and poured the hot water into the teapot. "I hope French vanilla tea is all right with you."

I didn't have room for anything after my croissant at Chocolate, but I said yes.

"This way." Carrying the tray, Angelica guided me through the foyer, down the front stairs, and around to the right. Her hair fluttered in the breeze. "The studio is in the back. My mother wanted it situated where she would receive the best afternoon light. Artists can be very particular about light."

She escorted me to a building that was separated from the rest of the house. When we entered the one-room studio, I felt as if I had been transported in time. It was an airy room that would have made Monet proud, with a wall of windows and two skylights overhead. Each bulb in an array of running lights attached to the pitched ceiling was aimed at a piece of art hanging on the walls.

I was amazed by the amount of furniture: a practical oak work desk fitted with architectural-type tools like pencils, drawing paper, and X-ACTO knives stood next to the far wall; two easels—one modern, one antique—were set on the multicolored area rug; a cart carrying paints stood beside the desk; and an eight-drawer cabinet, to store canvases, was tucked into the corner.

Against the opposing wall, directly to our left, stood a workbench. I set my purse down and examined the tools, which were similar to the ones I had seen at Willow's shop: palette knives, paintbrushes, a couple of blowtorches, glasscutters, and more. Beyond the bench, rustic shelving held empty wine bottles and assorted sheets of metal. Past that, a Jenkins kiln.

Along the wall of windows was a grouping of glass garden ornaments, each dangling from wires inserted into a Styrofoam planter. Beside the ornaments stood a wrought-iron bistro-style table with two wrought-iron chairs. Angelica set the tea service on the table.

"Pour you a cup?"

"Sure. Two sugars."

Using the sugar tongs, she dropped the cubes into the hot liquid and handed me a cup. As I stirred it, I noticed the scrolling on the miniature spoons. "These remind me of spoons Bryan owned." I had shared tea with him a couple of times, which is how I had become familiar with the art he had in his home.

"You're right. He gave these to Mom. They're French. He knew how much she had enjoyed that trip. How could he not? She talked about it all the time. They were a little token, he said." Her smile was bittersweet.

With teacup and saucer in hand, I roamed the studio. "Wow, your mother's artwork is incredible and so varied. I particularly like the impressionist French carnival piece." It was an oil painting that made me remember a time when Derrick and I had traveled to Paris and taken in a ridiculously brutal Punch and Judy show. We'd laughed until our sides hurt.

"That's one of my favorites. Mom always wanted to go back. Dad wasn't much of a traveler. I think the farthest they traveled was to Chicago for a wedding."

Angelica left her teacup on the service tray and wandered the studio, fondly touching items as she passed. The brush of her fingertips set off a tinkling of glass wind chimes. In a whisper she said, "It's sad, isn't it? Dad couldn't part with any of this.

Not a thing has been moved since she died. He, and only he, dusts it."

"Give him time," I said.

"It's been fifteen years."

"Everyone handles grief differently."

Angelica sighed. "You're right. After Grandpa died, Grandma wouldn't get rid of his clothes for even longer than that."

The door to the studio whipped open, and Lyle strode in. "There you are."

I tensed. Something about him seemed off. It wasn't just that he was wearing all black and reminded me of a bad guy in a B movie, but his eyes were beady, and he was sweating. He marched to Angelica and threw an arm around her shoulders, but he didn't kiss her. He looked like he wanted to throttle her.

"What's up?" She freed herself from his grasp and discreetly inched away. She must have picked up on his distress, too.

He stood there, hands clenching and unclenching. Out of the side of his mouth, he said, "Hi, Mimi."

"Hi, Lyle. Care for some tea?" I would gladly relinquish my cup and give it to him so his hands would be occupied and mine free.

He waved me off and faced Angelica. "I'm sorry, but this couldn't wait. The hotel manager, Jorianne, told me you two were meeting here."

How did Jo know where I was? Heather must have clued her in.

"We need to talk," Lyle went on.

I said, "That reminds me, Angelica. I saw your father in town. He needs to talk to you. I'm not sure about what. He didn't say. Maybe you should call him."

"It'll wait." She maintained eye contact with Lyle. Had being a talk show host taught her how to stay so composed? I was impressed. "Sweetheart, what's wrong?"

"Money," Lyle hissed. "The bridge loans. The bank is calling them in, and I . . ." He scrubbed his hair and paced in a circle. "I don't know what I'm going to do."

Here it comes, I thought. Her father and Bryan were right. He wanted her help financially. A theory scudded through my mind. Did Lyle steal the Fabergé egg so he could sell it and buy himself time with his loans? Did he hope to talk Angelica into selling off the rest of Bryan's artwork straightaway to bail out his company?

Angelica said, "Mimi, give us a little space, would you?"

"Sure." I set down my teacup and circled the room, taking in the pieces of art while listening in.

"We'll call the banks and negotiate," Angelica said, the voice of reason.

"I tried that, don't you see?"

"We'll try again. They haven't dealt with me, and you know how I am with money people. Tough as nails." She forced a laugh.

Lyle moaned. "I never should have gotten into this mess. I'm so weak."

"Sweetheart, you're not weak. You wanted to make sure the family business stayed afloat. You're loyal. How much are we talking about?"

"Three hundred thousand."

Angelica's mouth dropped, but she didn't gasp. She held herself together. I would imagine on her talk show she'd had to hide her shock numerous times. Celebrities could unload major zingers. "I've got half of that in savings. I'll figure out how to get the rest."

"I need it ASAP!" Lyle slammed his right fist into the palm of his left. "I need cold, hard cash."

"Lyle, honey, stay cool."

"I talked to my father. He doesn't have this kind of money. Paula laughed in my face. And Kent . . ." He whirled on her, his fists raised.

I gasped. Would he hurt her if she didn't comply? Did I need to tackle him?

"Lyle, lower your arms," Angelica ordered. "Take a deep breath. What did Kent do?"

Lyle dropped his arms to his sides, but even so, I moved in the direction of the workbench, where I had set my purse. My cell phone was tucked inside. I would call Tyson and alert him. If he wasn't available, I would call Edison for help. He wasn't a big man, but if his outburst with me less than an hour ago was any indication, he would fiercely protect his daughter. On my way, I paused in front of a fused glass sculpture—a deep-green heart that reminded me of the one hanging in Bryan's office. He told me once that a special lady had made it for him. Had Angelica's mother given it to him?

"What are you staring at, Mimi?" Lyle demanded.

I spun around. He was gawking at me.

"Speak, Mimi," he ordered.

I reached for the heart and lifted it off the wall. "Angelica, this is very pretty."

"My mother made it. She made two, but I don't know where the other one went."

"I think she might have given it to—"

The door burst open, and Edison stormed inside. "Give me that!"

Chapter 25

Edison charged me, hand extended. Instinctively, I recoiled. He took hold of the fused glass heart and wrested it away, but he lost his grip. It flew out of his hand and hit the wall with a *crack*. The glass was so dense that the heart only broke into two pieces.

As I bent to gather them, I noticed initials etched on the flipside: *AB* for Adele Barrington, Angelica's mother.

"Dad!" Angelica charged her father. "What is wrong with you?"

"He was a playboy." Spittle flew out of Edison's mouth. "He didn't deserve your love."

Angelica threw a sharp look at her husband.

Lyle shook his head. "Liquey, I would never cheat on you. I promise."

"I tried to warn you," Edison went on. "He didn't love you."

Didn't, I thought. *Past tense*. Maybe he wasn't talking about Lyle. Maybe he had some previous boyfriend or fiancé in mind.

"I told him to take a hike," Edison continued.

Lyle splayed his hands. "Sir, you never said—"

"I told your mother he would never settle down."

Lyle gawked at Angelica. "I never met your mom."

"Dad, stop it!" Angelica cried. She ran to her father and gripped his hands. "I feel like we're on a merry-go-round spinning out of control. Can you please slow down and tell me what is going on?"

Edison's eyes grew teary.

Suddenly I felt like I was caught in the movie *Charade*, where Cary Grant and Audrey Hepburn are standing near the carousel in a park, and they figure out where the treasure is hidden. But my realization wasn't about a missing treasure. It was about carousels and hearts. I took in the artwork on the walls. I examined the broken heart in my hand. Looking closely, I spotted an infinity sign etched between the letters *A* and *B*—infinity, meaning forever—which confirmed my suspicion. The *A* and *B* on the back didn't stand for Adele Barrington; the letters stood for Adele and Bryan. On further inspection, I spied the tiniest etched words at the bottom of the piece, and my heart skipped a beat: *Love fully before love leaves.* I recalled the story Willow had told me about an art student confiding to a teacher about a man—a *rover*—who had left her. Was the student Angelica's mother and Bryan, Adele's lover?

I glanced at Angelica and at the necklace she was wearing—the necklace her mother had told her that her father had entrusted to her—and a new thought occurred to me. What if Edison wasn't her father?

I glanced at Edison. What had he said to me earlier on the street when I'd asked about the stolen egg? *Angelica is innocent, do you hear me? She is like her mother, beyond reproach.* Had he been trying to convince himself that Adele was pure?

"Edison," I said carefully, "when did you guess that Bryan was Angelica's father?"

"What?" Angelica turned to her father for the answer.

Edison glowered at me. "I don't know what you're talking about."

"Sir, you're not accusing Lyle of being a playboy," I went on. "You're accusing your brother of being one, aren't you? He told me once that he met the love of his life on a carousel. He met Adele, didn't he? In Paris. But Bryan was like his father. He couldn't settle down. He—" It suddenly occurred to me what had been missing on my dry-erase board. I had drawn lines connecting Paula and her father, but I hadn't done the same for Angelica and Edison. Had I subconsciously wondered about Angelica's paternity because Bryan had left her his estate?

The photographer's proofs, I thought. I peeked at Lyle, who was no longer smoldering over his bridge loan issue. He seemed truly concerned for his new wife. "Lyle, do you still have the wedding proofs with you?"

"They're in my car. Why?"

I peered at Angelica. She was quivering. "Angelica, do you remember all of us commenting on how much you, your father, and your uncle looked alike? You said you were like your dad, through and through. But you aren't. Not entirely. Yes, your eyes are the same, but your hairline is exactly like Bryan's. And you have a dimple in your chin, like he did."

"You're right," Lyle said. "I'll get them."

"No, you won't." Edison grabbed Lyle by the arm and hurled him across the room with a force I didn't know he possessed.

Lyle slammed into the eight-drawer cabinet and crashed to the ground.

Angelica raced to him and cradled his head. "Dad, what is going on with you?"

"Lots of families look the same," he said.

"True," I said, "but you and Bryan had different fathers, so you didn't have the exact same gene pool. Angelica looks a lot like you, but she looks more like Bryan."

Angelica blinked back tears. "Dad, is it true? Was Bryan my father? Is that why you raged off in your Jaguar the other day? You said I was blind to the truth. You said I didn't understand that a marriage was a partnership in all aspects of the word. Were you talking about Mom? That she wasn't really your partner?"

Edison strode to the center of the area rug. He stared daggers at me.

"The fused glass heart that you demanded I hand over"—I pointed to the other piece on the floor—"Bryan has one exactly like it hanging in his office. When I visited him, I commented on it. He said a special lady had made it for him. She would always hold a place in his soul." I turned to Angelica. "You said your mother made two. I believe she gave the other one to Bryan. And the necklace you're wearing?" I continued. "Your father found it in your wallet that afternoon before the out-of-towners' dinner. When he asked you about it, you said your mother said your *father* gave it to her." I eyed Edison. "That's when you realized that Angelica wasn't your daughter because you didn't give it to Adele, did you? Bryan did. Adele was the woman who had stolen Bryan's heart so many years ago on that carousel. I'm guessing you had seen the necklace before, though."

Edison moaned.

"Bryan must have shown it to you. Maybe when you were kids. What is it, a family heirloom? That's why you arrived drunk to the out-of-towners' dinner. Seeing it sent you over the edge, and then hearing Angelica say that her father had given it to her mother . . ."

Angelica whispered, "Dad?"

Edison lowered his gaze, dejected. "Bryan's grandmother made him promise to give that necklace to the woman of his dreams, except he never met her—or so I thought. He dated a few women and said there was one who had stolen his heart on a carousel, but he never told me who."

I said, "You never guessed it was Adele?"

"No. Not until—"

"The day of the out-of-towner's dinner."

"He never got engaged or married," he snarled at me. "What tipped you off?"

"The painting of the carousel plus the missing Fabergé egg with the carousel inside. You stole it, didn't you? Because it reminded you of their love." I eyed Angelica. "You told me that Bryan said, 'No matter what, follow your heart. I didn't, and I'm sorry.' He rued his mistake, Angelica. He must have loved your mother until the end. And he loved you. But he respected his brother enough to keep quiet about being your birth father."

"He didn't respect me," Edison snapped.

"Dad!"

"You are my daughter, not his. I loved you." He jammed his thumb into his chest. "I raised you. He didn't have the right to walk you down the aisle and take you away from me."

Angelica's eyes grew misty. "He wasn't going to walk me down the aisle."

I said, "He wasn't going to take her away, either." I glanced at Angelica out of the corner of my eye, unwilling to take my full focus off her father. "That night, Bryan admired your necklace and said your mother would be so proud of how you had turned out. He recognized the necklace, and yet he didn't break his vow of silence, did he?"

"No."

"He must have promised your mother to keep quiet until his last breath." I regarded Edison. "Did you sense Bryan and Adele were attracted to each other?"

"Who didn't fall in love with Bryan? Every woman he met tried to tie him down. But when he took off for a world tour and Adele married me, I set aside my worry."

"Bryan regretted always being on the go," I said. "He told me so." I offered Angelica a reassuring glance. "But apparently he had the good sense not to tell you that he was your father. He didn't want to hurt you or your mother or even his brother."

Edison snorted. "Ha!"

"It didn't help that he bailed you out so many times, did it, Edison? You gambled and lost, and he gave you money every time, didn't he? That had to irk you. It must have made you feel like less of a man."

Edison stood taller.

"It annoyed you that he was paying for the wedding, didn't it? What was the last straw? When the photographer took a picture of the three of you instead of just the two of you?"

"The éclairs." His bravado failed. His chest sank inward as if he were a blow-up doll losing its air. He gazed at his daughter. "When you and he gushed over the éclairs, I couldn't breathe. I knew you were never going to be mine again. You would be his. You would grow to hate me. I'm a loner. I'm weak."

"I love you just the way you are," Angelica said while she continued to stroke Lyle's head. He hadn't budged. Was he okay? Did he have a concussion? Did we need to call 9-1-1?

"But that wasn't good enough, Angelica, don't you see?" I said as I inched toward my purse. I needed to get to my cell phone without upsetting Edison. "Your father wanted you to know the truth. He wanted you to hate Bryan as much as he hated him. He wanted you to despise him for abandoning you and for keeping you in the dark all these years. Edison, why couldn't Bryan commit to Adele?"

"You pegged him. He was exactly like his father. Within weeks of him taking off on a world tour, Adele visited me. Steady Eddie, she called me. She flirted with me. She baked for me. She made me feel special. She even took an interest in the vineyard. What a joke. Obviously she was pregnant and didn't want to raise a kid on her own. I thought you were mine, Angelica. All this time. What an idiot I was." He spread his arms to encompass the studio. "Do you see this? A couple of years later, Bryan waltzed back into our lives, and he paid for this. Every penny. He said he recognized your mother's talent, and she deserved to be spoiled. I said it was wasteful to build it. Bryan didn't care. He gave her the money for her birthday; he never asked to be repaid. I should have guessed then, I suppose, but I was blind."

"The night of the out-of-towners' dinner," I said gently, "you took my cell phone from the kitchen. Why?"

"I wanted to have it out with him, man to man. I didn't think he would respond if I used my phone."

"Why did you wait until morning to text him?"

"I hadn't intended to. When the party broke, I was getting ready to call him, but then I heard Lyle and Angelica arguing, and knowing they were occupied, I thought I might help myself to the gems in his travel safe and dig myself out of a financial hole first."

"How did you . . ." I flashed on the moment I'd met him at the out-of-towners' dinner. The corner of a piece of paper had been jutting from Angelica's new wallet. I'd seen her tuck the paper into place. "Angelica keeps the code to Lyle's portable safe in her wallet. She has a terrible time remembering numbers. You saw it."

"How did you know what the numbers and letters meant?" Angelica asked.

Edison snickered. "The moment I heard that your fiancé traveled with it, I thought, *Aha*! I'd seen a combination code—L-4, R-3-30, L-2-20, R-1-10." He mimed the action. "Clear the tumblers by turning left four times, then right three times and land on thirty, then left, and so on. I have the same kind of four-three-two-one system on the vineyard safe."

I inched closer to the workbench, one slow step at a time. "You slipped into the inn and picked the lock to Lyle's room."

"Didn't need to. The door was ajar." Edison peered at his son-in-law, who still hadn't budged. "Gotta be more careful, son." He chuckled in a slightly unstable way.

"You took a handful of gems," I said.

"And stuffed them in my pocket."

"You took a few aquamarine stones, too, even though they weren't very valuable, so you could make a new keepsake for your daughter using her birthstone."

Edison cocked his head. "You're pretty intuitive."

"What happened next?"

"As I exited, Lyle and Angelica were still arguing. I heard what Bryan had done—how he was trying to prove Lyle was wrong for her—and the anger I'd felt before turned into full-blown rage. I didn't want my brother to play God anymore. He didn't have the right." He gazed at his daughter. "He wasn't there for your ups and downs. He didn't put Band-Aids on your scraped knees. He didn't nurse you through your childhood illnesses. He wasn't by your side when your mother died. He didn't have the right!"

"That's when you decided to punish him," I said. "Forget having a chat. You wanted him dead, but you had the where-withal to wait until morning, when there would be no witnesses. You contacted him—"

"And he came running."

"You didn't confront him. You attacked him with the chair. And you stuffed an éclair into his mouth. Where did you get it?"

"I grabbed one as I exited through the kitchen."

"Of course. You stuffed it in his mouth because—"

"I wanted him to choke on all the things he had in common with my daughter."

"And the single aquamarine?"

"I wanted to show him that he wasn't—" He coughed. "That he never—" The coughing turned into deep sobs.

"You'll be tried for murder, Edison."

"No!" Angelica cut a look at me. "He's sick, don't you see? He's mentally ill."

"I'm not unhinged," her father said, the coughing and sobs replaced with fury. "I am seeing clearly for the first time in my life. All those years, I convinced myself that your mother loved me. I told myself I was enough for her. But I wasn't. She was wicked." His voice rose to a crescendo. "Wicked!"

"No!" Angelica cried.

"She was wicked, and so are you. As long as I see your face, I will be reminded of how she hurt me. How she hated me and made a fool of me." He darted to the practical desk, lifted an X-ACTO knife, and raced toward her. She screamed but couldn't disentangle herself from Lyle. He rested on her like a dead weight.

"Dad, don't!" She threw up her hands.

He slashed at her but missed.

I hurled half of the fused glass heart at him. It hit him in the back. He whirled around and stalked me, aiming the X-ACTO knife at my torso.

"You," he said, "with your theories and your keen eye. If you would have kept quiet, I'd have protected the secret."

Realization dawned on me. "It was you. You were the person in blue who warned me in the mobile restroom at the jazz festival. You stole into the bistro and rehung my mirror on a faulty hook so it would crash. You were the one who left the éclair and note outside my door."

I inched backward and felt the edge of the workbench. I seized the first thing I could, a cup of pencils, and hurled it at him. The pencils shot out like arrows. Edison batted them aside and continued to move toward me.

Lyle stirred. "Edison, don't!"

"Shut up, you weak-kneed coward. I know the likes of you, preying on my daughter so you can drain her resources."

"Sir, I love her."

"Quiet!" Edison continued toward me.

With Lyle's distraction, I was able to spin around. I grabbed the blowtorch and turned back while trying to switch it on. It didn't ignite. Shoot! How long had it been since Angelica's mother had used it? Dust had to be clogging the insides. I flicked the switch again. And again. On the fourth try, it flared with a *splut-whoosh*. I brandished it at Edison. He dodged right.

I grasped the strap of my purse and slung it at Angelica. "Get out my cell phone. Call Sheriff Daly. He's on my speed dial." I waved the torch again, keeping focused on Edison. "Don't come any nearer. I don't want to hurt you."

He cackled and reached for my hand. The flame caught his wrist. He yelped.

As Angelica dialed Tyson, I heard another cell phone jangle.

The door to the studio opened, and Tyson hurried in, phone to his ear.

I cried, "How did you—"

"Jo contacted me. Heather was getting vibes."

Relief washed over me. Thank heaven for Heather and her *vibes*.

The next few minutes whisked by in a blur. I extinguished the blowtorch. Tyson cuffed Edison. Angelica ran to her father and threw her arms around him.

He melted into her. "I'm sorry," he repeated over and over.

"I'm sorry, too," she murmured. "I will always love you. I'll get you the best defense attorney. I promise."

She might want to consider a good therapist, I mused. *For both of them.*

Lyle, who had been sitting on the ground, head between his knees, rose to his feet and joined them, but he seemed to know better than to attempt a group hug. He hung back, chin lowered.

I retrieved my purse and mouthed *thank you* to Tyson.

He threw me a sour glare, as if I was the one who had put all this in motion. "We'll talk," he muttered and ushered Edison out of the studio.

Chapter 26

Angelica rushed to me the moment Tyson and her father dis-appeared and clasped my hands. "Mimi, what am I going to do?" She sucked back a sob. "He couldn't have been in his right mind. He loved Uncle Bryan." She hesitated. "Bryan," she revised and released my hands. "I guess I can't refer to him as my uncle any longer." She started to roam the room, running her finger along the tables, the artwork, the shelving. At the window, she turned and wrapped her arms tightly around her body. "I wish my mother had told me."

Lyle joined her and slipped a comforting arm around her, his financial worries far less important than her current situation. "Babe, we'll figure it out. Family is drama, and drama is family," he said glibly. He knew from firsthand experience.

Leaving Angelica and her beloved to determine their next move, I returned to the bistro. You would have thought I was a hero with the welcome I received. Heather did some kind of goofy cheerleading leap. Where had she learned that? From one of the kids she used to teach, I decided. Stefan whooped like a crane. Our bartender Red tapped a wine bottle with a spoon. Oakley and the rest of the waitstaff applauded. Even Chef C came to the front of the restaurant to give me a two-kitchen-mitt thumbs-up.

Within minutes, Jo arrived, looking as intense as the neon-blue blouse she was wearing. "I'm so glad you're okay," she gushed. She couldn't have hugged me harder if she were a mama bear.

"Tyson is upset with me," I whispered.

She fanned the air. "Don't worry about him. I'll fix that."

I breathed easier. If anyone could pacify Tyson Daly, it was my pal Jo.

*

On Saturday, though Angelica was bereft over the incarceration of her father, she held a memorial for Bryan in the Bazille Garden. The sky was blue. A gentle breeze wafted through the trees and roses. Birds chirped merrily. Jo had arranged a lovely tea-style spread, with lemon scones, orange cardamom madeleines, and of course, éclairs—Bryan's favorite. Lyle and his family attended. Francine and Kent had hung around to support Lyle and Angelica.

I joined Paula Ives by the buffet as she was refilling her tea-cup. Her hair was coiffed, and she was wearing a pretty dark-green ensemble.

"Darn it all," she hissed. The lacy cuff of her blouse was ready to dunk itself in the hot water urn's drip basin.

"Let me help you." After I rescued the sleeve, I said, "Could you spare a minute?"

"Sure," she murmured, though her shoulders visibly tensed. What did she think I was going to do, strike her?

"The other day, you and I exchanged a glance at the bistro."

Her jaw ticked. "I don't know what you're talking about."

"You were on your cell phone and making notes on a legal pad. We locked gazes."

"Oh, that."

"An hour later, I caught you following me in Yountville."

"I wasn't following you. I—"

"You revved the engine of your BMW and glowered at me."

Paula tittered. "My, what an active imagination you have. I wasn't glowering. I was surprised and excited to see you. I had concluded a transaction with my realtor—that was who I was on the phone with at the bistro—and I wanted to tell you about what I bought and about, well, something else, but then Angelica's father showed up."

"Why did you rev your engine?"

She laughed again. "Because the heel of my pump snagged on the floor mat, and I accidentally jammed the accelerator trying to loosen it."

That all sounded reasonable. Maybe I did have an active imagination. "So what property did you purchase?"

"A precious bed-and-breakfast not far from your mother's vineyard. It's six rooms, which is the perfect size for me. It needs a little work, but I'm not afraid to paint a few walls and pound a few nails. And the garden? Did I mention the garden?"

I smiled. Exactly when would she have mentioned it?

"It needs a total overhaul, but it's going to be perfect," she said, waxing rhapsodic. "We'll serve breakfast. There's nothing better than omelets with fresh herbs, don't you think?"

How could I not agree? She was glowing.

"I hired the most adorable omelet chef. She's young and eager, plus—" She halted.

I waited. When she didn't add anything more, I said, "Is there something else you want to tell me?"

She peeked over her shoulder. At her father. "Move. That way." She prodded me toward a corner, away from him. "I'm seeing Raymond, and I don't want you to tell me I can't."

"I would never consider your love life or his my business. However, what I really think is that you don't want your father to have a say."

"Daddy"—she sniffed—"can be overbearing."

That was an understatement. I smiled. "Look, you are strong. You are making a huge break from the family and the family business. Tell him what you want to do, and don't let him bulldoze you. Believe in yourself."

She squeezed my arm in thanks.

Out of nowhere, Scoundrel bolted across the patio and stopped at Paula's feet. He gazed up, his tail curling in his characteristic question mark. She bent to pet him. "Hey, girl, how are you?"

"Girl?" I squawked.

"Didn't you know?"

"He's . . . she's Heather's responsibility." I had stroked him and picked him up. I hadn't inspected him. "He's a *she*, really?"

"Indeed she is." Paula giggled again. I was truly enjoying her happiness. She was an entirely different woman than the one who had shown up a week ago. "And she's pregnant!"

I burst into laughter. We were going to have six or seven mousers? Gee, I couldn't wait for them to come prowling around my cottage, bringing me trophies. Ack. "I'll see you later. I've got to find my sweet assistant and give her a piece of my mind."

*

An entire week passed before things totally settled down at Bistro Rousseau. Large crowds continued to flock to the place, which pleased me, but they were no longer gossipmongers hoping for a story; they were customers hungry for delicious food. The *Gourmet's Delight* review had been a rave, which had prompted two more wily food critics to show up unannounced.

Knowing the bistro was now a target for more surprise guests, I stepped up our game by increasing our three specials a day to five. Today's menu was on the dry-erase board in my living room; I had been eager to write a new project on it after I had erased my theories about Bryan's murder.

Appetizers would include individual fondues made with Gruyère cheese and white wine, each served with small baguettes of bread so the diner could tear off portions to dip. We would also offer my take on Jacques Pepin's choucroute garnie, with a base of sauerkraut and pork ribs, and featuring bacon, ham, three different sausages, boiled potatoes, and herbs. For the entrées, we would have Chef C's specialty, *coq au Riesling*, which meant "chicken in Riesling"—a nice tweak to coq au vin, which was usually made with Burgundy—as well as *matelote*, a scrumptious fish stew cooked in cider. I opted for a floating island dessert, which consisted of poached meringue set atop *crème anglaise*. In my opinion, it was downright incredible.

As I was standing at the hostess podium, watching Heather dash to the kitchen to deliver the menu I had scribbled for Chef C, the door whisked open, and a very distinguished black man entered with my mother.

"Darling," my mother cooed. Dressed in a wine-colored top over a flouncy skirt and strappy sandals, she looked as vivacious as a vineyard hostess. She bustled to me and kissed me on each cheek. "You won't guess who this is."

I whispered, "I know exactly who he is, Mother."

"You do?"

I nodded. Anthony Alston. Stefan's father. A renowned financier in the US government. Had he made the suggestion to dine at the bistro in an effort to touch base with his estranged son, or had my mother unwittingly made the invitation? She didn't know Stefan's last name. Luckily, my adorable sous chef was in the kitchen. I didn't need sparks flying.

"How did you two meet?" I asked.

"He came to San Francisco for a conference—a very *private* conference—and decided to spend his day off in Napa. We bumped into one another at the jazz festival, literally. My fault. His wineglass went flying. I bought him a refill."

"Why didn't you tell me you'd met someone when we had breakfast at Chocolate last week?"

"We hadn't reconnected yet. Doesn't he remind you of Johnny Mathis with his boyish good looks?"

Upon further inspection, he did. So did Stefan, come to think of it. The broad smile, the intense, romantic eyes.

"We had such a good time that I mentioned he should come back for another visit. I didn't think he would take me up on it, but"—my mother bumped her hip against his—"he did."

I about choked. Was she flirting with him? Had she taken what I had said about dating to heart? He was definitely dating material, but was she ready to date someone with such a high profile? My father had been very low-key.

"Nice to meet you, sir," I said.

"Call me Anthony." His voice was so melodious, I wondered if he was in fact channeling Johnny Mathis. No wonder he had swept my mother off her feet.

"Between us"—she winked at me—"Anthony recently decided to step down from his position because he's not a fan of the current administration. He wants to run for Congress, so he's thinking about resettling here."

"Here?" I gulped. "In Napa?"

"In Nouvelle Vie. There's a nice place up the road. Jorianne's father showed it to him."

I gulped again. How would Stefan feel about his father living in his backyard? He had worked so hard to keep his distance.

"By the by, I've been thinking about selling the vineyard."

"What?" I squealed. "Mom, you're making my head spin with all the news. Why?"

"It's daunting running a vineyard at my age. And with the possibility of ghosts—"

"There are no ghosts."

She giggled. "I know. But I should live a little, don't you think? Travel a bit. Your father and I didn't because I was tied to the vineyard." She tweaked Anthony's arm. "Anthony thinks it's a great idea. We both want to take a cruise or two. Maybe visit France. He's never been. Think of the sites I could show him."

"But Nouvelle Vie Vineyards is our history, our home."

"Then you buy it. You run it."

"Ha! Like I don't have enough on my plate." I caressed her arm. "We'll figure it out."

Anthony said, "Is Stefan here?"

I nodded. "He's working hard."

"Could I see him for a moment?"

I sighed. No sense putting off the inevitable. I went and fetched Stefan without telling him what was up. He emerged from the kitchen, spotted his father, and did an immediate about-face.

Anthony said, "I'll handle this." He pushed past me and strode toward the kitchen. So much for asking permission. I would imagine a man in his position didn't have to do so often.

Heather waltzed up to us. "Hey, Mimi," she said coyly, "there's someone on the patio who wants to see you—" She balked. "Wait a sec! Who is that guy?" She pointed at Stefan's father just as he disappeared into the kitchen. "I know him." She snapped her fingers. "It's on the tip of my tongue. He's—"

Seconds later, Stefan blew through the kitchen door, his father hot on his heels. He dodged me, my mother, and Heather and made a beeline for my office. His father followed him inside. As the door closed, Stefan yelled, "I can't believe you're dating my boss's mother!"

"Anthony Alston!" Heather shouted. "The moneyman for the United States of America. Yipes! Stefan is his son? No wonder he didn't want us to know. He's only a few feet from the seat of power. Knowing Stefan, I'd think he would have treasured an introduction to the White House chef. He's got big dreams."

He might have high aspirations, I mused, but he wanted to achieve them on his own terms, without any help from his father.

I headed toward the office.

"On the other hand," Heather continued, trailing me, "he probably didn't want anyone to know that he, a left-wing radical, was related to a centrist."

"Mother," I said over my shoulder, "did you know when you met Anthony that he was Stefan's father?"

"I figured it out. The eyes. The nose. The mention that his son was a sous chef. Like my daughter, I'm pretty good at deciphering clues." She snickered. "By the way, I believe Anthony's political views might be heading more in Stefan's direction, hence the career change."

I inched closer to the office door. Heather and my mother followed.

"I don't want to be hounded by the secret service," Stefan said loudly enough for us to hear.

"You won't need secret service," his father retorted. "I'm not running for president."

"You say Congress now, but I know your aspirations, Dad."

"Fine. Change your name."

I gulped. We didn't need to hear the rest of Stefan's angst. He and his father would work it out. At least I hoped they would.

"Heather, you said someone wants to see me on the patio?" I asked.

"Right this way."

I lifted a menu and beckoned my mother to follow me in that direction. I trailed Heather, hoping her surprise was Nash, but he wasn't there, and my heart sank. I hadn't heard from him since before Edison was captured. Even though he'd mentioned taking me ballooning, I knew I shouldn't have counted on having another date with him. Willow had probably cajoled her way back into his heart. She was clever and beautiful, and they had history. And yet I had held out hope because of Bryan. He always said, "If you don't wish for something, you might not get it. So dream big." Oh, how I missed him.

"This isn't some kind of blind date setup, is it, Heather?" I did not need her to be my matchmaker.

"Hardly." She strolled ahead of me, her blue sheath hugging every curve and showing off her trim figure. "C'mon. It'll be fun."

I directed my mother to an empty table and handed her a menu. "I'll be right back," I said, and then I joined my quirky hostess at a table where a thickset, pale man sat hunched over a laptop. A hank of dark hair hung low on his forehead. Heather cleared her throat. The man peered up and smiled a toothy grin. He had the most beautiful blue eyes with thick long lashes, like Heather's.

He closed his laptop. "Hello? Who's this?"

"Henry," Heather said, "this is Mimi. Mimi, this is my husband, Henry."

He was real? They didn't quite match, but their eyes did. Interesting. "Nice to meet you."

"Nice to meet you." He started to rise, but the table blocked his belly. Quickly he steadied the table with his palms and settled back on his chair. "Sorry about that. I always forget to scoot back." He waved. "Thanks for hiring Heather. She loves it here."

"Mimi, you see?" Heather cocked a hip and gave me a sassy look. "I told you he was real. Henry is working on a sci-fi novel."

"About Glonkirks?" I teased.

Henry's eyes widened. "You know about them?"

"Do I ever."

"They're real." He forced a conspiratorial wink.

Heather punched him in the arm. "They're real, mister."

"I believe." He raised his hands. "Oh, lordie, I believe."

"Oh, you!" Heather eyed me and giggled. "Okay, they're not real, Mimi. I admit it. But to tell the truth, I love the reactions I get whenever I share my stories. It's like people *want* to believe."

Her Glonkirks and my mother's ghosts. *What next?* I wondered.

Laughing, I headed back to the office. Stefan and Anthony emerged. Stefan plodded toward the kitchen. Anthony offered a beatific smile worthy of a lifelong politician. "Don't worry. We'll be on good footing soon. Where is your lovely mother?"

I gave him directions and he headed off. Before I could disappear into my office to find some much-needed breathing space, the front door of the bistro opened, and Jo entered on Tyson's arm. I nearly fell over. As predicted, the two seemed perfect for one another. Both were tall and fit. He wasn't in uniform but rather a crisp white shirt and chinos. She was wearing a pretty turquoise sundress and a cropped sweater.

"Where have you two been? You look spiffy."

"We gave up on taking a hike and toured the art galleries in Yountville instead. Afterward, we enjoyed a picnic." Jo tilted her head in Tyson's direction and batted her eyes at me. "Since it's late in the afternoon, do you think we can simply come in for two cafés au lait?"

"Sure. Pick a table. I'll bring the coffees myself."

Jo gave Tyson a nudge and said, "Find us a good one." As he set off, she turned to me and whispered, "Our first date was fabulous! He didn't lie. Does he ever know deli."

I didn't know if that was code for he was a good kisser, but I was ecstatic. Grinning, she hurried after him to a table by the window. I personally made their beverages, set a rock candy swizzle stick on each plate, and carried them over. They weren't holding hands, but both were leaning forward, their gazes locked on each other. I cleared my throat. The two snapped to attention.

"Here you go. Enjoy." I turned to leave.

Jo said, "Mimi, don't leave. We specifically took a table for four so you could join us for a minute." She stirred her coffee with the swizzle stick.

I perched on a chair. "What's up?"

"Tyson told me Edison Barrington will stand trial. His daughter is hoping for a temporary insanity plea. Have you spoken to her since the memorial? How is she holding up?"

"As well as can be expected." I glanced at Tyson. "May I speak freely?"

He aligned his cup on the saucer. "I'm not on duty."

"Angelica and Lyle went back to Los Angeles to start their new life, but she's going to be coming up weekly to make sure Kaya Hill—that's the attorney she hired—is doing everything she can for her father."

"And what about Paula Ives?" Jo asked.

"She's staying in Napa Valley. She quit her job at the family business and purchased a six-room bed-and-breakfast. Her father is not pleased about her choice to leave the business, though I know he would do anything to make her happy. He feels guilty about everything his children have suffered."

"I think she might be dating Raymond," Jo said. "I saw them kissing in the garden."

I nodded. "She is."

Jo took a sip of her coffee and set down the cup. "Boy oh boy, it was like a soap opera when those people were here, with all the hookups. That Francine. She was never my favorite, but she went right back to work with more than enough fodder for her society column. And I heard she and Kent remain an item."

"I'll bet she didn't see any of that coming with her palm readings," I joked.

A breeze cut through the restaurant.

Jo glanced across the room and back at me. "Ahem. I think you have company."

Nash, dressed similarly to Tyson, though he wore his standard leather jacket, stood by the hostess podium. He appeared worried. He was squinting; his mouth—such an attractive mouth—was drawn in a thin line. A quiver of unease vibrated through me until he spotted me, and a huge smile spread across his face. He strode across the room.

"Join us?" Tyson asked.

"Sure." Nash eyed me. "Can I get one of those? Hold the rock candy, add a dash of cocoa."

"Coming right up."

Before I departed, he clasped my elbow and whispered, "I'm sorry I've been out of touch. Something came up."

"Let me guess. Willow wants you back."

His mouth curved up on one side. "Woman, you've got Willow on the brain. Did she do a mind trip on you or what?"

"Sort of."

"I'm crazy about you."

And how many other women? I wondered.

"Look, I've been in absentia because my dad took a spill."

"A spill?"

"On a motorcycle. I told you he's a daredevil. Anything Evel Knievel did, he wants to try." He grinned. "Don't worry, he's all right, but I had to hurry to his side and nurse him through the first few days."

"Where was your mother?"

"I thought I told you about her. Guess not. My mother passed away a few years ago. Heart attack. I warned my father that he was the cause of her death with all his reckless behavior, and if he weren't careful, he'd give me a heart attack, too. Did it change him? Not a whit. He is what he is. We're nothing alike."

My mother joined us. "Nash Hawke. What a pleasure to see you."

"Ginette."

They kissed on both cheeks.

"Nash," my mother crooned, "seeing you has given me an idea. How would you like to run my vineyard?"

He gawked at her. "Ma'am?"

"Don't 'ma'am' me. I want to travel. I need someone who knows wine. A little birdie told me you'd always had your heart set on owning a vineyard."

He gazed at me.

I held up both hands. "Not I."

"We could do a test run for a year," my mother pressed on. "If you like it, maybe we could work out a lease-option deal until you own it."

Nash beamed from ear to ear. "Ginette, I don't know what to say."

"Say you'll consider it."

"I'll consider it, though I have to say, I really like my current job. It offers a lot of freedom."

"You don't like to be tied down?" my mother asked and threw me a look, clearly fishing on my behalf.

"That's not what I—"

"It's neither here nor there. I knew from the moment I laid eyes on you, young man, that you had a special something. Think on it. This is a solid offer." Mom poked me with a finger. "Darling, do you think you could bring some wine to the table so Anthony and I can celebrate my possible independence?"

"I'm on it!"

As she sashayed away, Nash said, "Mimi, wait a sec."

"Truly, I didn't say a thing to my mother. I—" A realization hit me. "Bryan must have. You and he talked often. He liked you a lot. He always saw potential. What do you bet he wrote her a note and suggested the idea?"

Nash's eyes brimmed with thankfulness. "I will consider it."

"Great. You'd be good at it."

"One more thing before you go," he said. "How about this coming Tuesday for ballooning? It's supposed to be seventy-five degrees all week and very little wind. Perfect conditions. Unless, of course, my ex has scared you off for good."

I still had concerns about him. I wasn't sure that I could rid myself of them yet. Was he or wasn't he a player? I liked him, that was for sure. Softly I said, "I'll let you know."

Recipes Included

Eggs Benedict

From Mimi:
I love this recipe. It's my mother's. It's a speedy version, yet consistently good. It was one of the first things my mother taught me after teaching me the five basic French sauces. It is what I consider the perfect comfort food.

(serves 2)

Hollandaise Sauce

3 egg yolks
¼ teaspoon Dijon mustard
1 tablespoon lemon juice
1 dash hot pepper sauce, like Tabasco
¼ teaspoon white pepper
½ cup butter (one stick)

In a blender, combine the egg yolks, mustard, lemon juice, hot pepper sauce, and white pepper. Blend for about 5–10 seconds.

Put the butter into a microwave-safe bowl or measuring cup and melt completely, about 30–45 seconds.

Set the blender on high speed and add the melted butter to the egg mixture in a thin stream. It will thicken up fast.

Neat trick: You can keep the sauce warm until serving by placing the blender itself in a pan of hot water.

To Make the Sandwich

4 eggs
1 tablespoon vinegar
2 English muffins, sliced in half (using a fork)
4 slices Canadian bacon
2–4 teaspoons butter
2 tablespoons chopped fresh chives

Preheat oven to broil.

Meanwhile, to poach the eggs, fill a large saucepan with about 3 inches of water. Bring the water to a simmer (small bubbles forming around the edges) and then add 1 tablespoon vinegar.

Carefully break eggs into simmering water and allow to cook for 2½–3 minutes. The whites try to get away. Don't worry. They'll return. When done, the yolks should be soft in the center.

Remove the eggs from water with a slotted spoon and set them on a warm plate.

While the eggs are poaching, heat a medium skillet on medium-high heat and brown the Canadian bacon, turning once. Also, set the halved English muffins on a baking sheet and toast them under the broiler until lightly brown, about 3–4 minutes.

To Plate

Set 2 halves of English muffins on 2 plates. Butter lightly with 1–2 teaspoons butter each. Top each half with a slice of the Canadian bacon followed by a poached egg.

Drizzle warm Hollandaise sauce over each half of the sandwich and sprinkle with chives.

Serve warm.

Balsamic Vinaigrette

From Mimi:
This is my mother's recipe. She swears the white pepper makes the difference. It is wonderful over a simple green salad and delicious over a chopped salad, as well.

Tip: When you emulsify a dressing, it holds together and doesn't separate once it is set in the refrigerator. FYI, an emulsion is a mixture of two or more liquids that are normally unblendable, like oil and water.

(makes 1 cup)

¼ cup balsamic vinegar
2 teaspoons sugar or brown sugar
½ teaspoon salt
½ teaspoon white pepper
¾ cup olive oil

In a blender, mix the vinegar, sugar, salt, and white pepper. Slowly add the olive oil in a stream to let the mixture emulsify.

Whatever portion you don't use, refrigerate.

Onion Soup Gratinée

From Mimi:

This is one of those go-to meals for me. I could eat onion soup every day of the week. It's so easy to prepare that you will, too. It keeps well in the refrigerator. The aroma in the kitchen after you've cooked it will knock your socks off. Enjoy!

(serves 4)

2 large Maui sweet onions, sliced thin
½ cup unsalted butter
4 cups chicken stock
½ teaspoon salt
½ teaspoon pepper
2 bay leaves
4 slices French bread, about ½-inch thick, lightly toasted
8 ounces Swiss cheese, shredded
more salt and pepper, to your liking

In a large saucepan, melt the butter over low heat. Add the onions and coat well with the butter. Cover and cook until tender, about 20–30 minutes, stirring occasionally.

Remove the cover and raise the heat a bit—just a bit. Sauté, stirring often. Do not let the onions burn. They will turn a deep caramel brown in about 30 minutes to 1 hour.

Add the stock and bay leaves and sprinkle with salt and pepper. Bring to a boil. Reduce the heat and cover. Simmer for about 15–30 minutes more.

Meanwhile, divide the shredded Swiss cheese into four portions.

Discard the bay leaves. Taste the soup and add more salt and pepper to your liking. (I prefer 1 teaspoon salt and 10 grinds of a peppermill.)

Ladle the soup into four oven-safe bowls and top each with a slice of lightly toasted French bread and 2 ounces shredded cheese. Set under the broiler for 3–4 minutes to melt the cheese. Serve hot.

Gruyère and Mushroom Quiche

From Mimi:

This quiche was one of the first I ever attempted. I think I was fourteen at the time. It takes minutes to throw together and minutes to cook and always satisfies an appetite. I particularly like the thyme in it. Here's a little history note: thyme has been around since Hippocrates and has lots of medicinal uses. Enjoy!

(serves 6)

Pie Ingredients

1 piecrust (9 inches)
1½ cups Gruyère cheese, grated
1 medium yellow onion, chopped
1 tablespoon unsalted butter
¼ pound sliced mushrooms
½ teaspoon salt
½ teaspoon white pepper
2 tablespoons fresh thyme, chopped, stems removed
½ teaspoon paprika

Daryl Wood Gerber

Custard Ingredients

4 eggs
1½ cups whole milk
3 tablespoons flour
¼ teaspoon salt
¼ teaspoon mustard powder
dash of garlic powder

Preheat oven to 375 degrees F.

In an unbaked piecrust, sprinkle the Gruyère cheese. Set aside.

In a frying pan, melt the butter and then sauté the chopped onion until soft and translucent, about 3–4 minutes.

Add the sliced mushrooms, salt, white pepper, and thyme to the onions. Sauté for 5 more minutes.

Spoon the mushroom mixture over the Gruyère cheese in the piecrust.

In a medium bowl, beat eggs, whole milk, flour, salt, mustard powder, and a dash of garlic powder.

Pour the custard mixture over the mushroom-and-cheese mixture until the pie is full. (Hint: If there is any custard mixture left over, you can cook it in a small ramekin. Decrease the cooking time for the ramekin *only* by 15–20 minutes.)

Sprinkle paprika over the top of the quiche and bake for 40–45 minutes.

Serve warm.

Note: if you would like to make this quiche gluten-free, use a gluten-free piecrust and substitute the flour in the custard mixture with cornstarch.

Steak au Poivre

From Chef C:
It is important not to overcook this steak. It is best served medium-rare. The sauce continues to cook the steak on the plate. Allow the savory sauce to melt in your mouth. This recipe comes to me from my mother, a Frenchwoman with a very strong will, to put it mildly.

4 tenderloin steaks, 6–8 ounces each and no more than
    1½ inches thick
Kosher salt
2 tablespoons whole black peppercorns
1 tablespoon unsalted butter
1 teaspoon olive oil
⅓ cup Cognac, plus 2 teaspoons
1 cup heavy cream
salt to taste (about 1 teaspoon)

It is important to remove the steaks from the refrigerator about 1 hour ahead of time and bring to room temperature prior to cooking. Sprinkle all sides with salt.

A Deadly Éclair

Crush the peppercorns using something hard like a mortar and pestle or a mallet on a cutting board. Spread the peppercorns evenly in a pie plate. Press each fillet, on both sides, into the pepper and coat the surface. Set aside.

In a medium skillet, melt the butter and olive oil over medium heat. When the butter and oil turn golden and start to smoke, carefully place the steaks in the pan.

For medium-rare, cook about 4 minutes per side; for medium, about 5 minutes per side. Remove the steaks to a plate, cover with foil, and set aside.

Pour off the excess fat from the skillet, but do not wipe or scrape it clean.

Now, with the skillet still off the heat, add the ⅓ cup Cognac to the pan and carefully light the alcohol with a long match or battery-operated lighter. Carefully shake the pan until the flames die.

Return the pan to medium heat and add the heavy cream.

Bring the mixture to a boil and whisk until the sauce becomes thick and sticks to the back of a spoon, approximately 5–6 minutes. Add the extra teaspoons of Cognac and season to taste with about 1 teaspoon of salt.

Add the steaks back to the pan, spoon the savory sauce over them, and then set them on plates, adding more sauce once plated.

Mimi's Seasoning Blend for *Poulet Rôti* (Rotisserie Chicken)

From Mimi:
I love roast chicken. I love playing with the spices. If there is a spice in this mix that you don't like, remove it and replace it with something you do like. You can always add garlic powder or garlic salt, but go lightly. You don't want to overwhelm the other flavors.

(serves 4–6)

2 bay leaves
2 tablespoons dried thyme
1 tablespoon dried rosemary
1 teaspoon dried basil
1 teaspoon dried oregano
¼ cup kosher salt
2 tablespoons paprika
1 teaspoon ground ginger
¼ teaspoon ground nutmeg
¾ teaspoon ground coriander

A Deadly Éclair

½ teaspoon ground white pepper
½ teaspoon ground cloves
1 chicken fryer (4–6 pounds)

In a small bowl, mix all the spices.

Set chicken fryer in a roasting pot. Use the seasoning blend as a dry rub and pat the rub all over the chicken. Cover the chicken with the roasting pot lid or with a tent of foil.

Bake in a slow oven, 300 degrees F, for 1 hour and 15 minutes. Remove the lid or foil.

Raise the temperature to 400 degrees F. Roast another 15 minutes until chicken is a warm brown.

Orange Cardamom Madeleines

From Chef C:

These are one of my favorite cookies. They are so simple to make, yet so elegant because of their shape. Perfect for afternoon tea. I am also sharing a gluten-free version of this cookie below, as my daughter has celiac disease and must eat gluten-free. You did not know I had a daughter? I do. Her name is Chantalle. She is living in New York for the time being and working as a sous chef. Wish her luck.

(makes 12)

For the Cookies

¼ cup unsalted butter
1 tablespoon honey
1 teaspoon pure vanilla extract
¾ cup flour
1 teaspoon baking powder
¾ teaspoon ground cardamom (*you may substitute nutmeg)
¼ teaspoon salt
¼ cup granulated sugar
2 large eggs

For the Glaze

¾ cup confectioners' sugar
1 teaspoon finely grated orange zest
2 tablespoons orange juice, no pulp

Brush the molds of a madeleine pan with butter and set aside.

In a small saucepan, melt the butter over low heat. Remove the pan from heat and stir in the honey and vanilla. Let cool about 10 minutes.

In a small bowl, whisk the flour, baking powder, cardamom, and salt; set aside.

Preheat oven to 325 degrees F, setting the rack in the center.

In a medium bowl, stir together the sugar and eggs. Add in the flour mixture and stir until combined. Add the butter mixture and stir gently until butter is completely incorporated. Cover the bowl with plastic wrap and refrigerate at least 30 minutes.

Spoon the batter into the madeleine pan, filling each mold halfway. If necessary, use moistened fingers to press the batter into the mold.

Bake the cookies 7–8 minutes. They will have puffed up, and the edges will become golden.

Remove the pan from the oven and let the cookies cool slightly. Unmold the cookies onto a wire rack and let them cool completely. This is very important.

In a small bowl, stir together the sugar, orange zest, and juice until the glaze is smooth and thick. Using a pastry brush, coat the ridged side of each cookie with the glaze. Let set 15 minutes.

Orange Cardamom Madeleines
Gluten-Free Version

(makes 12)

For the Cookies

¼ cup unsalted butter
1 tablespoon honey
1 teaspoon vanillin
¾ cup sweet rice flour (or a gluten-free blend you enjoy)
1 teaspoon baking powder
¾ teaspoon ground cardamom (*you may substitute nutmeg)
¼ teaspoon salt
¼ teaspoon xanthan gum
¼ cup granulated sugar
2 large eggs

For the Glaze

¾ cup confectioners' sugar
1 teaspoon finely grated orange zest
2 tablespoons orange juice, no pulp

A Deadly Éclair

Brush the molds of a madeleine pan with butter and set aside.

In a small saucepan, melt the butter over low heat. Remove the pan from heat and stir in honey and vanillin. Let cool about 10 minutes. Why vanillin? Because some gluten-free eaters can be sensitive to pure vanilla.

In a small bowl, whisk the gluten-free flour, baking powder, cardamom, salt, and xanthan gum; set aside.

Preheat oven to 325 degrees F, setting the rack in the center.

In a medium bowl, stir together the sugar and eggs. Add in the gluten-free flour mixture and stir until combined. Add the butter mixture and stir gently until butter is completely incorporated. Cover the bowl with plastic wrap and refrigerate at least 30 minutes.

Spoon the batter into the madeleine pan, filling each mold halfway. If necessary, use moistened fingers to press the batter into the mold.

Bake the cookies 7–8 minutes. They will have puffed up, and the edges will become golden.

Remove from oven and let the cookies cool slightly. Unmold the cookies onto a wire rack and let them cool completely. This is very important.

In a small bowl, stir together the sugar, orange zest, and juice until the glaze is smooth and thick. Using a small pastry brush, coat the ridged side of each cookie with the glaze. Let set 15 minutes.

Crème Brûlée

From Mimi:

For this luscious dessert, I pride myself on finding the best vanilla beans available. Because the dessert keeps well, we always have ramekins on hand. If you're planning this recipe for a party, remember to remove them from the refrigerator a few hours ahead so they can warm to room temperature before applying the vanilla sugar and heating the top. I like a utility blowtorch from a hardware store, but you can always spring for a pretty one from a kitchen store.

Tip: Vanilla sugar can be costly, but it's worth it. However, you can prepare it at home by combining approximately 2 cups of white sugar with the seeds scraped from one vanilla bean. Put it in an airtight jar. Let the mixture age for about 2 weeks and then use 2 tablespoons in place of one packet of vanilla sugar. Make sense? Each time, replace the sugar that is used, and the vanilla beans will last indefinitely. By the way, the little scrapings resemble ants! LOL! Don't worry. Your pantry has not been invaded.

(serves 6)

1 quart heavy cream
1 vanilla bean, split and scraped

A Deadly Éclair

1 cup vanilla sugar, divided
6 large egg yolks
2 quarts hot water

Preheat the oven to 325 degrees F.

Place the cream and the vanilla bean and its pulp into a medium saucepan set over medium-high heat. Bring to a boil. Remove from the heat, cover, and allow to rest for 15 minutes. Remove the vanilla bean and discard.

In a medium bowl, whisk together ½ cup vanilla sugar and the egg yolks until well blended and just starting to lighten in color.

Add the cream a little bit at a time. Stir continually.

Pour the liquid into 6 ramekins (7–8 ounces). Place the ramekins into a roasting pan or a 13 × 9 cake pan. Pour enough hot water into the pan to come halfway up the sides of the ramekins.

Bake the ramekins until the crème brûlée is set but still able to shake a little in the center, approximately 40–45 minutes.

Remove the ramekins from the roasting pan and refrigerate for at least 2 hours and up to 3 days.

Remove the crème brûlée from the refrigerator for at least 30 minutes prior to finishing the top.

Divide the remaining ½ cup vanilla sugar equally among the 6 dishes and spread evenly on top. Using a torch, melt the sugar and form a crispy top. Allow the crème brûlée to sit for at least 5 minutes before serving.

Gas torch safety: Propane gas torches are really flammable! They should be kept far away from an open flame as well as prolonged exposure to sunlight. Children shouldn't use a torch without adult supervision. Ever! Not even really precocious young chefs. When lighting the torch, set it on a flat surface, facing away from you. Light a match or a lighter and then open the gas valve. Light the gas jet and blow out the match. Always turn off the burner valve tightly when you are finished using the torch.

French Raspberry Sour Cream Tart

From Mimi:
This tart is easy to make and so delicious. It's one of the first I ever attempted. My mother was a big help! I've made it with nuts and without. It's great either way. The topping gives it a lovely finish. For any of you who need to eat gluten-free, don't despair; I've provided a gluten-free version below. Plus I've added the recipes for my pastry dough and tips on how to make them come out perfectly. Enjoy!

(yields 1 pie)

Ingredients for Custard

1 pie shell (9 inches)
1 egg
⅔ cup sour cream
½ teaspoon vanilla
½ cup white sugar
pinch of salt
3 tablespoons flour
1½ cups raspberries, rinsed and drained

Ingredients for Topping

¼ cup brown sugar
¼ cup flour
2 tablespoons butter, cold, diced
¼ cup chopped nuts, if desired

Preheat oven to 400 degrees F.

In a medium bowl, beat the egg, sour cream, and vanilla until fluffy.

In a separate bowl, mix the sugar, salt, and flour. Add to the egg mixture and stir.

Gently fold in the raspberries. Pour the mixture into the pie shell.

Bake for 30 minutes.

Meanwhile, make the topping. In a small bowl, mix the brown sugar, flour, cold butter, and nuts (if desired) until the mixture is crumbly.

Remove the pie from the oven and cover with the topping. Return the pie to the oven for 10–15 minutes until nicely brown. Allow to cool before serving.

French Raspberry Sour Cream Tart
Gluten-Free Version

(yields 1 pie)

Ingredients for Custard

1 gluten-free pie shell (9 inches)
1 egg
⅔ cup sour cream
½ teaspoon vanillin
½ cup white sugar
pinch of salt
3 tablespoons gluten-free flour
¼ teaspoon xanthan gum
1½ cups raspberries, rinsed and drained

Ingredients for Topping

¼ cup brown sugar
¼ cup gluten-free flour
¼ teaspoon xanthan gum

2 tablespoons butter, cold, diced
¼ cup chopped nuts, if desired

Preheat oven to 400 degrees F.

In a medium bowl, beat the egg, sour cream, and vanillin until fluffy.

In a separate bowl, mix the sugar, salt, gluten-free flour, and xanthan gum. Add to the egg mixture and stir.

Gently fold in the raspberries. Pour the mixture into the gluten-free pie shell.

Bake for 30 minutes.

Meanwhile, make the topping. In a small bowl, mix the brown sugar, gluten-free flour, xanthan gum, cold butter, and nuts (if desired) until the mixture is crumbly.

Remove the pie from the oven and cover with the topping. Return the pie to the oven for 10–15 minutes until nicely brown. Allow to cool before serving.

Pastry Dough

(makes 1 pie shell)

1¼ cup sifted flour, plus 2–4 tablespoons for rolling
1 teaspoon salt
6 tablespoons butter or shortening
2–3 tablespoons water

Put flour and salt into food processor fitted with a blade. Cut in 3 tablespoons of butter or shortening and pulse for 30 seconds. Cut in another 3 tablespoons of butter. Pulse again for 30 seconds. Sprinkle with 2–3 tablespoons water and pulse a third time for 30 seconds.

Remove the dough from the food processor and form into a ball using your hands. Wrap with wax paper or plastic wrap. Chill the dough for 30 minutes.

Remove the dough from the refrigerator and remove the covering. Place a large piece of parchment paper on a countertop. Sprinkle parchment paper with 2 tablespoons flour. Place the dough on top of the parchment paper. Sprinkle with more flour. Cover with another large piece of parchment paper. This prevents the dough from sticking to the rolling pin. Roll out dough so it is ¼-inch thick and large enough to fit into an 8-inch or 9-inch pie pan, with at least a ½-inch border along the edge.

Remove the top parchment paper. Gently roll the dough into a tube, removing the bottom layer of parchment paper, and then place the tube of dough into the pie tin. Unfurl the dough. Press the dough into the pie tin. Crimp the edges.

Note: If using a tart pan, you do not need the crimped edge. Press the dough to the top of the fluted edge and trim, if necessary.

Pastry Dough
Gluten-Free Version

(makes 1 pie shell)

1¼ cup sifted gluten-free flour,* plus 2–4 tablespoons for rolling
½ teaspoon xanthan gum
1 teaspoon salt
6 tablespoons butter or shortening
2–3 tablespoons water

Put gluten-free flour, xanthan gum, and salt into food processor fitted with a blade. Cut in 3 tablespoons of butter or shortening and pulse for 30 seconds. Cut in another 3 tablespoons of butter. Pulse again for 30 seconds. Sprinkle with 2–3 tablespoons water and pulse a third time for 30 seconds.

Remove the dough from the food processor and form into a ball using your hands. Wrap with wax paper or plastic wrap. Chill the dough for 30 minutes.

Remove the dough from the refrigerator and remove the covering. Place a large piece of parchment paper on a countertop.

Sprinkle parchment paper with 2 tablespoons gluten-free flour. Place the dough on top of the parchment paper. Sprinkle with more gluten-free flour. Cover with another large piece of parchment paper. This prevents the dough from sticking to the rolling pin. Roll out dough so it is ¼-inch thick and large enough to fit into an 8-inch or 9-inch pie pan, with at least a ½-inch border along the edge.

Remove the top parchment paper. Place the pie tin upside down on the dough. Flip the dough and pie tin. Remove the parchment paper. Press the dough into the pie tin. Crimp the edges.

Note: Why flip the dough and pie tin? Because gluten-free pastry dough, unlike regular pastry dough, doesn't roll or fold and has a tendency to break. This flip technique works best for me. If your dough does break, don't worry. Use a little water and fingertips to press any breakage back together. Nobody will see the bottom of the quiche.

Second Note: If using a tart pan, you do not need the crimped edge. Press the dough to the top of the fluted edge and trim, if necessary.

* I use a combination of sweet rice flour and tapioca starch; you can use store-bought ingredients like Bob's Red Mill or King Arthur gluten-free flour.

Chocolate Éclair

From Chef C:
Éclairs are not easy to make. They take patience. They require cold butter. You should have everything ready on the counter as you get started and be patient. The result is divine!

Filling

2 cups whole milk
½ vanilla bean, split lengthwise
6 egg yolks
⅔ cup sugar
¼ cup cornstarch
1 tablespoon cold unsalted butter

Pastry

1 cup water
8 tablespoons (1 stick) unsalted butter
½ teaspoon salt
1½ teaspoons sugar
1 cup all-purpose flour
3 eggs, plus 1 extra, if needed

Egg Wash

1 egg
1½ teaspoons water

Chocolate Glaze

½ cup heavy cream
4 ounces semisweet chocolate, coarsely chopped—use the best
  brand you can find

To Make the Filling

In a medium saucepan, heat the milk and vanilla bean to a boil
over medium heat. Immediately turn off the heat and set aside
to infuse for 15 minutes.

In a bowl, whisk the egg yolks and sugar until light and fluffy.
Add the cornstarch and whisk vigorously until no lumps
remain.

Whisk in ¼ cup of the hot milk mixture until incorporated. Whisk
in the remaining hot milk mixture, reserving the saucepan.

Pour the mixture through a strainer and back into the saucepan. Cook over medium-high heat, whisking constantly, until
thickened and slowly boiling.

Remove from the heat and stir in the butter. Let cool slightly.
Cover with plastic wrap, lightly pressing the plastic against the
surface to prevent a skin from forming.

A Deadly Éclair

Chill at least 2 hours or until ready to serve. The custard can be made up to 24 hours in advance. Refrigerate until 1 hour before using.

To Make the Pastry

Preheat the oven to 425 degrees F. Line a sheet pan with parchment paper. In a large saucepan, bring the water, butter, salt, and sugar to a rolling boil over medium-high heat.

When it boils, immediately take the pan off the heat.

Stirring with a *wooden* spoon, add all the flour at once and stir fast for 30–60 seconds until all the flour is incorporated.

Return to the heat and cook, stirring for 30 seconds.

Scrape the mixture into a mixer fitted with a paddle attachment (or use a hand mixer). Mix at medium speed. With the mixer running, add 3 eggs, 1 egg at a time.

Stop mixing after each addition to scrape down the sides of the bowl. Mix until the dough is smooth and glossy and the eggs are completely incorporated. The dough should be *thick* but should fall *slowly and steadily* from the beaters when you lift them out of the bowl. *If the dough is still clinging to the beaters*, add the remaining egg and mix until incorporated.

Using a pastry bag fitted with a large plain tip, pipe fat lengths of dough (about the size and shape of a jumbo hot dog) onto the lined baking sheet, leaving 2 inches of space between them. You should have 8–10 lengths.

To Make the Egg Wash

In a bowl, whisk the egg and water together. Brush the surface of each éclair with the egg wash. Use your fingers to smooth out any lumps that remain on the surface of the dough. You want them to be sleek.

Bake 15 minutes, then reduce the heat to 375 degrees F and bake until puffed up and light golden brown, about 25 minutes more. Try not to open the oven door too often during baking.

Remove from oven and let cool on the baking sheet. Fit a medium-size plain pastry tip over your index finger and use it to make a hole in the end of each éclair (or use your fingertip).

Using a pastry bag fitted with a medium-size plain tip, gently pipe the custard into the éclairs, using only enough to fill the inside (don't stuff them too full).

To Make the Glaze

In a small saucepan, heat the cream over medium heat just until it boils. Immediately turn off the heat. Put the chocolate in a medium bowl.

Pour the hot cream over the chocolate and whisk until melted and smooth. Set aside and keep warm. The glaze can be made up to 48 hours in advance. Cover and refrigerate until ready to use and rewarm in a microwave or over hot water when ready to use. If rewarming in a microwave, use medium heat and zap in spurts of about 15–30 seconds.

Dip the tops of the éclairs in the warm chocolate glaze and set on a sheet pan, chocolate side up. Chill, uncovered, at least 1 hour to set the glaze. Serve chilled.

Acknowledgments

Don't let life discourage you; everyone who got where he is had to begin where he was.

~ Richard L. Evans

Thank you to my family and friends for all your support. As I said in the dedication, *I am so blessed.*

Thank you to my talented author friends, Krista Davis and Hannah Dennison, for your words of wisdom and calm. Thank you to my brainstormers at Plothatchers: Krista, Janet, Kaye, Marilyn, Peg, and, yes, another Janet (we all have aliases, I think). Thanks to my blogmates on Mystery Lovers Kitchen: Cleo, Krista, Sheila, Leslie, Mary Jane/Victoria, Roberta/Lucy, and Linda/Erika. What fun it is to cook up "crime" with you.

Thanks to those who have helped make *A French Bistro Mystery* series a success: my fabulous editor, Faith Black; my keen-eyed copy editor, Megan Grande; my agent, John Talbot, for believing in every aspect of my work; and my brilliant cover artist, Teresa Fasolino!

Sheridan Stancliff, as I've said before, you are an Internet and creative marvel. Thank you. And thanks to Kimberley Greene. You know how much I appreciate everything you do for me.

Thank you to my street team, the Cake and Dagger Club! Thank you to all the cozy mystery lovers in the Delicious Mysteries group! I cherish your enthusiasm.

Thank you to Lieutenant John Crawford of the Napa County Sheriff's Office for his invaluable input. If I've made mistakes in any regard, they are not his fault. He was extremely patient and forthcoming.

Last but not least, I've said it before, but it bears repeating: thank you librarians, teachers, booksellers, and readers for eagerly jumping into a new series. I hope you embrace Mimi Rousseau and her family and friends as you have embraced my other casts of characters.

Savor the mystery!

Read an excerpt from

A SOUFFLE OF SUSPICION

the next

FRENCH BISTRO MYSTERY

by DARYL WOOD GERBER

available soon in hardcover from
Crooked Lane Books

**CROOKED
LANE**

NEW YORK

Chapter 1

"Mimi, whoa!" Stefan, my sous-chef, reeled back as I pushed through the swinging doors leading to the kitchen. "Hot stuff!" he yelled. He wasn't referring to me, sorry to say. He was commenting on the preparations for crème brûlée with caramel flambé that he was carting into the main dining room. The delicious aroma of burnt sugar permeated the air. As if reading my thoughts, he said, "Though you do look good."

"Kiss up," I said.

Stefan let out one of his rollicking laughs. "I'm not stupid."

I looked the same as I always did, clad in my work uniform of khaki pants, white shirt, and clogs, my toffee-colored hair slung into a bun. It wasn't a *hot* look but not unattractive, I'd been told. And I was always ready for whatever the day might bring. The only fashion statement I wore was the pink tourmaline necklace my father had given me when I turned sixteen and the matching tourmaline studs I had recently purchased to go with it. A little sparkle did a girl good.

I said, "Thank heaven you have young legs or I'd have been toast."

"Your legs are almost as young," he said. *"Almost."*

At thirty-five, I was ten years his senior. "Go!" I chuckled. "Someone is expecting a delectable dessert after their lunch."

"*After* lunch? This *is* lunch." Stefan winked. "You know the Friday crowd. People splurge!"

Humming, he pushed the cart into the main dining room. As he deftly wove between tables, I glimpsed multiple images of him in the mirrors that adorned the bistro's walls, and I couldn't help thinking how much he resembled Johnny Mathis in his heyday. His father did, too, right down to his espresso-colored skin and chocolate brown eyes. Did Stefan's twin sister look like Johnny, as well? I'd never met her. Last week was the first time I'd heard of her. Stefan could be secretive, and for good reason. He had wanted to follow his own path without his influential father's help. Fortunately, my gifted sous-chef oozed talent in the kitchen; he had never wanted for a job. When I was his age, I'd been equally precocious.

"Chef C!" I called as I reentered the kitchen and moved past the white farmhouse-style table where I ate most of my meals. "Chef!" I zigzagged through the busy kitchen crew.

Camille Chabot, or Chef C as she liked to be called by the staff, was standing by the eight-burner stove. She twirled a wooden spoon, acknowledging that she'd heard me, but she didn't take her focus off her task. How I adored her. She was a talented French-born woman with a lust for food as well as a hunger for excellence. Lucky me; I had discovered her a year ago after a statewide search in California for someone to head up the kitchen in my new bistro.

I said, "A birdie told me—"

She shook her head, indicating she couldn't catch all of what I was saying.

I knew how she felt. I'd once been a full-time executive chef. The cacophony in the kitchen could be daunting. I drew nearer.

"What is up, Mimi?" she asked with a hint of a French accent.

She had worked hard to get rid of it after moving to America as a child. She tilted her head to make eye contact. I wasn't that tall, but she was a cube of a woman. Her toque teetered on her head. I steadied it for her. "*Merci*," she said. Although she was in her forties, her hair was snow white. She claimed it was because her daughter—now a sous-chef in New York—had been a hellion in her teens.

"A birdie told me your sister Renee is doing a bang-up job setting up the Sweet Treats Festival at Maison Rousseau."

"*Oui.* I have been told the same."

After I'd given up my career as a chef—long story, not so short—I'd moved home and caught a break. A generous benefactor was willing to sponsor my dream of owning a restaurant. With wings on my feet, I tossed aside my toque and chef's coat and set to work. Soon after, I owned Bistro Rousseau. Rousseau was my maiden name and I was proud of it. My family had produced quality wine in Napa Valley—specifically in Nouvelle Vie, an unincorporated enclave in Napa between Yountville and St. Helena—for six decades. In addition to the bistro, I owned the neighboring and growing-in-popularity inn, Maison Rousseau.

"Renee is having the best time. She is on cloud nine." Camille cranked off the burners for the three huge pots of boiling water—a large pan filled with pasta that had been cooked al dente sat on the nearby counter—and redirected her attention to the four skillets in which she was sautéing fresh herbs, oil, and garlic. The aroma made my mouth water. "Renee has not told me much about it, and I will not ask. She does not need my two cents."

I usually served as chef on Fridays so Camille could relax before the weekend rush, but a few days ago she'd advised me that she was too excited to sit still. Now I understood why. If she had taken the day off, she might have been tempted to butt into her sister's business.

"Help, please," Camille said to me rather than to a sous-chef. She directed me to finish making the pasta appetizers. "And make it snappy, missy." At times she could be gruff. None of the staff seemed to mind. They had soon come to realize, as I had, that she was all bark and no bite and had a wicked sense of humor.

I saluted. "Yes, Chef." I plated four servings of pasta and topped them with the fresh herbs, oil, and garlic sauce. I added a basil leaf and a slice of *chabichou*, a traditional non-rind French goat cheese. "Ready," I said.

One of the waitstaff loaded the dishes onto a serving tray and hurried out of the kitchen. A sous-chef removed the skillets and replaced them with fresh ones plus the fixings for another batch of pasta toppings.

Camille went right to work. "Setting the festival at Maison Rousseau was a coup for Renee. Thank you for allowing her to do so. This is the first of many such events for her."

"I heard she acquired the rights to the festival from another woman."

"That is correct. The woman could not make a go of it. She could not get advertisers on board. She did not have the—what is the word—*knack*." Camille punctuated the word with a wave of her spoon. "Renee is a dynamo. To spread the word about the festival, she came up with the brilliant idea to donate ten percent of the proceeds to a local charity that helps promote education. Plus, she is going to include a bake-off competition."

"She sounds industrious."

"She is." Camille beamed. "Both the fundraiser and the bake-off helped her secure five prominent sponsors. The rest is history."

"The festival is going to be a huge draw for us," I said. Most festivals in the valley ran Thursday to Sunday, but Renee had decided a weeklong Saturday-to-Saturday event might really get people talking. The event, which would open tomorrow, would feature bakers, ice cream makers, and dessert beverage mixologists. Businesses from all over the valley had signed on to sell their wares. And hopeful amateurs had entered the bake-off. "Festival employees and volunteers are busy setting up tents, tables, and demonstration areas in the inn's gardens right now," I said. "I'm going over after lunch to take a peek."

Camille clacked her spoon on the rim. "Renee has told me each festival area will match the gardens' color schemes."

"How lovely."

With my benefactor's help, we had built the inn in the style of Monet's Giverny, each wing of the two-story building boasting a pink crushed-rock façade with green windowsills and shutters. There were three primary gardens, which we had named after Monet's family and artistic friends. Behind the inn, there was an idyllic lily pond and a walkway covered by arches of climbing plants.

I said, "Before the festival gets under way, you should stop by and take a peek, too."

"I will if I can. We have been packed with customers."

Every year in October, Napa Valley was busy. But this year, in particular, it was going to be busier than all get-out. In addition to the festival, people were flocking to the area to attend Crush Week—the time when grapes were pressed at the vineyards. There were going to be hoedowns, hayrides, and farm tours. At some vineyards, they celebrated the fall release with wine and food tastings. I loved how the heady scent of ripening fruit mixed with the excitement of those who grew the grapes as well as those who came to participate made the valley brim with energy. A walk through a vineyard preparing for a crush could be intoxicating.

"Renee has spoken highly of the inn's staff," Chef C went on. "She says they are very cooperative."

"That's great to hear."

"Plate," she ordered.

I set to work, preparing the pasta again as I had moments before. "You know, I have yet to meet her."

"You cannot miss her when you do. She is nothing like me. She is taller, for one thing, and she is colorful and tells the best jokes."

"You tell pretty good jokes."

"She is also a slob." Chef C slid the skillets aside and fetched six petit filets from a nearby platter. "Perhaps she is not . . ." She laughed as she prepared the filets for *steak au poivre* by rolling them in cracked pepper. "Perhaps I am a solitary person who prefers everything in its place."

"Like your kitchen."

"*Exactement,*" she said in a full French accent.

Renee hadn't always been a festival operator. Up until two weeks ago, she had managed a chicken-and-egg farm with her husband. Mid-September, she had announced to her husband that she had tired of the life and had secured the rights to the festival with savings she had amassed over the years. She'd also informed him that she had grown weary of their marriage and needed a breather. That afternoon, she'd moved into her sister's house. Talk about major life changes!

"I also heard she's touring a few more places this morning, looking for her next festival site." According to my source, Renee hoped to grow the festival business. She wanted to put on one a month.

"Yes. She went with Donovan." Camille's eyes glistened with excitement. Donovan Coleman, the son of a local vintner, was her new boyfriend. Well, sort of. I knew she had fallen for him; I wasn't sure how he felt about her. He was quite a bit younger and a tad impetuous. At the ripe age of thirty—he was all of thirty-five now—Donovan had shunned the family wine business to become a baker. Camille raved about his cookies, especially his bite-sized French *macarons*, a meringue and almond flour sandwich cookie filled with icing. "Renee and Donovan have gone to Calistoga."

"What's there?" I asked.

"The Bookery. Do you know it?"

"Indeed, I do." The Bookery was a charming bed-and-breakfast that held literary events. In my spare time, I loved to read, and I enjoyed attending book fairs and meeting authors. I'd visited The Bookery at least a dozen times. One of my favorite mystery authors, Kate Carlisle, who'd written a series set in San Francisco as well as the wine country, had appeared at a book event there a few months ago.

"Donovan is checking out the bakery," Camille said.

The Bookery boasted a thriving bakery and café. The owner's motto was "Nestle in and get comfortable." She believed one couldn't read a book without a cup of tea and something sweet in hand.

Chef C said, "*Shh*—it is a secret—but I believe Donovan is hoping to steal some ideas. He wants to open his own bakery. He does not wish to teach cooking classes forever, although the position has provided him a steady income." She sighed. "Men. They dream big, do they not?"

Yep, I thought. *The man had won her heart.* "I hope he gets what he wants."

"Me, too."

"Mimi!" Heather, my hostess and right-hand woman, breezed in via the kitchen's rear door. Her curly blonde tresses bounced on her shoulders. Her cornflower-blue dress clung to her lithesome frame. "You'll never guess what I did all day yesterday."

Dare I ask? I thought, suppressing a giggle. Heather had taken the day off. Who knew where she might have gone? When she'd first started working for me, she'd claimed that she had been abducted on numerous occasions by aliens—*Glonkirks*, she'd called them. Soon after, however, she disabused me of that notion, saying that talking about aliens was her way of pulling people's legs. The truth saddened me. I had enjoyed the stories, as fanciful as they were. I'd often fantasized about her visiting Mars and soaring outside the Milky Way. *Yoo-hoo, Scotty, beam me up.*

"Let me guess," I said. "Did you trip the light fandango? Or take tango classes? Maybe you've been typing your husband's latest manuscript." Henry wrote science fiction novels. For a long time, I hadn't believed he was real, either, until one day when she had finally brought him to the bistro. He was a dumpling of a guy.

Her bright eyes crinkled with amusement. "No, silly. I was playing with my babies."

"Your furry babies?"

"Yes!"

A few months ago we'd found out that Scoundrel—a gray-and-white mouser that dwelled in the neighboring vineyards and visited the bistro for real cat food and affection—was female, not male, and pregnant to boot. It wasn't my fault for the error. Heather had been the primary caretaker. I hadn't thought to, um, look. Six weeks ago, Scoundrel had given birth to a litter of kittens.

"You'll be pleased to know I've found them all homes." Heather rattled off the names of the new owners. A former math teacher, she was terrific with facts and figures. "Do you have a minute? Come see them. I'm not needed in the dining room at the moment."

"They're here?"

"Henry had a meeting with an attorney in the city. When he's done, he'll drop by and pick them up. It's okay, isn't it? I hate leaving them home alone. They're in the shed."

After completing the construction of the bistro, we'd realized we needed more storage. We'd added a small air-conditioned space where we kept staples like flour, sugar, and spices.

"It's fine."

"The kittens are so much cuter now."

"I hope so." When I'd first seen them, they'd looked like pinch-faced, furless rats. Growing up, I hadn't owned cats—my mother was a dog person. As a chef, I hadn't acquired any animals for fear of transporting their hair to my cooking area. Since then, fellow chefs had advised me that I needn't worry. Bobby Flay was a huge cat lover; if he could own a cat, so could I. Nowadays, Scoundrel often made her way to my cottage at the rear of Maison Rousseau—it had once been the caretaker's unit. She would meow a hello, as if she was there to visit me, but I believed she was more interested in getting to know my resident goldfish—intimately. *Yum.*

"Come on." Heather beckoned me.

She exited the kitchen, and I followed her to the shed. In the corner, inside a wire crate, huddled six mewing kittens.

"Ooh," I murmured. "They're adorable." One with gray-and-white markings reminded me of Scoundrel. Another was black with white paws. Three were charcoal gray. The sixth was black with a white stripe down its nose. "And each of them has a new home?"

"Yep." She buffed her nails on her dress. "I'll turn them over to their new owners in a couple of weeks. One couple is taking three of them, one for each of their little girls. How sweet is that?"

As I bent to unlatch the door, a flash of black whizzed between me and the crate. I started. "What the heck?"

Heather steadied me. "Bad Scooter!" She wagged a finger at a retreating feline.

"Who's Scooter?"

"Sorry, Mimi. I forgot to close the door to the shed."

"Who is Scooter?" I repeated.

"Scoundrel's significant other."

"He's a black cat," I murmured, my heart chugging from the fright.

"As black as lava and faster than a bullet train."

A shiver ran down my spine. I was not superstitious by nature. Fantasies and folk tales didn't suck me in, but I had to admit, a black cat crossing my path unnerved me. Black cats signified imminent danger, didn't they?